PRAISE FOR

THE NEVERLAND TRANSMISSIONS SERIES

"Sullivan builds tension and excitement in this space opera refashioning of Peter Pan."

—PUBLISHER'S WEEKLY

"... fantastic twist on a classic."

—THE LITERARY VIXEN

"A fast-paced romp through space with a Peter Pan flair!"

—MERADETH HOUSTON, SOMEONE ELSE'S SOUL

"...an enjoyable and creative retelling of Peter Pan!"

—C.A. GRAY

NEVER BOUND

A Neverland Transmissions Novel

J.M. SULLIVAN

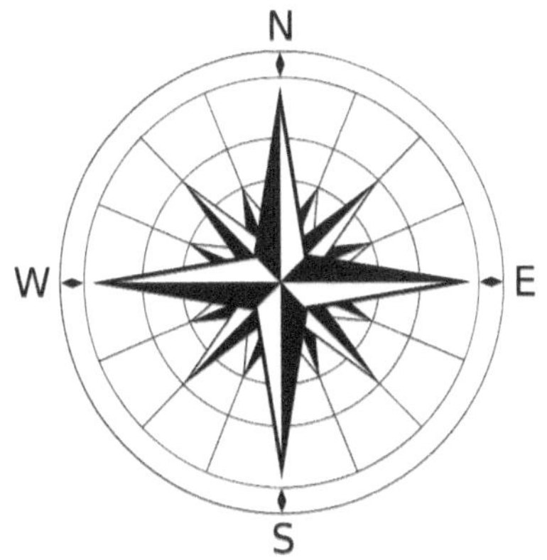

OWL HOLLOW PRESS

Owl Hollow Press, LLC, Springville, UT 84663

Neverbound: The Neverland Transmissions, Book Three
Copyright © 2023 by J.M. Sullivan

Library of Congress Cataloging-in-Publication Data
Neverbound / J.M. Sullivan — First edition.

Poem used: "The Gentle Maiden," Harold Boulton, available in the public domain.

Summary: Wendy's world is unraveling as she is forced with an impossible choice: defy the Fleet and endanger her remaining team, or disregard and doom the man she loves—and quite possibly, the world?

Cover Design by Sherry Ficklin

ISBN: 978-1-958109-45-8 (paperback)
ISBN: 978-1-958109-46-5 (e-book)

For Grandma Kay.
May you always sing in the stars.

There's one that is a pure as an angel,
As fair as the flowers of May,
They call her the gentle maiden
Wherever she takes her way.
Her eyes have the glance of sunlight,
As it brightens the blue sea wave
And more than the deep sea treasure
The love of her heart I crave.

Though parted afar from my darling,
I dream of her everywhere,
The sound of her voice is about me,
The spell of her presence there.
An whether my prayers be granted,
Or whether she pass me by,
The face of the gentle maiden
Will follow me till I die.

The Gentle Maiden,
Harold Boulton

PROLOGUE

COMMANDER AIDAN BOYCE

<< ERROR://LOCATION://UNKNOWN>>

Time is a cruel mistress.

Heartless, she speeds through the moments we cherish, then drudges through those we hate—turning dark minutes into darker hours, days, and weeks, seamlessly merging them into a lifetime of depthless despair.

It makes it difficult to remember who I am.

Aidan Boyce, Commander of the Londonniere Brigade. Rank Identification C-397v4. Assigned Liaison Officer to the Fede Fiducia—but... that's not where I am.

I don't know where I am.
I only know I'm no longer with her.

I was, briefly—and there was a spark, a pure, burning moment when her lips touched mine, and she pressed so closely against me that I almost felt her soul. But time turned it into a flash, an instant sped through so quickly that I've been reduced to wonder if it was simply my imagination, a construct from my mind made to save itself from the endless void time has plunged us into.

I wouldn't be surprised.

My mind . . . is not as it once was. Here in the dark, I am scattered. I feel myself slipping in and out, but from what, I cannot say. Consciousness? Or something else?

Once, I knew. The edges of my mind gripped the answer, but as I reached to claim it, it slipped away, sinking into another stretch of black.

Time is a cruel, cruel mistress. But she will not break me. She can't, or I won't survive.

I am not alone.

What I once thought an abandoned vessel has proven something else entirely. Cursed might be a more apt description.

I discovered it in the silence. Trapped in yet another stretch of emptiness, I was interrupted by a discordant sound. It began as little more than an itch in my ears, but soon transformed into brazen clawing through the walls that scraped under my skin and swelled to a loud, skittering echo to roar through the metallic hull surrounding me. Curious, I ven-

*tured further into the ship—the skeleton of a lost vessel—
but found nothing. Until they found me.*

*I have no name for them—they are like nothing I have ever
encountered before—maniacal monsters with devils in their
eyes. Hidden in the dark, they chased me through the shadows with their hissing cries. Fending them back, I retreated
to my holding cell, where I barricaded myself from their
ravenous whispers.*

I may have killed one, but I can't be sure.

*I'll have to find out soon. My supplies are rapidly diminish-
ing, and though time covets my happiness, it is quite content
to leave me with my quickly growing hunger. I wish I had
something more pleasant to help mark time's passing, and
perhaps I do.*

I wonder if I will ever see her again.

I wonder if she would care to see me.

THE RETURN FLIGHT

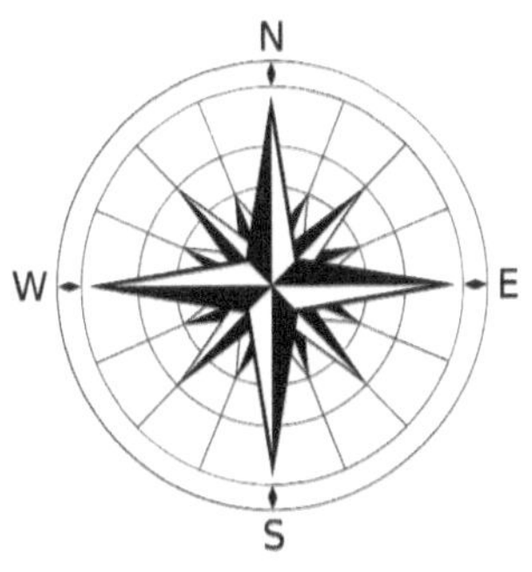

I
CAPTAIN WENDY DARLING

THE JOLLY ROGER

The ship was hot. Too hot. Stifling.

Not because of another glitch in the system. Mercifully, the repairs to *the Jolly Roger* had held, maintaining the ship's projected course to Earth and home to New London.

It was stifling, Wendy thought as she tugged her strangling collar, because it was nearly time to present her official report of the Neverland files. A report that was being given unusually early. Most briefings occurred upon mission completion, once the assigned crew docked and locked. However, due to the unexpected complications with Hooke and the Shadow, along with the Stjarnin's intervention, the Fleet demanded an expedited, in-depth review.

Though it made her anxious, Wendy agreed. Her intel would provide necessary time and information for the Fleet to prepare for their return—which would require housing for Peter and the Lost Boys, along with procuring cells for Hooke and his remaining pirates while they awaited trial for their crimes.

Still, understanding did nothing to settle her nerves. She wasn't naive enough to believe her performance wouldn't be harshly scrutinized. The Fleet would certainly have a long list of inquiries, many of which she wasn't prepared for. Even if they were the same questions she constantly asked herself.

Ready or not doesn't matter, Wendy thought with another nervous tug of her coat. As captain, Admiral Toussant would still expect her thorough report. The only problem: Wendy was unsure how many she could provide.

Glowering, Wendy moved to smooth her jacket once more, but her hand was stilled by the brush of a rugged palm.

"Don't worry, Cap, the hard part's over," Peter assured, his emerald eyes sparking over a crooked grin. Flecks of gold hovered inside his stare, matching the contented sparks trailing from the nanobot circling his shoulder. Tinc's echoing jangle might have been encouraging, but since Peter was the only one equipped with her cochlear translator, Wendy could only guess.

Ignoring the bot, Peter stepped closer to Wendy and slipped his hand firmly around hers. A small shiver rushed through her as she studied him. Newly outfitted in one of Michaels' spare suits, the mechanic looked even more dashing than usual. It wasn't just because his wiry muscles tightened against the uniform, filling out the dark navy fabric better than Jensen ever could. The pristine lines and sharp angles of the suit brought a polished edge to the scruffy mechanic, highlighting his rugged features against a sleek backdrop. Catching her stare, Peter quirked a confident smile.

"After all we've been through, this briefing will be a breeze."

"You obviously haven't met the Admiral," Wendy replied, stamping down a flare of nerves.

"Impressive, scary lady with a suit and gray hair? I remember," he nodded before gently raising his hand to her cheek. "I just happen to know another impressive woman who is just as intimidating, but much prettier." He teased, before turning serious. His carefree smile vanished under her smoldering gaze. "You saved a *world*, Cap. That's not something anyone could do perfectly. Sure, some bad stuff happened, but no one is going to hold it against you."

Peter moved his hand to gently caress her face. Wendy almost pressed into it, allowing his rough palms to cradle her cheek, but his words caught her in a tailspin. Peter was wrong. Someone absolutely would blame her, even if that someone was only herself.

That was why the hearing worried her so much. How could she face the Admiral to account for the mission when she couldn't even face herself? Wendy closed her eyes, and an unwanted vision flickered behind her eyelids—Commander Boyce crushing her in his powerful embrace, clutching her like his last anchor to reality before he kissed her like she'd never been kissed before. It was wonderful—dazzling, electrifying, and slightly terrifying—and then he vanished into the sky.

Not an easy memory to forget.

Her gut wrenching, Wendy swallowed her guilt and stepped out of Peter's gentle embrace. "I should have saved him," she whispered.

Peter frowned. "Boyce made his decision," he countered, failing to hide the tinge of disappointment in his voice. "The commander knew what he was doing. What had to be done. Don't discredit that."

His troubled stare made it difficult for Wendy to find the right words to say. Peter was right. Boyce had made his choice, but their knowledge of the commander's reasons hung so heavily between them it was almost palpable. Aidan had chosen to save *her*. If Wendy hadn't known before, the heart-wrenching kiss Boyce wrapped her in confirmed it—upending her childhood belief that his only feelings for her were contempt and disdain. And then, with the same suddenness of his confession, the commander disappeared, sacrificing himself to save the ship from the Shadow, defeating the Darkness and leaving Wendy with the aftermath—a swirling vortex of rage, guilt, longing, and despair.

It was all very confusing.

And yet, she was expected to have answers. The bitter sentiment flitted through her mind as the scanband on her wrist vibrated, chiding her elevated blood pressure and erratic pulse. Annoyed, Wendy shook her arm, silencing Nana while she expelled a heavy sigh. The Fleet wouldn't care about her fraying emotions. They only wanted facts.

Which is what I will provide, Wendy thought before turning to Peter. He deserved answers too. The steadfast mechanic had defied all odds to reach her, faced the Stjarnin, and partnered with his worst enemy to warn her about the Shadow's infiltration. It wasn't his fault that he had been caught in the crossfires of her conflicted heart.

"Thank you," she said, offering the warmest smile she could muster before slipping her hand in his.

Responding to her touch, Peter drew her into his embrace. His heart thrummed against her as he angled his face toward hers. Heat burned between them, and Wendy wished she could engulf herself in it—wished she could lose herself in *him*, but a tight cough sounded behind them.

"Captain?" Lieutenant Arielle Dawes' bright voice chirped through the room as the pilot addressed her. "I hate to interrupt, but the Fleet signaled. They're ready for you."

Embarrassed, Wendy slipped away from Peter. Although Dawes and everyone else aboard the *Roger* knew about their relationship—thanks to Lieutenant Johns' incessant teasing— propriety made her uncomfortable being seen in any capacity outside her Fleet-assigned duties. It was another complication to add to her growing list.

The *Roger* was a very small ship.

"Thank you, Dawes," Clearing her throat, Wendy excused the pilot before turning to Peter. A disappointed look flickered over his features, but he squeezed her hand before hooking his thumbs in his pockets and twisting to face the screen.

"Ready when you are, Cap," he said, quirking a lazy smile. Smoothing her hair, Wendy silently fought the urge to tame the mechanic's unruly mane. Standing at easy attention with his loosened collar, it was amazing how he could make even a uniform seem casual. She itched to straighten his appearance, but the comm buzzed, announcing the Admiral.

Focusing on the screen, Wendy issued a stiff salute, her jaw tightening at Peter's slack posture. She gritted her teeth and made a mental note to train him on comm protocol. At this point, she could only hope that the Admiral wouldn't notice, although the cool look that flickered over Toussant's deep features indicated she had. Angling her attention to Wendy, the Admiral offered a brief nod as the screen panned wide, revealing a panel of Fleet officials flanking an elaborate table. Stoic, they stared, revealing nothing.

Heart racing, Wendy forced her chin high. A silent beat pulsed through the air, suffocating her until finally, the Admiral began.

"Captain Wendy Darling," Toussant announced, briskly glancing from the file in front of her to Wendy's tethered gaze. "I realize this communication goes against standard protocol, and I appreciate your accommodation of our request. We are eager to gather your insight to the Neverland excursion. I trust you have had sufficient time to compile a thorough investigation, and that your team has proved helpful in the matter." Her steel gaze zeroed on Peter, betraying no emotion as she folded her hands and pierced Wendy with her stare.

"At this time, the Fleet is ready for your official report."

2
CAPTAIN WENDY DARLING

The room shrank around Wendy, turning her claustrophobic under the panel's expectant stares. Five sets of unwavering eyes waited for her story. Wendy's heart lurched in an uncomfortable flutter, and she tugged firmly on the ends of her coat.

"Of course, Admiral," she replied, coughing to clear the tremble from her voice. "Where should I begin?"

Toussant glanced at her file. "Since this briefing is rather unprecedented, I see no point clinging to tedium. We have already accessed your crew's files, identification signatures, and ranks, so an introductory statement isn't necessary." Steepling her fingers, she looked at Wendy thoughtfully. "I would imagine the start should suffice," she decided. "Although we have received several reports from yourself and Commander Boyce post landing, due to current circumstances, the commander's data has been deemed unreliable. It will be included with the full report, but for judicial integrity, it can only be considered supplemental—in the event that it is able to be corroborated."

Wendy nodded, understanding. As the liaison officer, Boyce had been tasked with compiling the original briefing from their journey to Neverland. Though she had reviewed most of his reports, she had no idea what information he later relayed under the influence of the Shadow. Her lips pursed as she conjured a memory of the commander, standing before her, his cornflower eyes wild with pain and desperation as he struggled against Itzala's dark control. A familiar wave of emotion rippled through her, drowning her words, but a quick squeeze of Peter's hand moored her to the present.

"I understand, Admiral."

"Very good." The Admiral said, gesturing for Wendy to continue.

Drawing a breath, Wendy paused to consider everything that had transpired over the course of the mission. Though it had only been a few months, it seemed a lifetime.

"Our arrival on Neverland did not go according to plan," Wendy stated, deciding the crash was as good a place as any to begin. "The *Fede Fiducia* suffered technical difficulties en route and we were forced into an emergency landing. The daring maneuver damaged our ship beyond repair, but ultimately, we reached our destination."

Wendy paused, allowing the officers to digest the information. A few members scratched notes in their files, but no one spoke, so she continued.

"The nature of our entrance into Neverland's atmosphere promptly notified the planet's inhabitants of our arrival. Before we could offload, we were met by Peter Pan and his nano-companion Tinc, and soon after, Neverland's natives, the Stjarnin. We originally classified them as merely a hostile alien race but have since amended our intel to include their role as the original keepers of Itzala—the entity better known as the Shadow."

Quiet murmurs erupted through the room but were quickly silenced by the Admiral's sharp glare. "We need the events of your report in order, Captain," she reminded, towering her fingers once more. "At this time, did you know about the Shadow?"

Wendy shook her head. "I didn't learn about the Shadow's presence until after I met with Captain Hooke."

"Then it should not yet be considered," Toussant declared, quickly notating her file. "Right now, we simply require the facts."

"Yes, Admiral," Wendy agreed, exhaling a wobbly breath. "The Stjarnin sent a small party to the *Fiducia's* crash site. They attacked, but with Peter's help, we escaped and found refuge in the base he founded with his crew; a small group they called the Lost Boys."

Another rumble of intrigued murmurs rippled through the room. This time Wendy noted the panel eyeing Peter with interest. Holding her impassive stare, the Admiral continued. "And, at this time, Captain Hooke was not present?"

"No, Admiral," Wendy answered. "The pira—*Hooke's crew*—resided in a separate camp they established upon the *Roger's* initial arrival."

"Do you know why this was?" A squat officer with squared glasses questioned, his curiosity breaking the panel's silent wall. The inquiry earned an annoyed glance from the Admiral, but Toussant nodded to Wendy, allowing it to stand.

Turning toward the man, Wendy noted his rounded features and too-snug colonel's uniform. The dark navy fabric stretched tight over his barrel chest, puckering his badge toward the ceiling. Still, Wendy could make out his printed name in neat Fleet script—Osbourne. Wendy racked her brain, trying to place it with his rank. Obviously he had been relegated to desk duty for quite some time, and she couldn't place his name with any notable exploits. More than likely, he was an administrative officer who could quote every protocol, but who had little understanding of active missions. The thought distracted her, and she struggled to refocus under the panel's impatient stares.

"Because Hooke was a pirate," Peter interrupted, squaring his shoulders as he stepped to address the panel. "He betrayed the Fleet and his crew, and our attempt—*my attempt*—to stop him was what got us stranded in the first place."

A crackle of feedback exploded through the comm as questions peppered from the panel, filling the room in a clamor until the Admiral motioned for silence.

"Ensign Pan," she bristled, meeting Peter with a cool stare, "you will be asked to share your findings in due course. Please refrain from doing so until after Captain Darling has completed her report."

The Admiral's reprimand elicited a tight clench of Peter's jaw, but the mechanic stepped down, leaving Wendy the floor.

"I had the same inquiry. Peter—*Ensign Pan*," Wendy amended, mimicking the Admiral's formal address, "indicated a rift between the two groups. During this time, he expressed explicit concerns about the captain before taking me to the *Jolly Roger*."

"He voiced these concerns, and still, you went?" A pinched-faced woman to the left of the Admiral asked, her mousy voice matching the dull tinge of her hair. Leaning forward, she studied Wendy over narrow spectacles and their flashing glare reflected the woman's waspish scowl.

"Our directive was to retrieve Hooke and his crew. Regardless of Pan's intel, in order to complete the mission, I had to locate the captain and bring him home."

"Which you have still not managed," the mousy officer added, cinching her lips as she annotated her file.

"We are doing our best, Ma'am," Wendy said, leveling her bristling temper. She glanced at the woman's badge and frowned as she noted her name—Colonel Matheson. At the Academy, she had heard several mentions of Matheson, and none of them had been complimentary. Taking a breath, Wendy gestured to the colonel's open file. "As the report states, we experienced several rather substantial complications."

"Yes," Matheson clipped, looking at Wendy as though she were something the colonel might have discovered under her shoe. "This *Shadow* creature. Quite the fairy-tale monster. Much like the bogeyman in children's nightmares."

A chill gripped Wendy as she recalled her first encounter with the Shadow. How its slick voice invited an emptiness that seeped through her bones, gripping them in an endless, hollow ache that threatened to overtake her with a single breath. It filled her mind with a whining keen, nearly swallowing her thoughts until Peter's warm hand tightened around hers.

"If so, then I very much understand their fear," Wendy clipped, angling a pointed gaze at Matheson before turning resolutely to the Admiral. "When I met the captain, I discovered Pan was correct. Hooke imprisoned me, then attempted to complete a summoning ritual for the entity we now know as Itzala. To fulfill the ritual, Hooke had also captured the Stjarnin princess, Tiger Lily. I believe his intent was to offer her as a sacrifice."

"And how did Hooke, a Fleet captain from Earth, have any knowledge of a ritual meant to revive an unknown alien entity?" Colonel Matheson interrupted.

"I don't—"

"If you really want to know, why don't you ask him yourself," Peter snapped, pushing between Wendy and the screen. Tension crackled through the room as he glared at the officer, whose dour expression pinched tighter. "We have him on board."

"That is not necessary," the Admiral interjected with a quick rap of her knuckles. The sound shot through the small conference room, making Matheson flinch. "Our records state that shortly after the attempted summoning, Hooke's crew was apprehended but Itzala and the captain disappeared. Is that correct?"

Wendy nodded. "Yes, Admiral."

"Good," the Admiral replied, unsmiling. "To this point, all records coincide," she announced, scanning the file once more. "What happened afterwards?"

Shuffling uncomfortably, Wendy hesitated. After was where things got muddled. She took a steadying breath then exhaled.

"After Itzala's escape, we corralled Hooke's crew and returned them to the *Fede Fiducia*, where my team worked tirelessly to get the vessel flight-bound. Unfortunately, the *Fiducia's* damage was irreparable, leaving us with only one option. We had to harvest the ship in an attempt to restore the *Jolly Roger*. It took a great deal of effort, but eventually we were able to get the *Roger* operational. There was a minor setback during the launch, but with Pe—Ensign Pan's help, we were able to begin the return voyage home."

Wendy turned to Peter with a warm smile. He caught her look and a sheepish grin darted across his face before he motioned to the panel. Spinning toward the officers, Wendy noted their mixed expressions. A brief silence hung in the room, leaving only the comm's soft vibrations thrumming through the air until another officer broke the quiet.

"And what of the Shadow?" he asked, shifting in his seat beside the Admiral. His thick mustache twitched as he spoke, scrubbing his lips with every word. "Were you aware at this point that it had infiltrated the ship?"

"No," Wendy answered. Clasping her hands behind her back, she focused on the officer—Colonel Hahti, according to his badge—and smoothed her frown. "We believed the Shadow fled into Neverland, taking Hooke as his prisoner. Our plan was to return earthside and alert the Fleet so they could determine the best course of action against Itzala's threat.

"And what of your mission?" Matheson challenged with a mean grin. Wendy felt Peter bristle at the Colonel's scathing tone and quickly stepped forward, filling her voice with as much authority as she could muster.

"Before the launch, several search parties attempted to locate the captain. Neither our men, nor the assisting Stjarnin found any traces of Hooke or the Shadow. Considering the captain's abandonment of the Fleet and his subsequent actions, I determined it was more essential to ensure the safe return of our loyal soldiers—the ones who dedicated their lives *to* the Fleet, not those actively fighting against it."

"A wise choice," Toussant interjected, denying Matheson's response. Wendy thought a warm smile flashed over the Admiral's face. "It is the Fleet's duty to execute missions that individuals alone could not. But that is not the question at hand," Toussant said, meeting Matheson's pinched scowl before redirecting her keen stare to Wendy. "Please Captain, continue."

"Of course, Admiral," Wendy said, coughing to clear her throat. "After the *Roger's* launch, we planned an immediate return. Unfortunately, the vessel's repairs proved unstable. We began experiencing technical distress. It manifested first as simple system glitches, but the issues soon became more severe."

"How severe?" The woman sitting beside Colonel Hahti asked. Though she had watched Wendy intensely throughout the briefing, it was the first time she had spoken, and her throaty accent caught Wendy off guard. Searching the officer's uniform, Wendy located the colonel's surname, Jimenez.

"The *Roger* became inoperable," Wendy answered, holding steady under the woman's starched gaze. "We took extensive efforts to repair the damage, even going so far as to venture off-vessel to scavenge parts, but little could be done. It was then the Shadow revealed itself and Ensign Pan stepped in to intervene."

Wendy paused, remembering the way Peter charged the room, his eyes wild as he careened toward her with Hooke in tow. The fire in his gaze had blazed so bright she'd thought it would burn through the room until Boyce—having briefly escaped Itzala—stepped forward to unravel her with a kiss. Choking under the memory, she fought to maintain her calm.

"Unfortunately, the Shadow had grown stronger during its time aboard the *Roger*. It fought bitterly to maintain control of Commander Boyce and utilize him to do its bidding. Ultimately, instead of allowing Itzala to succeed, Boyce sacrificed himself to destroy the Darkness. He saved us all."

Wendy's voice broke as she finished her admission and she looked down, hot tears pooling as she avoided the panel's stares.

"Thank you, Darling," the Admiral said. She paused to notate her folder, then flipped to another sleek page. "I assume that brings us to the present. Tell me, how many souls are currently aboard your ship?"

After a moment's thought, Wendy answered. "Twenty-one," she said briskly. "From our initial voyage, starting with myself and Dawes, DeLaCruz, Johns, and Michaels. Then Pan and five of his Lost Boys, plus Captain Hooke and eight of his men. We are also currently being accompanied by Tizari, a Stjarnin warrior who requested to remain on board."

A fresh murmur swept through the panel at Wendy's announcement, but the Admiral continued.

"What of the other Stjarnin?" she asked, her slate eyes shining with interest. "To what extent were they involved?"

Hesitating, Wendy glanced uncertainly at Peter. Although she had spoken briefly with the Stjarnin, Peter's understanding of their people was much stronger than her own. Catching her worried stare, the mechanic stepped forward.

"The Stjarnin are determined to contain Itzala," he answered, his stance firm as he addressed the Admiral. "But Captain Darling's interactions with them has been minimal. If you really want to know about their contributions, there are others better suited for your questions."

Her gaze trained on Peter, only a quick twitch of the Admiral's brow indicated her surprise at the mechanic's interjection. "If you think you can provide better insight than the captain, Pan," she began, unable to still the amused quirk of her lips, "by all means, continue."

3
FLEET MECHANIC PETER PAN

THE JOLLY ROGER

Meeting the Admiral's steely gaze, Peter squared his shoulders. "As you are aware," he started, then paused to issue a challenging glare at the remaining officers, "as *all* of you are aware, a system failure during the *Roger's* returning launch left only myself stranded on Neverland. During this time, the Stjarnin invited me to their camp and disclosed more about their past than we had previously known. Most interesting was, for many years, they had *kept* the Shadow bound to Neverland so it couldn't spread its darkness. It was the reason they had been so hostile. Our presence was a threat—a means the Shadow could use to escape—which in the end, is exactly what it did."

Peter paused to take a breath, and Matheson hurried to speak. "And how—"

"It was confirmed when we found Hooke," the mechanic breezed, cutting the colonel off with a smirk. "The Stjarnin sent me with two warriors to search Skull Rock, their original holding place for Itzala. We found Hooke, wounded and left to die after being discarded by the Shadow."

Nervous silence hovered over the panel. Peter allowed it to hang for a terse moment, then continued.

"When we realized Itzala was no longer Neverbound, I was able to convince the Stjarnin to help me locate Wendy—Captain Darling—and her crew. Using the Stjarnin's vessels, we followed them, chasing the Shadow."

"Was it the Stjarnin's intent to retrieve the Shadow to Neverland?" Admiral Toussant asked, her expression serious. Breaking her gaze, Peter glanced at Wendy, hoping the captain hadn't noticed his nervous edge. A reassuring smile pulled the corners of her perfect lips, her quiet confidence bolstering his own before he turned to Toussant.

"The Stjarnin wanted to retrieve the Shadow," he confirmed, "but they were concerned it had infiltrated the ship. They warned me that if Itzala had taken control of the *Roger*, they would not hesitate to destroy it." Wendy's sharp inhale sounded behind him, followed by a ripple of the panel's sweeping murmurs, but Peter pressed on. "To ensure the Stjarnin's cooperation, I agreed."

"But that wasn't true once you reached the *Roger*," the Admiral guessed, aiming an approving smile at the mechanic.

Peter shrugged mischievously, "I've never been good at just letting things go."

"And that's the reason we're in this mess," Matheson huffed, her snide tone needling under his skin. The scathing remark earned a surprised glance from Colonel Osbourne, but his bushy brows merely scrunched as the officer was promptly silenced.

"Colonel Matheson, while I appreciate your input, it would be much easier if you reserved your comments for your annotations," Toussant clipped. Training her stare, she finished her admonition. "It will resolve the tribunal much more quickly."

"Tribunal?" Wendy exclaimed, the color draining from her face. Her panicked expression brought a mean smile to Matheson's paper-thin lips, while beside her, the Admiral released a heavy sigh.

"Yes, Darling," Toussant laced her hands. "Due to the mission's unsettling turn of events, concerns have been raised about the way things have been handled."

Daring a glance at Wendy, Peter was caught off guard by the beauty in her intense stare. Though her hands balled in nervous fists, the captain faced forward, betraying no emotion against the harsh revelation. He longed to sweep her away, to whisk her free from the Fleet's condescending accusations, but standing firm before the panel, the fiery glint emanating from her rigid stance held him back.

Unfazed, the Admiral pressed on, her stoic mask a near reflection of the captain's. "There are some people," Toussant paused, and Peter caught the subtle flicker of her eyes toward Matheson, "who are questioning your capability as Captain."

"But—" Wendy started, her furious blinking unable to scatter her gathering tears.

"There was nothing Wendy could have done to change anything!" Peter interjected defensively. Behind him, Tinc jangled indignantly, cascading purple sparks to the ground. "If it wasn't for her, Itzala would have won on Neverland," he argued. "Her actions are the only reason it didn't succeed in its plans."

"Not according to Captain Darling," Matheson jeered. "From her iteration, it would seem that you, the Stjarnin, Commander Boyce, and even Captain Hooke—a man currently imprisoned for mutiny—have contributed further."

"It's a stars-damned monster!" Peter exploded, unable to restrain his temper. He knew the outburst wouldn't help, but the colonel's smug grin provoked his fury. "An evil, inhuman *thing* that took the dedication of an entire race just to restrain it! What do you expect her to do? *Command* it into submission?"

Watching Peter, Matheson's features twisted in an ugly sneer. Before she could retort, the Admiral's fist banged against the table.

"Enough!" Clearing her throat, Toussant turned to Wendy. The captain's face was devoid of color, offsetting her pale features beautifully against her navy suit. "Captain Darling, my intent was not to worry you, but rather to inform you that your actions are being carefully monitored. At this time, it is my opinion—my *decision*—" she amended, earning a sour look from Colonel Matheson, "that there is no evidence indicating a lack of competency in your captainship. There will be no corrective action taken, and you will retain full jurisdiction until the *Roger* returns." She closed her file with a snap, ignoring the colonel's fuming. "If there are no further questions, captain, you are dismissed."

Heavy silence lingered until a loud screech whined through the comm. The harsh sound stirred the panel, with Colonel Matheson rising first, abandoning her chair with a glower. Watching silently, the Admiral met her sneer then turned, excusing the rest of the panel.

Still scowling, Matheson lingered, dawdling until the Admiral's intentionally averted gaze sent her skulking from the room. It was only after the door swished shut that Toussant cast a furtive glance over her shoulders. Alone, Toussant slumped in her chair, gently massaging her temples. For the first time, Peter wondered exactly how old the Admiral was. The silver notes weaving through her hair indicated she was older, but this was the only time he'd seen her worn down. Beside him, Wendy took notice too. A troubled pout marred the captain's delicate features as she patiently studied her superior.

"I'm not going to downplay the situation, Darling. The state of your mission has gotten the Fleet in an uproar. Those who aren't raving over the introduction of the Shadow are already busy horning over Hooke's supposed mutiny. The bizarre turn of events and the lack of clear explanations to any of them is proving worrisome." Her lips pursed as she stalked to the center of the comm screen, where she stood close enough for Peter to note the dark flecks dotting her slate stare. "So tell me. Is there *any* additional insight you can provide? Anything that might prove useful in helping you return unscathed?"

Beside him, Wendy sucked in a breath. There was a weighted pause, followed by her firm response. "No," she answered. "All of our intel has been disclosed. We aren't hiding anything, Admiral."

Mollified, Toussant slackened her rigid stance. "Very well," she allowed. "I see no reason not to take you at your word." Gripping her file, the Admiral started toward the exit, then paused after a few steps. "But Darling," she added, angling her chin over her shoulder. "If it turns out that anything *has* been overlooked, I cannot guarantee indemnity."

The Admiral allowed her words to hang in the air before quickly exiting, leaving Peter and Wendy to stare at the empty table in front of them. For a moment, the only sound in the room was the crackle of Tinc's processor until—with a gasping, ragged breath—Wendy folded. Worried, Peter knelt and lifted her chin, moving her face to reveal streams of silent tears coursing down her face.

"Wendy," he asked, his chest tightening at her sunken frame. "What's wrong?"

A harsh scoff erupted from the captain, bringing with it a fire that filled her storming gaze. "Were we not just in the same briefing?" she asked through a bitter laugh. "I'd say just about everything." She wiped her cheeks, revealing an embarrassed flush before she sighed. "I'm sorry, I shouldn't have exploded, it's just—"

"That you're only one person who has been dropped in the middle of an impossible situation?" Peter guessed, angling in front of her once more. "Cap, I wasn't lying when I told the Admiral what I thought. There's not a single person in the 'verse who could handle this as well as you are. And if we asked around, I'm sure the crew would agree."

"But you heard what Matheson said," Wendy countered, glancing at the comm.

"Matheson can shove it," Peter shot back. Instinctively, the captain shot a nervous glance at the screen, but Peter dismissed her worry. "She's gone, Cap. She can't hear us. And even if she could, I wouldn't care. I've never met an Offie that I've wanted to throat punch so badly in my life, and I crewed with Hooke for years." He smiled, and Wendy begrudged a weak laugh. "Look, I know that wasn't the way you wanted the briefing to play out, but from my end, it sounded like a win. It's clear the Admiral is on your side. She even shot down Matheson a few times. Yeah, it sucked hearing that people are questioning things, but also— now you know," Peter explained with a shrug. "Honestly, the Admiral probably did you a favor. Since you know that old shrew Matheson has it out for us, you can plan accordingly. Then, when we make it back to terra and celebrate our trium- phant return," he drew her close, illuminating the delicate angles of her face under the cabin's soft glow. "It will make it all the sweeter."

He stroked her cheek and it felt like velvet under his cal- loused thumb. Caught in the moment, he leaned forward, erasing the distance between them with a soft kiss. Their lips touched, sparking a supernova in his chest. The need to protect her nearly overtook him as he clenched his arms around her slender frame. Deepening the kiss, he wished he could use it to show Wendy all his desires—his longing to care for her, to keep the wretched Colonel at bay, to show her how impressive and fierce and inspiring he really thought she was, but mostly, his want to keep her close forever.

Spurred by the thoughts, he pressed harder against the captain and a soft moan escaped her. She sank into him, returning his gesture with fervor, until the outside world couldn't be kept any longer at bay. The soft whir of the door sounded behind them, followed by a polite cough.

Peter glanced at the intruder then frowned when he recognized Wendy's pilot. Once more, he had to stamp down a pang of jealousy as he realized his stolen moment was about to be taken back. Squeezing Wendy's palm, he let her go, allowing her to briskly smooth her hair before facing the waiting officer. Still at the door, Dawes offered an apologetic smile to Peter before stepping obediently inside.

"I'm sorry to interrupt Captain, but if you have a moment, the boys have something they'd like to show you."

4
CAPTAIN WENDY DARLING

THE JOLLY ROGER

Still recovering from her embarrassment at being caught, Wendy stepped farther from Peter, and the heat between them ebbed. Turning toward Dawes, she quashed the breathy tremor in her voice with a tenor of authority.

"Something the Lost Boys wanted to show me?"

"Yes, Captain," Dawes' grin widened, her sea blue eyes sparkling as they darted from Wendy to Peter. "They said it was important, otherwise I wouldn't have bothered you."

A snicker sounded and Wendy silenced Peter with a murderous glare. Returning to the pilot, she discovered the lieutenant covering her own laugh with a pathetic cough.

"It's quite alright, Dawes," she said with a haughty sniff. "We were just finishing."

"Speak for yourself," Peter grumbled, earning another stifled giggle from the lieutenant.

"What do the boys need?" Wendy asked primly. Heat still flushed her cheeks, but she grew less flustered the longer her lips were away from Peter's.

"They wouldn't tell me," the pilot answered. "They said it would be best if you were there before they tried to explain. It sounded important."

"As you keep saying," Wendy grumbled, tugging on her jacket before casting a last glance at Peter. He met her stare, his burning gaze sending another thrill through her.

Watching their exchange, Dawes' grin widened, but the pilot tipped her head. "Yes, captain," she said, her apology poorly concealing another giggle. Fighting a scowl, Wendy forced Peter out the door in a quick retreat.

In the corridor, Wendy's steps synchronized with Peter's as they hustled across the ship, their steady gait punctuated by Tinc's soft jangles. Moving at a steady click, it took only a few moments to cross the *Roger*. Around them, the vessel thrummed vibrantly, the brightly-lit corridors banishing the worrisome shadows that used to linger at each turn. They had all disappeared, taking Itzala's whispers and lingering cold, leaving only the bustling sounds of the crew.

"Should we take bets on whether the boys actually found something, or do you think Nibs just trapped Curly in another antique?" Peter teased over hurried steps. Behind him, a shower of green sparks rained Tinc's jangled response. Laughing, he nodded at the bot. "Tinc's going with the antique. Your thoughts, Cap?"

"Hopefully not another vase," Wendy answered, shaking her head. "It took DeLaCruz twenty minutes to get Curly's head out of the last one, and that was *after* she broke it."

Peter grinned, "At least you don't have to worry about giving it back to Hooke."

"No, but it will be part of the Fleet's inventory," she pointed out. "Catalogued with all of Hooke's other stolen items." Her words were met with a quiet pause. After a few steps, Wendy peeked sideways. "I'm sure it will be an update on the map," she added.

"It better be," Peter replied. "Or I'm gonna wring Tootles' neck." He scrubbed his hand over the nape of his neck, his expression thoughtful.

"I don't think Tootles is the problem," Wendy pointed out, grimacing as she imagined the small boy studying a stack of charts while Nibs and Curly played catch with a Faberge Egg.

Peter laughed. "Probably not," he agreed, "he's always been the one who listened best."

"Hopefully Johns will keep the others on track," she added. As the words left her mouth, she visualized her lieutenant booming a laugh as he joined them in a very expensive game of Monkey in the Middle. Picking up her pace, she added, "I'm sure we'll find out when we get there."

"It's gonna be fine, Cap," Peter assured, but cast a pointed look at Tinc.

With a haughty jangle, the bot darted down the corridor, dusting them in a trail of sparks. Peter snorted.

"Thanks for your help." He shook his head after the snarky bot then reached for Wendy, his gentle pull slowing her anxious pace. When the captain finally stalled, he met her with his determined gaze. "I mean it, Cap. Everything will be fine. *Everything*."

"That's a lot of things," Wendy sighed.

"Yeah," Peter nodded, "But luckily, we've got a top-notch Captain." He lowered his voice to a throaty growl. "She always figures it out."

Wendy lowered her eyes. "Doesn't always seem that way," she protested.

"Oh, it does," Peter rebutted, guiding her gaze to his. "She just buries herself so deep in her own head that she doesn't realize it."

Smiling, he leaned in, meeting her with the trace of a kiss. The heat had barely transferred from his lips to hers before he pulled back to softly smooth her hair.

"Don't want to get interrupted again," he whispered, surprising Wendy with the sadness lacing his features. "Even now, I'm not done fighting for your attention."

A guilty pull tugged at Wendy and she stepped away, stealing her hand from his. "The perks of being captain," she joked, her words falling flat. Unwilling to meet his stare, she resumed their path and gestured for him to follow. Nodding, Peter matched her silent lead. They nearly reached the research room when the mechanic stopped suddenly, allowing her a few steps before a murmur escaped his lips.

"Cap," he began, looking intently at his feet. "Have you ever thought that maybe it would be better if the panel sided with Matheson?"

His question tightened Wendy's chest. Through all of her worrying, she had never truly considered the implications of what would accompany a ruling of her incompetence. But Peter's simple statement crashed around her like a tsunami. Everything she had worked for—years of training, all of her future goals and dreams, and most importantly, and her crew— ripped from her in a matter of seconds. The thought was almost too painful to bear. Blinking, she pushed her breath through the crystallized cavern in her throat.

"What?"

Peter shifted uncomfortably. "I'm just saying—" he paused to scratch his mop of fiery hair. "I don't want you to get in trouble, but if you weren't captain, you would be free to do whatever you want—with *whoever* you want... like... me," he suggested, glancing shyly at her.

Wendy bit her lip, unsure what to say. She wanted to pacify him, but unerring certainty promised she could never willingly abandon her post. Bile rose in her throat, bringing sick with the thought that she may just as well throw her life away. Her thoughts raced so quickly, she couldn't form coherent words. Watching her struggle, Peter stepped forward with a brazen resolve.

"Think about it," he urged, his eyes flashing as he spoke in an anxious rush. "Leaving the Fleet wouldn't ground you. It would open the sky. With your training and my mech skills, we could do anything—man our own rig, travel wherever we want. We'd have all the adventures you could dream of, without all the complications."

Like my crew, the unbidden thought left Wendy gaping at Peter's hopeful expression.

"I can't abandon my ship, Peter."

"But you wouldn't be," he argued, "It will be docked with the Fleet. And then—"

"If I start thinking that way now, part of me would be leaving them," she interrupted, straightening her shoulders. "For now, I am still captain of this vessel and that is where my attention is needed. If that should change—" she paused to clear her suddenly thick throat, "well, then that is something I will have to address. But at present, there are other things that require my attention."

She braced for an argument, but Peter only sighed. "You got it, Cap."

In silence, they continued toward the research room, where Tinc greeted them with an impatient buzz. Waving the bot away, Peter activated the access pad, his expression pulled in a tight frown. The door whirred open, revealing Nibs and Curly hanging toward the back of the bay, scanning files while sporadically checking the books stacked around them. Occasionally, the two would cast quick glances to where Johns thumbed through a hefty book of his own. At the front, Tootles sat with Seven curled beside him, snuffling under a series of holoscreened sketches. Hearing the door, the Neverbeast chirped then rushed toward Wendy, abandoning the boy to his jumble of papers.

Following Seven's sudden movement, Tootles turned, his chubby cheeks pulling in a bright smile. "C-captain!" he exclaimed, hurrying clumsily to his feet. Puffing his chest in a determined salute, the Lost Boy stood, waiting patiently while Wendy tried to break free from Seven's excited pawing.

"At ease, Tootles," Wendy allowed, laughing as she forced the chirping Neverbeast to sit. Giving Seven one last pat, Wendy directed the creature back to Tootles then moved to examine his projected diagrams. It had been a while since Wendy had checked in, and she was interested to see what the Lost Boy had learned about the secret etchings she had discovered in Hooke's mahogany bookshelves. She'd had the boys transfer the marks so they could study them independently—away from Wendy's quarters. It had been a tedious process, but thanks to Tootles' determination and SMEE's attention to detail, the maps had been transferred successfully.

Looking carefully at them now, Wendy stepped closer to the charts displayed on the far wall. The largest map was the focal point, a massive screen that the Lost Boys referenced as they scoured the others, constantly referencing its swirling designs in hopes to find a match.

"That's what we w-wanted to show you, actually," Tootles said eagerly. "I think we found something. Although," he corrected, "it *was* Lieutenant Johns who pointed it out."

Wendy's brows raised as she turned to where Johns lounged, looking bored as he leafed through an aging journal.

"Johns?" She asked, addressing the lieutenant with a teasing grin. "What could you possibly have promised to make him say that?"

Shrugging, Johns discarded his journal and started to reply, but before he could, Tootles rushed in. "N-no Captain, r-really! If the L-lieutenant hadn't pointed out the b-b-blip, I w-w-would have m-missed it!"

"Blip?" Wendy frowned at the vague term. Curious, she glanced at Johns, but he only gestured back to Tootles.

"Ask the kid," he said. "We all know he's really the one in charge."

Beaming at the compliment, Tootles wriggled as he bounced on his toes, eagerly waiting to explain.

"Alright. You found a blip. What does that mean Tootles?" she asked, formally redirecting her question.

"A b-blip is, well, th-that's just what w-we've s-s-s-started call-calling it," Tootles began, hardly able to get his words through his anxious rush.

Placing his hand on the Lost Boy's shoulder, Peter let out a gentle laugh. "Okay, kid. Slow down," he said, slinging his arm around Tootles' neck. As he did, Wendy couldn't help but notice how the smallest Lost Boy didn't seem so little anymore. Standing next to Peter, his shoulders now reached closer, and in their smiles, Wendy could see how Tootles' rounded cheeks had started to thin out with the rest of him. Unfazed by the changes, Peter continued with a scruff of the boy's tawny hair. "You're losing the Captain. Start at the beginning."

"Oh. R-right," Tootles let out a shy laugh, then hurried to the holoboard. He shuffled his maps until a shimmering blue replica of Hooke's charts displayed along the wall. "Th-this is the picture we f-found hidden in the back of Hooke's b-bookshelves. We f-figured it was a map, we just didn't know wh-what it charted," he stated, his stammer settling as he fell into his explanation. Using his fingers to guide the holomap, the images shimmered and moved, shifting the upper corner of the translucent diagram to his reach. "W-we've been studying it and we think we've found out what the Captain was m-marking." He pointed to a large swirling whorl hovering diagonally over another, smaller etching.

"The Second Star?" Wendy guessed, recognizing the familiar designs.

Turning to her, Tootles nodded then leaned forward, his lowered voice filled with intensity. "N-not just the Star. All of the nebula surrounding it."

5
CAPTAIN WENDY DARLING

Wendy's brow furrowed. "You mean, Hooke *charted* the Uncharted Sector?" she asked, looking wonderingly at the maps. Behind her, Peter and Johns pressed in, studying the marks before the lieutenant let out an incredulous scoff.

"Well, that information would have made our mission a hell of a lot easier," Johns said.

Wendy's laugh echoed her agreement. "Hooke must have found a way to map the nebula and kept his records hidden from the Fleet," she said, still eyeing the charts with disbelief, "It would have been difficult—"

"But not impossible," Peter interjected. "The whole reason we got stuck on Neverland was because I found out Hooke was keeping secrets. I tried to step in, and not knowing the skies, got us caught in the planet's pull. It was a freak accident that could have been totally avoided." He ended his thought with a frustrated bang of his fist. "Trapped for a hundred years, all because I was too stupid to realize Hooke's plan."

"But you were the one who caught it," Wendy said, offering an encouraging smile before turning to address the crew. "And now that we have a proper map, we can figure out where we are."

Pressing his lips together, Tootles raised his hand. "N-not y-yet, Captain," he said. "I have Nibs and Curly working on that," he indicated to where the two Lost Boys leaned over their table, giggling as they flicked a small spinning chip across the charts. Embarrassed, Tootles shook his head. "It's taking longer than I thought."

Frowning, Wendy signaled Johns, who grumbled and moved to hover over the laughing boys. Withering under the lieutenant's serious gaze, the two shrank away from each other, erasing their grins as they quickly resettled into their task.

With Nibs and Curly taken care of, Wendy turned back to Tootles. "So our current placement is taking longer than expected," she clarified, making a mental note to direct the charts to Dawes. "That can be worked around. Is there anything else we need to know?"

Tootles squirmed. "Well, I *did* notice something else," he paused to look shyly at the captain, who didn't miss the curious stares the boy's confession earned. "I didn't tell the others because I thought they'd laugh. They think I take things too seriously."

"That's one of the things I like most about you," Wendy encouraged, patting him on the shoulder. "What did you find?"

Grinning, Tootles scanned the cluttered room. He scratched his head as he searched, looking momentarily like a mini-version of Peter before he located a folded section of charting. Carefully, he unfolded it and held it up to the holoscreen. Pointing from the upper corner of the projected image to the corresponding corner of the tattered paper, Tootles' eyes sparked. "They're almost the same."

"Lots of maps are almost the same, Tootles." Peter said, looking at the boy curiously.

Tootles nodded. "Y-yes. But this one," he paused, wiggling the map in his hands, "w-was made about three h-hundred years before this one." He pointed to Hooke's uncovered star chart. "And if y-you l-look here," he gestured to a small inscription at the bottom of the page, "you can see where it c-came from."

"The Stjarnin!" Wendy exclaimed, recognizing the jagged characters. "Where did you get this?"

"It was tucked inside one of Hooke's books," Tootles explained. "I think it's what he used to help make his chart. But—there are some differences I can't explain," his face screwed in concentration as he reexamined the maps.

"That is strange," Wendy mused. Her lips pursed as she thought, and she turned to Peter. "You never saw anything like this when you were with Hooke?" She asked.

"No," he answered earnestly. "Most of my time was spent in the mechbay with Tinc. Any time I *did* see Hooke, it was to get his orders. On mission, he preferred to keep to himself."

"I can see why," Johns said, pointing to the yellowed map. "Apparently, he had quite the collection of contraband."

Wendy snorted, then considered the charts. "It doesn't make sense. Why would Hooke bother making a replica of a map he already had?" She wondered "Especially if it was unsanctioned. All that would do is provide evidence against him if he ever got caught."

Her question lingered until Johns let out an awkward cough.

"Not to state the obvious," the lieutenant asked, "but why don't we just ask the 'esteemed' captain?"

"Absolutely not," Wendy declared. "Hooke's secrecy regarding the map is the whole reason we are in this predicament.

I sincerely doubt his current position will encourage him to be forthcoming now."

"He's already a prisoner," Peter countered thoughtfully. "Couldn't we use that as leverage? Maybe it will give him a reason to talk."

"Yeah," Johns agreed. "A little, 'you scratch my back, I'll scratch yours' action," he said with a laugh. "Works with Rissa every time."

"No one wants to hear about your love life, Johns," Wendy snipped before turning curtly to Peter. "To authorize that, I'd have to get approval from the Admiral. Which won't happen without the entire panel finding out." She sighed, imagining Colonel Matheson's scathing sneer. "Which is the last thing we need."

"Panel?" Johns asked, his levity dimming at Wendy's frown. "Is something wrong?"

"Johns, there's been something wrong since this mission launched," she answered, evading his question with a scoff. "It's nothing anyone needs to concern themselves with. Just one more hoop to jump through before we get home."

Unconvinced, the lieutenant's brow dipped as he looked from Peter to Wendy. Met with only Wendy's steely gaze, he finished with a shrug. "If you say so, Darling. But with all the hoop-jumping you've been doing, you might consider adding ringmaster to your CV."

"I'll consider it." Wendy laughed before turning to the foreign marks dotting the weathered chart. "But that won't help us with this. Tootles, I don't want to interrupt your work, but would it be possible for me to take the Stjarnin map? If you scan another one to keep here?"

Tootles shrugged. "I w-wouldn't know how to m-make one."

Grinning, Johns wrapped his arm around Wendy's shoulder. "Well luckily, we have a sweet little techie downstairs who happens to love us," he barked a laugh. "Our own greasy-godmother."

Groaning at the lieutenant, Wendy turned to the forgotten boys. "Nibs, Curly," she commanded, scurrying them to attention. "I need you to get Michaels. You might reach him on the comm, but more than likely you'll have to physically pull him from the bay. Tell him I said it was urgent."

With an awkward salute, the boys hurried from the room, happily abandoning their charts. Before they scurried off, Curly stopped at the door and swept a quick salute to Wendy, highlighting the healing scar on his face. Nodding at the two, Wendy waited for the door to hiss shut behind them before returning her attention to Tootles.

"Tootles, when they get back, brief the commander on what you found and why you need the copy. I'm sure he'll be able to work something out. And Johns," she addressed the broad-shouldered officer sternly, "be nice to Michaels. And make sure he eats something while he's up here."

"Yes mom, I mean, ma'am," Johns mimicked Curly's stumbling salute with a wide grin. "Anything else?"

Wendy thought for a moment. "Yes, actually. Make sure the pirates in holding aren't acting up. I know things calmed down after—" her voice caught on her next words, "after the Shadow disappeared, but I'd still rather keep tabs on them than get hit with any more nasty surprises."

Johns nodded. "You've got it. Is that all?" he asked with a grin, "But fair warning" anything else is gonna cost extra," he winked.

Wendy snorted. "In that case, when you get a chance, tell DeLaCruz that she deserves a Medal of Honor for putting up with you."

Her dry jab made Johns' smile split further. "Don't you worry Darling," he teased back. "DeLaCruz knows all about the prize she's won," he said, kissing a flexed bicep. The mechanic stifled a snicker as Wendy urged him to the door.

"You shouldn't encourage him," she scolded, "It only makes his jokes worse."

Peter snorted. "Something tells me Johns would make those jokes even if no-one in the 'verse laughed."

"You're probably right," Wendy admitted with a begrudging smile. "I wasn't kidding about Rissa earning an award."

Eyes sparking, Peter shrugged, his lips curling as he changed the subject. "So, where to Cap?"

Wendy sighed. "Back to Navs. I need to check in with Dawes and I want to be onsite when Michaels delivers those charts. I have a feeling there's important information hiding in them, we just have to figure out how to find it."

"You know, Johns' thought wasn't terrible. If anyone on board could make sense of the maps, it would be Hooke."

"What did I say about encouraging Johns," Wendy replied, picking up her pace. If they made it to her quarters quick enough, perhaps they could avoid the conversation.

"Johns isn't here," Peter pressed, speeding to match her. "But think. You want to know what's in the maps; Hooke has already figured that out. We've got him on board, why not use him as a resource?"

"Because he's a traitor!" Wendy argued. "Because he betrayed the Fleet and *imprisoned* me to summon a demon! All things considered, I think the better question is, 'what makes you think we could trust him?'"

"I'm not saying we follow him blindly," Peter countered. "I just think he might be able to point us in the right direction."

"Or he could send us right into another shytestorm," Wendy clipped. "Which is just as likely."

"I doubt he'd fling the whole ship into oblivion," Peter said. "Hooke's untrustworthy, sure, but not suicidal. He's in no condition to be picking fights right now, and he knows it. If there's one thing to say about James, it's that he understands strategy."

"James?" Wendy questioned, balking at Peter's casual address. "Since when are you back on a first name basis?"

A frustrated groan escaped Peter. "For *years*, Cap," he said. "True, when we met, I was pissed at Hooke—and rightfully so—but it doesn't just cancel our past. Or the risk he took in helping to get me back to you."

Wendy's lips pressed together as she considered. Peter's point held some merit, but she wasn't convinced.

"It's not a good idea," she decided. "Hooke may have made an honorable choice in coming back, but enlisting him as an advisor is a risk I'm not willing to take."

Peter looked like he wanted to argue, but after a moment, he simply nodded. "You're the captain," he said. Hearing his frustration, Wendy almost pressed the issue further, until she realized they were still in the center of the ship. Unwilling to risk an audience, she simply nodded before resuming silently down the hall. She didn't wait to see if Peter followed, but the absence of Tinc's soft jangles told her he wasn't.

6
FLEET MECHANIC PETER PAN

THE JOLLY ROGER

Peter had nearly made it to the mechbay before he calmed enough for Tinc's worried jangles to translate through his cochlear implant. Growling, he whirled on the bot, unleashing his pent agitation.

"What do you mean we can't go sublevel?" he snarled, then ducked to evade the twitching swoop Tinc aimed at his head. "Oh, right." he said. "Michaels is with the Cap."

With an exaggerated huff, he spun to stalk back the way he came. It wasn't that he couldn't go down to the bay on his own. There wasn't a part down there that he hadn't been entrusted to fix. But ever since Wendy had taken control of the *Roger*, everything had changed. And now the bay—*his bay*—the place he went to escape…

It wasn't his anymore.

"So now what?" He groaned, stuck in place. He rocked on his heels, debating, when a rumble escaped his stomach. "I guess that's as good as any option," he said, starting toward the kitchen. "C'mon Tinc."

Releasing a happy jangle, Tinc swept forward, circling Peter before shooting down the corridor with a hum. Following the bot, Peter clipped through the *Roger*, his sour disposition lightening at the idea of food. Urged on by his stomach, Peter hurried his pace, rounding the main hall past the newly rigged MedBay. Sterile lights streamed through its transparent window panels, making Peter blink. Normally, the screens remained dimmed unless the residents activated them, but Wendy had ordered them to remain open during Hooke's stay, constantly revealing the bay's contents.

Inside, DeLaCruz flitted through the rooms, lost in concentration as she leaned over her medpad, swaying to a silent beat while in the farthest cabin, Hooke slept, seemingly unbothered by the restraints tethered to his wrists and ankles. Although some color had returned to the captain's pallid skin, he still looked surprisingly frail. His once dark hair draped his face in a silvery sheet that emphasized his shrunken cheeks. The protruding bones matched his emaciated form, turning the captain into a shriveled husk. It was hard to reconcile him to the strong, daring captain who had recruited him to the *Roger* so many years ago.

Wrestling his memory, Peter hesitated outside the bay, fighting emotions he couldn't quite place. Unbidden, his fist thudded softly against the pane and the captain began to stir.

"Pan?" Hooke's question was muffled, but his voice was steady as he pushed up on his elbows, to look curiously through the transparent panel. An arrogant smirk flitted across his gaunt features, restoring a hint of the man Peter remembered.

Watching Peter intently, Hooke's brow quirked, issuing a silent challenge that drew Peter into the MedBay. Defiantly, he stepped into the chilled cabin, crinkling his nose against the strong smell of disinfectant mingling with metal. Soft music rumbled from a back room, the booming notes a stark difference from the airy tunes Dawes always played.

"Hey Pan," DeLaCruz greeted, annotating her file before she lowered her chart. "If you're here for the synTrack you're welcome to it, I'll just have to allocate a channel for your personal biometrics."

"I'm alright," Peter said, waving his hand. "I'll save the machinery for Johns and the captain," he grinned. He had sat in on enough of Wendy's physio sessions to know he wanted nothing to do with the automated laps and maneuvers the track ran its victims through. "Just passing through."

"The MedBay?" DeLaCruz asked, not bothering to hide her disbelief.

"Yes—erm, no. I mean…" Peter huffed as he scratched his head. "I saw Hooke was awake, and—" he paused to search for the right words. "He looked like hell, so I thought I'd make sure he wasn't going to die on us," Peter dropped his hands to his pockets, hoping to bolster his bluff. Tinc's spark echoed over his shoulder, affirming his lie.

Studying them, DeLaCruz pursed her lips before hoisting her medpad to the crook of her arm. "Hooke's condition is fully stable and his vital scans are better than can be expected. You're more than welcome to check," she offered, refocusing on the charts projected before her, "but per Captain Darling, his restraints stay in place, and all non-medical personnel are required to keep a two foot perimeter." She side-eyed Tinc, "And that includes tech."

The medic's sharp gaze earned a surly flare of sparks from Tinc, but Peter nodded emphatically. "No need to get any closer," he agreed. He shot a warning glower at his protesting nano-companion and made a note to adjust the bot's sensitivity settings. "We'll just be a minute."

DeLaCruz nodded, but her attention had long slipped from the pair. With an absent-minded wave, she slipped away, focusing on her glowing medpad. Releasing a quick breath, Peter waved at the bot hovering over his shoulder.

"C'mon Tinc, let's get this over with," he started, still hardly believing he was heading toward the deceitful captain. Tinc jangled obediently, then nestled in the crook of his neck, her processor thrumming wildly. "We won't stay longer than necessary."

Tinc's soft reply was overshadowed by Hooke's surprised laugh. "Visitors?" he asked, a sly grin crawling over his face. "I was told those rights were revoked from traitors to the crown." He clucked his tongue before leaning tiredly against his pillow. "I'll have to ask your captain what she thinks about this."

Peter crossed his arms with a scowl. "Or we could just leave," he said, his temper flaring. He wasn't sure what he'd expected, but now he felt stupid for not anticipating Hooke's mocking. "Let's go, Tinc. He's alive and well enough to be a complete arse. He'll be just fine."

He hurried toward the door until a hacking cough erupted, slowing his quickened gait.

"Pan—wait." Hooke's moan creaked through the room.

Turning impatiently, Peter studied the bedridden man and an unwanted jolt of sympathy panged through him. Up close, he could see the angry red marks from where Hooke's bindings rubbed against his skin. They were covered by the remnants of an ointment that DeLaCruz had used to mitigate the damage, but it didn't quite work against the chapped rings. The area around the raw edges were tinged in a sickly purple, showing streaking bruises that trailed up his yellowed forearms. Taking a ragged breath, Hooke grimaced as he shifted to sit higher in his bed.

Silently, he met Peter's even gaze, his brows raised in a haughty challenge.

"You'll have to forgive me for not looking my best," he said, indicating the room with a flippant wave. "I was rather under the impression I shouldn't expect anyone."

"Being a prisoner tends to have that effect," Peter sniped.

A powerful rumble rippled from the captain's throat. "And yet, here you stand," he said, raising his peppered brow in a silent question.

"Got turned about," Peter shrugged. "It's been a while since the *Roger* and I have been acquainted."

Hooke laughed again, honest mirth lighting his sleet stare. "Come now Pan, both you and I know that we could have been caught on Neverland for a thousand years and you would not have forgotten one millimeter of our ship."

"Our ship?" Peter challenged. "We've had many discussions about the *Roger* over the years, Captain. I don't recall once being assigned ownership."

Hooke shrugged before resting against his bed. "On paper, perhaps," he ceded, "but in your heart you always saw the *Roger* as yours—otherwise, you wouldn't have taken such care with her." He paused, studying Peter shrewdly, "Unless I assume incorrectly?"

It was Peter's turn to shrug. Hooke knew he was right, there was no reason to boost his ego. Instead, the mechanic scanned the machinery surrounding the captain, searching for a way to change the subject. He didn't know why, but the conversation had brought a queasy feeling to his stomach, like the antigravity had fritzed and launched his guts into space. "It seems the Fleet is doing a good job keeping you alive."

Hooke scoffed and examined the bindings on his arm. "If you can call this living," he said, his features darkening against the wrinkles in his cheeks.

"Would you rather have been left on Skull Rock?" Peter asked, shivering as he recalled the ragged piles of skin and bones they had discovered on the craggy floor. Rough as he looked now, Hooke looked a lifetime better than the breathing corpse they had found on Neverland.

Hooke's lips pressed in a tight line. "That is not something I would wish on my worst enemy," he murmured, his voice soft as he sat, quietly brooding. After a moment he refocused his gaze. "However, it would seem that I have traded one cage for another," he nodded to his altered bed. "Regardless of how much more comfortable this one appears to be."

Peter's shoulders stiffened. He wasn't sure what to say. Though it was true that Hooke's position on the *Roger* was infinitely better than the condition Peter had found him on Skull Rock, he was also acutely aware that Hooke's decision to accompany him to the ship had led to his imprisonment in the MedBay. Once the Shadow had been defeated, Wendy had seized the captain, proclaiming his crimes against the Fleet.

"It's the captain's decision," Peter replied, reminding himself as much as Hooke. He cleared his throat, disliking the guilt seeping into his stomach. "One that I'm sure will be reevaluated once we reach New London."

"Ah yes," Hooke said with a withered smile. "A decision that will no doubt turn in my favor." He sighed, then adjusted his bed. Lying flat, the captain looked immensely frail. "I'll take your leave now, Pan. This conversation grows dreary." Shifting away from Peter, Hooke waved his hand, dismissing the mechanic.

Waiting for a moment, Peter studied the captain until Tinc's soft hum whispered through his implant. Nodding at the bot, Peter followed her from the bay, the captain's echoing words ringing heavy over the music still throbbing through the rooms.

7
FLEET MECHANIC PETER PAN

Peter's mind lingered on his conversation with Hooke long after he left the MedBay. Nagging thoughts chased him through the corridors, whirling him through a dizzying cycle. It was easy enough to say Hooke needed to be held accountable for his crimes, but seeing the man he once called a mentor reduced to a shackled, sliver of the captain he used to be was a jarring difference. Hadn't one hundred years trapped on Neverland been enough penance? Surely his cost of hosting the Shadow could have been some sort of peonage? Simply seeing the toll the brief exchange took on the captain's physique could attest to that.

But Wendy doesn't see it that way, he thought. *She only sees a man who betrayed the Fleet and caused the death of her friend.* Or, whatever classification she truly assigned Commander Boyce. The unwanted idea flipped his stomach. Before, he would have been sure Wendy only saw the commander as her subordinate.

Then he saw their kiss.

Jealousy flared through him as the memory replayed in his mind. Wendy, tilting her face to the commander as he closed the distance between them. Boyce pushed against her, and Wendy leaned in, pressing her body to his, allowing her dark curls to cascade around them, tethering their two forms together.

Grimacing, Peter rubbed his eyes to erase the imprinted image, but it was no use. No matter what words were said, emotion like that couldn't be faked. It was pretty clear to him Wendy felt something more for the commander; he just wondered if it was obvious to her, too.

Peter let out a frustrated growl and a concerned buzz thrummed in his ear. "It's nothing, Tinc," he lied. "Let's go find that sandwich."

Tinc jangled doubtfully, but shot off, leaving a trail of golden sparks. Shaking his head, Peter departed after her glimmering path, focusing on the way her cascading trail dispersed into the air. Distracted, he made his way through the *Roger*, until he turned a corner and nearly careened over a silent, sitting figure.

"Whoa! Sorry, I didn't see—"

"Peter Pan." Tizari's throaty accent rippled through the corridor, matching the amusement rumbling from her chest. "It is hard to see when one isn't looking where he is going."

Peter let out an embarrassed laugh. "That would do it," he agreed, offering the Stjarnin his hand. Tizari studied it quizzically, then rose to her feet, the motion as fluid as water pouring into a glass. Pocketing his useless hand, Peter met the alien's gaze. The warrior was taller than he was, composed of slender angles and lithe grace emanating from her mossy skin. "Why are you sitting in the hall? I know the *Roger's* far from a luxury brig, but there's got to be a more comfortable place for you to—erm—do whatever it was you were doing."

Tizari smiled. "There are not as many available places as one would think."

Peter's brow furrowed. "What do you mean? The rig has loads of places to... sit."

"Perhaps," Tizari agreed, "but few are without interruption. Your hallways are meant for passing. Rooms are a destination. I find it is less awkward for the other passengers if they can move around me, instead of encountering me where they intend to rest."

Peter's frown deepened. "Was someone rude to you? It might have been a miscommunication," he explained. "Wendy told the others you were welcome to stay."

"My translator ensures no miscommunication," Tizari motioned to a quicksilver disc pinned to her ear before offering a gilled smile. "No unkindness has been shown to me," she assured. The Stjarnin rested her willowy hand on Peter's shoulder and a subtle warmth seeped from her touch to his skin. "My people are watchers. We see things others do not. And as much as humans think they disguise, there has not been a race I have found worse at concealing their emotions."

She laughed and Peter felt a hot flare rush to his cheeks.

"I understand there is no ill-intent," Tizari added, removing her hand. "My presence simply brings too many unpleasant reminders of an event your crew are keen to forget."

"That shouldn't mean you have to hide in the halls," Peter argued.

"It is where I choose to be," Tizari said simply. "According to my understanding of human hospitality customs, that explanation should be enough."

Peter stifled his argument with a tight nod. "Polite manners would agree," he said. "Not that polite has ever been a key descriptor of my personality."

Tizari laughed again, shaking her shoulders so the beads adorning her dark braids tinkled in an echoing chime. "This does not surprise me," she ceded, before stepping back. "I did not mean to deter you from your destination. Do not let me keep you."

"I'm not in a hurry," Peter answered honestly. "Just killing time."

Tizari frowned at the figure of speech. "You humans are offered so much time that you choose to murder it?"

Chuckling, Peter shook his head. "Not anymore, I guess," he said, sobering at the thought.

Watching his reaction, Tizari's expression lengthened. "I have upset you," she said, an apology lining the timbre of her voice.

"No, just contemplating my shortened life span," he joked weakly.

"One should always be aware of their own mortality. It reminds us to make worthy each of our actions. It is a common belief among my people that those whose days are dwindling are the ones who leave the most impact."

Peter nodded, considering her words. Tizari's watchful eyes followed his action before she prodded further. "It may not have been my words, but I can see something is troubling you. Is there nothing I can do?"

"I think this one is out of your reach," Peter sighed. "Really, the only ones who can do anything about it are the Fleet."

"If nothing you do can change the outcome, why do you worry?" Tizari asked, with genuine concern.

"Good question," Peter answered with a scoff. "Part of me is still trying to figure out why I'm even bothered in the first place." Scratching his head, he finished his thought in a grumble. "It's not like Hooke would trouble himself if it was me."

Tizari stiffened. "Captain Hooke is…" she paused as she thought, "a sensitive subject. On the ship."

"You can say that again," Peter laughed. "Even for the few people who do tolerate him."

"Tolerate…" Tizari stretched the word. "Is this a human term of friendship?"

Another snort escaped Peter. "Not usually. Although with Hooke, it could be."

"You are concerned about how your planet will receive him." Tizari guessed, cutting past Peter's hedging. "That he will be punished for his involvement with the Shadow."

"No." Peter started, then hesitated. "Yes. Maybe?" He exhaled heavily. "Really, I don't know." He looked helplessly at the alien, feeling obligated to explain. "I don't think that punishing him is wrong; I just don't think the Fleet will be more concerned with justice so much as making an example."

"The captain's decisions created many incidents that could otherwise have been avoided," Tizari mused. "There are bound to be repercussions for the impact of his misdeeds."

"I get that," Peter sighed. "And I don't necessarily disagree, I just… wonder if he hasn't already been punished enough."

Tizari was quiet for a moment. The silence lingered, disturbed only by Tinc's intermittent sparks as she bobbed around their shoulders. Finally, the Stjarnin glanced up, trapping Peter in her ebony gaze.

"Captain Hooke is a murderer. A man hated by my people, who would not be offered our mercy of life." Peter's shoulders sagged, feeling the sincerity in her words. "However," she added, snapping Peter's attention to her mossy face. "I have seen more to Hooke. It does not excuse his actions, but it provides me understanding. Perhaps this is where you stand as well."

Peter nodded, feeling as though the alien's manufactured English had described his thoughts better than he ever could. Tizari attempted a smile and placed her hand on his shoulder once more.

"Waiting on the mountain is harder than being embedded in the valley. It offers greater perspective, but the climb is treacherous. Those who reach it can truly see but are burdened by the voices of others who didn't dare the climb." She removed her hand and took a small step back. "I have climbed the mountain with you, Pan. I can see your captain clearer than those who watch him from the valley."

"So what do you see?" Peter asked, hoping the Stjarnin might clarify his thoughts once more.

Tizari blinked. "I see a man who is searching desperately for something he has not yet found. Something he may never encounter because he doesn't know what it truly is. I see—" she paused, and the slits of her mouth pressed together. "To use the words of your crew, I see a Lost Boy."

Peter let out a considering hum. James had always seemed so untouchable. It had never occurred to him that Hooke's hardened exterior could be hiding wounds too. The thought was so encompassing that he almost forgot about the Stjarnin until she cleared her throat to speak.

"I can see you need some time alone. Thank you for your companionship, Pan. It has broken some of the silence." Tizari dipped her head in a polite excusal before disappearing into the dim. Still thinking, Peter hovered in the corridor until he was interrupted by Tinc's impatient jangle.

"Yes, we can go now," Peter grumbled, eyeing the swooping bot. "But I don't know why you're in such a hurry. You can't even eat the bloody sandwich."

Peter grinned at Tinc's translated snark as she sparked red and led him toward the kitchens, though his attention was only half on her showered path. The rest lingered with the lonely Stjarnin and the glimpse she provided into his own conflicted mind.

8
CAPTAIN WENDY DARLING

THE JOLLY ROGER

"You know Captain, if you leave your face like that long enough, it'll stick that way."

Dawes' teasing broke Wendy's furious concentration. Startled, the captain glanced up, surprised at the tension building in her jaw. Blinking, she unclenched her teeth and grimaced as they worked loose, earning a soft giggle from the pilot.

"Didn't your mom and dad ever teach you that?" Dawes asked.

"Surprisingly, no," Wendy answered, thinking how horrified her mother would be at the prospect of a permanently furrowed brow.

Dawes grinned. "It was one of my dad's favorite things to tell me. Especially when I pulled a face at my sisters. I think it's mostly because Arista always whined about it." She shrugged, and her smile dipped. "I didn't think I'd ever miss his jokes, but when we get topside, I might call just to have him say it."

Wendy smiled sadly. Missing home was something she couldn't relate to. Even with everything that happened, she longed more for the security of the Academy than Darling Manor, but she didn't doubt she was a minority in that case. During her time at school she'd observed enough family days to realize how severely her relationship with her parents was lacking. Probably the only one who had shared her sentiments was Boyce, and now—

Wendy closed her eyes as a thick lump caught in her throat. She tried to swallow, but it remained lodged in place as she toyed with the charm bracelet the commander had gifted her. The tiny spaceship dangling from the chain swayed as it moved, glinting dully in the cabin's lights. While it was far from fine jewelry, Wendy thought the aged metal gave it a charm that none of her mother's most exquisite baubles could replicate. It was beautiful in its simplicity, an attribute that Wendy now realized came from Boyce's understanding of her. The piece fit her just as well as he did, which made her love it all the more. Their rebellion against their parents' status-seeking had been one of the few interests Wendy knew they shared. They had been raised in it—mimicking perfection to appease distant parents and a fleet of their 'dearest' friends. Now, she was left wondering how many other things they might have shared.

"Are you okay, Captain?" Dawes' asked, her question breaking through Wendy's dark musings. "I lost you for a minute."

Nodding, Wendy forced a smile. "Just wondering what it must be like to have family who are actually excited to see you." She tugged the base of her coat. "I've heard stories from Johns and Michaels, but it's still somewhat of a novelty."

Dawes' smile withered. "I'm sure your parents have missed you." Her pretty features twisted in a thoughtful pout. "Do you think the Fleet told them anything about what's happened?"

Wendy felt her brow crease further. Smoothing the line with her fingers, she sighed.

"I doubt it. Even with how sideways everything went, I think the Fleet will hold off making any sort of official report for as long as possible. Less damage control. Unless something happened to make it impossible to avoid, I think things will probably be kept pretty well hushed."

"Do you think we'll be allowed to talk about it when we get back?"

"Do you really want to?" Wendy asked.

Dawes shrugged. "I mean, some pretty horrible things happened," the pilot admitted. "But it would almost be worse if we didn't." She picked through the loose strands of her flaming braid. "People are going to have questions." She dropped her hands into her lap before looking at Wendy. "I think that if we don't say what really happened with Hooke, and the Shadow, and most of all to Boyce—that it would be a disservice. Not talking about it won't mean nothing happened, it would just make it seem like we don't care." Quieting, she looked up at Wendy. "I care," she said.

"I know," Wendy nodded at the pilot. "I do too," she agreed, leaning against her chair. Dealing with Boyce's absence had been hard enough with just the crew's response to handle, she hadn't considered what the world might think too. Added to her rapidly growing pile of worries, it was just one more thing threatening to crush her. Wendy rubbed her temples and leaned over the StarBoard. Scanning through her files, she noted a new link and smiled. Michaels had already sent her the charts.

"I don't know what I did to deserve that kid," Wendy said gratefully.

"Who, Peter?" Dawes waggled her brows mischievously.

"No," Wendy laughed and shook her head. "I mean, he's great," she added with a flush, noticing the quizzical expression that flitted over the pilot's face. "But I was talking about Michaels."

It was Dawes' turn to blush. Her cheeks washed in a soft rose that offset her fiery hair. "Oh. *That* mechanic," the pilot coughed nervously. "Yeah, he's pretty great, I guess." She bit her lip to erase the sudden grin from her face.

"He is," Wendy agreed, enjoying the weight her teasing lifted from her chest. "Although, from my understanding, our reasoning is from two completely different angles." She gave Dawes a look of faux-disapproval, which sent the pilot's soft flush to completely overtake her face.

"I appreciate Jensen's care for the ship," Dawes retorted haughtily. "It makes my job much easier when the *Roger* actually functions."

"I bet it does," Wendy laughed. "I'll make sure and let *Jensen* know how much you appreciate his attention to detail," she tittered, "although, if you don't mind, I think I'll stick to calling him Michaels."

"He'd probably prefer that," Dawes agreed. "I just barely got permission, and it took some serious convincing."

Wendy covered her ears. "I don't want to hear anymore." Knowing Johns, she could easily assume what sort of tactics had been used but picturing them between Arielle and Michaels was difficult. "Let's just say I get it, and leave it at that."

Dawes giggled in response as she twisted her chair back to her command panel. Though the majority of her flush had disappeared, soft pink blotches still colored her cheeks as she playfully bit her lip. Watching her, Wendy was almost jealous of how easily the pilot displayed her emotions. Without care or embarrassment, Arielle was able to simply enjoy her feelings.

Wendy wondered if she would ever be able to do the same. She found it unlikely.

For a moment, she considered asking Dawes how she managed to stay so relaxed, but as Wendy glanced back at her StarBoard, something else caught her attention. At the end of the scanned files list, another document had been added with a secured encryption coded to her personal access key. Following the file, Michaels had keyed a simple note.

For your consideration.

Intrigued, Wendy clicked the document and an official report populated on the screen, filling the StarBoard with typed script.

Commander's Log, AIDAN BOYCE, Identification Code #33672 April 1, 2394.

Today marks the first complete day after our departure from Neverland, though departure might be too generous a word. Consistent with its acquisition of Hooke's men, the planet clung to our vessel, and did not relinquish its hold willingly. It resulted in the loss of a fleet mechanic, Ensign Peter Pan, a personal recruit of Hooke's whose complex involvement in the Neverland excursions leaves many questions yet to be answered. Personally, I find the mechanic's interference troubling—though helpful at times, I worry about his influence on the captain. While it is my belief that she has exhibited remarkable competency in a precarious situation, I worry that Pan's initial assistance might leave her feel indebted to a fleetman who, quite frankly, does not deserve it. I worry for her.

Swiping her hand across the screen, Wendy inhaled sharply as the message disappeared and was replaced by a subsequent report. Without pausing to read it, she scrolled through the re-mainder of the files, revealing a full collection of the commander's reports, official and unofficial entries compiling an entire dossier. Her head spinning, she cleared the message, replacing the extensive texts with her originally requested files. Clusters of stars and patterned trajectories swirled in the charts before, but Wendy couldn't clearly see any of them. Instead, her mind lingered on Boyce's reports and the frenzied questions they summoned.

Forcing them from her mind, Wendy twisted in her seat to focus on the task at hand, her gaze blurring until it narrowed on a small, barely noticeable mark in the corner of the displayed chart. Seizing the distraction, she examined the annotation until an idea struck. Running her hand over the chart to make sure she wasn't imagining things, she turned to the pilot when the spot remained.

"Dawes," Wendy called, her voice tighter than she intend-ed. "Come look at this."

"Sure thing, Captain," Dawes breezed, before walking over, bringing with her the faint scent of coconut. Her gaze narrowed expertly as she studied the maps Wendy displayed. "I've never seen these before," the pilot stated. "They definitely aren't any-thing from the Fleet database. Where did you get them?"

"These are the maps we discovered cut into Hooke's shelves. Tootles transcribed it onto a star chart, so I asked Michaels to upload it along with a few others that Tootles found in Hooke's logs. I think it's a recording of the Uncharted Sec-tor."

Dawes leaned closer, the end of her fishtail sweeping the panel as she studied the map. After a moment, she pressed her finger to a large constellation at the edge of the chart.

"I think you're right, Captain," she agreed. "It's hard to tell for sure, but I think I remember passing through that field of stars right before the *Fiducia's* systems went down. We were traveling this way," she traced her finger along the projected path, moving inward from the edge of the map, "when everything went haywire. And then," she paused, concentrating as she scoured the map, "we landed on Neverland." Her finger circled the landmark before pointing at two familiar swirls—a pair that clung together in the field of lonely lights. "That's the Second Star, isn't it?"

"That was my thought," Wendy confirmed, re-orienting the diagram. "I was just hoping someone could confirm it." She looked at Dawes, whose expression still puckered in confusion.

"I don't understand, though," the pilot questioned, "How was Hooke able to keep these from the Fleet's database? Even if he hadn't reported them, expeditionary rigs have auto-reporting systems installed to survey and capture the ship's surrounding coordinates."

"I'm not sure," Wendy admitted, "I guess that's something else we'll have to figure out. For now, I'm going to examine these further."

"Good idea," Dawes agreed, turning toward her seat. "I'll be here if you need anything."

Nodding, Wendy returned her attention to the diagram before her. Now that they had identified the segment of the Krawk Nebula, she could recognize some of the systems they had encountered. Looking back at the unidentified mark, Wendy traced it with her finger, wondering what it might be. She frowned as she scanned the rest of the map, until she noticed a familiar astral cluster. Matching its shape and energy signatures, her expression shifted. According to the readings, the segment she was studying should have been the floating graveyard, but the map's representation was too small. The graveyard—which the crew had unofficially dubbed the Shipwreck Belt—had spanned dozens of parsecs, with a battalion of vessels trapped in its wake. The field marked before her was much smaller, with only a few noted masses recorded through its body.

Confused, Wendy contemplated what could have caused the difference, when an idea struck. With an excited gasp, she furiously keyed a system coordinate retrieval. After a brief scan followed by a few concerning whirs from the StarBoard, only one other map matched; composed with the same boxy, severe lines.

Ignoring her brief disappointment, Wendy overlaid it on her coordinates, forming a new map. Scouring the chart, Wendy accessed the coded metadata and pulled up the author stamp. After several moments of searching, she finally located the file signature and clicked it open, her breath stopping as it flashed across her screen.

Krawk Nebula StarCast est. 1082 - - Tracing of the constellations assumed in the Uncharted Sector - - Data acquired from Stjarnin Intel. Transcribed by Captain James Tiberius Hooke, March 11, 2293.

Swallowing the words, Wendy minimized the report and returned to the secondary chart. Following the same path to its authoring data, she rushed to retrieve it. Another series of clicks and whirs summoned an identical report, bringing a glowing message flickering onscreen to hover alongside its brother.

Krawk Nebula StarCast est 1643- - Tracing of the constellations assumed in the Uncharted Sector - - Data acquired from Stjarnin Intel - Transcribed by Captain James Tiberius Hooke, March 11, 2293.

Heart thudding, Wendy's eyes widened as she toggled the charts, trying to confirm her theory that somehow, between two separate chartings, the strange mark had appeared. She took an extra moment to scrutinize the two maps, scouring every notation. Finding no other discrepancies, Wendy waved to her pilot.

"Dawes, could I borrow you one more time?"

"Of course, Captain. Did you find something else?"

"I think so," Wendy said, glancing at the lieutenant. "But to be sure, I need your help. Is there any way you could upload our most recent chart of the Krawk Nebula? The way it looked when we passed through?"

"You want a map of our current trajectory?"

"Yes," Wendy confirmed. "And include a data stamp of all the surrounding astral bodies."

"I should be able to handle that," Dawes nodded and began typing instructions into her command panel. It took a few minutes, but after a string of curses, Dawes cried out triumphantly. "Got it!" Her nimble fingers slid across the screen as she swiped a glowing chart from its center. "What do you want to see first?"

"All of it," Wendy said, striding to Dawes as she accessed the file and packaged it into a neat holobit. Unbothered by her shoulder hovering, the pilot shot the file, clearing it from the screen before Wendy's scanband buzzed. Glancing absently at the notification, she thanked Dawes for the file and stalked back to the StarBoard where she quickly pulled up the encrypted charts.

Keying in her access code, Wendy released the file, opening the map across her screen. It covered Hooke's maps, replacing the old charts with a current sector diagram. Navigating to the board's settings hub, Wendy opened the display and clicked through a series of commands. Finding what she wanted, she grinned as the holofile pixelated into a shimmering overlay of the maps below. The stack of images appeared to be a nearly identical tracing, with the exception of the clustered graveyard and the mysterious mark that had originally caught Wendy's eye.

Scanning the enlarged area, Wendy noticed how much it had grown since the time Hooke created his chart, which had already doubled from the original file. Making a mental note to look into it, she turned to the more concerning image—the unidentified whorl in the corner.

Faded and blurred, the mark might have been missed—there was nothing exceptional about the small flicker except for its strange appearance.

It's large enough that it registered on a cursory scan, but not so big that it drew Hooke's attention, Wendy thought, studying the blip. Accessing its metadata configuration, she discovered a faint energy signature resonating from the mark but no apparent pulse.

"What do you think it could be?" Dawes breathed, startling Wendy. The pilot hovered over her shoulder, studying the mark intently.

"I don't know," Wendy answered, then snapped to action as an idea struck.

She keyed a string of commands into the StarBoard, sequencing a long-distance scan of the given coordinates. With her automated instructions complete, she turned to Dawes with an eager grin.

"But I intend to find out."

THE LOST BOY

9
COMMANDER AIDAN BOYCE
LOCATION UNKNOWN

"Commander Aidan Boyce, officer of the Londonniere Brigade. Rank identification C-397v4. Assigned Liaison Officer to the *Fede Fiducia*, and the search and retrieval mission to Neverland. I was born April 4, 2372. My parents—my parents…"

The commander trailed off as his memory fogged, covering the conjured images with ghostly grey tendrils, immersing him once again in a darkened haze.

Cold.

Why was everything always so cold? He wondered as an unwanted chill swept down his spine. Turning in circles inside the tiny cabin, he examined the blockaded door. A large X had been slashed across the barrier in a dark, crimson substance too thick to be paint.

His brow furrowed as he studied the symbol until a loud growl ripped through his stomach, accompanied by a sharp pain. When was the last time he had eaten? He couldn't remember.

Searching the room, he found a small panel with a stash of ferreted nutripaks. Guided by the pangs in his stomach, he greedily pawed the meals, until a loose piece of foil fell loose and fluttered delicately to the ground. Confused, the commander watched until it landed, revealing another message left for him in stained red.

WAIT.

Replacing the packs, he retrieved the slip and paused as he noticed the bandage on his hand. Turning his palm, he discovered a dark slash seeping through the gauze, its color identical to the cryptic messages dotting the compartment.

Boyce groaned and scrubbed his face as he tried to remember what happened through his pocked mind. His only recollections were from the distant past—growing up, training, and always…watching her.

Wendy.

Through the haze, a vibrant memory flashed—of his arms wrapped around a beautiful girl with dark, sweeping curls tumbling around her as she pressed against his body, angling her face towards his. Her marble gaze searched him intently, the golden flecks in her stare like stars sparkling in an endless galaxy before she collided into him; their gravity creating a universe of passion, desire, and hope in their burning kiss.

Pressing his lips, he felt a trickle of warmth blaze through the icy room, heating him as a succession of images played through his mind, all centralized on the girl—*the captain*—directing her team aboard a ship, enwrapped in a raging battle with a fierce alien battalion, unflinching as she faced down a writhing pillar of black—

Each memory was punctuated with another shard of golden light bursting through his fogged thoughts until suddenly, they slammed against an onyx wall then vanished again into the muted void.

Feeling the darkness, Boyce recoiled, his body wrenching as his mind retreated from the looming barricade. His gut twisted, and a menacing laugh echoed in the recesses of his thoughts. Boyce recognized the sound—a deranged cackle that deepened into a slithering, mirthless growl.

The Shadow.

Cold washed over the commander, reminding him where he was—trapped aboard the ghost of a ship—a vessel the Shadow had slunk into after Boyce's desperate attempt to protect Wendy.

And how has that worked for you, commander? The Shadow whispered; its voice carried on the rippling wings of another slithering laugh.

Ignoring it, Boyce glanced at his hand. He unwrapped the bandage and looked at the gash in his palm where an angry red line formed a throbbing, jagged cut. As he did, a half-memory played in his mind—a hazy vision where he barricaded the door behind him before smearing the dripping wound across it to create the macabre warning.

Absent-minded, Boyce traced the cut and stepped toward the door. Hesitating, he took a deep breath, then raised his fist to pound against the metal. The knock resonated, vibrating into the ship until the muffled echo faded into the steel. Boyce listened, not sure what he was waiting for until distant scratches skittered from the depths of the barge. They started faintly, then the scrabbling grew louder—claws scraping metal followed by hissing laughter that swelled to a roar until it slammed into the barricade with a deafening bang.

Shrinking back from the barricade, Boyce listened to the angry shrieks, his hands balling into uncertain fists.

My pets tire of waiting, Commander, the Shadow hissed, emerging from the recesses of Boyce's mind. *Soon, even your feeble door won't be able to deter them.*

As if the creatures heard the Shadow's slithered taunts, a yowl erupted outside the door, followed by hammered thuds against the trembling steel. Gritting his teeth, Boyce searched for a weapon he could equip should his stronghold fail. His gaze landed on the metal rods he'd used for his makeshift barricade and decided that if they fell, they'd at least make a decent bludgeon against the intruders.

As long as there weren't too many.

Cracking his knuckles, Boyce stalked from the door to the command panel nestled in the far end of the compartment. The box was ancient, pummeled and dented to a nearly unrecognizable piece of junk—save the shattered comm screen displayed across the top. Studying the uneven shards, Boyce swore as more of the Shadow's fog lifted from his mind. He had seen this. He had *done* this. But how many times?

More than you care to know, the Shadow answered with another wave of laughter.

A low growl escaped the commander as he pushed the voice away to focus on the screen. It was cracked and splintered, as though someone—or something—had taken heavy fists to it, but there was also a large portion that remained intact. Perhaps he could get it to function.

Deciding it was better than nothing, Boyce crouched to observe the panel. Erratic dents cratered its body, bending its access doors at a twisted angle. Pulling the mangled steel, Boyce revealed a compartment of tangled wires. They jutted at kinked angles—a handful of survivors from the wrecked system.

Muttering a low curse, Boyce rubbed his tired eyes. Conflicting memories flashed through his vision, punctuated by hazy grey gaps. He shook his head to chase them away, then narrowed his gaze at the decimated panel.

It would be much easier to work with if you had the proper training, the dark voice taunted.

"I have the best training in the entire galaxy," Boyce muttered, baring his teeth at the mess of wires. Trailing the individual cords to their origins, he worked to unwind the larger knots.

It doesn't seem to be doing you much good, the voice countered. *Earning a commander's title might seem honorable to some, but for the son of the General...* the voice trailed off in a low cackle. *How disappointing.*

"Not nearly as disappointing as the fact that I still have to put up with you," Boyce snapped, attempting to erect a mental blockade. He imagined a steel wall snapping into place, sealing his mind from everything beside the wires and tech he held in his hands. For a moment, it seemed to work, leaving him in blessed quiet until his imagined wall dissipated and a fresh bout of laughter seeped around his thoughts, carrying with it a new wave of fog.

Oh Commander, another door? It was fun the first few times, but now it does grow tiresome. It seems originality isn't one of the strengths garnered from your training. I wonder, do you think Captain Darling even notices your absence or is your presence just as easily replaced?

The darkness paused, allowing Boyce's fury to simmer. Gripping the wires, the commander tried once more to push out the taunting voice, but the colored wires blurred and faded as it continued.

We all know she's already replaced you once with the mechanic, it said with another cruel laugh. *A delicious irony, don't you think? The one who might actually be able to fix the mess before you is the one you hate the most. Tell me, what is it like losing everything to an inferior?*

"Shut up!" Boyce screamed, clamping his hands over his temples to drown the laughter billowing through his thoughts. His cry stirred the creatures outside, inciting a fresh wave of howls as they renewed their attempts against his blockade. Pounding the floor, the commander hunched on the ground, chest heaving as he steadied himself against the darkness creeping around his mind.

Why ever would I do that, the Shadow asked, holding him captive in his own personal hell. *When your rage is so delicious?*

Boyce pressed his lips together, biting a furious retort. Arguing would do no good. Who knew how many wasted conversations he'd already had. Every time his temper spiked, his wrath fed it and made it stronger. Instead, he cleared his thoughts, erasing everything except a deep green constellation, with dancing golden flecks that sparked and weaved through hidden divots of slate, creating a perfect hazel fog. Only he knew where the constellation could be found, and as long as he did not put words to it, he could keep it from the Shadow, establishing a galaxy where he could be free.

"Because I have work to do," Boyce growled, grabbing the wires once more to separate them from their tangles. He felt the Shadow shudder angrily, trying to press into the foundation he had laid, and after a furious roar, its wrath was deflected by the constellation wall.

Smiling, the commander worked deftly, focusing on the wires while training the back of his mind on the color of Wendy's eyes, drawing strength from her steady, reassuring stare. Outside his conjured galaxy, the Shadow's scream came again, followed by a trembling attack against his defensive wall.

Realizing time was running out, the commander examined his work, trying to create a mental imprint of his progress. Gritting his teeth, he turned his wounded hand and removed the bandage to slash his cut across the edges of the crooked door. As the darkness swept over him, clouding out his mental block of beautiful stars, Boyce dipped his finger in the pooling blood.

Finishing his scrawled message, the commander leaned back with a victorious smile. Though he felt the threatening pull of the Shadow's rage, the monster's taunting was stalled against a singular thought. He had discovered something essential.

Itzala might have become his own personal demon, trapping him in a strange, dying vessel that mirrored the shattered fragments of his mind; but he would continue to fight. His smile faltered as another shadowy shudder trembled through his brain with such ferocity that it sent a physical wave of pain reeling through him. Crying out, Boyce pressed his palm against his skull, as if it might contain the monster, before he smiled once more.

Because that was what the commander knew. Even though the Shadow might have him—might own his trapped and broken thoughts—Itzala's possession of the commander prompted a significant derivative.

As long as Itzala was in him, Boyce held the Shadow, too.

IO
CAPTAIN WENDY DARLING

THE JOLLY ROGER

Groaning, Wendy scrubbed her eyes for what must have been the hundredth time. She couldn't help it, the more she looked at the charts, the less they seemed to reveal. Even the strange mark, which now formed a crystal clear image whenever she closed her eyes, had begun to dance and blur each time she observed the projected maps.

"You really should take a break, Captain," Dawes said when Wendy flopped over the StarBoard and burrowed under her arms. "If I learned one thing from my exam cram sessions at the Academy, it's that smooshing everything into the last few hours only helped trigger some serious migraines."

"This isn't an exam," Wendy countered, sighing as she pushed herself into a proper sitting position. She glanced back down at the map and once again the lines began to wobble.

Shaking her head, Wendy turned to stare at the worried pilot instead. "Those weren't life and death."

"That's not what you said back then," Michaels' interrupted, causing Wendy to glance at his projected image in the comm screen. She glowered at him and he shrugged before intently studying the tech in front of him.

Watching them, Dawes suppressed a snicker then pulled Wendy from her chair. "All I'm saying Captain, is that sometimes, getting out of your head makes all the difference. It's been two days and you've hardly moved from that spot. I'm beginning to wonder if I need to ask DeLaCruz to hook you up with a catheter."

Wendy scowled at the pilot. "That won't be necessary," she said.

Even with SMEE's tidying, a mess of charts surrounded them, creating a battlefield of maps and correspondence dossiers around the room. Slogging through them, Tootles worked, his little brows furrowed in a golden knot. As he searched each file, the bags under his eyes seemed to darken with every page. Laying at his feet, Seven snored softly, her bushy tail sweeping over his discarded charts until the Neverbeast yawned and rolled onto her back.

Stifling a yawn of her own, Wendy nodded in agreement. "You're probably right, a break would do us some good. Tootles, why don't you go rest. I'll call you in a few hours."

Blinking, Tootles gave a small shake of his head. "I'm alright Captain, I just have a few more pages to read."

"I wonder where he learned *that*," Dawes said, giving Wendy a pointed look while the Lost Boy wobbled with exhaustion. "You're breaking the child," she said, before leaning in to whisper. "A good work ethic is important, Captain—we all know how well you model that—but so is rest. Maybe demonstrate that sometimes, too."

Wendy frowned as she considered the pilot's words, her stubbornness holding out for an extra beat before she gave in with a slump of her shoulders.

"You're right," she said before raising her voice. "Let's all take a break. We can meet back in a few hours."

Hearing the Captain, Seven chirped and sat up, her tail thudding happily as she plodded over to Tootles, who opened his mouth, ready to protest.

"SMEE, please take Tootles to the kitchens to grab some lunch," Wendy directed, cutting off the Lost Boy. "Once he's finished, escort him to his dorms. I don't want to see him back here until he's gotten at least a two hour nap."

"Yes Captain," the synth said, lowering a stack of papers before hurrying to Tootles. "Come young master, you heard the captain."

"But—" Tootles tried to argue, but his protests were hushed by the First Mate's whirring steps. Pushing the boy from behind, SMEE marched out with Seven chirping happily behind.

"Thank you, SMEE," Wendy called after them, stifling a smile. At the door, Tootles twisted to give her a final pleading look but she waved him off.

"Go rest. I promise, everything will still be here when you wake up."

Tootles tried to reply, but SMEE pushed him outside with a series of mechanized tuts. As they passed through the sliding panels, Peter appeared with Tinc in tow, carrying a small sack and an oversized mug. He grinned at the tutting synth as it urged the whining boy onward but shrugged helplessly at Tootles' plight.

"What was that all about?" Peter asked when the door finally shut.

"Oh, nothing," Dawes called over airily. "Just one of the best examples of hypocrisy I've ever seen," she needled, aiming a glare at Wendy.

Turning to the pilot, Wendy rolled her eyes. "You wanted me to set an example, I set an example. Now I can get back to work."

"That's not what I meant and you know it," Dawes grumbled, before brightening at Peter. "Anyways, I hope you haven't come looking for any of the Captain's attention. As you can see, she's quite preoccupied."

"Is there any other way I'd find her?" Peter teased back, earning Dawes' approving laugh before he raised the contents in his hands. "I figured she needed a break. I didn't realize that you could also use some backup."

"With the Captain? You need an entire army," Dawes jabbed. "I've never met someone so stubborn in my life."

"I can hear you, you know," Wendy called, her eyes still glued to the charts.

"Isn't that a wonderful surprise?" Dawes breezed. "Here I was thinking I was talking to a wall this whole time."

Wendy cast a withering glare at the pilot, who shrugged innocently. Looking for support, the captain turned to Peter, but he raised his hands defensively.

"I didn't come to choose sides. I just thought you might like some coffee," he offered her the mug, then smiled as he waited for her reaction. "I have food too."

"Coffee is perfect," Wendy said, gratefully taking the cup. The warmth from the mug seeped into her hands as she drew it close. "Thank you."

Nodding, Peter set the bag on the edge of the command panel. "Save the sandwich for later," he suggested. "In case you get wrapped up again."

A snort sounded behind them, followed by Dawes' wry grumble. "In case," she scoffed, typing grumpily on the Navs.

Ignoring the surly pilot, Wendy faced Peter. "I will," she said, peeking curiously into the bag. The smell of roasted turkey wafted up, cueing hunger pangs she hadn't noticed before. She closed the bag to smother the distracting scent. "It looks great."

Peter puffed his chest. "I made it myself."

Wendy's brow quirked, and the mechanic let out an embarrassed chuckle.

"I've gotten pretty handy in the kitchens," he murmured sheepishly, before meeting Wendy with an uncertain gaze. "I've been trying to keep busy."

Understanding brought a rush of heat to Wendy's cheeks. It was the first time she'd seen Peter since their argument. She'd been so preoccupied with Hooke's maps that she hadn't given it any more thought. Clearing her throat, she stamped down her guilt, both at the realization and at the part of her that had enjoyed the distraction.

"Right," she mumbled, tugging at her coat. "I'm sorry I haven't been by, I've just been work—"

"Don't sweat it, Cap," Peter raised his hand to stop her fumbling apology. "It gave me time to get reacquainted with the ship."

Wendy smiled, thankful for the out. "This is perfect," she said, taking a sip of coffee before returning her attention to the charts.

"What have we got here?" Peter asked, leaning toward the maps, which also brought him closer. His shoulder brushed hers as he carefully observed the diagrams. "I didn't think Tootles had so many maps."

"He didn't," Wendy explained, quickly accessing Tootles' original chart. "Just this one. The rest," she paused to adjust the remaining maps over the holoscreen, "were maps Hooke had hidden. I asked Michaels to transpose them into holofiles." Peter let out an impressed whistle and she nodded. "It's been… a project."

"No-one ever said Hooke was an unskilled captain," Peter muttered, his green stare flashing while Tinc jangled behind him.

"Just not a very honest one," Wendy agreed, allowing the mechanic to examine the charts dotting the walls. "Although, that might actually work in our favor for once—if we can figure out what everything he charted means."

"You don't know what the maps are showing?" Peter asked. His brow furrowed as he stepped toward the screen. He was so close that the glow from the fiber optic lasers tinged his cheeks blue.

"I'm almost certain they're the coordinates that make up the Uncharted Sector," Wendy explained, pulling her stare from his rugged features to the whorls composing the map. She pointed at some prominent landmarks. "Neverland is there, and right here, you can see the Shipwreck Belt. There's a lot of space we still have to chart manually, but I've instructed Dawes to mine our current and past netscans to help confirm the coordinates."

"They look like they fit," Peter agreed, eyeing the chart until Tinc's wide swoop pulled his attention to the far corner. His brow furrowed and Wendy could tell he was studying the mark she'd agonized over. "But what's that there? It's not like any constellation I've seen."

Wendy smiled at his observation. With a few quick swipes, she minimized all the diagrams except for Hooke's pilfered maps. "That's what we've been trying to figure out. It appears in both charts, so Hooke must have registered them somehow, but there's no data except for their approximate location."

Peter scratched his head. "What if it's another ship?"

Looking at the map, Wendy frowned. She'd thought the same thing, but had discarded the idea, finding it unlikely. "Don't you think it's reading a little big for that?"

Peter shrugged. "Maybe," he answered, pointing to the mass that formed the graveyard. "I mean, look at the size of the belt. It's almost four times the size of your unknown mark and there were some huge ships caught in the pull. We saw them on our way to you."

"He makes a good point," Dawes chimed in. "Fleet ships are pretty standardized, but there are a lot of birds that come in different sizes—cargo vessels, cruise liners, and resettlement pods to name a few—and those are just terran vessels. Who knows how big extraterrestrial barges could be?"

Wendy's lips pursed at the pilot's reasoning. Spoken out loud, it made sense and she felt foolish for casting aside such an obvious hypothesis.

"But why is it out there?" she asked, mostly to herself. "What happened?"

"What happens to any downed bird?" Peter answered with a question. "Could be a million different things—as you experienced firsthand. A ship gets finicky, feels unloved, then quits. There are not many people who get a personal space-tow from their home planet," he said, teasing Wendy with a wry grin.

"Be that as it may," Wendy pressed, eager to change the subject, "it still doesn't explain what a vessel was doing out there."

"Does it matter?" Peter shrugged. "Like you said, it might not even be a ship. That question seems preemptive if you ask me."

"Maybe not," Dawes' chirped, her voice raising excitedly. She leaned forward in her seat, pressing close to the comm screen. Her fingers flew across the keys and a chime rang through the room, announcing an incoming transmission. Walking to the board, Wendy hovered over Dawes' shoulder to follow along as she read the correspondence.

"Coordinate verification complete. Tracing starpoints 73 zeta 9 dash 258 omarion, originating via the outskirts of the Krawk Nebula. Verified. Onsite: Exploratory vessel. Raptor." Dawes trailed off, leaving Wendy to translate airman's jargon as the pilot mumbled the remainder of the message under her breath until she released a loud gasp. Her face blanched in confusion. "Preliminary Biometric Scan—positive."

"I know my time as a baybody might not have made me a Navs specialist…" Peter interjected, scratching his head as he studied the message, "but is what I'm reading—"

"It's a ship," Dawes confirmed, making Wendy's stomach flip uncontrollably. She stared disbelieving at the transmission before whispering in a shaky breath.

"And there's something inside."

II
FLEET MECHANIC PETER PAN

THE JOLLY ROGER

"Something inside?" Peter glanced at the worried captain and was struck by how beautiful she was, regardless of the deep worry lines etched into her forehead. "Like what?"

"I don't know," Wendy admitted, dropping her face to her hands. She rubbed her thumb in a small circle, silently massaging her temple.

"I guess now we have to find out why the ship got left," Dawes said, her suggestion earning a scoff.

"So it would seem," Wendy said, letting out an exasperated sigh as she crossed to the projected charts. Her gait was agitated, and Peter could practically see green sparks exploding from her every step.

"Cap looks almost as cranky as you, Tinc," Peter murmured to the bot. Jangling a smart reply, Tinc zoomed to hover curiously in front of the maps. Peter started to follow, then paused as a nagging thought struck, forcing his attention back to the transmission. Stumbling through the unfamiliar terminology, he skimmed to the end of the message.

Preliminary Biometric Scan—positive.

"It doesn't make sense," Wendy announced, her thoughts echoing his own. "That ship has been in the same spot for centuries. Even if it could maintain systems after it broke down, there's no way the power could last. It would have been depleted decades ago. How did the scan pull a reading?"

"It is strange," Dawes agreed before glancing at the small portscreen over her head. "Any ideas Jensen?"

Her question confused Peter until he followed her gaze to where the mechanic was projected, situated in the heart of the bay, surrounded by a sea of wires. Peter watched as Michaels adjusted a few cables, then turned to the pilot.

"Well, depending on the Raptor's energy source, its half-lives could vary greatly. Like when we experienced our issues on the *Roger*. For all intents and purposes, we were dead in the water—just like that vessel. You saw how fast we lost power, which was simply due to the capacity of our system's reserves. If we had experienced the same issues on the *Fiducia*, our ship would still have deteriorated, but at a vastly different timeline." Michaels paused to readjust his glasses. "That being said, it's highly unlikely that the positive biometrics are being caused by any sort of output from the ship. Even the most advanced vessels could only generate power on a downed bird for a year, maybe 15 months, max."

"So decades is a stretch," Peter snorted, then nodded to the mech. "Hey, Michaels, how's the old girl treating you?"

"Better these days," Michaels answered with a grin. "Your modifications have really helped. It was a good idea to recalibrate the gravity bracers and extend the transcalefactor's production range."

Peter was about to ask more about the adjustments when Wendy interjected. "Not the time to talk shop, gentlemen," she said, managing to communicate her disapproval with her gaze fixed firmly on the map. Sharing a guilty look with his fellow mechanic, Peter shrugged before Michaels picked up his oil-stained wrench.

"At any rate," Michaels continued, raising his voice over the roar of the *Roger's* engines, "I'd be more inclined to say there was an error in the read than there was anything putting out a signal."

"You think the scan messed up?" Dawes asked, looking hopefully at Michaels.

"No," Wendy answered, facing them with worry. "He thinks something is on the ship."

"But what could be hanging around on a dead bird?" the pilot prodded. Though her confusion was understandable, Wendy's words prompted a realization for Peter. His gut twisted as he looked at the captain, his shoulders sagging under the weight of understanding.

"It's the Shadow," he said, meeting Wendy's deadened gaze. "Itzala survived and made it onto the ship," he announced, feeling the fear cast by his words. Tinc whirred anxiously over his shoulder, showering him in a cascade of purple.

"But, the Captain ejected it," Dawes argued, searching the room for support. "There's no way the Shadow—or *anything*—could have survived that. It would have been crushed, then smothered, and frozen. That's three very separate and painful deaths. For it to survive one, let alone all three isn't just unlikely, it's physically impossible!"

"Itzala has been alive for thousands of years," Wendy said, the resignation in her voice ruining her reassurance. "We have no idea what it can and can't survive. Based on what we've learned about Itzala so far, I would venture that it is possible."

"Is there any way we can verify that? You know, with*out* going anywhere near the potential demon infested ship?" Dawes asked. "Maybe with another scan?"

"I don't know what good that would do," Wendy answered. "Aside from retrieving the same data. What we need is someone who knows more about the Shadow than we do," she explained, glancing meaningfully at Peter.

Peter nodded in understanding. "Tizari," he said. "The Stjarnin know more about the Shadow than any of us. If anyone could tell if it was really possible, it would be her."

"My thoughts exactly," Wendy agreed, accessing her comm. The screen remained blank until the connection linked, revealing the slender first mate. "SMEE," Wendy commanded, blowing past pleasantries. "I need you to find Tizari. Tell her I require her assistance."

"Certainly, Captain. Anything I can do to help," the synth declared, bowing with a giddy grin before he hurried to end the call.

"If I didn't know any better, I'd say ol' SMEE has a bit of a crush, Cap," Peter teased. "I mean, he was always obedient, but now, there's extra pep in his step."

"Synths don't exhibit human emotion," Wendy said before nodding in Tinc's direction. "Besides, if anyone had any right to be jealous, I'd say it was me," she grinned at the sparking nano-bot, whose curt reply played in Peter's ear. Raising her brow at the bright cascade erupting from Tinc's core, Wendy snorted then turned back to the map. Quickly shooing the bot, Peter followed, only to be interrupted by Dawes.

"Are you okay, Captain?" the pilot asked, her pretty features pulling in concern.

Wendy turned and nodded. "Yes," she said, unable to hide the anxiety in her voice. Her forced smile failed miserably, then broke with a tired laugh. "No." She admitted with a sigh. She examined the charts, and Peter couldn't help but notice the trembling tears lining her eyelids. "I just... don't know if I can handle any more of this," she whispered.

Peter reached for her hand. The captain didn't have to voice her feelings for him to understand. They mirrored his exactly. His heart lurched at the worry in her stare, and he pulled her towards him, wrapping her in a tight hug. Allowing it, Wendy folded herself against his chest as a soft smile sprang to his lips. While he and the captain had never been overly affectionate, her distance had affected him more than he realized.

Enjoying her embrace, Peter tightened his grip and the captain's wayward curls tickled his cheek. "Cap, you can handle anything you set your mind to," he assured before a thought struck. "But you might not have to," he said, reaching quickly for his pocket. "We've got backup—Tizari is already on board. And if she can't help," he pulled his hand to reveal a smooth, onyx stone. "I have a direct line to the Stjarnin," he continued, placing a hand on the captain's shoulders. "All we have to do is let them know what's happening and they'll take care of it."

Staring at him, Wendy's lips pressed together, forming a hard line. She didn't speak, but behind her galaxy gaze, Peter saw a silent war.

"What's wrong?" he asked.

"I don't know that we can let them," she answered miserably, surprising him with her conviction.

Peter quirked his head, but before he could press further, Wendy released another weighted sigh.

"If the Stjarnin come, they will destroy the Shadow."

Peter's confusion deepened. "Isn't that a good thing?"

"Maybe not," Wendy said, looking at him as though she wished she could will him to understand.

Bewildered, Peter returned her look with a dumbfounded stare.

"Why?" he asked.

Wendy drew back, turning from him to face the map. She was silent for a long time before her words whispered out, so soft that he almost missed them.

"Because" she paused, turning back just in time for him to see her cascading tear, "if the Shadow is alive, then maybe Boyce is too."

12
CAPTAIN WENDY DARLING

THE JOLLY ROGER

Wendy held Peter's gaze as long as she could bear before finally turning away, shamefaced. Watching the hope drain from his eyes to be replaced with hurt was too much, as was his care for her. Because, as fiercely as Dawes insisted Wendy hadn't broken from her post, the pilot's claim wasn't exactly true. There had been several stolen moments where the captain had slipped from her maps to venture into Boyce's dossier.

The files had been devastating, a collection of the commander's observations throughout the expeditions, imprinting on her conscience. Beginning with the moment they embarked for Neverland, Boyce's cool notations maintained detailed records of the voyage, first adhering to fleet protocol to the letter until slowly the tone began to shift. Following the return launch for

New London, discrepancies began to appear within his notes. The commander's voice, so clinical and collected, became disjointed, with sentimental undertones seeping into his reports.

At first, it caught her off guard as the timestamps progressed, and the commander's commentaries revealed the feelings she now knew he had for her. Slips of hand, where the report turned pensive, and he asked questions of her or shared secrets from their past before striking them through to return to his notes. More than once, the commander admitted to watching her, wishing to share his thoughts, with some of the admissions being so heart-wrenching, Wendy nearly abandoned the dossier. But as she continued to read, the sentiments diverged from ardent confessions to jealous allegations. The focus shifted from her to Peter, with a vehemence that terrified Wendy—even more so when she realized the truth of their origin. There it was, nestled in the text, evidence of the Shadow's influence. For with every progressing entry, the commander's remarks became less coherent until finally, Wendy had to close the file. It was too much for her to comprehend. Reading Boyce's proclamations felt invasive, like she was reading something not meant for her, building a rolling ball of guilt that only grew with every added note revealing his suffering under the Shadow.

It was her fault. All of it.

Standing helpless in front of the others, she had no way to explain how irrational she knew she sounded. That in all likeliness Boyce was gone, and his death was a burden she would have to carry for the rest of her days, but none of that mattered. She would not abandon the commander to Itzala. She would not just leave the soldier who saw her past and still believed in her future.

It was the very least she owed him, but how could she tell the others?

Watching her struggle, a stricken look covered Peter's features that took him a moment to recover.

"Cap— there's no way he could have survived that," Peter said, recovering with a quick jerk of his head. He stared back at her, his green eyes filled with hurt. "I mean, it's hard enough to believe the Shadow might have made it, but Boyce too? I saw what happened to Hooke after Itzala left—it wasn't good. Pair that with getting shot into the 'verse," he softened his voice, "I just don't see how it's possible."

"I know," Wendy said, closing her eyes to separate her feelings from the betrayal on his face. In the quiet, her years of training rose to the foreground. Countless hours of protocol, operations, and strategy while alongside every memory, daunting in his presence, was Boyce. Never far from where she was, the commander was a constant, the North Star guiding her forward. Without him, her skies seemed empty.

Straightening her shoulders, Wendy faced the room.

"It doesn't mean we can't try," she announced, bolstered by the conviction threading her words. "If there's any possibility that Commander Boyce is alive, it's my duty to pursue it."

Grimacing, Peter stood, his eyes darting everywhere except hers. Silence stretched through the room, growing heavy until he exhaled and faced her, his voice thick with emotion.

"Is he really that important to you?"

Wendy's stomach flipped. A dozen answers sprang to her mind, each more complicated than the last. "I'm the commanding officer of this ship," she finally answered, choosing the safest option. "Everyone on board is that important."

"And your willingness to throw them all into danger on the off chance that the commander might still be there shows that how?" Peter countered.

Calm settled over Wendy as she met his petulant gaze. Insubordination was easier to manage than hurt. She pulled at the edge of her jacket and straightened her shoulders before addressing the room with authority.

"It's what I would do for any other crew member," she stated boldly, daring a glance at Dawes, whose conversation with Michaels had been forgotten. Embarrassment twinged through Wendy as she realized her audience, but she quashed it before returning to the sullen mechanic. "You are all under my charge, and as such, my responsibility. It is not a task I take lightly. If there's even a chance I can get all of my men back home, I intend to take it."

Finishing her speech, she glanced sideways at Dawes and Michaels to gauge their response. Smiling, the pilot bobbed her head while Michaels twitched a tiny smile.

"Let me make sure I've got everything in order," he said. Abandoning his tools, he disappeared, leaving only the red glow of the bay as he grumbled off the screen. "Before you make me tear it up again."

Snorting at the mechanic's snark, Wendy turned hopefully to her pilot. "Dawes?"

"You don't even have to ask, Captain," Dawes said, settling eagerly into her Navs. "I'm guessing we'll need to adjust our course?"

Wendy grinned and started to respond, but the sweeping of the cabin doors cut in.

"Tizari," Wendy said, greeting the expected Stjarnin before angling her attention to her other guest. "And Johns?"

Johns grinned and offered a guilty shrug. "I overheard the synth's invite and got nosy. Besides, it's been a while since you've entertained anyone besides Dawes and I was getting jealous. I'm starting to think you're replacing me." He finished with a friendly elbow to Wendy's ribs.

Rolling her eyes, Wendy shoved the lieutenant. "How could I ever do that, Johns," she needled. "Dawes doesn't treat me nearly as good. I don't think she's ever bruised me."

"All in love, Darling. All in love," Johns breezed, striding across the room to settle into an empty chair. Fluffing the cushion, he made himself comfortable before grinning at the others. "So. What's our newest crisis? That's what it is, right? I mean, it's been a whole three weeks of calm, so we're about due, yeah?"

Wendy scowled at her lieutenant before turning to Tizari. "Crisis is a strong word. However, a situation has come up that we feel warrants your opinion."

Tizari's face was a blank slate as she waited for Wendy's elaboration. Unsure how to read the expression, Wendy glanced uncertainly at Peter, who shrugged petulantly. Bristling at his pouting, Wendy collected her temper before addressing the Stjarnin.

"Recently, we discovered a hidden cache of Hooke's star charts that had all been withheld from the Fleet. They presented us with data we had never seen. Upon further examination, we discovered some new astrals. When we completed a cursory scan to acquire additional data," Wendy motioned to Dawes, who quickly projected the report on the holoscreen. "This is what we found."

Tizari walked toward the screen, wearing her expressionless mask. Wendy was momentarily jealous of the alien's impassive features, wishing she could disguise her emotions so well. Unbidden, she cast a furtive glance at Peter, who fixed his stare on the projected transmission while Tinc hovered lazily over his shoulder. Suppressing a surge of frustration, Wendy tried to focus but the scan's holographic text wavered across her fuming vision.

"I am unfamiliar with many of these words," Tizari announced after reading, "but there is a ship in the distance that concerns you? Is it one of your enemies?"

Wendy shook her head. "No. I mean, yes, there is a ship, but it isn't an enemy—at least, I don't believe it was." Realizing her fumbling, she paused. "When we encountered the anomaly, we ran a diagnostic and checked its biometrics, which confirmed it was a ship. That in itself was not concerning, however, the signals we received from the vessel were. According to Hooke's charts, the ship should be dead. Considering the exceptional amount of time that passed, there's no way it should have produced any energy for the scan to pick up."

"You want to know what is providing the vessel with power," Tizari guessed, glancing at Peter's scowl. "But I think you already know."

"We think it's the Shadow," Wendy confirmed, eliciting a loud groan from Johns' corner.

"Here we go again," he grumbled, but Wendy ignored her lieutenant, keeping her attention on the towering alien.

"Itzala has always been cunning," Tizari ceded, her gilled lips pulling in a tiered frown. "I will notify my people. If it is the Shadow, it will not escape again." She moved to leave but halted after Wendy's sharp command.

"Wait," Wendy said, surprised at her intensity. The startled looks from her crew told her they thought the same. Clearing her throat, she straightened her posture before continuing. "How can the Stjarnin ensure the creature won't escape again?"

Tizari turned to the captain. "My people have contained Itzala for millennia. We have long since learned of ways to deal with its tricks."

"No offense," Johns called from his chair, "but those ways don't really seem super effective, considering all the messes we've recently found ourselves in."

Tizari took his criticism calmly. "Yes. For too long we have put off what has needed to be done," she said. "But my people are tired. Itzala will not go free again."

"What does that mean?" Wendy asked, thinking of how the Stjarnin's actions might impact Boyce if he remained with the creature.

"It is nothing for you to concern yourself with, Captain. Your government will be here shortly. They will return you all to where you belong. Your crew has already sacrificed enough to assist with the Shadow."

"But what if we want to see it through to the end?" Wendy's desperate questioning earned a suspicious look from the Stjarnin.

"What reason could you possibly have to risk another meeting with Itzala?"

Biting her lip, Wendy looked at Dawes, who offered a reassuring nod while Peter stubbornly turned the other way. "To make sure Commander Boyce isn't abandoned in its wake," she answered.

"But, Darling, there's no way," Johns spluttered, pushing forward in his seat. "You... *ejected him into space*," he whispered, attempting to soften the blow. Unfortunately, his lowered voice didn't stall Wendy's flooding memory, and a fleeting recollection of her last moment with Boyce overtook her, setting her skin aflame with the ghost of the commander's gentle touch as he cradled her against his broad chest before undoing her with his kiss. Her lips tingled where Aidan's lingered until he drew back, his phantom stare drowning her in a fresh wave of guilt.

"I'm well aware, Lieutenant," she declared, her attention unwavering from Tizari. "But if Hooke was able to survive his possession, perhaps Boyce can too."

"It is unlikely," the Stjarnin finally stated.

"But there is a chance."

Tizari shrugged. "There is always a chance," she said icily. "There is a chance that your commander's body has scattered through the stars. Is that something you would also risk?"

Wendy recoiled at the visual but answered Tizari's gruesome question with a serious nod. "If it meant there was a chance to bring him home, then yes. His family deserves as much. *Aidan* deserves that much," she declared.

A sharp inhale gusted behind her, and Wendy turned to find Peter, hurt lining his features. Wendy cast a pleading look, but the mechanic blinked once before he angled away from her to stare at the projected charts.

"He is my commander. He is my responsibility," Wendy explained, uncertain if it was to the mechanic or the Stjarnin.

Watching the captain through an endless ebony gaze, Tizari clasped her hands. "I admire your conviction, Captain, but it would be misleading to promise your commander's return. It would be better to maintain the understanding that he cannot be saved."

"Because you think he's dead?" Wendy challenged, rebellion bubbling through her resolve.

"Because if he isn't already, he will be," the Stjarnin stated firmly, earning several shocked gasps.

"What does that mean?" Johns exclaimed, his brow furrowing as he jumped to his feet.

Unphased by his outburst, Tizari looked calmly at the lieutenant before scanning the room. Her even gaze passed smoothly over each troubled expression before lingering thoughtfully on Peter.

"It is what my people believed when you wanted to rescue your captain, Pan," she said, sending a guilty flutter through Wendy's chest. "We will not allow Itzala to escape." She paused once more, giving the words a moment to sink in before she continued. "Last time, you interfered to save the girl, and it has allowed the Shadow to remain a threat." She met Wendy with a pointed look. "My people will not allow the same mistake."

Reeling at Tizari's admission, Wendy blinked as the Stjarnin's words settled, drowning her in a fresh wave of emotion.

"What if we can get Commander Boyce out before you destroy the Shadow?" Dawes offered, her cheeks pale as she faced the room.

Tizari shook her head. "Itzala must be stopped. We will rid the world of its dark influence by whatever means necessary. One life is not enough to risk the world." she said, frowning as Peter scowled and looked away. "I am sorry that I cannot give you the answers you want to hear, but it is important you receive the truth. I will relay the information you have given me and my people will use it against Itzala. They will not concern themselves with the well-being of your soldier."

Dipping her head, Tizari turned to leave. Fighting to contain her temper, Wendy bit her lip, allowing the Stjarnin to reach the door before she finally erupted.

"What will they do?" she challenged, attempting to gauge the power the Stjarnin held.

Tizari's shoulders stiffened as she answered in a husky tenor. "It will cost my people greatly, but Itzala's evil cannot be permitted to escape," she said before continuing toward the sweeping doors.

The admission startled Wendy, the Stjarnin's conviction hitting so hard that she almost forgot her next question.

"How long will it take?"

Looking briefly over her shoulder, Tizari met the captain's eyes with regret. "I will communicate with my people. They will move swiftly against the monster. It will not take more than a week."

A week, Wendy thought, balking at the brief window. Offering a curt nod, she squared her posture, despite the coils inside her threatening to explode.

"Send word to the Stjarnin and inform me once you receive correspondence. If actions are going to be taken against the Shadow, I will have to communicate it with the Fleet as well."

Accepting Wendy's command, Tizari took her leave, exiting with a quiet swish of doors as a rush of silence swept among the remaining crew. Her absence hung in the air until the others slowly turned to Wendy. She allowed their stares to linger while she took a breath, collecting the thoughts dancing through her mind. They blinded her vision with a million different pasts, presents, and potential futures until she pushed them away, leaving only the burning resolve coursing through her veins.

"Dawes, set coordinates for a new course. End point: Krawk Nebula - Galactic latitude -86.17, and longitude 273.9."

"But Darling, isn't that where—" Johns' query was cut off by Wendy's quick retort.

"Yes, Lieutenant," she answered, settling in behind the StarBoard. She looked at the others, meeting their confusion with a wry grin. "If the Stjarnin won't help, we will."

13
COMMANDER AIDAN BOYCE
LOCATION UNKNOWN

Finally, the scratching had stopped.

That was Boyce's first thought as he blinked awake inside the small chamber.

But what scratching noises, and how did I even know about them, he wondered as he rubbed his head, feeling like he was slogging through a daze.

Groaning, he examined his surroundings. The room was familiar, all metal panels and lifeless projector screens. They circled the room, creating a 360-degree command station, save the thin rectangular access point—a steel door that had been hastily blocked and marked with—*something*.

Trying to remember how he got there, Boyce searched for something to jog his memory, but his throbbing temple made it hard to focus.

"Dammit," he muttered, pushing himself to sit. A sharp pain laced through his palm, and he slipped back, cursing as he raised it to find a heavy bandage ruined by a blotchy crimson stain bleeding. "What the hell?"

He picked carefully at the tucked wrapping, pulling it loose to study the wound. It unraveled quickly, sticking only where the blood had dried into the binding, pasting it to his flesh. With a hurried jerk, he tore it loose, revealing a thick, jagged cut stretching from the pad of his palm to the base of fingertips.

Grimacing, Boyce flexed his hand and looked around, surprised to find a rusted multitool on the ground, its sharp edge stained bright red. Confused, the commander set it back down, then followed his trail of blood from where it dotted the floor to streak across the panel behind him.

"Start here?" Boyce read aloud, stumbling over the strange message. His brow furrowed as he followed a small, streaky arrow pointing to a chamber of tangled wires.

Pulling at the mixed cords, Boyce twirled a loose blue wire. Fragmented images flashed through his mind, half memories of hunching over a corded web before a shadowy fog billowed over his mind. He tugged another cable and a chill rushed up his spine, licking him with icy tendrils as he suddenly remembered where he was—trapped on an unknown vessel with the Shadow still clinging to his mind.

But why was there a barricade to the rest of the ship, the commander wondered, studying the hastily secured rods and the ominous scrawled *x*.

Why not open it and find out, a dark voice taunted, slithering from the recesses of his thoughts. Shooing the call, Boyce returned his attention to the cryptic message penned in his blood.

"Start here," he repeated, considering the message as he absently twiddled the cables. Plunging into the panel, he began the tedious work of untangling the knotted cords, separating colored wire and frayed copper tendrils, ignoring the ghostly footsteps shuffling beyond the door and the cruel whispers permeating his mind.

14
CAPTAIN WENDY DARLING

THE JOLLY ROGER

Wendy was pacing again. Fighting buzzing thoughts that never seemed to tire, she rounded the worn circular path she'd tracked for a third time to no avail; still they needled in.

Ever since she had read Boyce's journals, new memories kept resurfacing, moments that her mind had classified as inconsequential inconsistencies, now came to light with deeper meaning. Like the Yuletide Ball her mother had hosted two years ago and insisted she attend. The ball itself was of no importance—it was just another of her mother's dreary excuses for another party that Wendy was forced to attend. In fact, Wendy had done her best to avoid it—so far as enlisting in extra duties over the holiday to force her parents' hand in allowing her to stay. Even when she discovered Boyce's name on the holiday boarding list. Since only a handful of cadets ever volunteered, it took a great deal to get off the task-list once assigned.

But her parents found a way. With no excuses and a chartered flight back to West Brighton, Wendy had no other choice but to attend, to be entertainment fodder for her mother's elitist friends. After hours of entertaining their mind-numbing drivel,

and being forced to dance with the upper side's 'most eligible bachelors', Wendy was prepared to volunteer for the next Quirinus colonization when she looked at her dance card and—

'I believe the waltz goes to me," Boyce said, catching her around the waist.

Wendy was so surprised, the retort on her lips dropped as he stepped closer, his icy blue eyes sparking against his handsome navy tuxedo. He fell into step as the music slowed, dragging her further onto the dance floor and away from Marcus Willoughby, the next escort signed on her card.

"Don't look so disappointed, Darling. You know Willoughby smells like fermented herring. I loaned him a rugby jersey on summer holiday and had to burn the bloody thing. Wouldn't want you to have to do the same with that dress," Boyce murmured, tightening his hold on her waist, "it's far more captivating than an old West Brighton jumper."

"And far more uncomfortable," Wendy fussed, flexing against the ribbed bodice. Her mother had cinched the corset as tight as her ribs would allow, and Wendy was certain she was going to wake up with bruises. "I will never complain about fleetgear again."

"It suits you," Boyce said, rubbing a thumb against the scarlet lace.

"Perhaps if I could conceal a phaser inside," Wendy grumbled.

Boyce offered with a devilish grin. "I'd be happy to help you try."

"So I can find out exactly how many seconds it takes for me to pull it out to shoot you?"

Aidan's gravelly laugh rumbled over the orchestra. "If that's what you need," he said before whirling her in a dizzying spin. Wendy turned out, then twirled inside the cadet-commander's grip as he pulled her close, wrapping her in sandalwood while he rumbled the lyrics to "The Gentle Maiden" in her ear. Lost in his surprising baritone, Wendy didn't recall anything else until Boyce's steps slowed and he pulled back, releasing her to Arun Singh, the nephew of her father's executive financial adviser. Arun bowed and whisked her away, leaving Boyce's haunting hum blocking out everything except a fleeting image of his name scrawled at the top of the Academy's holiday task list.

Wendy didn't know why the memory had escaped her until now, but sitting in her captain's chair, the waltz' soft lyrics floated along the stars, their soft glow forming the lilting sheet music to the haunting tune.

Caught in the lyrics, Wendy closed her eyes and rocked until a sheen of tears threatened to overtake them. Refusing their presence, Wendy huffed and stood, stalking around the cabin in another agitated lap.

Watching from her pilot's chair, Dawes snickered softly. She had long ago given up on small talk and had picked up a book, snuggling down and humming softly as she paged through the paperback.

Exhaling, Wendy crossed the room to review the charts, but all she saw was a dizzying playout of Boyce discarded in the hull of a frozen barge. Chasing the vision with an agitated huff, Wendy tried to focus. She glanced at Dawes, wishing the pilot would put the book away, while realizing it would be pointless. In her kindness, Arielle would try and pull the captain into a lighthearted conversation and Wendy would shut her down before reverting to her obsessive spiral.

Like when she had shut down Peter and Johns. Johns' dismissal had been all business—sending him out shortly after Tizari left to fill DeLaCruz in on the new developments, with strict orders of discretion. There was no need to give anyone else the chance to weigh in—or to let slip to the Fleet before she was ready to share.

Not that she would ever be ready. Wendy was certain once the Admiral discovered her plan there would be more than just a disciplinary hearing on her horizon—most likely a forceful extraction followed by a public dismissal. Even if the Admiral agreed with Wendy's decision, the panel had made it abundantly clear what the higher-ups thought of her handling the mission.

This would be just another nail in her coffin.

A frustrated growl ripped from her chest as she scrubbed her tired eyes, questioning herself for just a moment. So far, all she had accomplished was to bring more strife to her ship: added authoritative repercussions, taxations on the *Roger* and its crew, potential re-exposure to Itzala's threat, and a clearly driven wedge between her and Peter.

Is it really worth it, she wondered, finally allowing the question she'd so intently avoided. She dropped her hands as the thought sank in.

Was it? Clearly, there were more than enough reasons she should walk away. But just considering it formed a pit of guilt in her stomach. It was unwanted and illogical, but she couldn't deny her queasiness at the mere thought of abandoning the commander.

She closed her eyes and pictured Aidan, sitting in his cabin on the Roger, all alone and typing an entry in his journal. She could practically see his brow furrowed as he pored over his pad, sweat dripping as he angrily struck through another keyed line.

The final entries she had read were filled with more slashed text than legible, and her gut twisted as she realized, fighting Itzala alone onboard, she had already all but abandoned him once.

It was all there, progressing from the beginning; the commander's dedication and finally his desperation to keep them all safe, even with the Shadow poisoning his mind. Without complaint, Boyce shouldered the weight of Itzala's grip, fighting against it while she was wrapped up in other things—in other people, making the whole situation more muddled.

Their time as competitors at the Academy had made her oblivious to the commander's feelings for her but faced with them now… it pained her to think about how he must have felt. And thinking about Peter waiting for her to make a decision she could never make—how could she have let things get so muddled?

"I don't have time for this," Wendy moaned, ending the thought with a miserable growl. If Tizari's predictions were correct, her window for an uninterrupted rescue would be approximately one week. One week to alter courses, locate the commander, and face a demon—all without being detected by an alien fleet and Earth's finest brigade.

No wonder she was stressed.

Starting another lap around the cabin, Wendy cast her thoughts, hoping to land them somewhere pleasant. To her dismay, they ended on the hurt in Peter's eyes as he stormed from the cabin with Tinc sparking furiously by his side.

After Johns had left, the room had cleared, with Dawes excusing herself and instructing Michaels to meet her in the main bay. Their quick departures left Wendy and Peter staring awkwardly at each other before the mechanic's rusty laugh broke the quiet.

"It's always something with you, isn't it, Cap?" He asked, forcing a broken grin. "I'm starting to think if you ever slowed down you might spontaneously combust."

Wendy's lips pressed in a failed smile. "There's no medical proof that's a viable outcome."

"First time for everything," Peter teased, studying her reaction. He was offering an olive branch, but Wendy was wound so tight, she wasn't sure she could take it. Instead, she turned to the projected transmission, widening the space between them.

"Medical anomalies aside, I'd be quite happy for things to settle down," Wendy said. "Unfortunately, that doesn't seem to be an option."

"It could be," Peter's hopeful tone caught her off guard. Hesitantly, he wrapped her hands in his, grazing her palms with his rough skin.

"How?" She asked, briefly gripped by his certainty. He was always so sure that answers could be simple; part of her wished she could have the same conviction.

Dropping his gaze to her hands, Peter clutched them tight as he drew her close. "We could just stay," he suggested.

"Stay?"

Wendy frowned, momentarily confused before an indignant understanding flared. "Stay here?"

Peter nodded. "We could comm the Fleet and tell them what we've learned. They're already headed our way; they could just as easily send a recon party. With primed vessels and a fresh crew—not to mention the Stjarnin's assistance—they'd accomplish the same things we could, and probably do it better." He slowed his breathing before glancing hesitantly at her. "Then for once, it wouldn't be you in the thick of it. You'd be safe. Here. With me."

He leaned forward, offering himself to her, but as he pressed his lips to hers, the final line of Boyce's waltz played in her mind, forcing her to draw away. Heart breaking, she met his emerald gaze, and the burning hope it held was too much for Wendy to bear.

Deep down, she knew Peter's argument made sense—that it would be safer to let the Fleet take over—but her years of training had also taught her things were hardly ever that simple. Sure, the Fleet had fresher crews with better equipment, but they also had no experience against the Shadow. Calling them in would be like sending armored lambs to slaughter.

"I told you, we can't—"

"You told us *you* can't," Peter argued, his tone hardening in frustration. "I could walk away, no questions, and so could the Boys. And SMEE—actually, there's an idea. Did you ever consider asking the synth? He's *programmed* to find the most logical outcome. I'd bet if you even asked Hooke, he'd tell you—"

"Why on Earth would I do that?" Wendy challenged. "Taking advice from a dishonored turncoat? From the man whose decisions caused this entire situation? Why should I trust anything that traitor has to say?"

"Because unlike you, Hooke has learned his lesson!" Peter exploded, backed by Tinc's rioting sparks. "He made a bad choice, and he knows it! He knows Itzala is too much to handle, but he's not so arrogant that he refuses to believe it!"

Wendy reeled at Peter's accusation, her anger stealing her words. Gaping at the mechanic and his rampaging nanobot, she stood dumbfounded.

"James Hooke is a disgrace to the Fleet and to himself," she seethed, startled at the venom in her tone. "He abandoned his crew to pursue his own selfish ambitions—ambitions which endangered the lives of countless others. He is a callous benedict who will likely spend the rest of his days behind bars… if he isn't met with a swifter punishment. He is the last person I would *ever* ask for help, and your eagerness to fall under his line makes me question your loyalty," she said, watching Peter stiffen at her accusation. A brief flare of guilt flashed through Wendy at the look of hurt on Peter's face, but she stamped it down. "I suggest you find another way to express your distaste in my leadership before you find yourself in a holding cell next to your beloved captain."

"I get it, Cap," Peter stepped back, creating a frosted chasm between them. "I won't bring it up again." Extending an exaggerated bow, he stormed from the room, followed by a zigzagging trail of exploding sparks.

Withdrawing from the memory, Wendy unclamped her hands, which subconsciously formed fists at her side. Shaking them loose, she glanced quickly at Dawes to make sure the pilot was still distracted. Arielle sat in the same spot, still humming quietly as she flipped to her next page.

Thanking the fleet for small graces, Wendy flopped into her seat. The heavy noise pulled the pilot's attention, and Dawes lowered her book.

"Everything all right, Captain?" Dawes asked, echoing the too-familiar question.

Wendy nodded, a silent lie. "Just wondering when we're going to hear from Tizari," she said, using the half-truth as a decoy. It seemed safe enough, considering it *was* one of her many daunting thoughts.

"It's only been a few hours," Dawes reasoned. "I'm sure she'll update you soon."

"As long as she's not trying to hide anything," Wendy murmured, massaging her growing headache.

"Like we are?" Dawes teased, earning a rueful grin from the captain.

"I have no idea what you're talking about," Wendy sniffed. "We are merely updating our course. There is no need to make everyone aware of such a mundane maneuver."

"Whatever helps you sleep at night, Captain," Dawes laughed before falling serious. "I'm glad though," she said, ending her statement with a decisive nod. "I mean, honestly, I'm scared shyteless, but it's only right that we try and get Boyce. He's one of us, and he needs to come home."

The pilot's validation stirred a wave of fresh emotion through Wendy. "Thank you, Dawes. I can't tell you how much that means—" she said, trailing off under a threatening flood of tears.

Grinning, Dawes waved her hand. "Don't worry about it," she trilled. "I just figured you probably hadn't heard too many arguments in favor of your decision. I thought you might like to know you weren't alone."

"It's a refreshing take," Wendy replied with a smile.

Dawes nodded before turning to her screen to tap a few quick commands. The panel chirped and the pilot slapped her knees.

"Everything is in order and we're well on our way. All things considered, we're making great time. If it keeps up, my calculations place us at the Raptor in three days' time."

"Three days?" Wendy asked, genuinely surprised. It was the closest thing she'd had to good news in what seemed ages.

"It's a generous guess," Dawes admitted, "and one that assumes no surprises, but yes."

"How did you manage that?"

"I wasn't assigned this mission for nothing," the pilot teased. "Creative maneuvering has always been one of my greatest strengths. Just don't forget to mention it when you're regaling the Fleet with my impressive contributions." The pilot winked before rising to her feet. "For now, I'm starving. We should grab some food."

Wendy shook her head. "I'm fine," she insisted. "You go. I'll stay and make sure everything remains on track."

"That's what the autopilot function is for," Dawes sighed.

"It's okay," Wendy protested, until a series of loud steps shuffled into the cabin.

"It's not a request, Darling," Johns said, booming through the quiet. "You've been holed up way too long. Dawes *just* told you she took care of everything. Thirty minutes won't kill you."

"I can eat in here just as well as in the commons," Wendy argued, wrapping her arms stubbornly across her chest.

The lieutenant gave her a skeptical look before gesturing to the untouched plate of food on her table. The incriminating evidence sat, screaming its abandonment to Johns' argument.

"That's not fair," Wendy spluttered, "I wasn't hungry, I—"

"I don't wanna hear it," Johns raised his massive hand. "You're getting out of this room, whether it's the easy way or the hard way."

"Surely there are more pressing duties on your task list," Wendy argued, attempting to distract the lieutenant. "I never received that update on holding I requested."

"The pirates are fine," Johns dismissed. "Mad as hell and smellier than six months' worth of space excrement, but contained and pleasantly devoid of batshyte crazy, so all in all, exactly as they should be," he said before eyeing her crankily, "unlike their captain, who is about to force her crew to take matters into their own hands."

"But I—" Wendy attempted to protest.

A devilish grin split Johns' chiseled features. "The hard way it is," he announced, a little too delighted as he glanced conspiratorially at the pilot. "Dawes, follow behind. The captain isn't going to go easy."

"Easy? What do you mean, *easy*? I—ahhh!"

With a burst of speed, Elias crossed the room and scooped up Wendy, throwing her over his shoulders like a sack of potatoes. Beating his massive shoulders, Wendy kicked against him, but for all the trouble it caused, she might have been a rampaging toddler.

"Johns! *Elias!* Put. Me. Down!"

"As soon as we get to the commons," the lieutenant answered with a laugh.

"But I have work to do!"

"The charts will be here when you get back," he promised, angling so they could both see the pilot's chair. "Isn't that right, Dawes?"

"That's what I keep saying," Dawes answered with a shrug.

"Hear that, Darling?" Johns beamed. "That's what she *keeps* telling you. It's almost like you don't listen."

Wendy scowled furiously. "Technically, I don't have to. *You're* supposed to be the ones listening to me," she said.

"Only until you prove to be a danger to yourself. And I have it under very good authority that our medic is very concerned about your eating habits. I'm quite certain she'd support our intervention."

"You mean your coup?" Wendy seethed, still struggling against the lieutenant's beefy shoulders.

Johns' laugh vibrated Wendy's ribs. "Call it what you want, but we're taking you to dinner," he stated, starting toward the hall. "You can thank us later."

15
CAPTAIN WENDY DARLING

"You should have seen her face," Johns pounded his fist so hard as he laughed that the aluminum plates clattered against the table. "I didn't know that shade of purple existed."

"You're lucky I don't have you keelhauled," Wendy grumbled, chewing her potatoes while Johns roared. He had just finished an embellished retelling of her abduction to his eager audience. "You too, Dawes," she pointed her fork at the pilot, who raised her hands innocently.

"I maintain it was for your own good," the pilot's eyes twinkled deviously as she nestled on Michaels' shoulder. "We were starting to worry about you."

Wendy snorted in disbelief, but as she glanced around the table, she was surprised to see multiple nods of agreement. Michaels, DeLaCruz, Tootles, and even one of the twins bobbed their heads as they looked back at her.

Face warming, she checked her side, where Peter sat quietly, poking at his food. A polite smile was stitched onto his face, but he hadn't participated in the conversation with the rest of the crew and he had yet to make any eye contact with her. Waiting for him to speak, Wendy watched as he speared a piece of meat then dragged it around his plate before abandoning it again. Clearing her throat awkwardly, Wendy quickly redirected her gaze to the lieutenant.

"Be that as it may, if you ever do it again, I'm reporting you for insubordination," she threatened, then glared menacingly at Dawes. "You too."

The pilot's jaw dropped in shock, but Johns only bellowed louder. "Well, shyte, Darling, if I knew that was all I'd have to worry about, I would have done it sooner."

Wendy bristled, but she couldn't stop her laughter. With everyone gathered around the table, it was almost possible to forget they were millions of miles from home in the middle of barely-charted space. Nearly everyone was there, talking quietly among themselves—Dawes leaned into Michaels while DeLaCruz and Johns laughed at a rousing tale from the twins while Peter—distracted by the Lost Boys—had relaxed enough to eat a bit of his dissected meal. Even Tizari had made a rare appearance, thanking the Twins with a polite bow before returning to her room. The Stjarnin had not provided any updates other than to say she was still awaiting correspondence, but from what Wendy could tell, the warrior had seemed sincere. Not long after Tizari left, even SMEE sat down, placing an empty plate before him.

"It's part of my training," the synth explained after Johns questioned his attendance. "My form does not require the sustenance as your human vessels, however, it is common knowledge that many disagreements are settled during human meals. I would be remiss to excuse myself, should my presence be needed."

"Trust us, there's no deal making going on," DeLaCruz laughed, taking a quick drink.

"Unless the Twins want to promise to make some more of that cobbler," Johns said wistfully, looking at his empty plate in dismay. "That's a deal I'd be willing to entertain."

The table echoed in agreement, filling the bay with a lightness the *Roger had* long been missing. Wendy reveled in the simplicity, appreciating the moment where they all could just be. Slowly, the tension in her shoulders started to release and she almost found herself appreciating Johns' terrible jokes when a shrill chirp erupted from Dawes' scanband. Looking at the notification, the pilot's smile fell. Straightening in her seat, she glanced across the table at Wendy, her brows pulled in concern.

"Captain. It's the Admiral. The panel is requesting an audience. You're needed in Commands."

Cold dread washed down Wendy's back, but she schooled her features before offering the table a gracious smile.

"Thank you, Dawes," she said, surprised that her voice remained steady. She was glad she had been sitting when the notification came in or she might have fallen on her ass. Looking at the crew, Wendy laid her utensils across her plate. "And thank you all. If you'll excuse me." She tipped her head in silent dismissal before falling into step with Dawes as they hurried to access the comm. Wendy's mind whizzed through a million blurred scenarios as they rounded the bend, but a low voice called after them, breaking the stiff silence.

"Wait, Cap! Hold up," Peter rushed to catch them, followed by Tinc's golden cascade.

Wendy turned, meeting him with genuine surprise. "Did you need something?"

Shaking his head, Peter stopped to face her. "I'm coming with you," he announced.

"It's really not necessary," Wendy argued, remembering his cold reception at dinner. "I'm more than capable—"

"I know you are," he said, stepping closer even as her words pushed him away. "But that doesn't mean I don't want to be there for you." He reached for the chain still dangling from her neck, gently turning the acorn he had gifted her, and the charm reflected the golden flecks of his gaze.

Swallowing, Wendy glanced awkwardly at Dawes, whose eyes widened as she grinned. "I'll go access the comm," she said, quickly excusing herself. "It'll take a few minutes to get everything ready on our end anyway." Grinning, she darted off, but not before Peter tipped his head at Tinc, instructing her to follow. The bot issued a sharp jangle and obeyed, shooting green sparks into the darkened hall.

With the pilot and bot gone, Wendy glanced around the empty corridor before turning to Peter, conflicted. He was trying, offering to meet her in the middle, but part of her wasn't ready to accept, leaving her stuck and deliberating.

Noticing her hesitation, Peter stepped closer. "Look Cap, I'm sorry," he apologized with a heavy exhale. "I was an idiot. I'm just—not used to this whole thing," he said, gesturing between them. "The most human interaction I've had for a hundred years is dealing with a pack of twelve-year-olds," he shrugged. "Not exactly the best place to find advice on romance—or jealousy," he admitted sheepishly.

"No kidding," Wendy deadpanned, but a smile tugged her lips as she gave him her hand. "It's just hard because I'm not all that great either. It's not like there were courses offered at the Academy."

A rumbling laugh erupted from Peter. "If there was, I'm sure you would have aced them."

"Probably," Wendy agreed, matching his smile before she sobered, remembering the Fleet panel. "Maybe," she amended, picturing Colonel Matheson's pinched scowl. "But I guess we'll never know," she finished, her gaze pulling down the corridor.

"It's just a comm," Peter said, reading her tension. "Everything is going to be fine."

Wendy's brow arched in skepticism. "I sincerely doubt that," she said. "But standing here isn't going to do anything but prolong the inevitable."

Peter looked at her, the green in his eyes warming like a summer forest. "Then we'd better not keep them waiting," Peter murmured, holding tightly to her palm. He gave it a reassuring squeeze then hurried forward, drawing her protectively behind him. Touched by the sentiment, Wendy allowed herself to fall behind, giving Peter the lead while she tried to pretend her fear wouldn't drown her out.

16
CAPTAIN WENDY DARLING

Wendy's quarters were cold as she walked through the automated doors, but the captain couldn't tell if it was the room or her nerves. Returning Dawes' nervous smile, Wendy queued the comm.

"Everything is ready, Captain, the panel is just waiting for your sign on." Dawes explained anxiously. "Would you like me to stay?"

Wendy returned her question with a terse grin. "That won't be necessary. Run a stasis scan to make sure everything is on track with our charted course then you are free to go. I'll debrief you later."

Nodding, the pilot quickly checked the system, her braid dangling over her shoulder as she peered through the readings. "It all looks good," Dawes announced when she finished. "Are you sure there's not anything else?"

"All I need is the room," Wendy said, motioning for the pilot to take her leave. "Head out and take Peter," she said, earning a surprised look from the mechanic.

"But Cap, I told you—" he started, but Wendy quieted him with a raised hand.

"I know. But this is something I need to do on my own." She said before gripping Peter's hand.

There was a long pause while Peter studied her knuckles. "Something you need to do on your own, or without me," he finally asked, his expression torn between hope and hurt.

Wendy tried to say the words he needed to hear, but when she opened her mouth, the truth escaped before she could stop it.

"I don't know."

A cold mask slipped over Peter's face, casting his expression in stone. "Then maybe I don't anymore either," he responded with an exasperated shake of his head. "But I'm tired of trying to figure it out." He motioned to his bot. "Come on, Tinc. The captain will let us know if she needs us."

He stalked away with Tinc zipping behind, leaving Wendy standing before her stunned pilot. Dawes' blue eyes widened with worry, but Wendy waved her off.

"It's fine, Dawes—you don't have to ask," she forced a wry smile. "You can go."

Nodding quietly, the pilot followed Wendy's dismissal, her braid swishing as she retreated. Wendy waited until the doors whirred shut, then twisted to the comm, her heart slamming against her chest. Tugging the ends of her jacket, she activated the screen. The Admiral flickered to life before her, her stern features broadcasted before a row of stoic faces.

Raising her hand in a tight salute, Wendy pulled to attention. "Admiral Toussant," she said. "Apologies for the delay."

The Admiral nodded, her expression revealing nothing as she met Wendy's gaze. "I trust *the Roger* is holding steady?"

"As well as can be expected," Wendy answered, feeling only a slight pang at the omission.

"Then there is no cause to be alarmed by the adjustments to your course?" Colonel Matheson interrupted, her pointy gaze narrowing dubiously at the captain.

Gripping her hands behind her back, Wendy forced a smile. "We encountered some minor turbulence from an unexpected comet. A c-5 variant with a sizable tail," she lied, before issuing an absolution for Dawes. "I instructed our pilot to adjust the course rather than risk damaging the ship with cast-off debris."

The Admiral scrutinized Wendy before nodding tersely. "Very well. Make sure Lieutenant Dawes annotates her log accordingly," she instructed. Glancing back at her companions, the Admiral leveled a pointed scowl at Colonel Matheson. "Unless anyone has anything else to add, we will begin our preceding."

"That won't be necessary," Colonel Osbourne answered curtly, his bushy brows twitching over his squared spectacles. "I think we're all quite ready to be done deliberating," he said, cracking his knuckles impatiently.

"Indeed," the Admiral agreed, clasping her hands as she turned to Wendy.

Under Toussant's slate gaze, Wendy shifted, her heart flipping uncomfortably. Mercifully, the Admiral did not wait for a response, but continued her verdict, pinning Wendy under her impenetrable stare.

"Captain Wendy Moira Angela Darling, First Class of the Londonierre Brigade: You have been brought before the disciplinary tribune to account for the events that transpired during the Neverland mission. You have already been debriefed on the circumstances and accounts being considered. Do you have any questions before we proceed?"

"No, ma'am," Wendy answered, barely able to choke out her words over the nerves caught in her throat.

"Very good," the Admiral's lips pursed tightly as she glanced at the file under her fists. Noticing her pause, Colonel Matheson's mousy cough rippled through the silent screen. The Admiral ignored it and sat silently for another beat before looking quickly at Wendy.

"Captain Darling," she began. "After much deliberation, the panel has decided that though the events that have transpired have been thoroughly documented, there is too little reliable evidence to come to a definite conclusion. Due also to the unprecedented nature of many key incidents, it would be unjust to act decisively until a full investigation can be conducted."

A startled cough erupted and the panel's gaze turned to Colonel Matheson, whose eyes bugged as she spluttered. "That's not what—" she started, her face narrowing as she recovered and looked furiously at the others. "I thought—"

"Because of this, it is the tribunal's decision," the Admiral spoke over Matheson's protests, silencing the colonel before pausing to allow her words to resonate, "that you retain your position as provisional captain of the *Jolly Roger* until your return to New London, at which point, your appointment will be thoroughly reevaluated. Should you prove your competency for the remainder of the voyage, your rank and position will be preserved. However, should any additional discrepancies arise, the panel will reconvene posthaste."

Finishing, the Admiral rapped her knuckles on the table. The harsh noise jolted Wendy's system, breaking her paralysis. She wasn't sure if she was expected to respond, so instead she stared, noting the cool masks on every face—except for Colonel Matheson. Angry red splotches colored the woman's face as she bunched her fists, holding them so tightly that her arms shook. Not wanting to meet her gaze, Wendy quickly redirected her attention to Toussant, who loudly cleared her throat.

"Is there anything that needs to be clarified, Captain?"

"No, Admiral," Wendy rushed, sweeping a neat salute. "The directive is clear. Thank you."

Behind Toussant, Colonel Osbourne grunted and stood before saluting the Admiral and nodding to Wendy. "Admiral. Captain. Safe travels and godspeed. I'll be glad to have these hearings over and done with."

"Yes sir, goodnight." Wendy said, ignoring the grouchy admonishment. With a grumbling cough, the colonel shuffled out, followed closely by Lieutenant Jimenez who smiled at Wendy before saluting the Admiral. Waving the two of them out, Toussant eyed the lingering officers. Catching the Admiral's stare, Colonel Hahti quietly excused himself, while Matheson stood in front of her chair, seething.

"Is there something I forgot to add, Colonel?"

Turning toward Toussant, Matheson's violent expression looked as though it could curdle blood. Her face flushed an ugly purple before she smoothed her scowl with a dainty sniff.

"No, Admiral. *Your* decision was quite clear," Matheson said, her resentment morphing into a sickly grin. "I'm sure the young captain is quite grateful for your lenience." She smirked wickedly at Wendy before turning pointedly back to Toussant. "Such grace would not be given quite so freely from or for many such-ranked officers of the Fleet."

"Undoubtedly," the Admiral agreed. "Which is why I'm certain there will be no need to discuss the matter further." She flashed Matheson a brilliant smile before following it with a wave. "If there is nothing else, Colonel, you are dismissed."

Colonel Matheson looked like she'd like to hit the Admiral rather than salute her, but after a quick twitch of her neck, the officer swept the customary gesture before quickly taking her leave. When the sliding doors finally swept shut behind her, Toussant let out a heavy sigh and dropped her head.

Unsure whether the Admiral had forgotten to end the comm, Wendy allowed her a moment before softly clearing her throat. "Um, Admiral, was there anything else that you needed from me?" she asked hesitantly.

Hearing Wendy, the Admiral turned to face the screen.

"Actually Darling, there is," the Admiral answered, a new sense of urgency in her voice. "As I'm sure you gathered, there are some members of the panel who did not quite agree with the decision to retain your captaincy. As a matter of fact—"

The Admiral's statement lingered until Wendy pressed softly. "Admiral?"

Jerking back, Toussant excused her question with a swish of her hand.

"Never mind," she said finally, "What's done is done." Grabbing the file, the Admiral moved to leave, then paused. "Perhaps there is one thing?"

"Yes, Admiral?"

"It was not by popular vote that you were granted an extension of your rank, Captain. The panel was quite divided, with several members voicing *explicit* opposing opinions."

"Colonel Matheson being one of them," Wendy guessed around the sudden dryness in her mouth.

"Not the hardest deduction to make," the Admiral smiled grimly. "What I'm trying to express is that there are still doubts around your capabilities—doubts that I do not share but must take under consideration. So hear me when I advise you not to force the panel's hand. Another gathering is highly unlikely to turn in your favor."

"Understood," Wendy said.

The Admiral's shoulders relaxed. "Very good, Captain," she said, looking fractionally relieved. "If there is nothing else—" she began, but Wendy stepped forward, her hand raised to the screen.

"Admiral?" she asked. The tension in the Admiral's shoulders returned, but Toussant's casual expression remained firmly intact.

"Yes, Darling?"

Hesitating, Wendy stalled for words. She had considered asking the Admiral her opinion on the *Roger's* new developments, but a closer look at the tired lines etching Toussant's face brought her pause. Part of her wanted desperately to consult superior, but another part worried the Admiral would force her to abandon the mission.

And the commander.

Chest tightening, Wendy saluted. "Thank you," she stammered, the shakiness in her voice disguised as emotion. "For believing in me. I won't let you down."

In the flickering screen, the Admiral quirked her lips.

"You're very welcome captain," she said. "Don't make me regret it."

Offering a weary nod, Toussant quickly ended the comm. It blipped on the screen, leaving Wendy to stare at her darkened reflection.

"I'll do my best," Wendy whispered, as a sick feeling plunged over her, filling her with doubt. For as much as she had meant her promise, she knew nothing about her undisclosed plans would change. She was still going to try and save Commander Boyce.

Now, it was just that much more important that she succeeded.

17
FLEET MECHANIC PETER PAN

THE JOLLY ROGER

Peter was restless. He had been for the past few hours. *Really, the past few days,* he thought as he stalked around his cramped dorm. He'd already knocked into the edge of the bed frame three times in his circular route, and a dull throb in his thigh warned of a blossoming bruise at the impact site. Rubbing it aimlessly, Peter tried to redirect his thoughts, but he could only think about Wendy.

He wanted to know how the hearing went. Certainly, it couldn't still be in session. At first, he'd decided to wait outside for the captain, not wanting to interrupt, but as the hours stretched, his patience had fizzled and burned through a range of complicated emotions. All the while he forced himself to follow her directive and stay back. Now, looking again at the clock, he wondered if perhaps she had forgotten about him.

Or maybe not forgotten. Just left.

Grumbling, he tugged his already disheveled hair and resumed his agitated pacing, once more smashing against the bed.

"Shyte!" Peter winced. Bending over, he directed a string of curses at the bed frame until a sharp jangle interrupted his trail of expletives.

"I know it's not the bed's fault," he muttered darkly at the flippant fairy. "Would you rather I curse at you?"

A colorful burst of language exploded in Peter's ear and he let out a barking laugh.

"Alright, alright. I get it. You swear better than I do," he said, the bot's crass language earning the first genuine laugh he'd released all night. "It doesn't have to be a competition."

Tinc's smart retort suggested otherwise, but Peter's only response was a rough chuckle. He smiled for a moment, but his mood sobered as the ache in his thigh returned. It was only when he narrowly missed the frame a fifth time that he decided to abandon his quarters.

"Come on, Tinc, let's get some air." Grabbing his jacket, he shrugged quickly into the gray leather before striding out the door. Sparking happily behind him, the bot zoomed ahead, looping his torso in a few wide circles before coming to rest on his shoulder.

"Where to?" Peter asked, pausing uncertainly outside the hall. It had been easy to decide to escape, but standing outside, he realized there was nowhere to go. Several suggestions tinkled in his ear, but Peter dismissed all of them. It wasn't that any of them were particularly bad, it was just that in his state, he was fairly certain any recommendation would sound the same.

"How about we just start walking," he countered. "Maybe we'll find something interesting along the way?"

When Tinc's noncommittal spark didn't offer any argument, he gave a firm nod.

"Walking it is," he announced, starting down the winding halls, his feet leading down the familiar paths. Even with all the changes made to *the Roger*, Peter could still navigate the old bird by heart. His previous residency had branded each corner into his brain and as he crept through the quiet halls, phantom memories shifted through every shadowed path; all of them centered around Hooke, dauntless in his pursuit of adventure and glory.

It surprised him that the memories were wrapped in fondness instead of the bitter cloud that always seemed to follow Hooke's name. So much in fact, that it was only a quick jangle from Tinc that saved him from barreling into the wall after a particularly sharp turn toward the end of the barge. Dodging the collision with a quick curse, Peter shook his head.

"Thanks, Tinc," he said, earning a sharp retort. Smirking, Peter shrugged. "I probably deserved that," he agreed, still unsure where he intended to stop. Just being out on the ship made him feel worlds better than being cooped up in his tiny room. He'd had so many years of roaming free over Neverland that it made the *Roger's* confines almost unbearable. Still, the weathered corridors set his nerves at ease until his steady footsteps pulled down an electric blue hall.

Surprised, Peter looked around, realizing he had approached the MedBay. Its open screen cast a dim glow, illuminating the room where Hooke rested, propped up by the elevated bed. Frowning, Peter struggled to reconcile Hooke's recovering frame to his old memories. Noticing his presence, the captain met his gaze with an assured smirk.

"I'll just be a minute, Tinc," Peter sighed, waving the bot's sarcastic jangle with a quick swat. "It's not like we were busy," he grumbled, altering his course into the bay.

"Trouble sleeping, Pan?"

Peter shrugged. "Guess I'm still getting my space legs," he answered casually. "The nightsims don't hold a candle to the starcast."

"I would have to agree," Hooke admitted with a soft smile. "I didn't ever think I'd miss it, and yet, here we are."

"Here we are," Peter echoed, waiting for the captain's point.

After a moment, Hooke fixed him with a firm stare. "But I have to wonder why," he mused. "Certainly there are other things to occupy your time and attention. Specifically, other captains."

Peter's hands jammed in his pockets. "I guess not everyone is having as much trouble adjusting," he offered coolly.

Hooke's smirk widened. "So it would seem," he gestured to a small stool resting along the wall. "You're welcome to take a seat. Generally, it's reserved for the medic, but it seems she is one of the lucky few not plagued by insomnia."

Peter's brow cocked at the stool, wondering how he'd found himself entertaining Hooke for the second time in as many days. It wasn't ideal but thinking about the restless pacing awaiting him, he nodded and crossed the room. "So, what's new?" he asked flippantly.

A soft snort escaped the captain. "Nothing terribly exciting, as I'm sure you can imagine," Hooke replied. "I would assume you have more interesting developments to share."

"You mean the frequency of your bowel movements isn't noteworthy?" Peter edged, hoping to turn the conversation.

The captain chuckled, a hint of arrogance returning. "Everything I do is noteworthy," he declared, zeroing on the mechanic. "But that doesn't mean it's the most pressing development."

Peter barked a laugh. "The fact that I'm here with you should show how much I know about any happenings," he said, crossing his arms as he sagged against the wall.

"Trouble in paradise?" Hooke asked, arching his peppered brow.

Peter inhaled deeply. "Paradise is a strong word, James. Especially for a junked old bird." He grinned, hoping to strike a nerve.

Hooke merely grimaced and shifted to sit higher. "She wasn't always this way," he retorted, glancing wistfully around the room. "There was once a time when the *Roger* was the finest vessel in the 'verse." He turned a thoughtful smile. "But you already knew that. So let's discuss what's really troubling you."

Peter squirmed under the captain's iron gaze. "And how do you know something's bothering me?" He challenged, bending to rest his elbows on his knees.

Hooke's chuckle ended in a harsh wheeze. "You were never very good at disguising your emotions," he said. "Your fire burns too bright. After all these years, I can still read you like a book."

Peter's temper flared at Hooke's observation, but not wanting to prove the captain's point, he leaned in his chair, hoping his angry fists didn't betray him.

"Fine then," he challenged. "If you're so knowledgeable, you tell me. What ails my spirit?"

Another snort escaped the captain, but Hooke only clucked his tongue. "Come, Peter. No one has ever appreciated petulance," he breezed, sounding bored.

Crossing his arms, Peter glared at the captain, but it fizzled as the mechanic studied his former mentor. Hooke wore no judgment, just quiet curiosity as he puzzled over Peter's stubborn silence. For a moment, Peter wondered what advice Hooke *would* have on facing the Shadow, if it was information he'd be willing to discuss.

Not that it was even a thought he should be entertaining. Wendy had been quite clear in her directive that Hooke remained in the dark regarding the discovery of the Raptor. No matter how Peter phrased the conversation, he doubted he could skirt his way around her orders neatly enough to claim innocence.

"It's nothing," Peter said. "Nothing worth the *esteemed* captain's attention, anyway," he needled, remembering the phrase he'd so often used in the past to snag Hooke's interest in otherwise mundane topics—generally those requiring the captain's sign off on tech expenditures.

"Oh bloody hell, don't tell me you want to purchase some energy extrapolater or gravity turbine," Hooke moaned. "That's a problem better reserved for the fairer captain."

Peter snorted at Hooke's call on his bluff, but his brows furrowed as he stared thoughtfully at the paneled floor. "Do you ever wonder if maybe the Shadow can't truly be killed?" he asked.

The room was so silent that only the soft beep of the captain's ECG monitor responded as it trilled Hooke's vitals. After a moment, Peter glanced up, wondering if the old man had fallen asleep. When he met the captain's iron stare, Peter coughed uncomfortably.

"I was under the impression that it was no longer a concern," Hooke ventured, only the crease in his forehead betraying his fear.

"It was—*is*," Peter answered, correcting himself with a wave of his hand. "Launched into the void, expelled to the great beyond, vanished into the unknown, and all that," he backpedaled in a rush.

Hooke's brow quirked. "Quite," he said, his lips hardening into a thin line before he leaned tiredly against his pillow to stare at the steel ceiling. "I would imagine there must be a way Itzala could be killed. Or at the very least, weakened enough to be defeated. But considering that claim has already been made, my more immediate concern is why you would ask," Hooke mused.

"Sleep deprivation, most likely," Peter answered with a shrug before turning purposefully to Tinc. "Probably our cue to head out, Tinc" he breezed. "Can't say it hasn't been fun, James, but well, can't say that it has been either," he grinned, moving quickly after the fluttering bot until Hooke's call stalled his tracks.

"Some nightmares don't wait for sleep," the captain murmured. "You know as well as I do that Itzala is undoubtedly one of them."

His stomach plummeting, Peter turned to Hooke. Though he was just a shade of his former mentor, Peter could see where the ghost of the captain remained.

"I just wonder—if we weren't successful—will the Shadow stay away, or will it try to reclaim what it has lost," Peter asked, picking carefully through each word.

Hooke twisted a simple band on his thumb. "Perhaps you're worried it will try to reclaim *who* it lost," he countered.

"I'm not scared of any old Shadow," Peter retorted. "It won't come after me."

"Reassuring," the captain deadpanned, looking bored. "However, you aren't exactly whom I had in mind," he explained meaningfully. "If memory serves, there was another who both Itzala and its host were quite intrigued with."

The words sent an icy chill through Peter's veins. His statement was meant to be a diversion. He had never considered that approaching the Shadow might give Itzala another chance at Wendy. Ashamed, he realized he had been so wrapped up in jealousy that he'd completely disregarded her safety.

"Captain Darling is more than capable of taking care of herself," he responded, partially to appease the man before him and to partially for himself.

"Certainly," Hooke nodded thoughtfully. "Then what has you worried? Unless," the captain paused as a shrewd smile crept over his lips. "You're troubled by the reason you might encounter Itzala. Tell me, what has our fair captain found?"

Berating himself for thinking he could evade Hooke's shrewd perception, Peter scowled. "Nothing has been confirmed. The captain has just noticed some irregularities on several charts she discovered—yours, I believe," he added, hoping the turn of topics would force Hooke's hand. "Discrepancies I'm surprised you didn't catch yourself."

"My old maps?" Hooke asked. His brows raised at the reveal before he smiled in understanding. "Of the nebula. Pity. I was quite hoping those might have remained hidden. But no matter. I would be most interested to hear what our Darling has found."

"I'm sure you would," a terse voice interrupted, causing Peter to whirl in surprise. Behind him, DeLaCruz stood, her tousled hair matching her disheveled uniform as she glowered at them through the sleep in her baggy eyes. "Unfortunately, that's not something Captain Darling has approved."

"Oh come now, Commander," Hooke coaxed, smiling pleasantly at the medic. "Surely two heads are better than one. I'm certain I could provide valuable insight to the captain's predicament."

DeLaCruz' scowl deepened. "That's not my call to make," she answered, turning pointedly towards Peter. "Or yours." She crossed her arms, strengthening her stance. "And unless you want to wake her up and bring it to her attention directly, I suggest you make your way back to the dorms."

Peter nodded, realizing he wasn't going to make it anywhere with the bleary-eyed medic. "Come on, Tinc," he said, tilting his head for the bot to follow. "She's right, we really ought to head back."

"I'm going to have to inform the captain about your meeting," DeLaCruz declared as he passed.

"Just add it to my list of screw ups," Peter shrugged. "Catch you later, Hooke. That is, if I don't end up in holding myself," he grumbled. He hurried to vacate the room but as the door whirred open, a call from Hooke stopped him.

"Listen, Pan. Although the conversation we shared was dreadfully ill-informed—to the point of uselessness really—" he breezed, betraying his ploy only with his surreptitious glance at the medic, "my one question is this: if Itzala were to find its way back into our path, would you be able to do what is necessary to defeat it, even if others can't?"

Understanding, Peter nodded slowly before tipping his head apologetically to the medic. Exiting to the hall, Tinc's crimson sparks wrapped around him, echoing her scathing tirade ringing in his ears. But for all her scolding, Peter's attention was a million miles away, tuned to Hooke's final inquiry.

Will you be able to do what is necessary to defeat it, even if others can't? The words echoed, chasing him with every metallic step.

That was the question. Because at this point, whether he liked it or not, Wendy was bound and determined to reclaim the commander —regardless of her probability of success. He needed to answer. If the captain was unable to see past her blind determination to rescue the commander, could Peter save Wendy from herself?

18
COMMANDER AIDAN BOYCE
LOCATION UNKOWN

I t was strange, freezing to death whilst covered in sweat. Cursing, Boyce wiped his forehead to mop the sweat from his eyes. It had been tedious work, but somehow, he had managed to piece together the majority of the switchboard. He'd had to sacrifice some of the less significant parts to parcel as repairs for the more important cords and board was far from pretty, but if his mandatory classes in mech repair were worth their salt, he might actually have something.

Now if he could just locate a power source.

Shivering, Boyce searched the small cabin. He'd been working for what he guessed was a few hours, and he knew there had been at least a couple interrupted sessions between when he'd started and now. Itzala wasn't making it easy, but the commander was determined not to let the darkness win.

He stepped around the room, his soft steps reverberating through the floor. The vibrations subsided and a wave of chitters crashed against the door, followed by a solid clang against the barred seal before the faceless voices scurried back into the depths of the ship. Turning toward the sound, Boyce's brow furrowed. The things outside—whatever they were—had grown bolder over the past few days. They'd never breached the barricade, but they'd recently begun testing the barrier on their own, occasionally resurfacing to batter the door before scurrying back from where they came.

Unwanted, a picture of a dozen wraithlike creatures formed in his mind—monsters with bleached, shriveled skin that hung over their emaciated frames. Their skeletons appeared humanoid, but they moved like animals, hunched on all fours as they chattered in harsh tones. *Espazi anjale*, Itzala had called them, when it conjured the image to Boyce's mind, attempting to distract him with taunts of the waiting demons. The commander wasn't sure how exactly the Shadow knew them, but the certainty of Itzala's projection promised the imagery was real.

Forcing the ghostly creatures from his thoughts, Boyce focused once more on the task at hand. It was hard enough remaining coherent without having to evade additional nightmares.

It was no wonder he was so tired all the time.

Rubbing his eyes, Boyce fought the urge to rest against the switch panels. He wasn't sure how much longer he had, and he needed to utilize every second of clarity. Shaking his head, he bent toward the panel. Almost done. Then he could find a way to power it and transmit his message.

Or that was the plan. He wasn't sure how, but he was determined to make it work. He'd seen enough of the ship to determine he was on an old exploratory vessel—a mid-sized raptor by the looks of it—and some rooting through the abandoned files in the pilot's station had provided the ship's name, *the Ohore Ehiza,* a Spanish vessel that had launched in 2308. Admittedly, the dossier was hard to decipher because it was largely written in the nearly extinct language of Basque, but it seemed his father's obsession with foreign affairs had finally paid off, and he cobbled enough from his mandatory dialect lessons to decipher the significant data.

The *Ohore Ehiza,* piloted by Captain Alesandre Ibarre in the exploratory voyage of the Krawk Nebula, was spurred by unofficial intel that there was a great, untapped power hidden in the vast quadrant. It wasn't too surprising that the Spaniards had sent their own vessel—the Brigade had long suspected the Spanish Batailoia of conducting unsanctioned missions outside the Nations Accord. Such speculations had splashed across news briefings off and on for years, but Boyce's presence on their old ship confirmed the deception. The thought was troubling if the commander spent enough time trying to figure out where the Batailoia might have received such information, but there was enough occupying his thoughts that he couldn't fixate on such a minor detail.

Glancing at the abandoned dossier, Boyce flipped through the yellowed pages. Captain Ibarra and his crew of eight all but disappeared, leaving the empty raptor floating in the vast nebula, more captives of the Neverland Sector. They all stared happily at him from the roster, completely unaware of the fate that awaited them. A fate ending in the empty shell of a ship overtaken by a scourge of nightmares, a god of shadows, and… him.

A winning combination, Boyce thought grimly. But he couldn't let it get to him. He wouldn't go down without a fight. If it took every last ounce of sanity he had, so be it.

So eager to volunteer your mind? The dark question slithered through his brain, the probing tendrils slipping through his mental barricade. *I'd be happy to assist.*

"Not today, demon," Boyce answered, grinding his teeth. Now that Itzala had breached his defenses, his time was limited. Ripping off his scanband, he hurried to remove the backplate and reveal the tech's power source—a pin-sized, crescent disc.

Plucking it from the band, Boyce searched the board for the open divot he'd located in the frame. If his calculations were correct, inserting the chip wouldn't be a permanent fix, but it might give enough charge to get out a comm.

"Please let this work," Boyce muttered, linking the chip to a loose, threaded wire, praying the conductor would recognize a compatible charge. Nothing happened, so he repositioned the wire, silently repeating his prayer. The screen remained blank until a small pop sounded and it flickered to life, issuing a groaning wheeze as it woke from its extended slumber.

An impressive feat, the Shadow's voice murmured. *Too bad it will be short lived,* it finished, threatening the perimeter of his thoughts with a thick wave of darkness.

Wincing, the commander shoved it back. "I don't need it to last forever," he said, rising quickly to the switchboard, "just long enough."

The commander's sudden movement made his head spin as his gnawing hunger overtook him. Knees buckling, he gripped the panel, using it to steady himself while Itzala hovered overhead, cackling at his weakness.

His hands still shaking, Boyce located the keystroke panel. It was hard to see through the partially backlit screen, but peering close, he was able to make out the familiar layout. The commander scanned the board then positioned his hands and quickly began to type.

A waste of precious time, Itzala's dark voice needled, pressing closer to his ear. *And all for a doomed message that wouldn't matter to anyone who received it.* The Shadow's whisper ended with a cruel laugh before it played a silhouetted image of a dark haired beauty curled in the arms of a wiry mechanic.

She's already forgotten you.

"Just one more reason to remind her I'm here," Boyce said, stamping his blockade back in place. It slammed shut and the Shadow recoiled, leaving the commander with precious clarity. Utilizing the distraction, Boyce managed a few more sentences, but it was difficult. He just hoped he provided enough intel that if Wendy received his signal she could send help.

Or maybe she'll just leave you to rot.

Gritting his teeth, Boyce tried again to banish the Shadow, but this time the creature was prepared. Burrowing further into the commander's mind, it found a foothold, a bitter memory to latch onto and poison his mind.

"Not yet," Boyce growled. Only a few more strokes, and his message would be done. It just needed a signature—

Stop, the Shadow seethed, its low voice filled with hate. *You cannot disobey me.*

Boyce paused, tensing as Itzala exerted its hold, moving from the roots of his brain. The tenuous shaking in his limbs that prompted every blackout had begun, signaling the breath between his transition of consciousness to the Shadow's. Before the darkness could take over, he pushed against it with every ounce of willpower he had.

"Bog off, you monster," he growled, entering the last digits of his Fleet ID. The Shadow howled as the message shimmered and vanished, leaving an empty glow. It flickered, dimming as the panel nearly puttered out, but a final message stamped across the screen.

<<Transmission spooled. Message cast: COMPLETE>>

The cabin shook as the Shadow's roar ripped through the small compartment, but the commander was unphased as he gaped at the notification.

"It got out," he breathed, releasing his hitched breath with a hopeful whisper. "Maybe I will too."

Boyce smiled, then in a dizzying blur, the room went dark. Carried on the last thrums of the dying panel, he slumped to the ground, falling to exhaustion. He sat for a moment, hanging limp before he pushed himself to his knees. Crawling across the cabin, he knocked softly against the blockade.

"Not if I can stop it," Itzala jeered, laughing through stolen vocal cords while chittering hisses rallied against the door. *"I'm not done yet, commander."*

19
CAPTAIN WENDY DARLING

THE JOLLY ROGER

"Wow, Captain. I know it's called beauty sleep, but you look like shyte," Dawes laughed as Wendy rolled out of bed. The pilot snickered as the captain approached the StarBoard, then offered her a steaming cup of coffee.

"No commentary until after the first sip," Wendy grumbled, blowing on the mug's contents. Peering through bleary eyes, Wendy studied Dawes, who looked as chipper as ever. "When do you even find time to do all that?" she asked, indicating the pilot's flawless face before taking a long drink.

"I don't usually make it a habit to stay up until all hours of the night, Captain. It's about *balance*—which is a skill I don't think you've mastered."

"My balance is great," Wendy countered. "Now *Johns* on the other hand—"

"Not the balance I'm talking about," Dawes giggled. "This is more about setting personal boundaries than your inner ear."

Wendy shrugged, more interested in the drink she held than her pilot's life coaching. "Either way, the coffee is wonderful. Thank you," she said, shuffling to the captain's chair. Still clad in her sleek black leggings and thin sleeping shirt, she needed to suit up but wanted to check the *Roger's* progress first. Stealing her jacket from the back of her chair, Wendy covered her shoulders and settled in, sipping her coffee as she ordered a progress audit.

Across the room, Dawes awaited Wendy's commands. Wendy ignored her pointed gaze, focusing instead on the data streaming before her.

"It looks like everything is on course," Dawes supplied, filling the silence. "And we're making decent time. Hopefully, we'll arrive in the raptor's quadrant within the next 72 hours."

Wendy nodded. "The faster we get there, the better," she declared, remembering why she slept so poorly. Dawes was partially right, she *had* stayed up into the early morning hours, her anxiety spinning her into hyperdrive. But when she finally managed to force herself to sleep, her worry didn't settle. It plagued her dreams with dark shadows, shards of glass, and Boyce, spiraling endlessly through space.

Taking another long sip to warm her suddenly chilled bones, Wendy stared pensively at the map. After a long pause, a soft question slipped from her lips, whispering through the cabin.

"Dawes, if our positions were switched—yours and mine—would we still be following the same course?"

"If our positions were switched, Captain, we'd have fallen out of the sky a long time ago," the pilot teased, fixing Wendy with a broad grin. "I'm talking about you downing our bird, by the way. *I* would do an excellent job." Dawes giggled and Wendy found herself echoing her infectious laugh.

"Very true," she ceded, with a dismissive head shake. "But supposing I *were* up to your caliber of piloting," the levity in her voice dissipated as she quieted, then finished her thought. "Would you have altered the course?"

Arielle's smile slipped. Fingering her braid, the pilot thought for a moment, then angled her chair to face Wendy directly.

"I don't know," she said honestly. "It's not an easy decision." The pilot paused; her expression marred by her severity. "Like everything, there are positives and negatives to each outcome, but *unlike* most decisions these positives and negatives are life-altering. It's not like choosing what you want to eat, or even your career path. You hold people's lives in your hands. It's a heavy weight to carry."

Wendy's lips pulled as she considered. "What do you think you would do," she pressed, uncertain what she was hoping to hear.

Realizing she wasn't getting out without answering, Dawes sighed. "I think," she said, weighing her words carefully, "I would have done the same—Aidan is one of ours, and crotchety as he can be, there's something to be said about bringing everyone home. It's dangerous, but he'd do the same for any one of us."

A lump formed in Wendy's throat, but she forced a smile. "Thank you, Dawes. I appreciate your candor."

The pilot shrugged. "Anytime Captain. Sorry I can't be of more help."

"You've been wonderful," Wendy promised, trying to bolster the crooked turn of her lips before she turned to her command station. It wasn't the pilot's fault that Wendy was one slip from coming undone. Exhaling, she leaned forward, allowing her mind to wander as she finished the protocol, waking the systems as data scans flickered over the holoscreen.

Searching through the swarm of reports, Wendy was relieved everything came back green—the ship was in stasis and keeping steady. A welcome change from recent scans. Reaching the end of her roster, she was nearly ready to close the file when a flickering notification caught her eye.

"That's strange," Wendy murmured, swiping the small icon. She leaned forward as the file downloaded and flickered across the screen. Her eyes darted over the message and when she finished, her legs buckled as she gasped, grateful she hadn't been standing.

"Captain?" Dawes asked, but Wendy could hardly hear it over the blood pounding in her ears. Rereading the transmission to make sure she hadn't hallucinated, Wendy glanced at the pilot, who had paled with concern. "Captain, are you alright?"

Wendy's head twitched in an involuntary jerk. No, she wasn't alright. The final thread had been pulled and she feared that if she even moved to speak, her body would spool across the universe. Standing as still as possible, she took in a slow, deep breath, unsurprised to feel a cold tear trickle down her cheek. Her hands knotted in her pockets, and even though they clenched tight in fists, she couldn't stop the tremor that ran through them.

"Captain, you're scaring me," Dawes insisted. "What's wrong?"

Blinking, Wendy turned, feeling numb as she met the pilot's anxious gaze.

"It's Boyce," she whispered, glancing once more at the projected transmission to confirm she wasn't insane. There, at the bottom, his FleetSig, the unique ID assigned to each soldier for emergency verifications such as this, glowed. Stamped at the end of the message, it confirmed every hope, fear, and guilty thought she'd battled the past few weeks.

"He's alive."

20
CAPTAIN WENDY DARLING

"What?" Dawes blinked from worry to disbelief. "Can you repeat that?"

"Boyce is alive," Wendy affirmed, her resolve growing after her first incredulous admission. Pointing shakily at the message, she offered the pilot a moment to scan the message. "Somehow, he made it."

"Where did this come from?" Dawes asked, her expression tight.

"The Raptor," Wendy answered. She accessed the transmission stamp then let out another startled gasp. "He sent it yesterday."

"But how?" Dawes pressed. "The bird is dead. Our scan confirmed it. There's no way he should have been able to push a signal, let alone spool a transmission. What happened?"

"I don't know," Wendy admitted, "but it's him. No one else would have his identification code."

"What about the Shadow," the pilot asked, her eyes wide. "Could it have, I don't know—*harvested*—it from the commander's brain?"

The thought sent a shudder through Wendy. Dawes' question made the Shadow sound like some creature in a bad horror movie; Wendy couldn't forget the power Itzala exerted as it grappled to control her body and how the icy chill of its grip wormed its way into the darkest recesses of her mind.

"It's possible," Wendy admitted miserably, fighting the visual of Aidan's possessed body standing at the helm of some long-abandoned ship, his eyes glowing red as he cackled evilly—a puppet to Itzala's darkest whims. "But we can't think like that," she declared, "For all intents and purposes, Commander Boyce has survived and officially sent a plea for help. It's our duty to assist him."

As she spoke, the smallest bloom of relief seeped through the tightness cinching her chest. Per Fleet regulation, any crew that received a helpSig from another verified Fleet signia was required to assist. The fine print might have dictated more specific methods of aid, but Wendy was thinking positive—now if the panel had questions about her unsanctioned detour, she had legs to stand on, weak as they may be.

Dawes didn't look convinced. Her frown lingered, but she gave Wendy a dutiful nod. "I'll start shooting out scans. Maybe now that the Raptor's got some zip I'll be able to gather more data."

"Good idea," Wendy said. "In the meantime, I am going to notify Johns and I'd appreciate it if you could fill in Michaels while I'm gone."

"Sure thing, Captain," Dawes agreed, sweeping a small salute.

"Thank you," Wendy said and hurried into her uniform before combing through her hair, inciting her curls into a riot before tethering them with a thick band. With one last trip to her panel, she keyed a quick command to spool Boyce's transmission to a filebyte on her scanband.

Her wrist buzzed as the transfer completed and with a grim smile, Wendy cleared the holoscreen, leaving the image stamped in her mind, a flickering undercurrent to her every thought.

5.16.2394//IntGal-LL:-86.17,-273.9//03:47
Mayday. Mayday. Mayday.

This is—this is—important. I have been trapped on the incapacitated vessel, the Ohore Ehiza from the Spanish Batailoia commanded by Captain Alesandre Ibarra and his crew in 2308. There is no evidence of what has happened to the team, but there are remnants of an attack, and potentially—

I ... I don't know how long I have been on board, nor how I arrived, but I fear time will soon run out. Requesting assistance from any nearby vessels—except—except hers. It's not safe for you here. I'd rather die than have It...

If anyone receives, please send help. Or tell her—tell her that I—that I'm glad it was me. I just wish it had been me for everything. I—I think she'll know what I mean. . .

Commander Aiden Boyce, Londonniere Brigade. Fleet

Insignia 33672. Status:
Severe.
Please hurry.

21
CAPTAIN WENDY DARLING

Wendy stalked through the *Roger*, Boyce's message replaying nearly a dozen times before she gathered her bearings enough to decide where to go first. Redirecting her aimless walk, she headed for the ship's main bay, angling for the research room, where Johns would be working with Tootles.

Moving with newfound purpose, she almost reached the bay when her scanband hummed and she twitched her wrist to access the notification. Reading the tiny print, she scowled at DeLaCruz' request, imagining a ploy to coax her into a physio session, but the medic's last lines brought her pause.

It's Hooke.

Frowning, Wendy typed a quick directive to Johns, instructing him to meet her at his earliest opportunity. Turning back, Wendy rounded the corridor, following the path to the dimmed

MedBay, where the darkened holoshade obscured Hooke's quarters.

Wondering what could possibly have happened to make DeLaCruz directly oppose her orders, Wendy hurried in, her determined stride making up for her brief pause outside the door. The medic flitted about, her shoulders bunched as she moved from task to task, her pen bouncing wildly between her thumb and pointer finger.

"I don't think I've ever seen you anxious before, DeLaCruz," Wendy said, her voice coming out much lighter than she felt. Usually, Rissa's seriousness was tempered by a streak of sarcasm and wit—the heavy agitation blanketing her athletic frame was unsettling. "It doesn't suit you."

"We can't all be infallible bearers of this world's burdens," the medic peppered back, but her words were flat, like her tired expression. Clasping her medpad, DeLaCruz quickly saluted. "Nice to see you, Captain."

"I find when one is requested with such cryptic urgency, it's best they make an appearance," Wendy said, glancing around. To the right, Hooke's door gaped open, but she couldn't see anything inside besides the green light seeping through the panel. She looked back at DeLaCruz, who had fallen to attention. "What did you need to tell me?"

Darkening, Rissa quickly pressed her palm to the access panel outside Hooke's quarters. The pad issued a soft beep before the door streamed shut, closing Wendy and the medic in the front room. Crossing to her workstation, DeLaCruz set down her pad and looked at Wendy, her lips forming a hard line.

"I'm not exactly sure how to say this—" DeLaCruz hesitated, flexing her jaw.

"Then just say it, Commander," Wendy ordered, the worry in her chest turning her impatient.

Nodding, DeLaCruz clasped her hands. "Of course, Captain," she said, her eyes darting to the closed panel behind Wendy. She waited a moment, as though she expected someone to walk in, but when it remained fixed in place, she let out a quiet breath.

"Last night as I was doing my rounds, I came to check on Hooke. Everything was fine: his vitals, his bindings…"

"If everything was fine, DeLaCruz, why is there an issue?" Wendy insisted, urging the Commander on.

"Because when I walked in, Hooke was not alone. Pan was with him. Discussing the maps."

"Are you sure?" Wendy asked, forcing the question around her anger.

DeLaCruz nodded. "Hooke was asking Peter what information you had pulled from them. I don't know what else they spoke about, but I stopped the conversation immediately."

Grimacing, Wendy's thoughts tumbled in a dizzying whir. "Did Pan have anything to say?"

Rissa shrugged. "I didn't give him much of a chance. I told him he needed to leave and informed him I would be reporting the incident. He didn't seem pleased, but he didn't argue, either."

The only smart move he made, Wendy thought, looking at Hooke's closed door. She debated interrogating the injured pirate but part of her screamed to find Peter and demand he explain himself. Briefly, she remembered Boyce's journaled concern about her misplaced trust in the mechanic, and nearly erupted in her rage until the bay's access door hissed, and Johns marched in with a lazy smile.

"Well, if it isn't my two favorite ladies—aside from my mom, of course," he breezed, then slowed at their sour looks. "Hold on, who died?"

"No one, yet," Wendy grumbled, "although it's not off the table."

Johns arched a bushy brow. "Do I wanna know?" He directed the question to DeLaCruz, who shook her head grimly.

"It would seem," Wendy answered curtly, "that old alliances die harder than we were led to believe," she snipped. "And it's something I intend to stop. Immediately."

Johns cracked his knuckles menacingly. "Is that why you called? What do I need to do?"

Wendy shook her head. "This is something I need to handle. But I have another reason for bringing you," she added, remembering the other pressing issue. "DeLaCruz, you probably need to hear this too, but considering recent developments, I think it best we keep our discussion within this room."

Exchanging a curious glance, Elias and Rissa stepped closer, forming a tight huddle for Wendy to whisper over the hum of the sanitization compressors. Glancing first at Johns, the captain spoke quickly.

"Some of this you already know, Johns, so I'm going to summarize, and you can elaborate for Rissa later," she paused long enough for the lieutenant to nod before continuing. "Not long ago, we discovered a moored ship—an old Raptor that died in the air. There wasn't anything particularly worrisome about it until Dawes' cursory scan registered it with positive biometrics."

"Positive biometrics?" DeLaCruz asked, her brow furrowing as she picked up on Wendy's meaning. "How long was it downed?"

"According to our timestamps, a few years prior to Hooke's crash on Neverland."

"So, one hundred years," Rissa approximated. Wendy nodded and the medic let out a low whistle. "That's a long time."

"Exactly," Wendy said, "Far too long for there to still be energy outputs from the original crew. We had a couple ideas about what could make that possible, but our concern was that the Shadow had somehow managed to claim the vessel after its escape." Wendy took a deep breath before looking grimly at her officers. "A concern we can all but confirm after our latest transmission."

"From the Admiral?" Johns asked. "How did she know about the ship?"

"She didn't," Wendy said flatly. "The transmission wasn't from the Fleet. It was from Commander Boyce."

"*Aidan* Boyce?" DeLaCruz exclaimed, abandoning her hushed whisper as she looked from Wendy to Johns in disbelief. "*Our* Boyce. Who was lost in the depths of space?"

Shushing the medic, Wendy nodded as she cast a wary look towards Hooke's closed door. "Yes. Our Boyce," she confirmed. "We received his stream early this morning."

"What did it say?" Johns asked, pushing in closer to hear the news.

"It was an SOS," Wendy answered, grateful they hadn't asked to see the comm. "He said he is in danger, and… and he needs someone to come quickly," she finished, concealing the more personal parts of the transmission. "We have already altered our course to reach him; Dawes is putting us about two days out. The only problem is that when we first discovered the Raptor, Tizari also alerted the Stjarnin. If they get involved, it with make things much more difficult for Aidan."

"But won't the Fleet help?" DeLaCruz asked. "Now that we've received an official helpSig? If it's official Fleet business, maybe they can divert the Stjarnin?"

Wendy's expression twisted guiltily. "So, not the *only* problem," she corrected, glancing once more towards Hooke's shuttered quarters. "We also haven't informed the Admiral."

"What?" DeLaCruz exploded, before Johns' warning look forced her to regulate. "What do you mean we haven't informed the Admiral?"

Straightening her shoulders, Wendy forced her most authoritative tone. "I wasn't planning on making this knowledge public," she said, exhaling a determined huff. "But I was recently requisitioned by the Admiral for a disciplinary hearing. Everything went fine," she added, noting her commanders' slacked jaws, "but I was *encouraged* against any further deviations from our course. I didn't inform the Admiral because I am uncertain the rest of the panel will be as supportive of assisting Commander Boyce as we need them to be."

"Darling, you—" Johns stopped incredulously before spreading a wide smile, "—are such a *badass!*" He swung her in a wild circle before righting her with a whisper. "Going rogue right after a disciplinary hearing? Who are you and what did you do to the old captain?"

"I think she got left somewhere on Neverland," Wendy answered, surprised at the sentiment's truth.

"Well, it's about time," Johns said, slapping her heartily on the shoulder. Wendy glanced at DeLaCruz, who offered a supportive shrug.

"He's always said you were the greatest captain ever," the medic smiled, "but you would be unstoppable if you got over your fear of the rules."

Wendy laughed. "The fear is still there, trust me. It's just not as strong as what we all know we have to do," she declared, looking for Rissa's affirming vote.

Understanding her questioning gaze, the medic nodded. "When you have a man down, you do whatever you can to save him. No one knows that more than a medgrunt."

Smiling at the medic, Wendy's tension eased. "Thank you," she said, allowing the moment to linger before returning to business. "Now that it's settled, we have to move. We've got a lot going against us and very little in our favor. We're going to need all hands on deck but also, a distinct level of secrecy. The only people I want to know about this are those who absolutely have to—you two, Dawes, Michaels, and myself should be more than sufficient."

Johns' brows raised. "And what about our secondary mechanic?" He asked. "Is he not included in the fun?"

Wendy exchanged a quick glance with DeLaCruz before answering with a tight jerk of her head. "At this time, only the original members of the *Fede Fiducia* should be entrusted with our plans. This may be amended later, but at present, let's hold things close."

The oversized commander still looked confused, but after a reassuring nod from Rissa, he shrugged, accepting the declaration. Squeezing his hand, DeLaCruz turned to Wendy.

"Thank you for the update, Captain, and for coming in on such short notice. I'm sorry I didn't have better news to share."

"It's alright," Wendy said. "It was important. I appreciate you keeping me informed. If anything else comes up, let me know immediately. In the meantime, I'm sure you have more than enough to occupy your time besides entertaining your captain."

"I'd be happy to if it meant getting in a few more rounds of physio for your knee," the medic jabbed.

Shifting uncomfortably, Wendy glowered when her knee responded with an incriminating pop. "I'll take it under advisement."

"Very good, Captain," DeLaCruz responded before excusing herself to retrieve her medpad.

"Catch you for lunch?" Johns called after, a spark in his eye as he watched her leave. Grinning, DeLaCruz nodded before she waved and disappeared into her office.

"Still going strong I see," Wendy murmured, fighting back a snicker at Johns' goofy grin.

"What can I say?" Johns said, following her from the MedBay. "She's great at playing doctor."

"Johns, I *cannot* hear that," Wendy grumbled, punching the lieutenant in the shoulder. "For so many reasons."

Johns shrugged unapologetically. "You asked."

"A mistake I promise never to make again," Wendy grumbled. Johns smirked, then looked at her, his expression softening.

"How are you doing, Darling," he asked, all levity gone. His caramel eyes searched hers, and for a moment, she was at the Academy, safe in her dorm. The flashback nearly broke her.

"I'm alright," she lied. "Just living the dream."

"That's right, this *was* your dream," Johns chuckled with a shake of his head. "How's that working out for you?"

Wendy grimaced. "Not as planned," she answered flatly. "I may consider a career change when we get earthside."

"Might be for the best," Johns said, the remnants of his smile fading to worry. "Did you really have a disciplinary hearing?"

Wendy let out a tight cough. "It was more a formality than anything," she breezed, surprised at how second-nature providing half-truths had become. "It's nothing to concern yourself with."

"Well, we all know you worry more than enough for all of us," Johns said, "but that doesn't mean we don't worry about you. For some reason, even with all your bloody overthinking you always manage to neglect yourself."

"I know what I'm doing, Johns," Wendy answered curtly, although she heard the wobble in her resolve. They walked quietly for a moment before she stopped suddenly. "Don't I?"

Slowing, Johns turned before emphatically dropping his heavy hands onto her shoulders.

"Darling, I wasn't kidding when I told the Admiral you'd be the greatest captain the Fleet could ever make. There's never been one time I've doubted your capability to make the best, most calculated decision," he said. "But what sets your judgment apart, is that it doesn't prioritize strategy, its focus is on doing the right thing. It's an innate ability that not many others have," he thumbed toward the MedBay. "Case in point being our grounded infirmary friend."

Wendy snickered as another thin layer of doubt peeled from her shoulders. "Thanks, Elias," she glanced at the broad commander. "That… means a lot."

"It should," Johns declared, before tapping her forehead. "Now if we could just get you to *remember* it. I swear, Darling, for all those smarts you can be incredibly thick."

"I get it," Wendy said, swatting his hand. "I'll add internalization to my self-improvements list."

"See that you do," Johns demanded before his scanband beeped and his expression soured. "Ah crap, I gotta run. I left the boys in ammunitions to complete inventory. Apparently Nibs found the old szikra conductors and is using them to terrorize Curly."

Wendy couldn't hold back her laugh at his defeated expression. "You mean, being in charge of the fun, carefree crew members isn't all it's cracked up to be?"

"I see what you're doing and I don't like it." Johns pointed at her before resuming his quickened pace. "We'll finish this chat later!"

"Can't wait!" Wendy yelled, although she was certain he couldn't hear. The commander had already disappeared, leaving the echo of his heavy gait ringing through the hall. Releasing the last of her laugh, Wendy turned toward her quarters, a smile lingering on her lips.

"Hey Cap," the sudden chirp nearly stopped her heart as its owner rounded innocently from a hidden bend. "Glad to see you're in a good mood."

22

FLEET MECHANIC PETER PAN

THE JOLLY ROGER

The smile on Wendy's face faded as soon she whirled to face him. Its quick disappearance stung almost as much as the wary look that replaced it.

"Pan," she barked, before hurrying to amend her stiff greeting. "Peter."

"I take it DeLaCruz found you," he guessed, noting her rigid posture.

"She did," Wendy answered, straightforward as ever. She studied him a moment before releasing an angry breath. "What were you thinking?"

"I wasn't," Peter answered, hoping he sounded apologetic. "I just—I couldn't sleep, and I was walking the *Roger,* and then—"

"And then you accidentally stumbled into the holding bay?"

"Yes—no. It's not as simple as that," Peter justified, trailing off under a fervent shower of Tinc's indignant sparks. Unfazed, Wendy glowered at the rampaging bot before returning her furious glare to Peter, arching a singular brow as she waited for him to finish.

Peter swatted at Tinc's processor and stepped forward, angling himself so the feisty bot couldn't swoop in. Sighing, he ran a hand through his disheveled hair before dragging it down his face.

"I really didn't intend to talk to Hooke," he started, picking through his words. "After our… dinner, I couldn't sleep, so I figured I'd round the ship to make sure everything was still in order. Old habits die hard, and all that," he forced a tight smile, hoping to defrost the captain, but her scowl only deepened.

"Right," he swallowed. His hand found its path through his hair as he coughed and pressed on. "I was on my way back when I passed the MedBay. Hooke saw me and—"

"And you should have kept walking!" Wendy exclaimed, supplying an end to his story. "You saw him, you ignored him, and you *went to bed.* Just like any other person on board would have done."

Peter opened his mouth to argue, but only a choked garble escaped. "You're right, I should have," he said, raising his hands helplessly. "But I—"

"But you didn't, and someone saw you deliberately ignoring my explicit command," Wendy countered, dropping her voice to a hiss. She glanced over her shoulder then stepped forward, the light in her eyes fueled with rage and desperation. "You realize the kind of position this puts me in, don't you? Even if I *wanted* to, I can't just overlook this! Was talking to Hooke really so important?" she asked, searching him with a silent plea.

Peter met her gaze, trying not to let her beauty distract him. Every part of him ached to clutch her close, but he knew her pride would never allow it. Instead, he offered the only reply he could.

"No."

"Then what the hell were you thinking?" Wendy exploded.

"I wasn't!" Peter yelled, his voice ringing through the rounded hall. "I *wasn't* thinking. I was tired, and upset, and—and I didn't know what else to do, so when I saw James, I fell back to a time where he was someone I could confide in. I know it sounds crazy and it doesn't make it right, but there was a point when he was the only person I could go to," he explained, adding a quick amendment after a sharp spark. "Aside from Tinc, of course."

After a moment that dragged through a Neverland minute, some of the fire fizzled from the captain's posture as she let out a weighted breath.

"I can't go back and change the past, Peter. I can't erase what Hooke was to you. But I also can't deny that he is a traitor who has repeatedly shown he can't be trusted. If you choose not to see that, you will find yourself in trouble. I can't control your view of him, but I can dictate what happens next. As the ship's captain, I can and will enforce the fact that he will not be interacted with, old habits or not."

Peter frowned. "I didn't mean—"

Wendy held her hand to silence him. "Whether you meant to or not, is irrelevant. I am *acutely* aware of the fact that all of us are held accountable for our decisions. Yours come with their own repercussions. You are in a position where your actions reflect on me, and I will not risk having unsanctioned actions threaten my leadership—not when I am risking so much already. You may or may not agree, but that is not something I am not willing to discuss further.."

With a curt nod, Wendy finished her speech and turned, the clicking of her booted heels emphasizing her hurried exit. After her departure, Tinc shot off, stalking her with an eruption of hateful jangles until Peter released a soft moan.

"Let her go, Tinc," he said, deflating as her footsteps faded. Wendy had hardly looked at him before she left, but one glimpse told him she was pulling away—and he had just forced her another step farther. The thought gutted him, but he needed to give her space or risk losing her completely. "We have to let her go."

Tinc jangled softly in his ear, but he ignored her, his mind a roiling starstorm until a smooth voice breezed behind him.

"Peter Pan."

Spinning to the sound, he found Tizari, poised as ever, her expression all hard lines and angles. "Am I incorrect, or were you just speaking with the captain?"

"You're correct," Peter answered tiredly. "But you just missed her. She got called to her quarters," he lied, not wanting to rehash the argument with the Stjarnin warrior. Hopefully she hadn't heard enough to pick out any incriminating evidence; he'd already got Wendy pissed and he didn't need the Stjarnin at his throat, too.

"I need to speak with her. I have received word from my people."

Of course you have, Peter thought bitterly. *Because that's exactly what we need. More shyte for the pile.* Grimacing, he rubbed his hand through his hair and tried to force a smile.

"You got word?" he asked, "What did they say?"

Tizari's gilled lips pressed close. "As I suspected, they will not risk Itzala's escape. They have charted their course to intercept the ship from Hooke's map. They will arrive shortly."

23
COMMANDER AIDAN BOYCE
THE OHORE EHIZA

The commander continues to evade me. I must admit, I find his stubborn defiance both vexing and delightful. Though it is bothersome to share this feeble body, the willful streak he holds is delicious in its own way. How delightful it shall taste when I finally break him.

Perhaps I will wait until his rescuers arrive.

Troublesome, I thought, when he managed his signal, but now I see the opportunity for what it really is, another chance to be free. And now, with my minions to assist me, it won't be long until I can lay claim to all that is truly mine.

Itzala's voice faded as outside the barrier, a chorus of scratches rippled, filling the compartment with ghastly reverberations. Aidan felt them under his fingertips as he pushed himself up from where he slumped against the barricade, his nails dug into a set of grooves scratched in the metal door.

Frowning, he twisted his hands to look at the browned blood crusting over them. He flexed his fingers, wincing as they unkinked from their stiff, clawed position. His brain muddled as he searched the room, slowly taking in the familiar space. A puff of air floated, hot from his breath and his mind registered another disturbing thought.

It was cold. Too cold.

Pulling his jacket tight, Boyce leaned against the wall, resting his head as he tried to gather his bearings.

He was in the cockpit. Of an old abandoned Raptor. And it was—*freezing*. His teeth chattered as an involuntary shiver washed through him, the room's chill infecting his blood. He rubbed his hands together, hoping to bring some feeling into them besides the prickling frostbite, but after a moment he slumped tiredly against the panel.

It was too much work. And he was so tired.

Closing his eyes, he allowed his head to loll as he peered around the room. He'd seen a space blanket somewhere—*there*—he thought as his dizzy gaze fell on the slick, discarded fabric. Using too much effort, he leaned to grab it, clutching it around himself as best he could.

He was in the cockpit of an old abandoned Raptor. And he had gotten out a helpSig. Wendy would hear it and she would come. Until then, he just had to rest.

Maybe if he slept, she'd get there quicker.

TIME CREEPS IN

24
CAPTAIN WENDY DARLING
THE JOLLY ROGER

Seething from her conversation with Peter, Wendy stormed into her cabin, a cascade of murmurs escaping as she practiced all the things she should have said to the infuriating mechanic.

Hearing her entry, Dawes turned to greet her, but faltered under Wendy's foul mood.

"Hey there, Captain," she offered instead, her voice uncertain as Wendy tromped into the room. "Everything—"

"Dawes, if you ask me that one more time," Wendy started, then forced herself to take a breath. Scrunching her face, Wendy registered her tension and slowly let it go, evaporating the haze of anger obscuring her vision.

"No. Everything is not alright," she answered honestly. Releasing a last poisoned breath, Wendy stalked to her chair.

Settling in, she accessed her command screens, positioning her charts over their current mapstream before toggling Boyce's transmission to the corner. Scanning once more through the urgent plea, she swallowed, her whole body thrumming with conviction. "But it will be."

She typed a few quick codes before swiveling quickly towards her pilot, who eyed her with concern.

"Dawes," Wendy ordered, "Comm Michaels. I need his help."

Leaving the pilot to her task, Wendy completed a Fleet data scan. She had only made it through the first pages when Michaels' voice needled through the room.

"Arielle, you know I love our talks, but at some point, I have to run the ship," the mechanic said, his words muffled by the wrench in his teeth.

Turning to the screen, Wendy had just enough time to arc her brow at the flushing pilot before Dawes angled the screen in front of her chair.

"Michaels, the *captain* is here," Dawes coughed, then cleared her throat. "She asked me to comm you."

Over the high back of the pilot's chair, Wendy saw Michaels' streaked lenses peek from his tech. She might have thought the mechanic had blushed, but the blue reflection from the holoprojector made it impossible to tell.

Pulling the wrench from his mouth, Michaels readjusted his glasses. "You need something, Captain?"

"I do," Wendy answered, raising her voice so he could hear. "Sorry to interrupt, but I had a few questions I wanted to run by you."

"Sure thing," Michaels said, wiping his hands on a towel. Finished, he flipped it over his shoulder and Wendy had to bite her lip to hide her smile at the tiny seashells embroidered on the end. She cast a wry glance at Dawes, who ducked her face while the mechanic continued. "What do you need?"

"I need to know everything you can tell me about the *Roger's* capacity. Max holding weight, defense traction, speed, everything."

"Ok?" Michaels said, "That shouldn't be a problem, I'll just have to run an inventory. It'll all depend on how our systems are running."

"That's what I figured," Wendy said. "And I want *specifics*. Can you do that?"

Michaels shrugged. "Seems simple enough. Is that all?"

Wendy shook her head. "I also need to know if there is any way we can boost our top speed. If it's possible without impacting other systems, I want to try. And if it does affect them, find out how much we can push without shutting anything down."

"I can't make any promises," Michaels said, "but it should be something I can work out. May take a bit, though."

"Then let's get started," Wendy instructed. "Unless you have something more pressing, I'd like this to be your new priority."

"Sure thing. Let me just wrap up with this ion modulator and I'll get right to it."

"Thanks, Michaels."

The mechanic's only reply was a quick salute and flash of his lenses before the screen blipped, leaving Wendy staring at charted maps. The dotted projections blinked before her, each scattered star seeming to represent her mounting problems. Sighing, Wendy leaned back, glaring at the marks until Dawes' soft cough pulled her attention.

"Is there anything I can help you with, Captain?"

"Can you make people less infuriating?"

Dawes' eyes rounded. "That's not generally my specialty," the pilot started, "but I can give it a go. Is there any *particular* infuriating person you have in mind?"

Wendy answered the pilot's question with a scowl.

"I see," Dawes said. "Do you mind if I ask what's bothering you?"

Wendy dropped her head in her hands. "I don't know," she moaned. "I mean I do, for some of it," she added, thinking about her last argument with Peter, "but there are some things I just… maybe there's something wrong with me." Wendy finished, unsure how else to explain.

The pilot watched sympathetically before turning a small smile. "Relationships are hard," she said. "No one does them perfect but that doesn't mean there's anything wrong with anyone. Sometimes, things just take work."

"What if I don't know if I want it to?" Wendy finally murmured, daring a glance across the room. She couldn't believe the words had escaped, but as they fell, the truth they carried was freeing. It wasn't logical; she couldn't explain it. Peter had been nothing but kind, had done nothing to deserve her betrayal, but her traitorous emotions didn't care. Unwrapped from the mechanic's captivating touch, her heart yearned for another.

One who she might never see again.

Dawes thought for a moment, then gave a soft shrug.

"Then I think you owe it to yourself and to him to figure that out."

"But *how?*" Wendy exclaimed. "I have other things to worry about, Dawes. This should not be a priority!"

Nodding her understanding, Dawes held Wendy's stare. "True," she admitted, "But you can't avoid him forever."

"I can try," Wendy's grumble earned a breezy laugh from her pilot.

"Not on this bird, you can't," Dawes grinned. "Besides, you're better than that."

Avoiding Arielle's stare, Wendy looked at her hands. Under the cuff of her suit sleeve, a tiny spaceship peeked out. Wendy thumbed it carefully, focusing on the cool metal to slow her dizzying thoughts.

"What if I choose wrong?" she finally asked, voicing her true fear.

"That's not something I've seen yet." Dawes assured, her warm smile thawing some of Wendy's worry.

"Thank you, Dawes," Wendy said, ignoring the whir of the cabin doors. "I really apprecia—"

"Uh, Captain," Dawes interjected, her eyes darting meaningfully to the panel.

Following her gaze, Wendy groaned as Peter rushed in, with Tizari alongside.

"I thought I made it clear that I had other things to attend to," Wendy started, her temper flaring as Peter strode brashly to the center of the room.

"I know you're busy, Captain," the mechanic said, coming to a halt. "But Tizari has something you really need to hear."

"Which required your personal escort?" Wendy jabbed, ice coating her words.

Peter frowned at her tone but straightened to meet her gaze. "No, I just thought it was important."

"Thank you for your keen assessment," Wendy said, her temper overriding her tongue. She was being cruel, but her anger demanded a target. "I assure you I am quite capable of doing the same."

"I know you are—"

"Good. Then, if that's settled, you are dismissed."

Peter's eyes widened. "But Cap—"

"I don't need any more information making its way around the ship, Pan. If I find myself in need of your services, I will ask."

Clasping her hands behind her back, Wendy turned to Tizari, angling Peter out. She felt his wounded stare on her back but didn't break as she waited. Finally, after a series of quiet steps the doors whirred, signaling his leave.

"Captain?" Dawes prodded, deflating Wendy's riled temper. Meeting the pilot's worried gaze, Wendy bristled over her guilt.

"Dawes, please see that Peter makes it to his dorm."

The pilot looked like she wanted to speak, but merely nodded. "Yes, Captain," she said, before also taking her leave.

With the room empty, Wendy turned to Tizari, who waited, watching the exchange through her endless stare. "Did you receive word from the Stjarnin?"

Tizari nodded, unfazed by their terse exchange. "They are going to fight. If Itzala has survived, they will find him."

And Commander Boyce with him, Wendy thought as Aidan's helpSig flashed through her mind. But she nodded, faking calm. "They believe this will be the case?"

Tizari's blink lasted an eternity before she replied. "I do not believe they would have altered their course otherwise."

"I see," Wendy said, fighting to maintain her facade. She hoped hers was half as convincing as the Stjarnin's slate reflection. Unwilling to risk otherwise, she cleared her throat. "Thank you for notifying me, Tizari. I appreciate your communication."

With a quick nod, Wendy turned toward her screen to hide her disappointment. Beside her, the warrior lingered, her willowy frame towering in the center of the room.

"I am sorry it is not the news you were hoping for."

Brow arched, Wendy whirled to face her. "And what news would you have brought otherwise," she challenged, her frustration resurfacing. "The outcome was known before you contacted the others. This was a mere formality."

Tizari accepted the captain's outburst with an understanding blink. "But one that brings much pain."

"It has certainly made things more difficult," Wendy agreed with a bitter laugh. Rubbing her temple, she issued a tired sigh. "But I don't blame you," she said, falling into formality. "As a soldier or a captain. It is how I hope my crew would respond as well."

A soft curve lifted Tizari's gilled lips. "I am certain they would."

Nodding, Wendy tuned to Dawes' routed trajectory, wondering how the Stjarnin's interference would impact their plans. The thought rattled her, but she waved her hand to dismiss the alien. "Thank you, Tizari."

Bowing politely, the Stjarnin moved to leave then paused, her green skin appearing mossy in the cabin's glow. "May I ask one question?" she asked, her blank face betraying no hint to her query. When Wendy didn't stop her, Tizari pressed in. "Why do you hold so tight to the one you lost, when it risks those you have found?"

Wendy paused, struck by the Stjarnin's frank assessment. Though she knew little about the warrior, Tizari's question resonated to her core. She had been preoccupied with saving Boyce—righting all her past mistakes—but in the process, was she gambling her crew?

Smoothing her uniform, Wendy thought of her team, of the brave soldiers who eagerly volunteered to follow her into the unknown, who trusted her implicitly. She thought of the times they had spent together: laughing over suppers, bickering in tight quarters, and banding together to overcome insurmountable odds. Each memory played stronger than the last, until Wendy's answer tumbled from her lips, resolute in her conviction.

"Because any one of them would do the same for me," she said.

"And that is what you would wish of them?" Tizari asked, her coal eyes boring into her. There was no judgment in her stare, only pure curiosity as she awaited the captain's response. Stumbling again, Wendy struggled for words, disliking the Stjarnin's forced revelations.

"I would want them safe," she admitted, "without myself or not."

"And what if your actions mean that they will not be?"

Turning from the Stjarnin, Wendy exhaled as she considered, her thoughts pulling once more to the commander's reports. She'd read through them so many times the words formed in her vision, the holographic text freed from its code.

This might be my last entry. ~~I don't know how much longer I can take this~~. I don't know who I am anymore.

I know who I look like. I see the same face reflected in ~~the metal tomb enshrouding us all, preparing to launch us to our doom~~ the halls, worn in its path. But too often now, those tired features seem like a mask, a cover to ~~something~~ someone I don't know. It grips me in the dark, stealing my thoughts to wicked recesses, where it whispers terrible instructions, commanding my obedience while wrapping me in lies.

~~It tells me it will kill her.~~

I don't know what hides in the darkness, but I recognize its power. I feel it as it shudders through the Roger, *infesting the vessel with its wrath and greed. I hoped containing it within might stop the spread, might trap it with me and away from the others, but I worry that I was wrong. Instead I gave this monster a place to hide, to bide its time before executing its devious ploy.*

~~I have doomed us all.~~

The darkness is coming. It bubbles from within, grasping its greedy clutches as it clamors for release, demanding my life. ~~I am afraid.~~ If it succeeds, I fear for her. I have heard its hopes. I have seen ~~its~~—

If there is any way to be freed from this darkness, I pray it arrives quickly, before there's nothing left to revive.

Wendy shook her head, chasing the message and the tide of emotions swelling behind as she faced the Stjarnin's patient question.

"What if our inaction means that no one will be?" Wendy challenged, recalling Itzala's brief, blackened hold on her own consciousness. Though she tried to force it out, she could remember the Shadow's chilling grip and its consuming thoughts as it wore her skin. The *plans* it had for its escape. If they couldn't extricate Boyce from its grip, and it used the commander to exercise them on the world. . .

"My people will not allow that to happen," Tizari promised, her expression turning apologetic before she continued. "They will ensure the commander's sacrifice was not in vain. So that life can move on."

Though Tizari's words were not cruel, Wendy struggled against the Stjarnin's clinical diagnosis. "Should I forget him so quickly?" she objected.

Tizari's beads clinked as she shook her head. "Not forget. Mourn," she answered. "Move on. It would be—" she paused, searching for the English translation. "Easier."

"Easier?" Wendy exclaimed, choking over the thought of surrendering Boyce to the stars.

"Maybe not," Tizari paused, searching for the right word. "But better. Less pain."

Tears gathered in Wendy's eyes and she blinked them angrily away. Everything inside her wanted to voice the question running wild through her brain, angrily demanding *'For who?'* Instead, she swallowed the rebellious thought.

"I'll take it into consideration," she said. Stiffening, she stared at her charts, fuming at the blurring marks until Tizari's footsteps signaled her leave. Rejecting further conversation, Wendy didn't turn until the Stjarnin's hushed steps stilled.

"It will take my people some time to reach the Raptor," Tizari revealed, her voice gentle, but stiff. "If Itzala truly is waiting, they will prepare for battle. It will slow them down. Perhaps enough time for another vessel to arrive."

Wendy's throat caught. "That's… good to know," she said, studying the Stjarnin critically. "But why are you helping me?"

Sadness flickered in Tizari's gaze. "Pan trusts you. It is evident in the way he speaks your name," she answered, gripping her staff. "And through our interactions, I have come to greatly trust him. Peter Pan is a boy in many ways," the Stjarnin added, maintaining Wendy's gaze, "but he has many qualities that evade the greatest men—attributes that many don't appreciate until they have gone."

Her gaze became distant, and she moved toward the door. Its gentle hum whirred as she stepped forward, the soft tone nearly swallowing her final words.

"Do not take for granted the gift you have been given, Captain. It will not stay forever."

Sitting in the quiet, Wendy contemplated the Stjarnin's words. Peter trusted her, and for all their conflict, she had to admit, she trusted him too. Tizari was right, the mechanic could be childish, but when push came to shove, Peter always showed up. It was what drew her to him on Neverland—his fierce protectiveness of the ones he loved; a parallel she reflected.

She sat for a moment, her mind wandering over the implications until a wild thought struck. Revisiting her conversation with the Stjarnin, she accessed her charts while mentally arranging her new plan.

Tizari's admission offered a huge advantage; she simply had to use it.

Engaging the autopilot, Wendy tapped a quick comm to Dawes, explaining her orders. She was certain she wouldn't be back before the pilot returned, but she trusted Arielle to follow her instructions without delay. Checking once more to make sure everything was in order, Wendy tugged her jacket in place before striding purposefully from the room. If she moved quick enough, maybe—just maybe—they could reach Boyce in time. But to do that, she was going to need all hands on deck.

25
CAPTAIN WENDY DARLING

Hating what she was about to do, Wendy had to convince herself nearly a dozen times to stay her course through the *Roger*. She was so distracted that she almost barreled into Johns, who stopped her with a surprised laugh.

"Whoa, Darling! What's with the hallway sprint?"

"It's nothing," Wendy answered with a distracted wave. "There's just someone I need to talk to, even though I'd rather not."

"Listen, I know the boys are rough around the edges, but they're not all bad once you get used to—"

"It's Hooke." Wendy admitted, cutting the lieutenant short.

"Hooke?" Johns spluttered, "What do you need to talk to him for?"

Glancing over her shoulder, Wendy lowered her voice to whisper. "The Stjarnin are on their way to intercept the Raptor.

I'm working on getting us there as quickly as possible, but I need Hooke to tell me if there's any way to get there faster."

"That sounds like a mech issue. Isn't that something you could just ask Pan? Or Michaels?"

"I've tasked Michaels with figuring that out, but I'd rather not risk adding extra stress to the *ship*. We're already running on bandaids, I really don't want to make it worse. We need a quicker route, and the only person who has any real knowledge about that is currently in holding."

"But do you really want him to know what we're doing?" Johns asked. "I thought it was kind of a 'the less people know about it the better' sort of situation."

"I know," Wendy answered darkly, "which is why this is so frustrating." She scrubbed her eyes. "Listen, I need you to come with me. Follow me, and *don't say anything*. I'd rather have a witness if this goes sideways."

"You mean, like everything else so far?"

Wendy grimaced. "So you understand my concern," she deadpanned, earning a snort. Gesturing for him to fall in step beside her, she resumed her pace, comforted by his heavy footsteps tracking to the MedBay.

"Are you sure about this, Darling?" Johns asked when Wendy stalled outside.

"Not at all."

Casting a weak smile at the lieutenant, she beelined to the captain, who laid against his pillow, his eyelids twitching in restless sleep.

"Hooke," she demanded, her voice flat and cold. It was enough to make the wizened man stir. A frown flitted over his features as he blinked tiredly, focusing on where she stood.

"Captain Darling," he murmured, conjuring a winning smile. "What a delightful surprise."

Wendy's only response was stamping her lips in a grim line as she impatiently crossed her arms.

"Or perhaps not," Hooke shrugged before leaning back against his pillow. "To what do I owe the pleasure?" he asked, his gaze briefly darting to Johns.

"Not for anything you've done," the lieutenant growled, and Wendy raised her hand in warning.

"Information," she said, offering nothing more. "A situation has arisen that needs remedied, and I'd like to hear what you know."

"I'd like to not be tethered to this stars-forsaken bed," Hooke retorted, pulling against his chains. "And yet, here we are."

"And there you'll stay," Wendy sniped. "Per protocol, there is nothing I can do about your accommodations," she said, eyeing the captain's bindings.

"Come now, Captain, don't you trust me?"

"I think it's quite clear that I don't," Wendy answered flatly, "nor do I delude myself into thinking I should. Unfortunately, that's no longer a luxury I can afford," she quipped before striding to Hooke's bedside. "I need you to tell me something."

"It seems even more unfortunate that I have no desire to do so," Hooke replied, twisting his shackled arm once more. "Unless I might receive something in return."

Wendy watched the motion impatiently. "Compliance in a Fleet mission will reflect well in your disciplinary tribunal," she prompted.

Hooke eyed her shrewdly. "Ah, but this excursion isn't Fleet sanctioned, Captain. And we both know it," he said with a sly grin. "Bad form."

Grimacing, Wendy cleared her throat. "What leads you to that belief?"

"My dear, if you had the Fleet's blessing, there would be no need for your presence," he answered. "For some reason, you have chosen to ask for my assistance in lieu of the great brigade and I must admit, I am desperately curious as to why."

"Proximity, mostly," Wendy lied, playing the situation to her advantage. "By the time the Fleet could act, their aid would come too late. Circumstances have made expedience an issue, which brings us back to you."

"I see," Hooke said, though his eyes retained his doubt. "And what is it you require?"

"Insight. We found your map of the nebula, a fact you already know, but our data is incomplete. I'd like to know if you could navigate it faster."

"And if I can?"

"You'll have my full support during the Fleet's cross-examination. I will not lie, but I will guarantee my endorsement." *For what it's worth,* she thought.

"I might be willing to help… since the situation is so dire," Hooke needled. "But at such a cost, I would require equal compensation—*generous* as your offer is."

Wendy scowled. "What did you have in mind?"

"First, I want free of these blasted chains," Hooke said. "They're doing nothing for my complexion. And then I'd like my restrictions lifted from this room."

"All MedBay decisions reside with DeLaCruz."

Hooke nodded his understanding. "But you would check, of course."

Wendy jerked her head. "Of course."

The captain's smile widened. "And for my other request?"

Knowing she had no other bargaining power, Wendy gritted her teeth. "Upon the implementation of certain safeguards, I believe that is a permission I can grant."

"How very gracious."

"Indeed," Wendy replied, before fixing an addendum. "But if I'm going to release you, there is one more thing I'll need."

"My, my Captain. I didn't realize you were so very shrewd."

Wendy ignored Hooke's comment, boring into him with her gaze. Sighing, the captain settled back into his bed.

"What is your request?"

Wendy paused as she carefully considered what she was willing to divulge. After a heavy pause, she met the captain's gaze. "I need to know what knowledge you have on Itzala."

Hooke's eyes tightened before he fixed his wily grin. "Ahh, the Shadow. What makes you think I have anything to give?"

"The color of your hair for starters," Wendy said, motioning toward his whitewashed locks. "And the night terrors registering on your charts these past weeks. You might have slipped from Itzala's grip, but something is still holding on—and you know it. I'm willing to bet that it has something to do with what you saw while the Shadow was inside you."

"Very clever, Captain," Hooke praised, though his smile had gone cold. "But what if your assumption is wrong? What if your astute observations are nothing more than the residual aftermath of a suffered trauma?"

"Then I guess I have no use for you," Wendy said dismissively, then turned to leave. "Put away the keys, Johns. Apparently the captain prefers to retain his residency with De-LaCruz."

"That's not what I said," Hooke growled, his ferocity startling her. Masking her shock, she twisted to meet the captain's steely gaze. Tapping her fingers impatiently, Wendy looked coolly at the bedridden man.

"Do we have a deal?"

Hooke stared her down, rage boiling beneath his expertly crafted expression. Finally, he released a sharp breath, his temper coiling in the iced hues of his gaze.

"What do you require?"

"Once you get us to the Raptor, I need to know what to expect. From whatever might be waiting."

"As you wish."

Nodding, Wendy drew herself to full height. "Very well, then," she started to walk away then hesitated. Gripping her fists, she debated the question that sprung to mind, then angled pensively back to the captain.

Watching her, Hooke's brow rose in interest. "Something more, Captain?"

Wendy gritted her teeth, regretting her pause, but steeled herself, refusing to balk.

"Peter—*Pan*—visited with you last night. What—?"

"I can assure you the mechanic's conversation provided precious little in means of intel," Hooke interrupted dryly. "It seemed my old ward's loyalties have definitively shifted," he said, eyeing her with amusement.

"I should hope so, seeing where loyalty has positioned your other men," Wendy retorted.

"Ahh yes, my *pirates,* as you are so intent on claiming. While I admit, I am sensitive to their plight, not one of those men earned quite the investment I put into young Pan."

Wendy's frown tightened. "But you abandoned him."

Hooke's lips pressed together. "A choice that, if you'll recall, was forced by Peter's own hand," the captain said, his expression darkening. "Had he spoken to me directly, our entire plight might have been avoided."

"You don't believe that."

Hooke sighed. "Do or don't, it is a claim that cannot be proven," he said, before looking tiredly at Wendy. "Now, unless there is a pressing reason for this interrogation—"

"Why did you accompany Peter? Back to the *Roger*?" Wendy asked, the question lipping out before she could temper it. "You must have known the risks."

The captain's icy gaze narrowed before he released a weary exhale. "Were it not for Pan, I would have perished on Skull Rock. He could just as easily have left me to die—as many others would have in his position—but he refused. Even though he thought me little more than a dastardly pirate." His steel eyes flashed as he studied Wendy, and he slowly expanded his grin. "But I would think, of all people, Captain, you would be the last to ask for reasons to act against a risk."

Wendy scowled as the pirate's settling words knotted in her stomach. Strengthening her resolve, she met the captain's gaze. "You and I are not the same," she seethed.

"Of course not captain," Hooke simpered. "I am by far the better dresser." Smirking, he leaned against his pillow. "And I will do as you have requested, but I can only begin once our conversation has concluded."

Ignoring Hooke's needling, Wendy nodded and turned to Johns.

"Lieutenant, release the prisoner and escort him to the helm. He is not to be confined, but do not let him out of your sight. I will meet you both presently to discuss our next steps."

Johns nodded obediently, though he watched her with concern. "Where are you going, Captain?"

Wendy smiled, invigorated by their course of action. "Now that we've got our informant, it's time to enlist the others. I'm going to round the troops."

26
FLEET MECHANIC PETER PAN

THE JOLLY ROGER

Y ou're sure she's coming," Peter confirmed, arching his brow at Tinc, who jangled impatiently then replayed Wendy's comm in his translator.

Peter, it's Wendy. I apologize for the abrupt message, but I need you to come to my quarters for urgent assistance. I will fill you in when I arrive, in the meantime, your discretion is expected.

The captain's voice wavered as though she prepared to sign off, but after a soft cough, her message continued.

Also, I'm sorry. I know you are doing your best to help—I... I'm doing my best too. I hope that it's enough.

A crackle of Tinc's processor signaled the comm's end, and a tenuous smile flickered over Peter's lips. After the way they had left their last conversation, he was certain Wendy wasn't going to speak to him for the duration of the voyage, let alone request his help. While her invite may not have provided great detail of his expected assistance, and admittedly, he was disappointed to discover her quarters filled with other crewmen awaiting her directives, Peter was simply grateful he was even invited. Maybe, it meant things were finally turning topside with the captain.

"Wendy wanted all of us here?" he looked around the room, hoping the question came out as nonchalant as he intended.

Toying with his scanband, Michaels shrugged, but Dawes leaned in with a nod. "That's what Johns said," she answered, following his antsy gaze to the notably vacant spots where the captain and her lieutenant should have been. "I'm sure they'll be here soon."

Tinc's jangled remark rang in Peter's ear, and he stifled a snicker. "Let's hope so," he murmured to the bot. Clenching his hands into a singular fist, he resisted the urge to drum them on the table. He was fidgety and less than thrilled that a crew meeting was the first way he'd see the captain after their fight. It felt like a demotion, which was exactly what he'd been trying to avoid.

And likely what he'd pushed right into.

Exhaling, Peter fidgeted in his seat as he tried to distract himself. He was intently avoiding DeLaCruz' stern stare when the access door slid open, revealing Wendy with two figures hurrying behind.

With a shocked crackle, Tinc swooped to the rafters, her electronic shrieks ricocheting over the crew's surprised murmurs. Peter glanced at the rampaging bot, allowing her volatile surprise to speak over his forced calm. Peering at Hooke, he searched the captain for a hidden tell to explain his sudden presence, but the pirate's wizened mask betrayed nothing.

"What is he doing here?" Dawes finally shrilled, voicing the question that Peter was certain the whole room shared. Following her gaze, Michaels and the Lost Boys all eyed the withered captain standing between Wendy and Johns with open fear and distrust. Only DeLaCruz and Tizari appeared somewhat calm, although the medic's pinched expression made her opinion clear.

Avoiding the pilot's question, Wendy directed Johns and Hooke to the empty bench flanking the room, impassive as they settled, the aged captain's hands massaging bruised wrists.

"Thank you all for meeting so quickly," Wendy began, jumping to business. "I am sure you all have questions, particularly regarding our new guest." She gestured to Hooke, who returned the crews' distrusting stares with a tired nod. "I assure you, answers will be provided in due course, but at present, there are more pressing matters to consider." Pausing, she let her words settle before she continued, her expression grim.

"We have found Commander Boyce. He relayed a distress signal from a downed Raptor on the edge of the nebula. Without going into detail, his situation is... dire. While we are unsure about how he reached the vessel, we are certain the Shadow has landed with him."

Hushed gasps rippled through the table at the mention of Itzala, but Wendy maintained her collected stance as she waited for it to quiet.

"This obviously presents unique complications to our situation, but nevertheless, the retrieval of our crew outweighs the risk. We are going to recover the commander and do whatever it takes to bring our family home."

"B-but Captain, wh-why d-do w-w-we need Captain Hooke?" Tootles asked, his stutter more pronounced with his nerves. "If h-he's b-better, sh-shouldn't he b-be w-with the other p-prisoners?"

Softening at the small boy, Wendy smiled. "No, Tootles. Hooke is going to help us," she explained. "I know you've been working hard to decipher his maps, but he knows them better than anyone. He's going to take us."

"Isn't there another way?" Dawes asked, unable to conceal her mistrust. "With a little time, I'm sure I could navigate a quicker path or—"

"I'm sure you could, too," Wendy assured, "but the problem is that we don't *have* the time. The Stjarnin have already mobilized," she glanced at Tizari to confirm her statement. "They are unwilling to risk the Shadow's escape, and, as such, will not allow us the opportunity to recover the commander. We need to make sure they aren't there to interfere."

Following her admission, the crew turned to Tizari, who bore their open stares. Studying the warrior's cool gaze, Peter wanted to interject, but he couldn't pull his focus from Wendy. Struggling to temper his response, he cocked a questioning brow.

"So you trust Hooke now?" He asked, a grated edge lining his tone. Pausing, he released his agitated breath, struggling to reconcile his understanding that the captain's shifted attitude had less to do with her faith in him than her hopes to save the commander. "I mean, I'm all for it, but I'm just a little confused, considering your previous stance."

To her credit, Wendy met his objection calmly. "Of all the people on board, I'd figured you'd have the least trouble with our solution," she quipped, bringing a hot flush to his cheeks. Scowling, Peter leaned forward, ignoring the tirade of curses translating in his ear.

"No trouble. I get it," he countered, his sparking temper matching his furious nanobot. "I'm just confused about the sudden change of heart. Unless, there's something else we should be aware of before we jet off in a massive game of interplanetary chicken?"

Wendy's expression was flat as she returned his aching stare, and Peter wished he could see what she was thinking. His better senses berated his outburst, knowing it was the exact behavior pushing her away. But at this point, it was too late, his temper had taken control of his tongue—common sense be damned.

"We asked for Hooke's help to specifically avoid that outcome. We all know he's a skilled pilot. What remains to be determined is whether we can trust him. Since you have assured me of his reliance, I see no reason why you should be troubled." Wendy replied, disguising any underlying emotion. Only the quick tug of her jacket indicated her agitation, and that passed as quickly as the smoothing of her hair. "Are there any other concerns?" she asked, pointedly avoiding Peter's flummoxed stare.

Tinc jangled fiercely, and while he echoed her furious sentiments, he held his tongue, as did the rest of the crew. After an uncomfortable silence, Wendy nodded.

"If there are no other questions, everyone is dismissed. I appreciate your understanding, and most importantly, your discretion. If anyone feels this request is inappropriate, I encourage them to speak now."

Finishing her announcement, the captain looked shrewdly around the room. Aside from several inquisitive glances and Hooke's lazy smirk, her audience was motionless, leaving only Tinc's barbed curses ringing in Peter's ears. After a moment, the hardened angles of Wendy's jaw softened in release.

"Thank you all for your time. We will provide updates as necessary. If anything changes, you will be the first to know." Turning to Johns, she signaled for him to collect Hooke and follow after her.

Allowing the rest of the crew to trickle out, Peter lingered in his chair as the oversized lieutenant exited with Hooke. Caught in his warring temper and pride, Peter almost let Wendy slip away until the whirring door spurred him on. Rushing toward her, Peter's booted steps clattered through the quiet room. Wendy turned quickly toward the sound.

"Yes, Pan?"

Peter coughed to expel the sudden dryness gripping his throat. "Captain, I—"

He paused, trying to figure out what he wanted to say. Recklessly barreling after her, he hadn't formed a plan; he'd just known he didn't want to leave things the way they had ended, and staring into her glittering galaxy stare cemented his decision. Gingerly reaching for the loose curl that framed her face, he caressed her cheek as he gently tucked it in place. His touch lingered until with an embarrassed cough, Wendy pulled back, her cheeks tinged pink.

"Peter, I—" she paused, swallowing her words before she blinked, her eyes filled with a swirling mystery. Searching his expression, she set her chin. "I can't," she whispered, her words conflicting with the yearning in her stare.

Gutted at her word, Peter stiffened, but nodded, unable to speak as he forced a tremulous smile. "Not the time, I get it," he fronted, before letting out a raspy laugh. "I was just wondering, is there anything I can assist you with?" he asked, hoping to keep her close.

"I didn't think you approved," Wendy edged, studying him cautiously. "You seemed—"

Before she could finish, Tinc cut in, swooping wildly overhead, her defensive jangles punctuated with illicit curses directed at the pretty captain. Swiping the bot with a furious scowl, Peter returned to the captain with a manufactured shrug.

"It's not in my top ten, but it beats KP duty with the Twins."

Watching his bickering exchange with Tinc, Wendy's lips twitched before she smoothed them with a curt nod. "I see," she said, the soft blush in her cheek spurring the cadence in his heart. After a brief moment of consideration, Wendy nodded. "Would you be able to run a systems scan on our Navtech?" she asked, "I'd like to ensure they are fully operational and it might be helpful to have you nearby."

A smile split Peter's lips. "I think I can handle that," he answered happily over Tinc's riotous cascade.

"Excellent," Wendy said. "But Pan," she added, her eyes crackling in an electric dare, "If you ever think about challenging me in front of my crew like that again, Tinc's potty mouth will be nothing compared to what you hear from me." She cast a knowing glance at the hovering nanobot and Peter let out a surprised snort.

"Sounds like Cap's got your number, Tinc," he chuckled before turning back to the captain. She studied him dutifully, awaiting his reply. "Understood," he agreed, swiping a jaunty salute.

"Wonderful," Wendy said, her wry smile blossoming as she allowed him to fall in step behind her. "Now, hurry up. We have a lot to get done and I have no intention of sitting around waiting for you."

Peter grinned. Following the captain, he admired how the strength of her stride flowed perfectly into the soft sway of her hips. It reminded him of the girl he met on Neverland, forged from steel and grace, whose starcast gaze transported him to another world. Hurrying after her, he crowed a delighted laugh.

"Don't you worry, Cap," he crowed, hurrying alongside her. "I wouldn't dare ask."

27
CAPTAIN WENDY DARLING

THE JOLLY ROGER

Wendy didn't speak to Peter again after he accepted the job. She didn't speak to anyone, preferring the quiet ring of her footsteps as the backdrop to her swirling thoughts. With Hooke's release, she had openly endorsed insubordination in front of her entire crew and destroyed any plausible deniability she might have claimed before the panel. That alone was enough to set her nerves over the edge, and she didn't need Peter and his smoldering gaze complicating things.

Insubordination, desertion, and treason, she thought, tiredly rubbing the wrinkles on her forehead. Sighing, she refocused on her plan. Now that she had involved the crew, she needed to follow through.

Striding purposefully into Navs, Wendy hurried to the command station where Dawes pored dutifully over her charts.

"Johns, find Hooke a seat. Make sure he's comfortable, but not so much so that he forgets his place," she instructed, looking sternly at the pirate. Meeting her stare, Hooke let out a wheezy snicker.

"I remember your reception being more inviting when we first met," he drawled. Though his expression was indifferent, Wendy didn't miss the shrewd glint in his eyes as they darted around his old quarters or the way they lingered on the antique urn that once housed his szikra.

"Yes, although by the end of that sit down, I was ambushed and slated as an offering for an ancient deity," Wendy snapped, not missing a beat, "so I'd say we're even."

Hooke's snort was cut short as SMEE breezed in, struggling behind a loaded cart. "Oh Captain, you're back. How delightful. I brought some treats I thought you might like after your meeting. How did it go by the—"

The cybernet's happy chatter was cut short as he twirled around, registering the gathered crowd. His synthetic skin paled as his golden eyes scanned Hooke.

"What is he doing here?" he said, exhibiting the first trace of anger Wendy had ever seen. Reaching forward, the synth grabbed a large pronged serving fork and waved it threateningly. "Shall I escort him to the holding facility?"

"It's alright, SMEE," Wendy said, grinning at the synth's brandished flatware. She nodded to Johns, who made a show of gripping the captain's loose arms. "I believe Lieutenant Johns has the situation handled," she answered, before adding somewhat guiltily, "Hooke has been invited as my guest."

"Guest?" SMEE's manufactured reaction was as realistic as her other officers'. He clutched his chest, only the flickering of his mechanical eyes betraying his fabrication. "Captain, should I remind you what happened last time?" He whispered, but the space between them revealed his question to the room. Behind her, Wendy heard Peter's gravelly laugh.

"I remember," Wendy answered, her affection for the synth earning a gentle tone. "However, we are at an impasse. For the time being, Captain Hooke is welcome," she explained before eyeing the greying soldier. "But that is subject to change."

Following her stare, Hooke shrugged lazily before glancing at the overstuffed seat behind him. "May I?" He gestured to the burgundy chaise before quirking a peppered brow at SMEE's still-raised utensil. "Unless the first mate would like to skewer me first?"

"I don't think that's necessary," Wendy said, motioning for the synth to return the fork. "SMEE, please make sure everyone receives some refreshment," she directed. A slight whir issued from deep within the synth's chest as his processor flickered, but he straightened his glasses and offered a polite incline of his head.

"Of course, Captain," he answered, scuttling away from Hooke and Johns in preference of Dawes. Again, Wendy tried not to snicker as she returned to her charts. Only a few hours had passed, but looking at the progression of their trajectory, a nagging fear told her it wasn't nearly far enough. How much time would it take the Stjarnin to arrive? Had Dawes altered their course fast enough to head them off? Try as she might, she couldn't find any answers in her display.

"We're gonna make it, you know," Peter's gravelly whisper sounded beside her.

Startled, Wendy jerked toward the mechanic.

"How—"

Peter smiled. "You're a lot of things, Cap, but mysterious isn't exactly one of them." He looked at her, and Wendy detected a trace of sadness lingering in his warm stare. "It's not a bad thing," he said, raising his hand to stall any potential arguments.

"It just means it's easy for people to see what's important to you—*who* is important to you."

"Everyone on this ship is important to me," Wendy said, before her stare darted to the captain. "Well, almost," she amended.

Peter's smile didn't quite reach his eyes. "I know," he said, reaching for her hand. "I just hope maybe there's one of us who you think is most important." He stepped closer, bringing smoldering heat with his proximity.

"Yes, because that is the most pressing matter at hand," a dry voice cut across the room, interrupting the moment.

Stepping back from the mechanic, Wendy scowled at Hooke. "I'll be the judge in matters of importance," she quipped, before redirecting her attention to Navs. "Dawes, pull up our coordinates, please. I'd like to see how we are progressing."

"Yes, Captain," Dawes responded, turning obediently to her station, leaving Wendy open to Hooke's piercing stare.

"Ahh, yes. Our coordinates. I must admit I am quite eager to see where exactly it is we are going. Since it is my property you are using. Tell me, Captain, how did you stumble across my maps?"

"It wasn't as difficult as you might have hoped," Wendy retorted coolly. Hooke didn't need to know they had been found accidentally nor the painstaking efforts it had taken to decipher them. Turning to the maps, she grinned. "They've proved quite helpful."

"I can imagine," Hooke murmured ruefully. "So then, my maps truly are the basis for this entire scheme?"

"We're utilizing all of our resources to create the best trajectory," Wendy answered curtly. "Regardless of how we feel about their place of origin."

Hooke sniffed a laugh. "Quite," he said. "And what other resources have you considered?"

"None that involve you," Wendy answered, cutting off the captain's probing.

"Actually, Captain," Dawes interrupted apologetically, "they might." Her expression taut, she turned to Wendy. Her normally fair skin had paled, revealing a dusting of freckles across her cheeks. The pilot's worry was unsettling, but it didn't bring Wendy pause until she saw Arielle's white-knuckled grip on her station. "We have a problem."

28
CAPTAIN WENDY DARLING

"Problem?" Wendy asked, the pilot's fear knotting her stomach. "What problem?"

"On our route. An uncharted phenomena just registered on our trajectory. We're heading right for it."

"Is the bogey that big?" Wendy questioned, examining the mark that had appeared on the edge of the holoscreen. "Can't we navigate around it?"

Dawes shook her head. "No, Captain. It's not an astral form," the pilot's voice faltered, and she swallowed. "It's a grey hole."

Wendy swore. Scattered throughout the 'verse, grey holes were almost as deadly as their more famous counterparts, the black holes, though some voyagers—Wendy included—feared them more. While it was true that encountering a black hole meant certain death, the pitch abysses were blunderers, announcing themselves with their bottomless appetites. Grey holes were their smaller brothers—deep gaps that had just enough escape velocity to create a ringed barricade of orbiting debris that disguised them enough to ensnare unsuspecting passersby.

Like them.

"How did this happen?" Wendy asked, scouring the chart. "Why didn't we see it sooner?"

"I couldn't detect it because of the conduit signature bordering the charybdis," Dawes explains. "It looks like the hole's found itself a ring of thorium conglomerates—"

"...which blocked the external readings," Wendy finished with a grimace.

"Which means…?" Peter's question was echoed by a crackle of Tinc's worried blue sparks.

"We flew straight into a shytestorm," Hooke answered tiredly, his hand resting heavy over his brow. Beside him, the lieutenant turned, bristling as he glared accusingly at the captain.

"Flew into, or were led into?" Johns growled.

"Pardon?" Hooke asked, power crackling through his steel stare.

"Weren't you just telling the captain how interested you were in our route? That was based on *your* maps? You could have walked us right into a trap and we would be none the wiser," the lieutenant said.

"Ah yes, the old 'don't chart a deadly chasm in the hopes that someone, someday steals your work' trick. One of my very favorites," Hooke said dryly, then scoffed. "Be reasonable. It seems rather pointless to lead you down a path so detrimental to my own well being," the aged captain said. "Self-destruction is more Pan's style."

Peter scowled at the jab, then turned to Johns. "Sorry as I am to admit, he's got a point. No one in their right mind would intentionally cane their ankles. Not even James."

"How touching," Hooke sniffed.

Johns glowered from captain to mechanic, unconvinced.

"Regardless," Wendy stepped in, pressing a warning hand to still the lieutenant's furious trembling. "We don't have time to argue. We've got more pressing matters at hand." She turned to Dawes. "How long until we hit the hole's gravitational field?"

"Less than a parsec," Dawes guessed. "Maybe less. Once we hit the thorium belt, I can get a proper scan, but by that point, we'll be sunk."

"Then we'd better not get that far," Wendy commanded, surging to action. "Dawes, get Michaels online. We need his boost *now*. Johns, get a message to SMEE and tell him he needs to get the others in a full security lockdown. Peter, you're on watch until he gets back," she said, nodding to the captain.

A frown pulled Johns' brow, but the lieutenant sidled away, allowing Peter to hover beside Hooke. A smug smile played on the edges of the captain's lips and Wendy stalked forward, eyeing him threateningly.

"We may not have the luxury of time to discuss whether or not this truly was your doing, but let me be very frank; if anything else on our path so much as *blinks*, I'll have you in to holding so fast your head will spin."

Hooke's smirk remained in place, but the skin around his eyes tightened at the threat. Catching the nearly imperceptible reaction, Wendy grinned menacingly.

"You might have not liked your quarters in the MedBay, but they were resort-living compared to the sardine box the other pirates are in. I don't think any have gone rabid since Noodler, but I could be wrong."

Her mention of the addled deckhand darkened Hooke's expression, but the captain merely shook his head. "I don't see any reason to worry," he claimed.

"Good," Wendy nodded, turning her back on him to address her pilot.

"Dawes, do you have Michaels?"

"Of course," Arielle answered, swiveling in her chair. With a keystroke, her holoscreen flickered to display the lower deck. Michaels was inside, buzzing around in the hazy compartment. "Hey, Jensen," she started.

"This really isn't a good time, angel, I—" Michaels began, pausing his work to glance at the screen. He froze mid-syllable, his eyes widening at his audience as he realized it was too late. From the far corner of the room, Johns doubled over.

"*Angel*?" Johns' snicker erupted into a full snort. "Wait—is it because she has—" the Lieutenant had to catch his breath after another wheezing guffaw, "*wings*?" He exploded again, laughing so hard he had to wipe tears from his eyes.

"We can address it another time, Johns," Wendy said, failing to hide the smirk the commander's infectious glee brought to her own lips. Clearing her throat, she turned back to the screen. "Sorry to interrupt, Michaels, but we need you."

"Yeah, *we*, not just *Dawes*," Johns teased.

"Unless you'd like me to share some of the things I've heard from DeLaCruz, Johns, I suggest you leave him alone," Wendy threatened, turning to the spectacled mechanic. "I'm sorry, Michaels, but I need an update on our systems boost."

"Well, it's not my finest work," Michaels admitted, wiping his hands on an oily rag, "but it's passable."

"Passable is all we have time for," Wendy answered, her grim response earning a puzzled glance. "I'll explain later," she promised. "But if the boost is ready, on your signal, we're going to initiate."

"I'm not ever going to argue over extra time, but if you need it now," Michaels shrugged and tapped quickly on his scanband. "I sent Arielle the command sequence. Just make sure everyone's strapped down before she launches."

"Already on it," Wendy said. "Find somewhere to buckle yourself down, too. We'll keep the comm live in case anything goes sideways, but if there are no other objections—"

"Way ahead of you, Captain." Dawes said, furiously keying the code from Michaels' file. The pilot's brow furrowed as she worked, her lips pursing until she leaned back with a proud smile. "There," she announced. "The boost is rea—"

Her announcement ended in a clipped cry as the *Roger* lurched, shuddering under a peppering of erratic impacts.

"Everyone hang on!" Wendy yelled, clinging to the Star-Board while the ship continued to rock. Swiping wildly over the panel, she enlarged their trajectory, zooming in on their vessel marker. A dotted red haze surrounded the ship, indicating the hazards that had just assaulted them.

"Dawes! What the hell is going on?" Wendy cried as another muffled barrage struck, vibrating the *Roger* from hull to nose. "What's hitting us?"

Training her stare on the screen, the pilot shook her head. "It looks like a meteoroid cloud, but… we passed it already." Frowning, she swiped the tousled strands from her eyes to look closer and gasped. "Its tail must have gotten caught by the grey hole," she explained breathlessly. "It's getting sucked in."

"And if it got caught—" Peter started.

"Then one can only presume we're next," Hooke finished his statement with an irritated huff. "Good show *indeed*, Captain."

29
FLEET MECHANIC PETER PAN

THE JOLLY ROGER

Wendy's biting retort was cut short by another tired groan as the *Roger* trembled again, shuddering under the trapped cloud.

"Captain, I need orders!" Dawes cried scrabbling to stabilize the ship. Worry covered Wendy's features, but before she could answer, Michaels reappeared on screen, scowling behind streaked glasses.

"Let me guess; things went sideways?"

Peter snorted. "What was your first clue?"

"I would imagine the shrieking alarms," Hooke needled, his eyes glinting dangerously as the ship rocked under the barrage of meteoroids. "Although the turbulence also indicates a certain level of alarm."

Bristling past the pirate's remark, Wendy turned to Michaels. "We couldn't complete the boost. The grey hole already had a hold on us. We need more power."

Michaels darkened. "That's where we're going to have a problem," he said. "To focus acceleration, I've already siphoned most of our extraneous energy sources to the turbines. If I start stealing power from other functions, the ship's integrity is going to suffer."

"If we don't get away from this hole, there's going to be a lot more suffering," Peter countered.

Michaels nodded, "True, but I don't see much sense hurrying to escape a quick death to rush headlong into asphyxiation. We almost did that once; I'd rather not play again."

Fear wiped Wendy's expression. Peter longed to comfort her, but she was absorbed in concentration. Looking at the flashing screen, Peter's mind whirred through alternative solutions. The blaring sirens made it hard to focus, so he closed his eyes and nearly jumped out of his skin when a light touch brushed his shoulder.

"Pan," Tizari greeted, unbothered by his shock. Her dark eyes searched the room, studying the scene in an eerie calm. "What has happened to the ship?"

Glancing at Wendy, Peter deferred his answer. "We have encountered some turbulence from the grips of a grey hole," the captain explained, tugging the ends of her sleeves. "We attempted to breach the pull but were unsuccessful."

"Basically, we've got to figure out a way to book it, and quick," Peter summarized, forcing a smile. "I don't suppose you've got any Stjarnin magic?" he joked, reaching into his pocket for the stone Tiger Lily had gifted him. "I've got this thing, but I don't think a collect call to the princess will do much good."

Tizari's eyes widened as she reached for the trinket. "Olskjata," she whispered, breathless as she turned it in her hands. The carved turquoise etchings flared under her touch then darkened, leaving nothing but black stone. "Do you know what you hold?"

Peter shook his head, surprised by the Stjarnin's reverence. "When the princess gave it to me, she just said I could use it to reach her. I thought it was some sort of communicator."

The Stjarnin's dumbfounded blink made Peter regret his admission. "The olskjata can act as a beacon," the warrior admitted, "but it has much greater uses."

Gripping the stone, Tizari turned to Wendy.

"It will provide the power needed to escape the hole," the Stjarnin explained, though the expression on her angular features remained grave. "But we must be very careful," she warned. "Once the olskjata's power is depleted, it cannot be revived. A mistake means we will not survive."

The warrior's quiet warning dissipated into the room, leaving the throbbing alarm blaring past her silence. For the briefest moment, Wendy hesitated until another violent tremble spurred her response. Looking at the warrior, her gaze hardened with certainty.

"Peter," she said, commanding the room like a modern valkyrie. "Take Tizari and the olskjata. Get it to Michaels, *now*."

30
FLEET MECHANIC PETER PAN

"Michaels! Where are you?" Peter called, sliding past the last few stairs. The muggy heat hit his face as he jumped inside the bay, immersing him in the steaming room with Tizari close behind.

"Back here," the mech responded from deep within. His voice was muffled by the *Roger's* hissing insides as she struggled to stay afloat. Following Michaels' call, Peter approached the baserig, where the swelling clang of metal pierced the groaning powergrids. With a last bang, Michaels appeared, standing behind a mid-sized tower with tangled pipes branching from its base.

"Did the catalyst go out?" Peter asked, quickly assessing the situation.

"Close," Michaels confirmed. "The compartment adapter failed and it's threatening the catalyst's integrity." He held up a small part that looked like a box with a circular mouth. "It's zapping power from all the other systems to sustain itself."

"And they can't handle it," Peter guessed.

Michaels shook his head. "Not with the bandage job that's already holding everything together. I had to cut the power to everything nonessential to operations," he said. "I redirected it to the catalyst so it would siphon energy from that system instead of our big rigs." He wiped the sweat from his forehead with a stained towel and sighed. "The boost might have worked had we not been caught in the hole's reach, but honestly, I don't know how long the ship would have lasted anyway." He wiped under his glasses, smudging the tired bags above his cheeks. "Getting it to a high enough gear to pull out *and* maintain itself might be a pipe dream."

Peter turned to Tizari. "Maybe not," he said, producing the olskjata from his pocket. "Tizari said we might be able to use this for what we need."

Michaels looked at the stone dubiously. "Listen, the Stjarnin's tech is incredible, but I don't see how that one piece is going to fix all of this," he gestured to the mechbay, whose red glow was filled with spitting steam.

"It will work," Tizari assured. "I just need to know what will best help your ship."

Michaels thought for a moment. "We need to avoid more leeching," he said. "The cannibalism of the parts isn't doing anything for the *Roger's* sustainability. Once we get everything stabilized, then we can find a way to manufacture some extra velocity."

Tizari looked at Peter. "If I can repair the catalyst, can you create more speed?"

"Actually, I have an idea for that," Peter said, "but I'm going to need a working alloy charge reductor."

An incredulous snort escaped the spectacled mechanic. "That's the first good news I've heard," he said. "I just finished maintenance on the reductor. It's one of the few parts that's holding together."

"Good," Peter said. "Let's keep it that way. Tizari, do whatever you need to fix the catalyst. Michaels and I are gonna get you that boost." He passed the stone to the Stjarnin, who took it before disappearing further into the bay.

With the Stjarnin gone and the mechbay sweltering, Peter unzipped his jumper. Shrugging out of the top half, he used the hem of his tank to wipe the sweat from his brow as he scanned the bay. "You said the reductor is good to go?" he asked, waiting for the mech to confirm.

When Michaels nodded, Peter smiled.

"Good," he said. "I need you to unplug it and bring it to me. While you work on the wiring, I'm gonna hook it up to the friction compressor. I know it sounds strange, but I'm hoping once everything is in stasis, we can activate it to reduce the opposing force on our thrust and boost our overall velocity."

"That's brilliant." Michaels said, wiping his foggy lenses. "If we can get the compressor to eat some of that pull, then we can use the excess energy to break free."

"I thought so," Peter said, "Now let's just hope it works."

31
CAPTAIN WENDY DARLING

THE JOLLY ROGER

An hour had passed and Wendy still hadn't heard anything. She knew, because she had checked her scanband every five minutes since Peter had rushed to the bay, leaving her to watch their ship getting tugged closer and closer to the grey hole's beckoning vortex.

Several times, she tried to hail the mechbay, but shortly after Peter and Tizari exited the room, everything but the cabin's emergency running lights and her main grid powered off. The absence of the blaring warning system was a welcome relief, but with no way to reach the lower deck, Wendy's nerves quickly began to spiral.

Looking at her scanband, she growled when she realized not even three minutes had passed. In a rage, she unfastened the

Nana and flung it across the room, ignoring the sharp beep it made as it hit the wall.

"Feel better?" Hooke's tired voice needled from his seat. Scowling, Wendy turned to the pirate, who leaned sideways while watching her with droopy eyes. Dark purple bags hung over his cheeks, and the rest of his complexion had taken on a yellowish hue. Ignoring him, Wendy stalked to the coursemap to review their trajectory.

Hovering on the map, the *Roger's* tiny vessel marker had started to stray from its projected course. Trailing from the holographic image, a dotted line followed, diverging sharply from the solid green line indicating where they were supposed to be. Far to the right, a hazard symbol had appeared, materializing once the vessel's sensors registered the grey hole's pull. It was still far enough that the chart hadn't issued an imminent danger signal, but it inched closer with every creeping moment.

Wendy rubbed her eyes, forgetting the last time she had slept. She was certain it must have been sometime before they arrived on Neverland. Bowing her head over the panel, she played through possible scenarios, calculating the chances they would arrive home free. Grimacing at the odds, she straightened.

Not long ago, Dawes had asked about her plan. The pilot had tearfully pulled her gaze from the screen to ask her what they were going to do. Wendy hadn't answered, and instead resumed her nervous pacing while her worst fears ran rampant in her mind. Still, Wendy had no answers that could provide even a semblance of a solution, but now at least she had a response. Loosening her shoulders, she turned to the pilot.

"Dawes," she said, forcing as much courage as she could muster. "Issue a comm. We have to call the Admiral."

"But Captain, comms are down," Dawes protested, her brow furrowing in concern.

"Then we will record the link and spool it when they are operational. But the situation is such that we need to notify the Fleet. Even if it is only for identification purposes."

The pilot's worried eyes glistened, but she obediently queued the comm. Stepping into the screen, Wendy swallowed and smoothed her hair. Quickly, she glanced around the cabin, then pointed at Hooke, who watched with interest from where he slumped.

"Stay quiet," she warned, before sternly addressing her lieutenant. "Johns, make sure he stays off screen. Just because we're revealing our hand doesn't mean we have to confess full-on insubordination."

Smirking, Hooke tipped his head in silent agreement. Behind him, Johns gripped the chaise and slid it farther against the wall to ensure the pirate remained off screen. Wendy waited until the chair's scraping feet quieted, then returned to the recording with a curt nod. Centering herself, Wendy tugged the ends of her coat and stood firmly at attention, preparing her address.

"This is Captain Wendy Darling of the Fede Fiducia, *manning the* Jolly Roger, *hailing the Londonnierre Brigade. If intercepted, please direct this transmission to Admiral Renee Toussant. Tell her—tell her I apologize."*

Pausing, Wendy looked down, averting her gaze so that whoever recovered the feed would not see her break. With a quick exhale, she looked up, fixing her expression in a cool mask.

"I'm not sure when you will receive this, Admiral, but I wanted it to go on the record. Against my crew's council, I made the decision to alter our course. Evidence presented indicating Commander Aidan Boyce's survival and relative proximity to our vessel. Following this data, I overrode the coordinates set by Lieutenant Arielle Dawes in an attempt to reach the com-

mander. On this new route, at approximately galactic latitude -64 and longitude 247, we encountered the gravity pull for a previously unidentified grey hole. Due to the unstable conditions of the Roger, *we have been unable to achieve escape velocity. Our mechanics, Lieutenant Jensen Michaels and Ensign Peter Pan are working to remedy this, but at present, I regret to inform you that our situation is dire. Most regrettably, it is through nobody's fault but my own. God save our souls, but at worst, I pray He forgive mine. Should anyone retrieve this message, we are requesting immediate transmission to the* Jolly Roger, *communication code xv1543f7-9, hailing the Londonierre Brigade.*

This is Captain Wendy Darling, signing off."

When her message finished, Wendy disconnected the comm and stepped away. Tears misted her eyes and she wiped them dry before turning to Dawes.

"Queue the transmission for release. As soon as we have power, I want our message going out. The Admiral said the Fleet was on their way; maybe we've earned a miracle."

"Yes, Captain," Dawes said, issuing the comm directives. Her face pulled in concentration until she hit the final button and her eyes widened in shock. "Captain," the pilot started, looking at Wendy in surprise. "Communications are back online. Our transmission has been released."

"What?" Wendy asked, stalking to the pilot's station. She meant to look at the directive code, but before she could, the screen over Dawes crackled, pixelating Peter's image.

"Peter!" Wendy exclaimed. "We've been trying to reach you but the comms were down."

"Yeah, those and about half of the *Roger's* other systems," the mechanic admitted. "Michaels had to pare down operations or else it would have been curtains for us all. There's a few extraneous functions we tried to save, but really, if it's not keeping us in the air, it's probably not operational."

"We noticed," Hooke called dryly, earning the mechanic's scowl. Passing the pirate an irritated glance, Wendy looked back at the screen.

"Right now, I want to know more about what *is* operational," she pressed, studying the mechs. "What can you tell me?"

"Systems are holding," Michaels announced, removing his glasses to wipe their collected fog. "Whatever Tiger Lily gave to Peter really did have some magic, because the catalyst is fully operational, which restored functionality to some other affected systems as well."

"Good," Wendy declared. "Does that mean we'll be able to reach escape velocity?"

"We're about to find out," Michaels answered, before turning to Dawes. "Arielle, on my count, I want you to access and initiate sequence FinWrap vx-32. Make sure you announce it to the crew and give them time to strap in. The maneuver is gonna pack a punch."

"Heard," Dawes said, moving to access the file. Locating the sequence, she looked back at Michaels. "Make sure you find somewhere to lock in, too. Captain's going to make the call."

"Good," Peter said, looking at Wendy. His eyes smoldered at her through the screen, making her heart thrum with their raw desire. "It's time to get out of here." Reaching forward, he disconnected, leaving her staring at a blank screen. Heat coursed through her cheeks until the intensity of the mechanic's ember stare fizzled, and Wendy found herself cold in absence.

Recalling Michaels' instructions, she strode to make her announcement. Clearing her throat, Wendy issued the protocol.

"Attention. Immediate lockdown notice activated. Sequence countdown initiated. Please locate the nearest safety harness and secure your position. Maneuver implementation in T-90."

Completing the message, Wendy hurried to secure her harness. Locked in her seat, she cast a last glance at the tiny vessel marker on the map, its tail end drawing nearer to the stretching abyss.

Closing her eyes, Wendy leaned back, preparing for the boost. With the countdown completed, the ship lurched, throwing her against the seat. Pressure crushed against her as the vessel thrust forward, the *Roger's* pained groans roaring in her ears as it worked to break free. For a moment, everything slowed as they encountered a perfect equilibrium, until with a snap, the ship launched forward, breaking free from the grey hole's chasm.

Riding the boost, the *Roger* hurtled through the nebula until its speed regulated to a cruise. Reaching a safe velocity, Wendy gave the all-clear while Dawes hurried to check the maps. Wendy had barely finished her call when the cabin whirred open, and Peter raced inside.

"Did we get it?" He asked, his green eyes flashing as he rushed to the StarBoard. "Did it work?"

Eagerly, Wendy listened, waiting for the pilot's answer over a tightly held breath.

Dawes turned, looking at them in surprise. "Actually," she said, "the jump was more effective than we hoped." She turned to Wendy, her smile trembling with disbelief. "We're going to arrive much sooner than we thought."

"How much sooner?" Wendy asked.

The pilot's grin widened as she enlarged the map. With the *Roger's* basic functions restored, it flickered to life, projecting the ship's path. On the holoscreen, *the Roger's* icon appeared, hovering beside its highlighted end point.

"A lot sooner," Dawes answered, before Wendy interrupted, unable to contain her shock.

"We're almost there."

32
COMMANDER AIDAN BOYCE
THE OHORE EHIZA

"No!" Boyce jerked awake, recoiling from the cold ground below him. A chill overtook him as the frigid air swept across the sweat trickling down his spine. Struggling against the panic crushing his chest, he fought to grasp the last traces of his dream.

It had seemed almost a memory, the beauty wrapped in his arms, her dazzling eyes staring into his as she pressed close, begging him to stay. Her rose lips brushed his and a fire ignited, scattering the churning cloud hovering over his shoulders.

The commander's brow furrowed. But who was she? He couldn't remember through the haze.

It's not important, a dark thought needled. *Go back to sleep,* it crooned, lulling him to the floor, but the slick voice spoke in writhes and slithers, filling him with dread.

Groaning, he closed his eyes and exhaled an unsteady breath. Behind his lids, a galaxy of stars danced, a glittering backdrop to an angelic face. The commander frowned as he tried to focus before the image dissipated into shimmering mist.

"Shyte!" He pounded the frozen floor as his temper flared then fizzled in an exhausted wave. It disconcerted him, the sudden fatigue when he had just awoken, but his worry was overrun by a sharp pang in his stomach accompanied by a ravenous grumble.

When was the last time he had eaten, he wondered. Discarded wrappers littered the floor but his dizzying confusion suggested it had been quite some time.

Just close your eyes. It will take the bite from your hunger, the hissing voice suggested, fogging his mind with a warm haze.

Obeying the command, Boyce worked to get comfortable against the hard metal. Once again, cold nipped his skin, sending a shiver through his bones. Sighing, the commander shifted into the cold, embracing the chill until he could no longer recognize its sting.

It won't be long now, the dark voice cooed, it's lilting tenor a disturbed lullaby. *All will be well very soon,* it said, its excitement palpable. Disoriented, the commander's eyes fluttered, but as he searched the empty chamber, the throbbing in his head nearly blinded him. Glancing at his hand, he frowned at the blurred crimson bandage.

There was a reason that had happened... one that he didn't remember being an accident.

Blinking at the wound, he tried again to spur his mind, but only succeeded in wincing at the pain that lanced through his head. Closing his eyes seemed to be the only way to make it stop, so he stayed in place, breathing slowly through the fever coursing his veins.

A little rest would probably do him good.

Yes, the familiar voice encouraged. *Rest. Everything will be better,* it agreed, though the commander couldn't chase the sinking feeling its promise summoned. Puzzling its meaning seemed far too much effort, so the commander sagged tiredly instead, his limbs drooping against the floor. Maybe while he slept, he'd remember the dream. Maybe, if he slept hard enough, he could believe he wasn't alone.

The thought was so laughable, Boyce nearly snorted, but the effort was just too much. It was far easier to succumb to the sleep crashing over him, allowing thick darkness to steal his hunger and pain. Utilizing the last of his willpower to focus on the beautiful spectre before the glittering stars, Boyce smiled as he drifted into the dark. The girl really seemed so familiar, if only he could remember her name.

You'll remember soon enough, the silky voice promised, laughing softly as Boyce drifted to sleep. *You won't have to wait long at all.*

Delighted, Itzala pictured the girl haunting Boyce's dreams. Though the commander couldn't place her, Itzala knew exactly who she was and how certain she was to appear.

Come and find me, Darling.

33
CAPTAIN WENDY DARLING

THE OHORE EHIZA

Docking the *Ehiza* was easier than Wendy had anticipated. Clad in their sleek spacesuits and fitted visors, the crew offboarded the *Roger* and crept into the dead vessel with only the clang of the emergency hatch to announce their arrival.

Peering into the access corridor, Wendy's stomach tensed as she imagined a billowing cloud of murky tendrils sweeping into the room to overtake them all, but after an excruciating moment, the ship retained its calm. Exhaling a breath, Wendy adjusted her mask so only the breathing apparatus remained. Frigid air nipped her cheeks, carrying with it the stale stench of metal. It turned Wendy's nose as she completed a quick weapons assessment, readying her phaser before mounting her magbeam beneath. Prepped, Wendy took in another must-laced breath before turning to her crew.

"Alright everyone, we made it onboard, but the hard part's not over," Wendy said,

addressing her crew in turn. Staggering around the batailoia's insignia, Johns and Peter flanked a dour-faced Hooke leaving Tizari standing left and Tootles, Nibs, and Curly filing around the right. Curly hovered closest to Wendy, his attention darting around the ship as he rubbed nervously at his scar, unable to keep still. Angling away from the fidgeting boy, Wendy turned to the others. "We're going to move as quickly as we can to get Boyce and get out. No reason to overstay our welcome."

Pausing, she glanced at Johns. The lieutenant flanked the group, his massive arms crossed as he monitored the team with mission-sharp eyes.

"Johns, I want you paired with Tootles. Hang close to Nibs and Curly in the center, and Tizari, I'd like you to watch the back. Peter and I will cover the front, with Hooke in between," she directed, grabbing the captain's arm in warning. "If he tries anything funny, he'll be the first to go," she smiled.

"Perish the thought," Hooke grumbled. "Though I daresay, Captain, your crew leaves something to be desired. Unless it was your intent to scrape the dregs of the barrel?" He cocked a salted eyebrow and smirked. "Perhaps in hopes of dissuading Itzala?"

"I think you more than suffice in that aspect," Wendy shot back, unwavering. "He's already discarded you once—"

Peter stepped forward, positioning himself between the sparring captains. "What's our next move, Cap?" he asked, Tinc's core illuminating him with her processor's soft glow. "It's cold down here and I'd like to be done."

Studying Peter, Wendy nodded. He was right, they were wasting precious time. Hooke's opinion didn't matter, he left his right to one on Neverland.

"We need to locate Boyce. I imagine he'll be wherever the transmission spool originated," she said, typing on her scanband. Nana beeped then cast a small holograph from her wrist to hover over their crooked ring. "The schematics I downloaded should point us in the right direction."

Studying the projection, she examined the layout, then pointed to a small compartment on the lower deck at the back of the *Ehiza*.

"There," she said. "It looks like their command center is on the base level. It's a bit of a trek, but the ship's no *Titania*. If we don't run into issues, it shouldn't take long."

Glancing around, Wendy allowed a moment for questions, but her crew only waited grimly for her to proceed. Confirming the path, she led them down the iced corridors, following her magbeam's illuminated beacon.

Her team didn't speak as they moved, leaving Wendy nothing to focus on save the unnatural stillness clinging to the air. It hung thick around her, lingering in the empty space, setting Wendy's hairs on edge as her primordial brain screamed against its wrongness. Fighting her hitching terror, Wendy pressed on, swallowed in the muffled footprints of her crew until a clattering echo shattered through the dark.

"What was that?" Curly's whimper registered through the auditory transponder. "Did anyone else hear that?"

Wendy didn't answer as she continued, focusing instead on her steps. *The Ehiza was a large ship,* she thought, justifying the noise. It had been abandoned and deteriorating for years. It was normal for strange sounds to—

"Okay," Johns' low rumble agreed after another grating screech ricocheted through the vent, "it's not just Curly's paranoia. There's something out there."

"Yes," Wendy confirmed, her face grim, "I heard it."

She peered down the darkened corridor, her magbeam reflecting the sleek panels, illuminating the space surrounding them before slipping into shadows. Deep within the whispering dark, Wendy couldn't tell from which direction the eerie chitters beckoned.

Craning her neck, she searched until the silence resettled, hovering on the frost-chilled air. Finally, she waved the group forward.

"Let's keep moving."

Inching forward, Wendy cringed after every clunking step until the angled corridor sloped, leading them to a forked hall. Slinking from the dark, vicious hisses skittered along the corridors, their strength growing as they drudged from the deep.

"Wh-where are w-we?" Tootles stammered, his tiny voice cutting through the stagnant air. His eyes were wide as he peered ahead, as though he might cut the pitch hall to reveal the vessel's secrets.

"It looks like the bridge," Wendy said, consulting her map. "The schematics say we go left, then look for an inset staircase." She peered closer at the glowing chart. "Maybe 200 feet after the fork."

Lowering her wrist, she signaled the team on. While they'd stalled, the distant chitters had snuck so close they now sounded like they were nearing from all sides.

"And ready your weapons," she added, mainly to Peter's men. Like her, Johns and Tizari were at the ready, but the Boys' years of grunt work had created laborers, not soldiers.

Fully armed, the team continued, ignoring the swelling murmurs in the stagnant corridor until they were overtaken by a reeking veil of rot. Gagging against the stench, Wendy forced the crew's progress as the rank smell thickened, wrapping them like a blanket until her magbeam's light shifted, revealing the *Ehiza's* access fork. Halting the team, she crept closer. At the divide, the rot wafted from the left—the access tunnel leading to Commands. It wasn't the only way to the lower deck's compartment, but based on the *Ehiza's* blueprint, it was definitely the fastest.

"Shyte," Wendy swore as peered blindly down the blackened hall, her hair standing on edge. Surrounded by chilled metal and the scent of decay, the *Ehiza* had fallen silent.

Tightening her grip on her phaser, Wendy crept through the corridor's opening. The air was so heavy it rested on her shoulders. Even the light on her magbeam seemed dimmed by the strange atmosphere. Wendy recalibrated the settings to adjust the light, but the beam only flickered before fizzling out. Cursing, she fumbled to fix it and the faint beam stuttered on, casting a needle into the dark. It pierced the hall, leaving a ring of black around its narrow glow.

Her hands trembling, Wendy expanded the beam to a wide-scanning arc. The radius doubled, illuminating a larger segment of the hall, but her body was angled too far towards the wall. Realizing her mistake, she adjusted her stance. The movement swiveled the light, revealing a ghastly figure hidden in the shadows. It erupted with a hiss, revealing rows of jagged teeth. Wendy jumped, narrowly avoiding its biting lunge as the creature swiped at her and landed in a crouch, the force of its attack vibrating through her heavy magboots.

"Get back!" Wendy shouted, training her weapon on the emaciated creature. Pushing to its feet, the monster snarled and cocked its head, angling its murky gaze at her crew. Sidestepping, Wendy altered her position, forcing its attention on her. It hissed loudly then let out a strange yowl before hunching on all fours, the unnatural stance appearing ghastly on its humanoid form.

Before Wendy had more time to assess, the creature lunged again, snapping furiously at her face. With two quick bursts, Wendy discharged, shooting two neat, sizzling holes through the monster's chest. Crumpling, the creature released a garbled shriek, its spindly arms scrabbling furiously before finally falling still.

"What the hell was that?" Peter's cry cut through the corridor.

"I don't know," Wendy said, inching toward the twitching corpse, still zeroed on the creature's skull. She knelt to observe the body, starting with its elongated head, where gauzy, hooded eyes stared blankly over hollowed cheeks. Its skin, parched and patchy, hung on thin bones that jutted in angular knobs, showcasing narrow joints. "It looks almost human, but it couldn't be."

"I've never seen a person act like that," Johns answered, a frown overtaking his easy demeanor. "And New London has all sorts roaming the streets. You remember that one time? We—"

Silencing Johns' reminiscing, Wendy turned to Tizari, who uttered a single word.

"*Adani*," she breathed, her onyx eyes trained on the creature whose straining had finally ceased. Blinking, she looked at Wendy, with what might have been fear. "A lost one. Not dead—like human *ghosts*, but rather—"

"A wraith," Tootles translated, earning the warrior's firm nod.

"Yes. *Adani*. Wraith," Tizari's statement was punctuated with a distant howl and Wendy shivered. Peering where the creature had appeared, she swallowed.

"These wraiths," she started, tightening her grip on her weapon as she prodded the fallen creature. "What are they?"

"*Nethtali*," Tizari began, bouncing her arm and looking to Tootles for help. "Like human toys." She made a pinching motion and the boy's brow furrowed before he took a guess.

"A puppet?"

Tizari nodded again. "Yes. Puppet. Adani are Itzala's playthings. Creatures whose souls were too weak to withstand his influence. He claimed them, turning them to his will."

Studying the wraith's grotesque figure, Wendy shuddered. A terrible image of Boyce transforming into a sinister puppet flashed through her mind and she forced it away with a grimace.

"But how could the Shadow have them here?" she asked, turning to the Stjarnin. "The ship has been dead for decades."

"There was something here they clung to. The spirits were grasping, unable to find peace. *Itzala* pulled them from their searching and revived them for his use. The Adani are what my people call 'the unrested.'

"Unrested, in the *plural* form?" Johns interjected, his nose scrunching as he nudged the creature with his boot. "You mean, there's more than one of these things?" He asked, his question chased by another spine-chilling shriek.

Tizari nodded. "Adani can be alone, but they often travel together. The larger their groups, the stronger their shadowed-spirit becomes."

"Then we need to get moving," Wendy decided, not liking the compounding skitters reverberating through the corridors. Her magbeam still illuminated the musty corridor, but its reach now seemed tragically short. "We're going to have to take the long way," she decided.

Waving for the others to follow, she fell back, retreating to the opposite hall, her boots thudding beneath her. She had no more than slipped out of the rotten corridor when another howl bellowed through the ship, ratcheting off the winding metal walls. Before Wendy could warn her men, the Adani struck.

Bellows erupted from the *Ehiza's* depths, and a terrifying chorus swelled around them as a swarm emerged, their ghostly figures tumbling into the steady beam of her illuminating maglight.

Gasping, Wendy recoiled as their smiles widened in evil sneers. The creatures' eyes, though filmed in hazy white, trained on her crew while they communicated in discordant chitters. For just a moment, time stilled as the pack thinned and a towering Adani stepped forward, glaring at her team before it released a howl that needled through her spine.

"Run," Wendy breathed, drawing back before the creature screeched and lunged, bringing with it the swarm of monsters. Sprinting down the hall, Wendy cried again, demanding her team to follow, to save them from the monsters.

SOMETHING WORSE THAN THE NIGHT

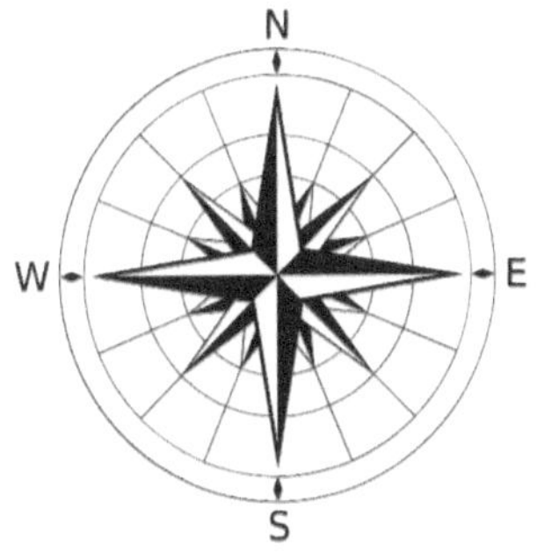

34
FLEET MECHANIC PETER PAN

THE OHORE EHIZA

"You heard her, let's go!" Peter yelled, guiding the Lost Boys down the forked path. Grabbing Tootles' hand, he tugged the smallest boy, whose panicked breathing hitched, while Nibs and Curly rushed ahead. Turning to the others, Peter ignored Tinc's terrified jangles as he turned to Hooke, whose chest heaved violently before he erupted in a massive coughing fit.

"James, come on!" He urged, but the captain only glowered as another series of coughs burst from his chest, leaving him hunched and wheezing.

Swearing, Peter looked past the pirate and his blood ran cold. The Adani had reached the gap and were swarming in, their eyes wild with rage.

"Tizari! Protect the boys!" Peter yelled, gesturing to their small frames. Directing Tinc to follow, he motioned further down the empty hall. "Find a clear room and hunker down. We'll find you when the coast is clear."

Nodding, the Stjarnin rushed to the boys, brandishing her staff as she ushered them to safety. Watching her defensive stance as they disappeared down the corridor guided by Tinc's flickering core, Peter's breath eased and he returned his attention to the shuddering pirate at his feet.

"Hooke! What's going on," Peter yelled, his brow furrowing at the captain's struggling frame.

"This blasted illness" Hooke wheezed, clutching his chest. "It's going to be the death of me."

Peter didn't want to admit it, but for a moment, he thought the old man might be right. Leaning against the wall, all the color had drained from Hooke's face, save the ugly tinge of yellow spreading up his jaw. Briefly, Peter wondered how he hadn't noticed the effects of the captain's Hinson-Braehls before.

"It's going to be the death of all of us!" Johns yelled, hovering anxiously between Hooke and Wendy, his loyalty torn between captain and charge.

Following his stare, Peter looked to where Wendy fended off the advancing monsters, keeping the swarm from overtaking the hall. Her phaser's deadly aim had amassed a small pile of corpses, but more surged forward, their screeches curdling in Peter's ears.

Staring them down, the captain was a force to behold, dauntless before the swarm. Sizzling beams hit every mark, each eliciting another furious howl until a rogue Adani lunged, tackling Wendy around her middle. With a surprised yelp, the captain scrabbled for her thigh strap and its deadly double-edged blade, but the creature swiped, tearing a gash in her shoulder, drawing crimson stains across her coat.

"Wendy!" Peter cried, aiming his shooter. With two sizzling bursts, the creature fell, pinning the captain to the ground. Abandoning Hooke with the lieutenant, Peter rushed to free her before another Adani cratered the panel where she laid seconds before.

"I'm alright," the captain assured, aiming her phaser to take out another wraith with a quick shot. "Take care of the others!"

"Tizari took the boys and Johns has Hooke," Peter explained. "You're the only one left!"

"But we have to get through!" Wendy argued, stalling at the fork. "Boyce—"

"Is still going to be stuck if we get killed trying to find him!" Peter yelled, cursing her stubbornness.

Hearing his words, the captain's expression pinched. Her phaser wavered as she considered, then fell back to join him. She turned, and in that moment, a wraith burst through a nearby access chute, its lips dribbling with spittle.

"Darling, look out!" Johns yelled from his guard, leveling his shooter at the shrieking wraith, landing a neat shot in its eye. The monster fell, but the damage was done. Its attack pulled their attention from the oncoming horde, bolstering the monster's ranks, swarming faster than phasers could match.

"Cap, come on!" Peter cried, tugging frantically at Wendy. "There's too many!"

Casting a final glance at the overrun corridor, Wendy swore, then followed Peter down the hall. Together they ran, loosing desperate shots at the Adani scurrying after them, while the monsters' deadly claws filled the narrow walkway with tinny scritches. Peter thought they might never make it until they rounded a corner to an open bay where Tootles waved wildly behind a propped hatch.

"Peter, come on!"

Crowing in relief, Peter rushed forward, closing the gap to safety. Suddenly from the opposite end of the bay, another group of monsters appeared. Crossing through the opening, they hissed, bearing down on the group to trap them between the pursuing horde. Gripping his wrench, Peter cut down the nearest Adani, allowing Wendy and Johns to mark the wraiths on the edge. Sizzling phaser beams whipped past in a dizzying blur until a large enough break formed for them to slink inside and seal the hatch with a resounding clang.

Safely barricaded, Peter sagged to the ground, laughing as Tinc sparked delightedly in his ear, thinking about what they had just escaped. Wendy, heaving breathlessly, did the same, her eyes alight as she smiled at Johns then the boys, assessing their group. It wasn't until her gaze flickered over Tizari that her grin vanished. Jumping to her feet, Wendy's face drained of color as she turned to Peter, worry in her stare.

"Where's Hooke?"

Frowning, Peter searched the room with a twisting gut. Unable to locate the pirate, he looked at Wendy, his eyes wide.

"I don't know. He was just behind us."

"Weren't you watching him?"

Turning defensive, Peter scowled. "I was a little preoccupied with surviving," he shot back over Tinc's tirade of angry curses.

"You said Hooke could be trusted," Wendy argued, her voice rising as she paced. "I didn't think it was a good idea, but *you told me—*"

"Darling, I really think you guys need to keep it down," Johns suggested, glancing at the shuddering hatch with concern. Wendy's eyes narrowed at the warning but she lowered her voice to finish her tirade.

"He is a wanted criminal and now he's vanished," the captain said, breaking with panic. Glaring at Peter, her angry shout cut into the air, trembling through the paneled room. "All because you convinced me to believe a bloody pirate!"

The captain's claim ended in a surprised shriek as the oversized cooling vent exploded in, admitting another crowd of Adani. They fumbled inside, clawing and crawling over each other to reach the crew.

"Shyte!" Peter yelled, jumping to his feet. He reached for his wrench, but Tizari's longstaff whipped past him, bludgeoning a set of advancing monsters. Striding to the front of the line, the Stjarnin twirled her rod, disabling another Adani with her powerful stroke. Peter thought for a moment she might single-handedly end their threat, when a massive wraith burst inside, rampaging in a frenzy. Before Tizari could reset her stance, the Adani attacked, swiping high then low, cutting under her legs. The strike tore a wide gash in the Stjarnin's earthy skin, causing dark green blood to trickle from the wound.

Dropping to her knee, Tizari blocked the massive creature's next attack, but it struck again, breaking her staff in two. Splintering, it tumbled from her grip, leaving the warrior exposed. Seizing its chance, the Adani reared back to strike, then launched forward, screeching as it impaled itself on the skewered ends of the broken club.

Blinking in surprise, Peter followed the end of the staff to find its wielder and gasped when he saw Curly, bracing it in the air, his eyes clamped shut. He held firm until the writhing creature slowed, taking its last breath.

"Curly!" Peter shouted, looking at the boy in pride. "That was amaz—"

Peter didn't get to finish his crow of praise. Turning toward his voice, the boy had beamed, taking his attention from the vent. With a wild roar, another Adani spilled in, all limbs and protruding bones. Hissing, it lunged at the Lost Boy and violently twisted his neck. With a sickening crack, Curly's body stiffened before it twitched and dropped with his smile.

"Curly!" Johns' roar swallowed Peter as the lieutenant gaped at the fallen boy. Raw fury boiled on his face as he trained his phaser and released a series of shots into the wraith's chest. The creature dropped and still the lieutenant fired, screaming wildly until the shooter emptied.

Blinking at the scene, Peter watched numbly as the others battled on, each facing their own wraith. Several forced their way closer, and he fended them off in a daze, screaming until his red vision ebbed and the room fell in silence.

Chest heaving, he looked around the crowded room, filled with discarded bodies. Vaguely he noticed Wendy and Tizari boarding the vent, but it didn't compute over Nibs' anguished sobs.

Shuffling toward the boy, Peter knelt beside him, looking blankly at the small form he clutched.

"Nibs—"

"He's gone, Peter!" the boy sobbed, his brown eyes brimming with tears. "I was teasing him for always being afraid, and then he went and…" Nibs' voice broke in an anguished sob. "I don't want him to be brave anymore. I just want him to be here!"

Peter tried to comfort the overwrought boy, but no words came out. Instead, he looked around the room and found Tootles, watching them silently, paling as he clutched a large gash in his stomach. Rushing toward the boy, Peter caught him just before he dropped, his breath coming out in uneven rasps.

"Tootles!" he cried, shaking the boy. "Stay with me, kid," he begged, looking desperately around the room. "Wendy—help!"

Staring at the Lost Boy, Wendy's expression broke. Rushing to his side, she leaned over Tootles' heart before frowning at the barren room.

"There's nothing we can do here," she said, her brow knitted in worry. "We have to get him to DeLaCruz."

"We can't risk sending him out," Peter spluttered in shock. "What if more of those *things* come?"

"I will take the boy," Tizari volunteered, stepping forward with a limp. Scooping Tootles in her arms, she turned to the group. "I will not allow him any more harm."

Looking at the Stjarnin, Nibs stuck out his lower lip. Wiping his eyes with the back of his hand, he grunted as he collected Curly's lifeless body. "I'm going with her," he said resolutely. "Curly needs to go home."

Peter placed a gentle hand on the mischievous boy's shoulder. "Nibs, he's too heavy. You won't be able to."

"He will if I help," Johns interrupted, stepping forward with tear stained cheeks. "I'll make sure they make it back," Johns offered, coughing back his emotion. "You two just keep it together long enough to get Boyce. Otherwise, we lost him for nothing." Looking at Curly's sunken frame, the lieutenant's features darkened.

Cowed by Johns' bluntness, Peter exhaled. "He's right," he turned miserably to Wendy. "You brought us here to find Boyce and now Curly's gone. He wanted to help the commander, so that's what we should do."

Avoiding Wendy's pained gaze, he motioned for Tinc, who flitted to his shoulder with a quiet jangle. Her garbled reassurances translated in his ear, but they fell deaf as he waged a silent war with himself—battling his guilt over the loss of Curly and the fact that even still, his jealousy outweighed the sting. Brushing the thought away with the bot, Peter set his chin.

"Tinc," he commanded, "We need the medic. Go ahead and tell her they're coming, so she can meet them as soon as they're off the raptor. It'll be faster that way." The nanobot sparked obediently before trilling a worried question. "I'll be fine," he promised, urging his companion on. "But be quick. And keep away from those things in the halls. I don't think they'll chase you, but no need to risk it. Fly high. And fast."

Finishing his orders, Peter turned to Wendy. The captain looked as though she wanted to speak, but he turned away, refusing her the chance as he hurried down the corridor, burning with fury and shame as his heart turned to stone.

35
CAPTAIN WENDY DARLING

THE OHORE EHIZA

Hurrying towards the *Ehiza's* command station, Wendy remained silent while darkness settled in. Stalking the hall behind Peter, the mechanic's tense frame tormented her as she replayed their argument in her mind. Guilt coiled in her stomach, ready to explode, until an abrupt recollection of Hooke's disappearance incited her rage. The cycle was exhausting, threatening to overtake her already tenuous grip, and she needed to keep her wits.

It was simply easier to banish Pan from her thoughts.

Redirecting her focus, Wendy referenced the *Ehiza's* blueprints and a grim smile tugged her lips.

"We're almost there," she murmured, locating the emergency access hatch leading to commands. Sliding back the concealing cover, she revealed the ladder descending to the lower deck. Reading the question on Peter's sullen expression, Wendy elaborated. "We can take this chute to the base deck, and then we just have to follow a couple corridors to Commands."

Peter frowned at the cramped hatch. "Are there any other options?"

"None that will get us there any faster," Wendy answered.

"Ladies first," Peter gestured to the narrow chute with a grin. "Make sure not to wiggle too much as you go down, or you might get stuck."

Wendy let out an amused snort. "I'll do my best."

Dropping onto the steps, the rusted rungs creaked under her as she crept below deck, the corridor encasing her like a frozen tomb.

Probably not the best time to be thinking of tombs, she scolded as she lowered herself further, the stale air clinging to her like a musty cloak. A loud creak above made her heart skip until she looked up and saw Peter carefully following her climb.

Expelling her frightened breath, Wendy forced her breathing to slow before continuing on. She made it several meters lower when another heavy creak echoed down the stairs.

It's just Peter, she chided, focusing on her steps. Pushing on, she dropped lower until a series of chitters rippled through the chute. The sound paralyzed her as she listened, her hair standing on end. When no other noise followed, she took another tentative step and almost slipped when a massive crash exploded through the chute, carrying with it a fresh wave of the Adani.

"We've got company, Cap!" Peter yelled, terror washing his expression.

"I see them," she cried, fumbling on the rungs. Glancing at the bottom of the chute, Wendy gritted her teeth and released her hold, dropping with a grunt. She rolled out of the way as Peter did the same, groaning as she hefted him to his feet to run, the Adani yowling overhead.

"It looks like they came back to finish the job," Peter grumbled, rubbing his shoulder with a wince.

"That's either a good sign or a really bad one," Wendy murmured, hoping the crew managed to escape. Scanning the corridor, she looked for the markers matching her blueprints. The command station shouldn't be far, they just needed to find the door—

"There!" Wendy pointed to the massive circular panel.

Rushing forward, she slammed into the metal, cursing when it didn't budge. Pounding the cold steel, Wendy's eyes widened as the Adani's shrieks grew.

"It's locked!" She yelled, searching for an access pad as she tried to pry the door open. Skittering footsteps drew nearer as she struggled, hindered by the blockade. Trying one last time to jar the door, Wendy cursed and readied her phaser, training it on the nearest creature. It charged forward, snatching at her flesh. Wendy steadied her aim, zeroing in on the creature until with a loud groan, Peter wrenched the panel open, leaving a tiny sliver to slip through.

"Wendy, come on!" he yelled, buckling under the gap. His wrench had been thrust between the metal edges, but it trembled under the pressure. "It isn't going to hold!"

Following his command, Wendy turned, discharging a warning shot before she squiggled through the opening, ducking through the frame as the wrench shot from the wedge and the door came crushing shut.

Leaning against the metal access point, Wendy closed her eyes, shutting out the Adani's frenzied howls until the wild screeches quieted, and her breathing slowly steadied. When she could finally inhale without her lungs threatening to collapse, she scanned the dim cabin, a small circular room with a row of nav panels lining the front and trash littering the floor.

Following the trail of debris, her gaze landed on a large mass in the middle of the room, a slumped figure with scraggly golden hair. Wendy choked at the sight, unable to breathe until the lump released an agonized moan, confirming it was alive.

36
CAPTAIN WENDY DARLING

"**B**oyce!"

Darting toward the commander, Wendy scooped him in her arms, flinching at his frozen skin.

"He's alive!" she called, her voice breaking as she met Peter's dumbfounded stare. "Find me a blanket or something to warm him up!" She commanded, clutching Boyce closer, hoping to warm his frigid bones. Leaning closer, she pressed her ear to his chest, praying for a heartbeat. At first, there was nothing but her own pulse thudding in her ears, but after a few hitched breaths, she found it. It was faint, only a shadow of its normal strength, but it was there.

"Peter!" Wendy cried, choking as her voice faltered. "We need DeLaCruz. Is there any way to reach her?"

Peter shook his head, his gaze lingering where Wendy's hands clutched Boyce's. "We don't even know if the others made it back to her. If they did, she's already got her hands full. If they didn't…"

Grimacing at his logic, Wendy pulled Boyce closer. He was so cold, and all her effort had only siphoned her heat into his icy core. Smoothing his disheveled hair, she swept the blonde strands neatly in place and cringed at the fever radiating through his frozen skin. The commander needed medical attention, and fast.

Cursing, Wendy looked frantically around the tiny room.

"Where is that blanket?"

"There isn't one," Peter answered, revealing the barren compartments. "Everything's been picked through. Boyce probably already used what he could. There's nothing here."

"There has to be something!" she yelled, scanning the cabin desperately. Nothing was there, nothing she could give him, unless—

Noticing the dark sleeve of her coat, Wendy rushed to unbutton her jacket. Shrugging out of the sleek fabric, she bundled it over Boyce, tucking it around him as best she could. She finished her swaddling and drew back to study his face.

"Boyce?" she asked, hoping the added warmth would help revive him. "Boyce, can you hear me?"

The commander didn't answer, but his eyelids twitched before his head lolled into the crook of her arm. A victorious sob ripped from Wendy's chest before she gestured wildly to the mechanic.

"Peter! Give me your jacket! We need to raise his temperature," she turned, ignoring his concerned expression. "Quickly!"

Sulking, Peter shrugged from his coat and handed it over, leaving his arms trembling against the cold.

"Thank you," Wendy said, through a clouded breath. Tucking the fabric around the commander, she laid him carefully on the ground. After a quick check of his fading pulse, Wendy went into autodrive, administering emergency medical protocol through her frozen tears. When Boyce didn't respond, an anguished cry ripped from her lips, and she renewed her efforts until a soft hand landed timidly on her shoulder.

"Cap," Peter started, scratching his head as he examined the commander. His expression was troubled and Wendy briefly wondered if it was because of the way her hands brushed Boyce's cheek. "Maybe you should let him rest."

"We need to improve his vitals," Wendy argued. Boyce looked so weak, if she wasn't careful, he might—

"He's breathing and he's warm," Peter asserted, "er—as warm as he can be…"

"But I need him to *wake up,*" Wendy pressed, despair turning her stubborn.

Peter watched her for a moment, then knelt with a defeated sigh. "The fact is, Cap, he might *not* wake up." His words were gentle, but Wendy bristled indignantly until he amended, "For a while. He's been through a lot and when he does wake up, he'll most likely be in shock. That's not something you want him to experience here."

"But—" Wendy countered feebly, "what if—"

"What if he wakes up and brings Itzala with him?" Peter finally snapped, his voice raising in frustration. He gestured to the commander's lifeless form, before tiredly scrubbing his face. "Honestly, it might be better that he stays unconscious until we can run a full screen on him."

Pulling a grease-stained hand through his coarse hair, Peter slowly leaned toward the captain. Carefully, he unclasped her hands from Boyce's, unable to hide the hurt in his gaze.

"Any way you cut it, he doesn't look good. You might need to start preparing yourself for the likely possibility that he's not coming b—"

"But I need him!" Wendy yelled, the admission escaping before she could stop it. The force of her cry sent Peter reeling, staring with open shock before his expression darkened and he turned away. He stood for a moment, then stormed towards the door, halting before the barricade, tensing as he clenched his fists.

Buttoning her lips, Wendy watched the broken mechanic guiltily. She struggled for something to say, but her brimming tears overflowed, casting a leaky stain down her cheek. Angling from Peter's gutted expression, Wendy focused on the commander, studying his too-pale face. Lying motionless in her lap, Boyce's hollowed cheeks sapped his handsome features, leaving a distorted relic of the man he used to be. It jarred Wendy's reality—fitting the specter before her with the soldier in her mind. Closing her eyes, she shut out the commander's wasting frame and an unsteady melody thrummed from her chest.

"Though parted from my darling, I dream of him everywhere, the sound of his voice about me, the spell of his presence there," Wendy rasped, clutching Boyce's waist the way he had as they waltzed. Brushing his brow, she watched his shallow breaths, remembering the lilting song's final line. Expelling a shaky breath, she whispered the words, adjusting them for Aidan. "And whether my prayers be granted, or whether he pass me by, the face of my gentle fleetman will follow me till I die."

The melody finished and Wendy's voice lingered in the frigid room, hanging on her frozen breath. Blinking away frosted tears, Wendy stared at the commander, her burning resolution blazing through the cold.

"We need to get him home," she added with a sniffle, wiping her face. "He's alive, and we can help him, *I*—can help him."

She ran her hand along the commander's frozen jaw, fumbling for a solution. Desperate, she laid alongside him, pressing her body against his. Her cheek rested against his cold jaw and as she huddled closer, a soft breath escaped his chest. Heart racing at the faint sign of life, Wendy inhaled shakily and tried the last thing she could think of—holding a gust of warm breath, she leaned in with the barest trace of a kiss.

Boyce's lips were so cold, it was hard for her not to surrender to despair. Drawing back, she searched the commander's face, praying for a response. A frozen tear crystallized in the corner of her eye, but before she could blink it away, Boyce coughed, expelling a rattling wheeze as he gaped at her, fighting over his shallow breaths.

"Boyce!" Wendy shrieked, lighting with joy. "Boyce— we're here. We're going to get you home."

Dazed, the commander blinked again, his expression widening into a slow grin as he lifted his hand to her cheek.

"Wendy," he whispered her name like a song. Sobbing with relief, Wendy leaned into his touch until Boyce drug his nails into her cheek, tearing her face in a jagged scrape.

Jerking back, Wendy cried in shock, but the commander only laughed. Raising his bloodied hand, Boyce's expression morphed, replacing the tenderness on his chiseled features with a hardened sneer. Looking at the captain, he let out a ghastly laugh that bubbled to a throaty growl.

"Oh, Captain, I knew you'd be back."

37
COMMANDER AIDAN BOYCE
THE OHORE EHIZA

"Wendy."

It was her. The girl from his memory—his captain, competitor, and comrade. The girl who had always been two steps in front of him, elusive, even in his thoughts.

But she was here now.

He smiled, gazing up at her, ready to confess everything she meant to him when an icy spectre clutched his mind. Wrapping its grip around his consciousness, the darkness threatened to overtake him. Turning frantically to her—to *Wendy*—he tried to warn her, but Itzala's grip was too strong. All he could do was thrash in protest as the Shadow gleefully washed over, smothering him with its wicked delight.

Many thanks, Commander, it whispered, hissing a mirthless laugh. *You've done your part. Now I will take over from here.*

Boyce thrashed again, directing all his fury against the creature confiscating his body, but Itzala directed its wicked sights on Wendy, who stared back with dread.

"Boyce!" she cried, clutching him tight. "Boyce—we're here, we're going to get you home."

The Shadow blinked slowly as it reacclimated, exploring its stolen body before summoning a wide grin. Refocusing the commander's feeble stare, it examined the figure hovering above. Delight washed over Itzala as it recognized the captain, sitting within its reach. It was too much to stand.

Using the commander's boxy hand, Itzala caressed the girl's cheek, igniting its desire to crush her. Stifling the urge, Itzala merely grinned.

"Wendy," it repeated, tasting her name. Unable to contain itself any longer, it stroked her face and dragged the commander's nails into her supple skin until it spouted crimson.

It took the captain a moment to register her pain, but when she did, she recoiled in surprise. Losing itself, the Shadow laughed, allowing its depravity to bubble from the commander's throat, growing to a merciless cackle before calming at her paralyzed gaze.

"Oh Captain, I knew you'd be back." Itzala rumbled as delicious fear overtook her. "We've been waiting for so long."

Glowering, Wendy stumbled to her feet. She wore her fury well, though it didn't hide the panic Itzala tasted in the air. "Where's Boyce?" She spat. "Give him back."

"I don't think I will," Itzala breezed, lazily marionetting the commander. "Besides," it added, with an evil grin. "I doubt he'd be able to even if I allowed it."

"Why don't you let him be the judge of that," a low growl erupted. Itzala turned toward the sound, and another delighted rumble escaped its chest.

"Ah. The Pan," it purred, glancing from Peter to Wendy. "I'm surprised you're here to defend the commander," it said, meticulously studying Peter's angry gaze. "Especially considering how he feels about your captain," it tipped Boyce's head towards Wendy. "You wouldn't believe the thoughts I've seen."

Peter's expression soured and Itzala laughed again.

"Maybe I should tell you about his dreams. Dreams in which you are nowhere to be found. I remember that being a fear of yours," the Shadow pressed. "Or perhaps you'd like to see the kiss—" A maniacal smile uncurled from Itzala's lips. "It's one of his favorites, based on how often it plays."

"Stop it!" Wendy demanded, pushing between the mechanic and the stolen commander. "Boyce, I know you're in there," she pleaded, her voice wavering in a pathetic whimper.

Itzala scoffed, but deep in the recesses of its hold, it felt an uncomfortable stir. It tried to stamp it away, but the disturbance grew, bucking against its command.

Ignoring the needling, Itzala rounded on Wendy. "Come, Captain, you must want to know, too. The girl who grew up so unloved and ignored, suddenly desired—the center of everyone's affection. I could let you know what *both* of them think of you," it paused, a sinister chuckle bubbling from its chest. "Perhaps it would make it easier for you to choose."

"Shut up!" Wendy yelled, earning a victorious sneer from the Shadow before it abandoned her to angle its gaze toward Peter.

"It seems we've found a sensitive subject for our captain. I wonder how it affects you," it mused, the glitter in its eyes reflecting from the mechanic's murderous stare. When Peter didn't respond, Itzala rumbled in delight. "Quite a bit, I see. Let me warn you, Pan, it would be better for you to let me stay. Especially if the commander's memories are truthful."

Closing Boyce's eyes, the Shadow pretended to revisit a memory. Wicked delight covered its features as it taunted Peter, who roared and lunged at the stolen body.

"Peter, wait! That's not Boyce!" Wendy cried, "He's trying to get into your head!"

"There's no trying, Captain," Itzala needled, directing the commander's fist to sledgehammer Pan's chest. Gasping in pain, Peter staggered back before gritting his teeth and lunging again. Behind the mechanic, Wendy's shouts fell on deaf ears as she fought to stall his futile attacks. After artfully dodging another swing, Itzala guided a smashing kick to Pan's kneecap. It crumpled under the commander's heavy boots with a pleasant crack and the mechanic dropped before Wendy let out another frantic shriek.

"Peter!" She cried, her dark eyes filled with guilt. She dove for the mechanic, pulling him from the commander's long reach then looked up, desperate. "Boyce!" She cried, appealing to Itzala's buried hostage. "Wake *up!* You have to stop this!"

Again, Itzala's smile lengthened, but this time, it was to disguise its shock. At the sound of her voice, the commander's consciousness stirred within, bucking against its hold. It was still in control, it could tell by the strength of its reach, holding firm in the commander's brain, but patches of light had broken through its shadowed skin, creating pockets that Itzala could no longer grasp.

"Apologies, Captain, but the commander cannot hear you," Itzala lied smoothly "I am afraid it's just us."

"Let him go, you bastard," Wendy seethed, supporting Peter while he fought to stand. The mechanic grunted as he staggered to his feet and the captain slung her arm around his waist to keep him from slumping back to the ground.

"I don't think I will," the Shadow cooed. "I'd much rather stay here with you. Besides, the commander wouldn't appreciate finding you like this," it indicated to Wendy's grip around Peter. "It might break what little remains of his heart."

Wendy's glare narrowed at the commander's stolen face. "Either you let him go," she threatened darkly, "or I will take him from you."

Boyce's head thrust back as the Shadow erupted in laughter. Tinny peals rippled through the cabin as the panels thrummed under its force, until finally, Itzala settled and the room quieted once more.

"And how exactly do you presume to do that?" Itzala challenged, flashing the commander's eyes a dangerous shade of black.

"Like this," Wendy said, unhooking her arm from Peter's side to charge at Boyce, before flinging her arms around his neck and trapping him with a forceful kiss. A shudder pulsed through the Shadow as Wendy's brazen attack sent a jolt of warmth coursing through the commander's soul. It wracked the demon with pain as the act of love severed its hold, cracking the inky shield it formed around Boyce's mind.

Responding to Wendy's touch, the soldier reared against the Shadow, desperate to reach her. It sent a wave of energy bursting from within, searing Itzala with its light.

Wendy, I'm here.

"No," the Shadow growled, shoving the captain away. It tried to strike, to hit her so she couldn't approach again, but Boyce stayed his hand.

I won't let you hurt her, Boyce thought, though dark spots had already started to overtake his vision. A wave of darkness rocked through his sight, and he felt his hold slip as the Shadow began to laugh. Still trying to fight, Wendy rose and lunged again, but this time was stopped by a square kick to her chest. Gasping, she staggered back, her eyes wide as the commander contorted in maniacal laughter.

"There's nothing you can do," Itzala taunted, addressing both captain and commander. Finishing his hissing laugh, it drew Boyce to his full height to loom over Wendy, whose face washed in terror.

"So tell me, Captain, what are you going to do now that you have failed?"

WENDY'S CHOICE

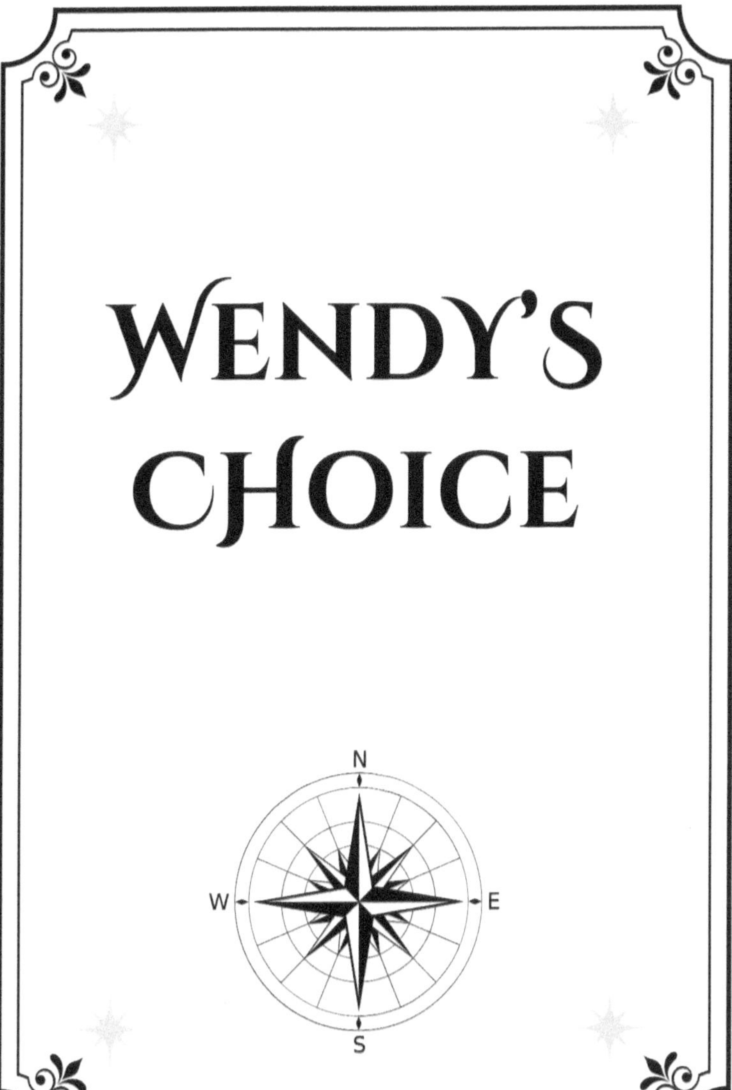

38
CAPTAIN WENDY DARLING
THE OHORE EHIZA

Wendy gritted her teeth at Itzala's stinging words. That the sharp barbs originated from the commander's tongue resonated even further. She *had* failed. The Shadow had claimed Boyce—it had long ago—but her emotions had made her reckless, putting everything in jeopardy. She was going to lose everything, and she deserved it.

Trapped in her thoughts, she had nothing to say. Her confidence had been replaced with a pit of self-loathing she doubted she could pull herself from. Seeing her misery, Itzala curdled Boyce's features with a sinister grin.

"Come now, certainly you must have something more formidable than tears," it taunted, before angling toward Peter. "Or perhaps her champion would step forward—second rate though he may be." Its laugh hissed from the commander's throat, flooding Wendy with ire. Fueled by its flame, she straightened to stand resolutely before the demon, her body coiled in rage.

Sucking in a breath, she narrowed her eyes, unwavering at the commander's stolen stare. "We're going to kill you," she growled, keyed with determination.

Boyce's expression blanked as the Shadow considered her words, before it burst into delirious laughter. "Dear Captain, you can't be serious." It shook the commander's head in a belittling taunt. "You've tried that. And failed. Twice. What makes you think this time is any different?"

Wendy bunched her knuckles into a fist. "This time I'm going to crush the life from you myself."

Itzala issued a soft laugh. "A noble sentiment," it said, lowering its voice in a dangerous growl. "Unfortunately, your claim is empty." Uttering the words, Itzala wrenched Boyce's arm with blinding speed and lashed out, striking her in the face. Wendy yelped and stumbled as the blow cracked across her jaw, her hand flying to where Boyce's fist impacted. She trembled as he hovered over her, its dark, wicked tendrils licking excitedly from its stolen form.

"You see, Captain, this time I have the advantage. I've not only taken your commander; here I have friends of my own."

With an evil laugh, the Shadow turned, puppeteering Boyce to the cabin's barricade. With a hefty tug, the blockade was removed, leaving only the weakened door. Sensing the breach, the Adani slammed against the metal, inciting their shrieks with revived vigor.

Realizing Itzala's plan, Wendy and Peter rushed to stop them, but there was nothing they could do. Frantic, scratching claws reached inside, shoving through as Itzala granted their entry. Stepping aside, Itzala laughed.

"You might have already met them. The Adani can be quite persistent when it comes to new people, reduced to their singular focus to feed," Itzala laughed cruelly. "They recognize humanity, you see, and are driven to reclaim it by whatever means necessary. Usually, this results in quite a mess. But as luck would have it, now I can give them exactly what they want."

With a final shudder, the door burst open, slamming against the wall as the last monsters barreled inside. Huddled together, Peter and Wendy faced the swarming creatures.

"Peter, there's too many! We can't fight them all!" Wendy cried. Her eyes darted around the cabin, searching for other options, but coming up short.

"I know," Peter said, gently slipping his hand in hers before sadly meeting her stare. "I'll head them off," he volunteered, glancing quickly at Itzala. "You stay here. Make sure he doesn't get away again," he commanded then silenced her protests with a kiss. It was so brief, Wendy barely registered it before the mechanic stepped toward the Adani.

Retrieving his rig wrench, Peter brandished it at the creatures. With a shriek, the nearest Adani struck hungrily, reaching with its clawed fist. Dodging to the side, Peter swung, filling the cabin with a resounding clang as the wrench connected and the Adani slumped to the floor, its cratered skull pooling crimson. Hissing, the other monsters shrank away, eyeing the mechanic and his bloodied weapon. Watching their response, Peter's smile widened, a confident spark reigniting his gaze. Casting a challenging glare, he squared against them.

"You hungry?" He crowed, nimbly twirling the tool. "Come and get me."

Leaping onto the dented switchboard, Peter sprang over the Adani. Their starving gazes followed as he arced over their heads and tumbled into the corridor outside, darting toward the shadows. With a laugh, he dragged the wrench along the wall, taunting them with its ringing call. Tracking him, the creatures screeched again, this time launching in a frenzied swarm, their bodies tangling as they surged into the open hall, their skittering footsteps fading in the dark.

Unholstering her phaser, Wendy turned to Itzala, who had stamped an ugly sneer on the commander's face. Thrilled at its fury, she stepped forward to attack, but a lingering Adani launched from the control board it had hidden behind, saliva dripping from its teeth. It swung wildly, its wide arc knocking her weapon from her grip. The shooter clattered to the floor, skittering over the paneling until it was far from her reach. Dodging back, Wendy narrowly evaded a second strike aimed at her head and kicked, catching the creature at the knee. Yowling, it tumbled and hissed before launching itself again, its hollow white eyes fixed in a frenzy. Wendy watched the creature until the last second, then struck again, delivering a crushing kick to its chest. The Adani's cry died in the air as its lungs crumpled and it fell, weakly pushing to its knees. Eyes still trained on Wendy, it scraped its claws along the floor as it crawled, blood dripping from its gnashing teeth. Wendy knelt to strike, but before she could, the commander's hands clamped around the monster's head. The wraith screeched as with a deft twist, its spine was severed, ending the creature with a defeated gurgle.

Looking up, Wendy had a fleeting hope of meeting Boyce's clear blue gaze, but as the commander's hands clapped clean, Itzala's stare met hers.

"That was disappointing," it said, eyeing the Adani with distaste. "You've cost me a pet." It reached for the door and pulled the heavy paneling shut before carefully stepping over the fallen creature. "No matter though," it said, twisting the commander's handsome features into a wicked smirk. "Now we're all alone."

39
FLEET MECHANIC PETER PAN

THE OHORE EHIZA

The Adani were fast. Faster than they should be.

But then again, they shouldn't even be alive, Peter thought over a hitching breath as he careened through the hall. *So any speed is surprising.*

Finishing the thought, he waited for Tinc's biting retort, but only pounding footsteps resonated in his ears as he fled alone, isolated from everyone.

Except the Adani.

The monsters howled as they chased him, their guttural cries stretching to herd him through the ship. At the front, two taller creatures headed the charge, their broad shoulders dwarfing the others. Screaming, they continued after him, their frothy sneers widening as they scrabbled ever closer.

Gripping his wrench, Peter instinctively altered his path, pivoting toward the Raptor's nose. His labored breaths came in painful gasps, but the pursuing creatures only yowled louder. Sprinting through the frigid corridors, he pushed until his muscles threatened to collapse, but the Adani continued, reaching for him with their jagged claws.

Swinging his wrench, Peter clipped the closest creature's jaw. The impact jarred his shoulder, but more importantly, twisted the Adani's neck with a sickening squelch. Fumbling forward, the monster's legs buckled and it toppled to the ground. Its comrades watched it fall, their bleached eyes wild. Closing in, the next Adani slashed, aiming for his neck.

Lunging out of the way, Peter cackled as the creature's wild swing sent it spiraling off balance. His victory was short-lived as one of the smaller monsters dove forward, its long, clumped hair draping across its face. Peter tried to dart out of its reach, but the first Adani had regained its footing and now advanced from the other side, cornering him in a dangerous triangle.

Stalking in unison, the monsters chittered, the unnatural sound gurgling from their skeletal throats. The closer they approached, the clearer their grotesque features became, from the withered hue of their rotting skin to the jagged protrusions of bone peeking through their flayed flesh. Grimacing, Peter tried not to gag at the stench of decay permeating the air. Taking a step back, he swore as his heel bumped steel, announcing the end of the hall.

Trapped by advancing monsters with a group holding their flank, Peter had nowhere to go. With a snarl, he gripped his wrench tighter, holding it threateningly before him. The wraiths eyed the tool but didn't slow. Peter sized the stalking pair, weighing the greater threat. Looking to his left, he decided on the male—at least, that's what the broad shoulders and rotting jaw suggested. The other was slighter, with thin bones that had already deteriorated so much that several of her ribs and smaller appendages were missing.

Picking his target, Peter squared towards the hulking Adani, planting his feet to power his attack. The monsters lunged and Peter smiled. Anticipating the male's wide swing, Peter dove at the creature's feet, aiming directly at its ankles. A crunch sounded as bone broke, and Peter rolled from the wraith's buckling legs to angle for the other monster.

Releasing a murderous cry, the female wraith advanced in a whirl of claws and teeth. Her speed was blinding, and before Peter could evade, she slashed again, catching his chest with her jagged nails. They tore through his jumpsuit, neatly slicing to the skin beneath. Crying out, Peter swung his wrench, flattening the Adani's skull. Shrieking, the wraith spasmed, spraying the corridor with blood as the creature convulsed, twitching in its last cursed pulses of life.

Watching the monster, Peter's nose curled. He fought the urge to kick the wraith before glancing at its snarling face. Though it was distorted—a shadow of a soul with sunken cheeks and a chalky stare—traces of humanity were still there. That's what the Adani had been, after all, a human—maybe not so different from him.

A guttural yowl sounded behind Peter, making him reconsider. The sound was so empty and filled with hate, it made his blood run cold. Whirling toward the sound, his eyes widened at the remaining wraiths, who had crept nearer in his distraction. Now, he could easily count six—four males and two females. They were all close in size and build, except the one at the rear. He was boxy and slow—*and big*. His emaciated form filled the narrow corridor and while it would have taken Peter a flying leap to reach the balustrades above, the approaching monster looked as though he might use them as a pull-up bar.

Cursing, he reclaimed his wrench and tried to scrabble away, but the others had snuck too close. With an ear-piercing cry, the nearest wraith launched herself, tackling him in the middle, ripping at any flesh she could reach. Her last hit cut deepest, carving a long, jagged gash across his chest, drawing a crooked line from shoulder to shoulder.

With a cry, Peter pushed her off, sending her sprawling. Slipping to the side, he ducked out of the way, but stars dotted his vision as he tried to steady himself. He was losing a lot of blood, and pain pulsed through him; the steady ache throbbed in his skull. He tried to grip his wrench to anchor it over his shoulder, but the tool felt too heavy in his suddenly clumsy hands.

Sensing his weakness, the wraiths circled, barricading him as they called to each other with their unearthly chitters. Swaying unsteadily, Peter watched them until, with a resounding shriek, the two middle wraiths sped forward in a double-attack. Closing his eyes, Peter swung his wrench, surprised when it sailed unhindered through the air. Peeking them open, he gasped at the Adani's smoking halves. The dissected remains sizzled as they burned, the stench of cauterizing flesh filling the hall. Peter swallowed, trying not to hurl as he searched for their attacker, but there was no time. The other four monsters were still whole and had turned their murderous gaze on Peter.

"Whoa, that wasn't me," Peter said innocently, though he knew it wouldn't matter. After another discordant series of howls, they launched, careening toward him with vicious speed. Readying his wrench, Peter prepared for impact, but a humming flare burned through the corridor, dropping two more creatures in its blinding light.

Turning toward the source, Peter's eyes widened at the same time the Adani registered their new threat. Brandishing a rusted szikra, Hooke stood in the center of the hall, glowering at the remaining monsters. Tired lines still traced his face but the captain's shoulders straightened as he gave a haughty sneer.

Eyeing the captain, the remaining Adani hissed, their glassy eyes narrowed in fury as they looked uncertainly from Peter to Hooke and his crackling szikra. Determining Hooke the greater threat, they howled and lunged, reaching for the captain with gnarled limbs. Smiling, Hooke flourished his weapon, and with a speed that rivaled his former glory, severed the first Adani's head. It dropped with a sickening pop and rolled to land at the pirate's feet, gaping at him through vacant eyes. Quickly, Hooke darted to face the last creature but the monster, anticipating the captain's move, had stepped wide. As soon as the captain turned, the Adani launched from the corridor wall, swiping furiously. It moved with blinding speed and before Hooke could reposition himself, the creature's jagged claws struck his arm, pummeling into the base of his rusting prosthetic. The antiquated hand sparked and released its grip on the szikra's hilt, sending the weapon clattering to the floor while Hooke grabbed at the base of his stump in a rage. Falling back as he cradled his arm, the captain roared, earning a victorious growl from the Adani, who circled back to finish him.

Watching from the corner, Peter glanced at Hooke's fallen szikra, which had clattered across the corridor to his feet. With a wild crow, Peter darted for the weapon and springboarded toward the exposed pipes in the rafters above. Stretching as far as he could, Peter gripped the pipe and swung, twisting out of reach as he gutted the final Adani.

The monster screeched as the szikra severed its spine, cutting it to the floor. It howled as it dragged itself across the grated paneling, its fury undeterred. Seething, Hooke rose, his torn prosthetic tucked under his arm before he unsheathed a hidden dagger and plunged it into the monster's heart.

Releasing a final shriek, the Adani writhed, seizing as the last of its life escaped. Sneering, Hooke stepped around the corpses, avoiding their pooling blood before silently extending his hand.

"Well, I can't say I'm not glad to see you," Peter said, allowing the captain to help him to his feet. He shook his head at the carnage before him and immediately regretted it as a lancing pain exploded from the base of his skull. Dizzy, he leaned against the corridor's frigid paneling and shrugged. "But I think I had them handled."

Hooke let out an ungentlemanly snort. "Quite," he mused, eyeing Peter warily. "As the loss of blood would indicate."

Following the captain's gesture, Peter prodded his wound. "That's nothing," Peter said with a wave, then paused at his crimson stained hand.

Hooke chortled as he reached for his pocket. "Here," he said, tossing a stolen bandage roll to Peter. "Cover that before you faint."

"Only if you fix yours before it electrocutes us," Peter said, pointing at the captain's sparking prosthetic.

Grimacing at the hand, Hooke did his best to configure it before securing it with the remaining wrapping. It let out a tired hum as the fingers twitched erratically, but it remained attached to the base of the captain's arm.

"That'll be another repair," the pirate mused, before turning to Peter. Recovered from his shock, he stood before Hooke, assessing him through a leery gaze.

"What are you doing here, James?"

The captain sniffed. "Saving your arse, it would seem," he breezed.

Peter's eyes narrowed. "No, what are you *doing?* First, you run off looking like death, then all of a sudden, you're back and cutting monsters down like it's some sort of clip through the galaxy!"

"Don't worry, Pan. It wasn't intentional," Hooke assured boredly. "I was looking for an escape pod to commandeer, and instead, I found you."

"And the szikra?"

"A rather happy accident. Although little good it does me now," he said, frowning at the fritzing prosthetic. He attempted to flex the fingers, but they spasmed disobediently. Looking at the lame hand, Peter stalked to the captain.

Removing the bandage, he reached for his multitool. "Hold still," he commanded, working busily on the severed wires. In just a few moments, Hooke waggled his fingers triumphantly.

"My, my, Pan," the captain said approvingly. "It seems you aren't completely useless after all."

Snorting at the backhanded compliment, Peter shrugged. "Right. Well, fun as this has been, I've got to get back. Wendy needs me."

Hooke's brow arched skyward. "Does she, though?" he asked, an icy glint in his gaze. "From what I can tell, the captain seems incredibly self-sufficient," he mused.

"Oh, she is, but that doesn't mean she doesn't need help every once in a while."

Hooke nodded sagely. "What if she preferred her help from elsewhere? Is it worth endangering yourself if she'd rather have another?"

"You don't know what you're talking about."

"Don't I?" Hooke pressed. "I've seen the passion that grips the captain when she speaks about the commander. It differs greatly from the way she looks at you."

Scowling, Peter turned from the pirate. "Listen, I'm not going to ask you to come. You have more than enough reasons to want to get away. Maybe if I was smart, I would too." He scratched the nape of his neck and winced as he grazed the gash on his head. "But us mechs aren't generally known for mental acuity," he said. "And I've got someone waiting for me."

A tired groan escaped the captain. "Nobility is so droll," he said, dismissing Peter with a wave. "Do what you must. Just know, if you leave for your captain, I won't assist if more wraiths appear."

Peter smiled. "I wouldn't expect you to," he said. "Clear skies, Captain."

Hooke's lips twitched in a begrudging grin. "I'd wish you the same. Do try not to get yourself killed."

"Can't make any promises," Peter said with a wink. "Though that would be ideal." Releasing a crow, he nodded to the captain before heading back. Back through the frozen corridor, back to the tiny compartment, back to more complications.

But more important than all of that, Peter reminded himself, the thought beating his paces in time, *back to her,* he grinned.

"Back to Wendy."

40
CAPTAIN WENDY DARLING
THE OHORE EHIZA

The door was too far.

It was Wendy's first thought as she watched the Shadow navigate Boyce's feet nimbly around the pooling blood in the center of the room. The Adani it spurted from scrabbled weakly, trying to pull itself up from the ground.

It hadn't registered that it was dead yet.

Glaring at the Shadow's prowling figure, Wendy knew she wouldn't run. Even though Itzala wore Boyce like a twisted suit, pinching the commander's features and distorting them with an edge of cruelty, it was still Aidan's face.

He had to be in there somewhere.

"We knew you would come," the Shadow gloated, creeping ever closer as it skirted the small compartment. "Well, *I* knew you would come. The commander certainly *hoped* you would, but then—well, things have been hazy for him as of late."

Wendy scowled. "I'm sure you had nothing to do with that," she challenged.

Boyce's face twisted in false innocence, before the Shadow curled it in a wicked grin. "I had everything to do with it," it boasted. "At least until the fever set in. Human bodies are so tragically weak. It's part of the reason I'm so grateful you arrived. I was beginning to worry I had run out of time."

Wendy's brow narrowed in suspicion. "What do you mean," she asked, mirroring the Shadow's meticulous steps.

"Think now," Itzala chided, marionetting its disapproval. When she didn't respond, a distorted tsk-ing sound escaped its lips. "And the commander always thought so highly of your intellect," it lamented, shaking Boyce's head as it took another step closer. "I needed you here before his shell expired," it explained, as though it were the most obvious thing in the world. "While it's possible to maneuver without a physical form, the effort it requires is staggering. It's much more pleasant to employ a host."

"What does that have to do with me?"

The Shadow widened its twisted grin. "As I have mentioned, the commander is insufficient. His frame was useful in the interim, and physically, not a complete disappointment; but overall, much too weak to sustain my needs. You see, most forms I inhabit do not—*appreciate*—my presence. They tend to rebel. This, unfortunately, has rather undesirable effects on their psyche. Unless it is resolute enough, they tend to disintegrate."

"Maybe that should be enough to communicate they aren't that into it," Wendy bit back, stalking the devil's moves.

Itzala released a hissing laugh. "Indeed," it agreed. "Sadly for them, that is not a requirement."

"And what are your requirements," Wendy asked defiantly.

A look of exquisite pleasure flitted over Boyce's face. "Oh, Captain, I thought you'd never ask," the Shadow said, the sheer joy it emanated setting Wendy on edge. "Primarily, it must have a functional body, which I admit, your commander does. An additional advantage is retaining a position I can leverage—figures of authority, where questions aren't nearly as meddlesome. This is not an imperative, however, merely a boon."

Wendy snorted. "Trust me, if you think inhabiting me is going to help you avoid questioning, I've got a panel of raging Fleetwardens who can prove otherwise," she said, fighting a laugh at an imagined inquisition between Itzala and Colonel Matheson.

"A trifle," Itzala sniffed, leveraging its path to block her from the door. It studied Wendy thoughtfully before shaking the commander's head. "My secondary requirement is much more important, and a discovery I've made only recently, thanks to my current *residence*," he said, plucking distastefully at Boyce's uniform.

"It's in the mind, I've realized. This husk—it deteriorates too rapidly. I couldn't figure out the cause at first, and I'm afraid I took out my frustrations on the commander, which did not help. Then, during one of his brief stints of control, and another session spent dithering over his pathetic *feelings*, I realized something."

Itzala paused to cock its head at Wendy, as though considering her for the first time.

"You see, after becoming so incredibly bored of you, I finally wondered—what was it that captivated him so? I had to find out. So I revisited each of our interactions, from first meeting on the endless planet, to living alongside you in the stars. There is something rather fantastic about you, Captain. A fire that burns when everything else would succumb to the darkness. It is that fire I need to fuel my return."

"If it's all the same, I'd like to keep my fire where it is, thank you. But I have something else you can shove right up your—"

"There it is," Itzala chuckled, watching her hungrily. "So tempting. The commander never could match that passion. But you, Captain. *You*—"

The Shadow's tell was so subtle, Wendy almost missed it. She was so enthralled by its story, had it not been for years of combat training, she would have. But as Itzala spoke, its steps had fallen into a steady cadence, matching the pace of its tale. On its last words, its steps had slowed, stalling to plant the commander's heavy boots. Without shaking her gaze, she marked its stance, and when Boyce's taut muscles bunched in a crouch, hers did the same.

Diving out of the way, Wendy narrowly avoided the Shadow's sweeping grab and rolled to the ground, jarring her shoulder as she reached for her phaser. Fumbling for the hilt, she gripped it and aimed, discharging a sizzling beam into the commander's chest.

Recoiling, Itzala looked curiously at the wound. "I didn't think you had it in you," it mused.

Directing the commander's hand to the blooming stain, it grimaced then pulled away, eyeing the dripping crimson with interest.

"Such a peculiar life force," it murmured, rubbing the commander's fingers as it considered the liquid. "No wonder humans are so weak."

Itzala went unnaturally stiff as a shudder pulsed through the room. When it stilled, Boyce flinched, his body spasming as his shoulders arched, jerking his face to the sky. A deafening scream ricocheted through the cabin, and Wendy covered her head, afraid the piercing shriek might splinter the cabin and empty it to the abyss.

Daring a peek, Wendy issued a choked sob at the unfurling scene. Dark, writhing smoke—more liquid than air—churned from every opening in Boyce's body, slithering from his nose, mouth, and ears in undulating tendrils. Even the commander's eyes leaked the substance, like sinister tears. Wendy reached for him in an attempt to help, but his blood curdling scream filled the room, whipping the air into a roiling tirade. Debris ripped past her, carried on the churning wind, the small projectiles battering her body before getting caught in the funnel once more.

"Boyce!" Wendy cried, praying he might somehow stop the madness—whatever it was. But her voice was lost in the terrible discord of the shrieking wind. Finally, the billowing substance pouring from him began to slow, trickling until it joined the thrashing cloud above him. As the last of it streamed away, the shriek dissolved, leaving deafening silence until Boyce collapsed to the ground.

Wendy tried to rush forward, but the Shadow's cloud hovered in front of the commander's body, forming a solid black wall that coiled together to create a wicked golem. The monster loomed before Boyce, siphoning his life force through the thin tendrils connecting them. They pulsed and shuddered as they fed Itzala, strengthening its crafted body while leeching the remnants of the commander's strength.

"I told you already; the commander is much too weak," Itzala crooned through the darkened whorls. "And soon, he will be gone." The golem glanced at Boyce before turning to Wendy with dead eyes. "Then it will be just you and me."

"Not if I have anything to say about it," Wendy growled, pulling her trigger. It discharged, but no beam came out, only the hum of an uncharged pulse. Cursing, Wendy shot again, emitting nothing more than fizzling sparks.

Watching her struggle, Itzala's golem swelled in laughter. "Oh, Captain, you do amuse me," it wheezed. "How I'll miss your antics once I claim you for my own."

Cackling, the golem strode forward, its dark wisps licking in anticipation as it drew near, reaching for Wendy. Scrabbling back, the captain rose, raising her hands protectively. She dodged a slow swing from the hulking golem, but when she struck out, the creature's tendrils imprisoned her wrist, dragging her into its shadows.

Recoiling against the demon, Wendy tried to fight, but there was little she could do. Trapped under its bulk, she choked, unable to breathe as Itzala pressed down on her, stealing her air. A cry formed on her lips, but it stayed caught, held hostage in her lungs as they grappled for oxygen. Head spinning, Wendy tried to force the creature off, but it only laughed, filling the room with its evil rumble while its shuddering form rippled through her grip.

Around her, the room began to fade as the steel edges blurred in her failing vision. Wendy tried to fight it, blinking to clear the distorted haze, but Itzala pressed harder, wringing a disturbing gargle from her throat. Pain blossomed, setting fire to her mind, screaming for her to breathe, but she couldn't. All she could do was shut her eyes while allowing her thoughts to drift to a different place, somewhere so far in the stars that the evil taking hold of her mind couldn't reach.

Slipping away, she heard Itzala's victorious laugh, and a pang of regret coursed through her as she remembered her crew on the ship. Loyal to the end, and she'd never get the chance to thank them. She'd end up like Boyce, a discarded husk, broken from the Shadow's abuse.

"I'm sorry," she whispered, wishing just one of them could hear. All the words she'd left unsaid, hindered by duty and pride. She shouldn't have waited so long, she thought, succumbing to the darkness. *I should have told them—*

Her thoughts were interrupted as the Shadow's gleeful laughter turned to a furious growl. Confused, Wendy tried to look around, but Itzala held her down, leaving her blind to the commotion clattering through the room and the voice that pierced the black.

"Wendy—don't let it win!"

41
FLEET MECHANIC PETER PAN

THE OHORE EHIZA

Crashing through the door, Peter thought it was too late. Wendy's body sprawled like a discarded rag, her injured leg at a grotesque angle. Overhead, Itzala hovered, writhing in gleeful anticipation.

"Wendy!"

Surging forward, Peter tried to slide beside her, but a thick fist smashed into his stomach, slamming him into the wall.

This isn't your fight, Pan, Itzala seethed. *She doesn't want you. She lied, pretending you held her heart while unrepentantly granting it to another. Her cruelty should not be rewarded. Perhaps I should just take it instead.*

For a moment, Peter hesitated. Carried on Itzala's poisoned whisper, all the jealousy, bitterness, and rage pent in his heart slicked to the surface, fighting to drown him. But seeing Wendy, face down on the floor, her unkempt curls framing her delicate features, Peter knew he couldn't. Now, he needed to be strong.

"And what would that accomplish except giving you everything you want?"

A shuddering laugh rippled from deep within the Shadow's form. *You were the cleverest of my hosts*, Itzala offered. *Each one a different strength. Hooke, the conniver. Boyce, the brawn. Wendy the unrelenting. And you, so bright, but so painfully unwanted.*

The admission hit like the whipping gusts stirring the room, but Peter didn't flinch. Holding his stance, he faced the Shadow, his jaw gritted tight.

"The only unwanted one I see around here is you," Peter bit back, fixating on the demon while inching closer to Wendy. "And yet it hasn't seemed to chase you off."

Itzala laughed, a harsh, cruel note. "It won't. Not when you produce such delicious misery." Without warning, it struck Peter with a whipped tendril, slicing through his cheek.

Crying out, Peter jumped to the side, biting through the pain to crawl closer to the captain. Wendy lifted her head, terrified.

"Peter, don't," she panted, tears forming in her galaxy eyes as a million starbursts exploded in her gaze. "It's too late, you have to run."

"I don't think so, Cap. You've got a lot of people waiting for you back on that ship and I promised I'd bring you back."

Scooping her in his arms, Peter shifted the captain to stand, but the Shadow struck again, slashing the mechanic's neck. Gritting his teeth, Peter tried once more to move her, but was stopped by another roiling blow. Itzala's rumbling laugh filled the room as Peter gently lowered the captain and stood before her, blood streaming from his newly carved wounds.

Come now Pan, it could be so much easier if you would just walk away.

"I've never been a fan of easy," Peter said, gunning for the Shadow's writhing tendrils. His wild blitz caught the creature off guard, but the golem was too fast. With a crushing blow, it slammed the mechanic in the chest, dropping him to his knees.

Gasping, Peter struggled to stand while the golem stomped over, pinning him to the ground. Peter thrashed against the monster's weight, but the creature only smiled and kicked, sending Peter sliding across the room before it chucked a heavy metal panel on top of him, eliciting a pained yelp as the mechanic was pinned in place.

"No!" Peter cried, struggling against the steel. His legs burned as he tried to escape its crushing weight, but he didn't care. He only saw Wendy. "You can't do this!"

Ignoring his helpless attempts, Itzala turned and with an exuberant roar, coiled, ready to strike. Its billowing body condensed into a compact cloud when a solid figure lunged, hurtling past Peter with a ferocious cry. It barreled into the Shadow, severing its link to Wendy, who spluttered as she breathed. Her lungs filling, color returned to her lips as she looked at her rescuer and let out a raw gasp.

"Hooke?"

Brandishing his szikra, Hooke answered dryly. "In a shocking turn of events."

"James?" Peter asked, his confusion greater than Wendy's. "But I thought—"

"Turns out, Pan, I would rather die briefly a hero than live forever in chains."

"But you aren't dead yet," Peter pointed out, grinning at the proud captain.

Chuckling, Hooke gripped his szikra. "A fact I am certain is disappointing to all," Hooke deadpanned, his wry smile turning feral as he faced the Shadow. Stepping closer to the raging monster, a fierce glower painted his brooding features. Smoldering resolve ignited from his chest, filling him with a strength Peter thought long lost. "It seems I have unfinished business to tend to."

"You?" the Shadow seethed, its hungry gaze trained on Hooke in disbelief. "But I—"

"Thought you'd bested me?" Hooke challenged, a mean grin pulling his sunken features. "I've always heard pride comes before the fall."

The command station shuddered as a violent roar ripped from the golem, pulsating through the compartment. Peter's teeth chattered as the ground shook, buckling under the Shadow's fury. The golem pulsed as it raged, its shrouded body rolling into a billowing cloud that ripped the panels from the walls in a swirling cyclone. Its eyes narrowed on Hooke before it moved its hand, directing a jagged sheet of metal directly at the pirate.

Hooke's face paled as he dove, registering the creature's attack, but the steel corner caught his hip and sliced down his leg, fileting his thigh. Hooke roared in pain, but the Shadow was not finished. With another slash of his arm, a razored screen shot towards the pirate's chest, aimed directly at his heart. Unable to move, the captain flung his prosthetic defensively, filling the room with a shower of sparks as the mech collided with a pop. Under the force of the shock, the pirate convulsed against the wall, hanging from his skewered leg.

Gloating at the captain's fallen form, Itzala twisted, angling its furious gaze to the next available target. Gritting his teeth, Peter met the monster's devoid stare and bucked against the door, struggling to break free. Though the metal scraped and slid, the weight was too heavy for him to shift. Grinning evilly, the Shadow advanced, transforming the golem's boxy, wisping hand into a bladed point.

"Poor form, Pan," Itzala hissed, edging closer to Peter. "And to think, you never stood a cha—"

The Shadow's cruel taunt dissolved into a surprised garble. Tearing his gaze from the creature's spasms, Peter turned to Wendy, grinning fiendishly as she lunged, brandishing Hooke's prosthetic in one hand and his stolen szikra in the other. A sharp cry tore from her chest as she thrust the metal appendage deeper into the golem's chest, running it through with the szikra's deadly current.

Watching in a haze, Peter thought the Shadow's agonized roar might crumple the *Ehiza*. Steel fragments groaned and screeched as they ripped from the ship, leaving the compartment in utter ruin as the shadow writhed, its tendrils crackling with the throbbing current. The shock jerked through the creature, but Wendy stabbed harder, skewering the golem until her grip slackened and the Shadow flung her across the room.

A sickening crack echoed through the cabin as Wendy struck the wall. Slipping to the ground, the captain landed, her body unmoving.

Releasing a furious growl, the Shadow collected its disintegrating coils, summoning them to reform its golem. The inky creature staggered to the captain, glaring at her with open hatred.

"I think killing you is going to be the most exhilarating," the Shadow seethed, towering over Wendy's incapacitated form. Raising the golem's arms, it prepared to strike when, with a deafening hum, a szikra's crackling beam sizzled into its back.

Howling, the Shadow flung its manifested arms toward the source of the new attack and released a surprised hiss. Staggering in the center of the room, his sword arm sagging under the szikra' weight, Boyce stood, his eyes flashing with contempt.

"I was thinking the same about you."

42
COMMANDER AIDAN BOYCE
THE OHORE EHIZA

Boyce grinned as the Shadow flickered, shuddering its roiling tendrils into airy wisps before they pulsed back into a thick cloud.

Training his gaze on the golem, Boyce drew to full height, using the command panel to steady his weight. Beads of sweat dripped down his brow, but he forced his stance to survey Itzala's destruction. Near the door, the discarded bodies of Captain Hooke and his mechanic Pan crumpled together, bloodied and bruised while an unfamiliar corpse laid in the center, its decaying skin hanging from knobbed bones. And across the way was Wendy, huddled behind the Shadow, her hazel eyes wide as they followed him in disbelief. He turned a smile as he met her gaze, then returned to Itzala's churning form.

"I think you've forgotten something important."

The Shadow's laughter was deafening as it rumbled through the cabin.

"Forgotten? No, my dear Commander, nothing has been forgotten," Itzala's words slithered under his skin, chilling him with their hate. "My use for you has simply shriveled, much like I anticipate Captain Darling's has, now that she's witnessed your pathetic state."

The Shadow's condescending titters ignited Boyce's temper. Mustering all his strength, Boyce lunged at the curling golem. His sudden attack caught the creature off guard as he clipped its side, tackling it to the floor.

Flailing under the force of the commander's attack, the golem's shadowed form slithered from his grip. Grappling with the beast, Boyce fought to restrain it but with a deafening roar, the Shadow swiped a malleted fist against his head.

Groaning, Boyce staggered as the cabin swirled in a dizzying blur. From the far side of the room, the Shadow's wicked cackle swelled until it loomed above him.

"I cannot express how glad I will be to rid myself of you," the Shadow growled, towering over Boyce's unsteady figure. "You have been a thorn in my side for far too long."

Boyce chuckled, hoping it sounded more confident than he felt. "Funny. I was going to say the same about you." The Shadow hissed, but Boyce continued, his confidence growing with every shaky step. "You thought for so long that you were in charge, that you were using me, stealing my secrets for your own twisted gain," he said, moving to defy the monster. "But what you didn't realize, is that the whole time we were here, I was doing the same."

Reaching for the szikra, the commander stared at Itzala, his gaze unflinching. Without a word, Boyce activated the sparking blade and with a final, longing glance at Wendy, dove for the creature. Wrapping his arms around the golem's shivering core, the commander pressed against the writhing mass, reconnecting with the monster one final time. Gripping it tight, he angled the blade to pierce Itzala's back and plunged it through, thrusting it into his own exposed chest.

Bellowing, the Shadow thrashed to escape, but held captive by Boyce's tenuous bond, Itzala had nowhere to turn. The *Ehiza* rocked as the creature's power stormed through the room. Though it slashed and hissed, the commander only grinned as the szikra's thrumming blade emitted its final pulse.

An eerie calm fell over the cabin and with a garbled gasp, the Shadow's writhing power dissipated. The whipping wind whooshed past, biting as it funneled in on itself, until Itzala's last fragments disintegrated, leaving nothing but a scorched black mark.

Teetering, the commander smiled at Wendy before glancing at the dulled szikra piercing his chest. Choking over a sickly gurgle, he fell to his knees before tumbling sideways to the ground.

"Boyce!" Wendy's voice was a flickering light in the inky dark. He felt her tugging him, pulling at his shoulders, maybe, but the numbness invading his body made it difficult to tell. All he knew was that here, alone in his twilight bubble, warmth had finally started to reach his frozen bones.

"Boyce, wake up stars-dammit!"

The captain's frantic yell sparked a blinding light into his cocoon, and he turned, shrinking from its painful brightness toward the welcoming pool of black. Again, his body rocked in a pulling wave as he slipped farther away, chasing peace.

"You can't go yet—" Wendy pleaded as the shaking around him stopped. Freed from the disorienting jostles, Boyce paused to listen, torn by the pain hanging on her voice. "I still need you."

Her last words were a whimper he nearly missed under the beckoning roar swelling in his ears. Forcing it back, he turned to the captain's fragmented light, which cut through the dark, casting her in a golden halo.

"Wendy," he whispered, ignoring the agony it caused. He wasn't even sure the word escaped until the captain froze, silhouetting her in glimmering shards. Soft light danced on her hair and caught the flecks in her gaze, illuminating her with an ethereal beauty not even her glittering tears could mar. "Why are you crying?"

Summoning all his strength, he forced his phantom limbs to move. Cutting through the glow, his boxy hand appeared, pale and trembling, to brush the tears from his captain's face.

"I love you," he rasped, oblivious to the pain coursing through him. "I always have, I just didn't know how to tell you."

Dipping her forehead to his, Wendy let out a trembling laugh. "Surely there had to be a better way than this," she joked weakly, glancing around the destroyed compartment. Blood and debris coated the room, making it look more like a desecrated wasteland than the heart of a spaceship.

"I don't know," Boyce said, redirecting her stare. Cradling her face in his hand, he drew her close, ignoring his muscles' protest as he angled his body towards hers, eliminating the distance between them. She allowed him, her eyes darting nervously over his figure as though he might break, but he smiled reassuringly. "Then I wouldn't be able to do this."

Closing the final inches between them, Boyce met her in a reckless kiss.

The moment Wendy's lips touched his, all the pain enveloping his body seemed to fade. He was certain it was still there, waiting, but for that one instant, he didn't care—the only truth he knew was her. Clutching the captain closer, he reveled in the moment, hoping his touch had the same effect on her. Before long, he had to pull back, his trembling lips unnoticeable as the rest of his body was wrapped in violent shudders.

Smiling, he reached for Wendy as the world around them faded into thundering explosions. Worried, he fought to stay awake, but as the room filled with shadowed figures, Boyce could only tune to Wendy.

"I love you," he whispered urgently. He needed to tell her, to make sure she understood before everything went dark.

43
CAPTAIN WENDY DARLING

THE OHORE EHIZA

"Boyce?"

Wendy's nerves spiked as the commander went limp in her arms. Around her, surprised murmurs filled the room as Fleet soldiers swarmed in, their visored expressions betraying no emotion as they assessed the damage. Vaguely, her mind pieced together what that meant—the brigade had arrived, and all her deceptions would finally be revealed. But even though atonement was closing in, Wendy was surprisingly numb to its threat. Instead, her attention remained on her fallen soldier.

Clutching Boyce tighter, she fought to revive him, but the commander laid slack while his head lolled weakly against her chest.

Sobbing, Wendy scanned the room, begging for help and a dark-suited soldier directed two others to her aid. The grunts nodded obediently and rushed to her side before attempting to extricate Boyce from her grip.

At first, Wendy struggled against their outstretched hands, unwilling to release him to the strangers. She hovered over him, barricading his upper half until a muffled command ordered the soldiers to pause. Booted scuffles sounded in her ears and she wiped her tears on Boyce's jacket before facing the officer kneeling beside her.

"It's going to be alright," a steady voice assured, placing a warm hand on her shoulder. "The Fleet will take care of him."

Drawing back, Wendy looked at the fleetman. It was the same officer who had ordered Boyce's collection. He had left his post to join her, his expression blank, but not unkind. Peering closer, Wendy realized he was older, closer to her father's age than her own, with umber hair and eyes accenting his deep bronze skin. His uniform revealed more than his expression, with a colonel commander's badge emblazoned prominently over his heart. Stitched above was a small patch displaying his initialed name, R. Amin.

When she didn't respond, Amin gently squeezed her shoulder. "The commander needs medical attention," he prompted, his shrewd gaze pulling in concern as he inspected Boyce. "And he won't get that here."

Glancing down, Wendy nodded weakly, slowly releasing her grip on Boyce's torn jacket. Her fingers cramped as she unclenched her fists and leaned back to allow the field lieutenants forward. Beside her, one of the lieutenants pulled a small card from his pocket and pressed the center, emitting a small beep as the plastic lengthened and unfolded into a portable gurney. When it finished, they hoisted Boyce to the bed then carefully wheeled him from the room while their commanding officer lingered at Wendy's side.

Staring after them, Wendy's chest hitched. She wondered what would happen to him and if she would ever be allowed to find out. The worried musings crowded her mind, running rampant until a husky tenor rumbled past her thoughts.

"Hey, Cap," Peter called, leaning against the wall with a wince. "Looks like we finally did it."

"I think we did," she agreed. She glanced from him to Hooke, who grimaced as he pressed his hand to a bandage on his forehead that was damp with sweat and blood. Several other blood-roses blossomed from his wounds, dotting his once pristine suit with crimson. A frown pulled at her lips as she studied the pirate, conflicted. She might have thanked him, but her tired brain couldn't comprehend what happened, let alone what to say. Instead, she peered down the dark corridor the commander had been taken into and started to follow.

"One moment, Captain," Amin called, stopping her before she left. "I'm afraid you'll have to stay here."

Brow furrowing, Wendy glanced at the stoic officer, who stood with his hands clasped tight behind his shoulders.

"It will only be a moment," the colonel commander assured. "We've been instructed to retrieve all the evidence and return as quickly as possible."

"The evidence?"

"Yes," Amin nodded. "As I am sure you are aware, the Admiral is quite displeased."

Wendy flinched at the colonel's admonishment but stood firm. "I am happy to answer your questions, Colonel, but first I'd like to ensure the well-being of my commander."

"Understandable," Amin said, "and I can assure you my crew will take every measure to resuscitate Commander Boyce. However, at this point, I regret to inform you that he is no longer your charge."

"No longer—" Wendy's chest tightened as she choked on her understanding. Coughing, she fought to regain her composure, but before she could inquire further, Johns stormed in, crackling with rage. Colonel Amin's soldiers followed closely behind, their faces red as they pursued the bristling lieutenant, who ignored their protests as he scanned the room.

Chest heaving, Johns' eyes landed on Wendy and the tension in his chest evaporated.

"Darling!" He rushed forward to crush her in a hug. The trailing soldiers attempted to intervene, but Amin stilled them with a patient hand. "You have to stop doing this to me," Johns said, pushing her lightly on the shoulder. She rocked back, wobbling on weak legs and he cursed and lunged to steady her.

"I'm fine," Wendy assured, before narrowing her gaze. "But what are you doing here Johns? Why aren't you on the ship? Is everyone safe?"

Johns nodded. "They're peachy. Dawes is a little shook up from the specialist act the Fleet pulled when they rolled up, but otherwise all is good. We were worried about *you*," he shook his head incredulously. "When those grunts carried Boyce in, we were worried that—"

He paused at Wendy's expression, letting the sentence die on his lips.

"He's in the MedBay with Rissa now," he explained, anticipating her next question. "There's another medic there too, a blonde guy I heard another grunt call Sully. He seems like a decent sort, but I don't think she's thrilled to share her space."

Wendy nodded. "I can imagine," she said, picturing DeLaCruz' pristine bay being overrun by tromping soldiers while she tried to tend the crew. "What about the others?" she asked, remembering the boys. "Nibs? And Tootles?"

"Everyone is fine, Darling," Johns assured, before his jaw clenched. "Well, almost everyone," he inhaled sharply, looking pointedly around the room to hide his misting gaze. His attention landed on a group of waiting fleetmen and he bristled. "They said they'd give a full briefing when we boarded the return ship, but that we'd have to wait for our new captain to issue the statement."

Coughing, Colonel Amin stepped forward, silencing the lieutenant with a raised hand. Meeting Wendy's wide gaze, he nodded to address her.

"Thank you, Lieutenant. That is just what I was trying to explain," Amin said, clearing his throat. "As of this point, the *Jolly Roger* and the rest of your crew have been reassigned to my command. I will be escorting you all earthside before the commencement of Captain Darling's trial."

"Trial?" Johns asked, "Don't you mean for Hooke?" He thumbed at the wounded captain, pointing out the guards hovering protectively over him and Peter.

Amin's eyes narrowed at the pirate, his head quirked in a silent question, but he brushed it off with a tight edge. "For Captain Darling," he answered tersely. "The tribunal would like to revisit the Neverland charges."

Johns erupted in a spluttering objection, but it was quickly silenced by Wendy's furious glare. "He's right, Johns," she said, setting her jaw. "This isn't a surprise."

"But he—"

"It's all right Elias," Wendy warned, standing to full height. The motion stretched her bruised muscles and she bit back a whimper. "Colonel Amin is just doing his job."

"No, he's doing *your* job," Johns muttered angrily.

Amin let out a haughty sniff before turning to his team. "Let's wrap it up," he announced, pointedly ignoring the lieutenant as he directed the soldiers imaging the room. Datapads chirped as the fleetmen completed scan after scan, annotating the state of the *Ehiza* and its inhabitants. When they indicated they were done, the colonel commander cleared his throat.

"Well done, men. Please escort the acquisitions to the ship. We will reconvene from there."

Flagging another soldier, Colonel Amin relinquished Wendy to their care, leaving her watching his proud stance as he oversaw the usurping of her crew. Bitterly, Wendy allowed the soldiers to lead her away before realizing with a pang that she had officially lost it all.

44
FLEET MECHANIC PETER PAN
THE FIDELIS ETERNA

"Come on, Pan," Peter's designated officer instructed, offering a gloved hand. The field lieutenant was slighter than the two flanking Hooke, but the dark visors the trio wore obscured any other distinguishable features. Studying the rest of the officer's uniform, Peter located the name plate bearing the lieutenant's ID: M. Kirova.

Hefting him to his feet, Kirova groaned alongside him—Peter at the pain jostling his muscles while the soldier grappled with his nearly dead-weight. His escort was kinder than Hooke's. The captain's lieutenant, though much taller and broader than Kirova, didn't offer any assistance. Instead, he aimed a kick at Hooke's ribs before barking at him to get up.

Delaying a moment, Hooke angled his head to peer at the soldier. "I see the Fleet has lost their attention to manners," he grumbled, glowering through his unobscured eye. It sparked as dangerously as his flashing szikra before, exhausted, the captain fell against the wall, his chest hitching in shallow breaths.

"This can't be the guy a whole crew risked their necks for," the officer, identified as Hanson, laughed and elbowed his partner, Lieutenant Moss. "Although, it seems like they were second rate too, needing us to save their asses like this."

Peter bristled at the masked officer, but with Kirova gripping his bicep, all he could do was seethe.

"Come on then," Hanson egged, prodding Hooke once more. The captain sneered, but before he could act, Peter leaned forward.

"Here, Hooke," he interrupted, offering his hand. It startled Kirova, who glanced uncertainly at Hanson. The visored man scoffed, but simply crossed his arms as Peter hoisted the captain to his feet. It was difficult, with Peter's limbs protesting as they supported Hooke's buckling frame, but he managed with a grunt. "Can't bring down the bureaucracy until you're on your feet," he whispered.

Smirking, Hooke gripped Peter's shoulder. "True," he said, before shooting a murderous glance at Hanson. "But much less effort is needed for only one," he growled, spurring the soldier to quickly unholster his phaser. Peter snorted. At least the man wasn't stupid.

"Hanson," his partner warned, "The Fleet wants them back alive."

Hanson didn't flinch. He aimed his weapon at Hooke a moment longer before jabbing it angrily in the captain's back.

"Move," he finally muttered, urging them forward with a jerk of his head. Spurred onward, they exited the flickering cabin to enter the frigid corridor. Peter tried to ignore his clamoring wounds, but with little to distract him, they felt like knives cutting with every step.

Passing by them, another visored fleetman hurried through the *Ehiza*, his stiff posture mirrored by the slight soldier he escorted, her hands bound behind her back. Frowning at the cascading curls and torn uniform, Peter longed to call for Wendy, but realized it would do no good. Her assigned guard matched every step, keenly attuned to the captain while allowing her the freedom to direct herself.

"She is intriguing, I'll give you that," Hooke's gravelly murmur interrupted Peter's buzzing thoughts. "Though, I daresay, more trouble than she's worth."

"And what would you know about that," Peter challenged.

A wheezing laugh escaped the captain. "More than you might guess," Hooke said, his gaze going distant as the fleetmen directed them further through the ship. The captain was quiet so long, Peter thought their conversation ended until the old man's rasp broke over their muffled footsteps. "Are you going to tell her?"

"Tell her what?" Peter asked, "that the Fleet will steal her soul? Pretty sure she knows that. I think it's in the fine print of the enlistment form."

Hooke let out a rumbling laugh. "Indeed," he said, testing the photobracers around his wrists. Electric blue beams sizzled coolly until he pulled too far, then the flickering light crackled and ignited to burn hot against his skin. Grimacing, Peter dropped his hands to deactivate the bracer's harsh energy. "Though that's not exactly what I meant."

A husky chuckle escaped Peter before he quieted under Hanson's glare. Taking a few silent steps, he cast a sideways glance at the pirate, who limped proudly down the hall, spurred by the barrel of Hanson's phaser.

"I don't know if she wants me to," Peter finally admitted. He wasn't sure what prompted the confession, outside the crash of his thoughts against the corridor's gnawing silence.

"Does that make it any less true?" Hooke asked, his gaze surprisingly void of judgment.

Peter thought for a moment, then shook his head.

"Then what could it harm?"

"I'd have to hear her admit she's in love with the commander." Peter said bitterly.

Hooke nodded. "It sounds like you already know that."

Slowing, Peter blinked at the pirate. Hooke was right. He did know—he *had* known—he just hadn't been brave enough to admit it. Now that the words had escaped—

"Perhaps if you went and stranded yourself on that blasted planet again…"

The captain's suggestion earned a bitter scowl. "I didn't mean to get caught there the first hundred years, Hooke. I have no intention of doing it again."

Hooke snorted. "If it didn't seem I was about to spend the next century in a Fleet holding cell, I might offer to take you with me."

Peter let out a surprised laugh. "Still planning grand adventures?" he asked, before offering the captain a shrug. "If you weren't right about your upcoming incarceration, I might agree to join you."

A wry smile quirked the captain's lips, then disappeared as Hanson shoved him forward, directing them into a large storage compartment that had been hastily converted into a containment bay. At the far end, the pirates' holding cell had been transferred from the *Jolly Roger*, complete with the remainder of Hooke's crew. The captain's steely eyes flickered over his men, but he didn't speak as the soldiers angled to the opposite reach.

Striding across the bay, Peter noticed a collection of artifacts from the *Roger*. They had been gathered and tagged, then designated to the room. Looking closer, Peter realized most of the ship's usable supplies had been transferred, including

SMEE, who bustled around the items, worrying over each piece. Peter almost called to the first mate but stopped when he saw Tizari.

Standing strong in the center of the bay, the Stjarnin observed the officers bustling from the *Ehiza*, her cool gaze taking in every movement until it landed on the soldiers flanking Peter. Silently, she stepped forward as Hanson and Kirova slowed, cautiously assessing her imposing features.

"You were successful," she greeted, her gilled lips turned in a stoic smile.

"How did you know?" Peter asked, his brow furrowing in confusion.

Tizari's ebony eyes flashed. "Itzala's presence began with my people," she said, pressing a hand to her heart. Pulling the top of her banded shirt, she exposed the skin beneath, revealing a shiny gray mark. Faded and faint, it matched the brand Itzala's presence had left on Peter's skin, which after the Shadow's defeat, had shrunk to no larger than the size of Tinc's microprocessor. Within a few hours, he was certain the imprint would dissolve completely.

Meeting his gaze, Tizari nodded.

"His absence will end with us as well." Adjusting her collar, she bowed to Peter. "Our people owe you a great debt," she said, before eyeing the waiting soldiers. "Soon your people will realize they do, too."

"One can only hope," Peter grumbled, feeling the manacles lick his wrists.

"When they do," Tizari pressed, "will you go home?"

Peter frowned, considering. Glancing around the room, his eyes fell on Wendy. She had been led to the front of the bay, where she waited proudly; her expression a cool mask as she sat with her bracers locking her hands in place. Staring, Peter couldn't help but feel a pang of regret. Even now, she was beautiful, unwavering in her convictions. She stayed that way, un-moving in her calm, until for a brief instant, her gaze pulled to the corridor leading to the MedBay.

To Boyce.

Fighting a raging pang of jealousy, Peter averted his stare. Forcing an easy grin, he returned to Tizari. "I don't know that I have much of a home anymore," he said simply, surprised at the ache from his admission. "I hoped I might—" he swallowed, losing the rest of his words before he re-plastered his smile. "I'm considering my options. Don't want to tie myself down just yet."

Tizari simply nodded. "Lendare sene je ani," Tizari said, dipping her head politely, before surprisingly repeating the motion to Hooke. "Until we meet again," she translated, then continued her solitary path. Hanson watched her exit, trailing the Stjarnin's willowy frame with a sneer.

"Colonel is offering a lot of freedom to a crew full of prisoners," he grumbled, tightening his grip on Hooke.

"The Stjarnin is not a prisoner, and neither are any of Darling's crew," Kirova countered, her exasperation evident. "Not yet anyway. That will be determined by the Admiral once we're earthside," she looked apologetically at Peter. "And from what I hear, most of them will walk free. Sounds like the only one who's in deep is the captain."

Casting a quick glance at Wendy, Kirova's eyes darted over the bracers around her wrists, the electric blue tinge perfectly matching Hooke's.

"Well, captains," she amended, urging Peter forward with a shrug.

"I don't buy it," Hanson declared. "You can't tell me there's no-one on this busted bird that didn't know what Darling was up to." He grunted as he dragged Hooke along, glowering at the suddenly limp captain. "They had to be in on it."

"Not if she was smart," Kirova countered, "and from what I've heard, she absolutely is. I'd be willing to bet she had the whole thing worked from the get go," she said, studying Wendy with a note of admiration in her voice.

"I'll take that bet," Hansen said with a scoff. "She's going to be in the brig for a long time." He shook his head. "It's too bad, she's cute."

"Maybe," Kirova shrugged. "It was pretty ballsy going against direct orders from the tribunal like that. I heard Matheson lost it."

Hansen snorted. "Matheson's had her panties in a wad longer than I've been in the force," he argued, but Peter heard his begrudging approval. "Guess if it was me who needed saving, I'd be glad she went rogue too."

"You mean the General's son?" Kirova asked. "It'll be interesting to see what he has to say about it."

"Guess that depends on if the kid makes it or not," Moss interjected, breaking his quiet stance. "I saw him on the way out," he added darkly. "Didn't look good."

The soldier's admission made Peter stumble in his stride. Ignoring Kirova's strange look, Peter dissected what the lanky soldier had said.

Boyce didn't look good.

Did that mean he was still alive? Or that the commander was too far gone to save? If Boyce didn't make it . . .

His heart squeezed as he wondered what that would mean for Wendy. Then, with another wrenching twist, he wondered what it would mean for him. He knew he was being selfish, but the thought had been too prominent the past few weeks to ignore.

With Boyce gone, maybe I can keep Wendy.

Allowing Kirova to guide his steps, Peter focused on the war in his brain. He got so wrapped up, he hardly noticed when she lowered him onto the containment bench until a crackling light exploded in his sights. Emitting a burst of sparks, Tinc swirled around him, her processor a screaming whir.

"Hey! You can't have that here!" Hansen growled, grabbing for the bot. Tinc flitted from his reach before barreling into the man's arm, knocking it forcefully out of the way. Watching her fiery outburst, Peter smirked as she rampaged, her tiny frame bobbing in agitation as she continued her garbled string of obscenities.

Scowling, Hansen lunged forward again but Peter held up his hands. "I wouldn't do that if I were you."

Surprised, the soldier turned to Peter. "What—" he growled, sending Tinc into another furious tizzy. Speaking over her tirade, Peter let out a cocky laugh.

"She's a bot. My bot. And she can get a little possessive. And stubborn," he added, noting the way Hansen eyed Tinc's hovering form. "Get on her bad side and she won't stop until you're broken, or she is, but fair warning—" he said, a dangerous glint in his eye, "I can rebuild *her*."

Hanson turned an ugly shade of purple, and Kirova stepped in. "Leave it, Hanson," she said, grinning at Peter. "It's his pet. It's cute."

Beside him, Tinc let out a string of curses that showed exactly what she thought of Kirova's assessment, but she landed on his shoulder, her processor crackling with agitation. Peter turned to thank Kirova, but before he could, he was tackled from the side.

"Peter!"

Tootles' cry was followed by a delighted burst of laughter as the Lost Boy snuggled against him. Smiling, Peter wrapped his manacled arms around the gangly boy, careful to avoid the heavy bandaging around his torso.

"Hey Tootles. Glad to see you made it."

Pulling away, sobered, for the first time Peter noticed the age settling on him. Just over the past few days he had stretched and his rounded baby face had begun to narrow and thin out.

"Yeah," Tootles said with a sheepish chuckle. "I just wish…" the boy's voice broke, and Peter knew what was left unsaid. Squeezing his shoulder, Peter nodded.

"Me too, Tootles. Me too."

Standing silent, Peter and the Lost Boy grieved, mourning Curly while Tinc flickered around them, omitting blue sparks. Moisture collected in the corner of Peter's eyes, and when he moved to wipe it, his gaze landed once more on Wendy. She really was beautiful, standing tall and proud, even in the center of an individual holding cell, facing down the Fleet. Part of him wanted to run to her, to free her from the bay and run with her without stopping. But as he looked on at the captain, and the way her gaze kept shifting, searching though he was right there waiting, he knew. It wouldn't be enough.

He wouldn't be enough.

The thought burned, filling him with a painful understanding that he wasn't ready to face. He might have thought more about it, and maybe he would later, but as he sat, waiting with uncertainty, Tinc hummed in his ear while Tootles quietly guarded his feet. Looking at the two of them, Tizari's question breezed through his thoughts, and Peter realized that maybe he'd been home all along.

FAMOUS LAST WORDS

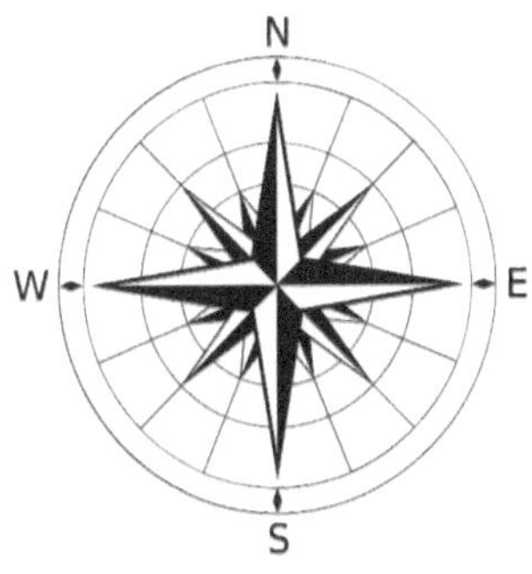

45
CAPTAIN WENDY DARLING
LONDONNIERRE BRIGADE
HEADQUARTERS

"Do you have anything to say for yourself, Captain?"

I did it to save the man I loved, Wendy thought, though her lips never formed the words. That was what it all came down to. She'd realized it in the brig after Amin took her crew and relocated them to a new barge—the *Fidelis Eterna*. He'd had a series of questions of his own and though he was not unkind, Wendy saw the Fleet in his gaze. Amin was a soldier through and through, and her defiance was the only feature his stare reflected. 'I did it for love,' didn't compute in his mind—not when it defied direct orders.

Especially when it failed.

Tears rimmed Wendy's eyes as she recalled Boyce's lifeless body being escorted from the ship. Amin and his men had promised they would take care of him, that they would get him the medical attention he needed. It was the only reason she let him go.

She shouldn't have let him go.

Boyce disappeared and she'd been thrown in the brig, treated little more than a pirate as she was shackled away from her crew, barred from everything until they returned her to New London.

To pay for her crimes.

A loud cough resounded through the room, startling Wendy from her thoughts. Blinking, she met the panel's solemn stares as they considered her, awaiting an explanation.

"Well, Captain?" Colonel Hahti prompted, studying her with his ebony gaze.

Shifting her weight from her achy knee, Wendy looked ahead, keeping the rest of her stance fixed at perfect attention.

"I don't believe I do," she finally answered, inciting a hushed murmur from the outer crowd. Wendy tried not to roll her eyes. Too much of this trial had been an elaborate display, an intentional act to maintain Fleet appearances.

Her mother would be impressed.

At least, she would have been if Wendy weren't the sacrifice. Now Mrs. Darling sat, lingering near the back of the room with her silk handkerchief covering her hair and Wendy's father beside her, both watching behind cold stares. Wendy had no delusions that they were there to support her. It was damage control. She knew her mother was shrewdly dissecting every piece of intel, dedicating it to memory, waiting to be first to hear of Wendy's guilt so she could soften the impact when she presented it to her friends.

'Clearly there has been some mistake, our daughter could never do something like this...'

Cue crocodile tears.

No. Her parents' attendance was nothing more than an act for the show, and Wendy was so completely tired of it.

Leaning forward, Admiral Toussant folded her hands and stared meaningfully at Wendy. "You're sure about this, Captain Darling?"

Swallowing a lump, Wendy peeked at the crowd behind her, stopping at the first row. Filling the front stand, her crew waited, sitting side by side: DeLaCruz and Dawes flanking Johns and Michaels, with SMEE and Nibs ending the line.

Though her brothers smiled encouragingly, Wendy felt a small pang at the noticeable gap where Peter should have been.

It wasn't fair for her to feel that way, she knew. It was just one of the many terrible things she had done to the mechanic. But as much as she had wanted to want him—as much as she had no reason *not* to, Peter had seen what she couldn't. Then he did the kindest thing he could and made the decision for her.

She hadn't known right away. Her isolation on the *Eterna* ensured that. Preceding her inquisition, the directive had come from the panel—Matheson specifically, she later found out—that Wendy be isolated in order to 'maintain briefing fidelity,' as Amin put it, without Wendy *influencing* her crew's reports.

Not that it mattered. Wendy would have never asked them to lie. She had made her decisions fully aware of the repercussions. She had known what was at risk and what was at stake.

But Amin, under direct orders, did what any proper soldier would do—he obeyed. And so, Wendy spent the final days of her maiden captain's voyage stowed in the brig, waiting.

For her trial, for word on Boyce, for anything.

"Captain?" Toussant prodded, reminding Wendy of her audience. Shaking her mind clear, Wendy straightened her coat.

"I believe everything worth saying already has been," Wendy met the Admiral's firm gaze. "Unless there is something specific the panel requires," she finished, directing her statement to Matheson, whose face pinched as the Admiral responded.

"There is," Toussant confirmed, her lips drawn in a hard line. "We know the main events and have covered them extensively—among the panel and within this trial—but as for recent developments, I need your confirmation."

Wendy nodded and the Admiral sniffed in response.

"Very well then," Toussant said, accessing her file. "Let me make this very clear. Captain Wendy Darling, you are currently standing trial for events occurring during the return voyage of the Neverland mission—the research and rescue expedition intended to retrieve Captain James Hooke and his crew."

Again, Wendy nodded.

"During these events, you were contacted by the Disciplinary Tribunal, where you were explicitly informed that your actions would be closely monitored due to previous debacles, including the loss of Liaisons Officer Aidan Boyce. Do you agree so far?"

"Yes, Admiral, I do."

"In that same meeting, you were also instructed that the Fleet had directed a team to retrieve your ship and to employ a holding pattern until they could meet you."

She paused for Wendy's approval before continuing.

"Is it then true, that directly after that communication, you made the decision to initiate an unauthorized excursion to an unsanctioned location upon the assumption that Itzala might be there."

"And Commander Boyce," Wendy added, glancing at each panel member. Her gaze lingered on Matheson's sneer before she cleared her throat. "Yes."

Frowning at Wendy's confirmation, the Admiral pressed on. "And during that time, though you confirmed Itzala's presence and located the commander's body, there were additional casualties, including the loss of a young ensign, Curtis Jones, whom I understood went by the name of 'Curly.'"

A guilty pang ripped through Wendy's stomach, but she held her gaze. "Yes, Admiral."

"From there, our understanding is that Itzala attacked, which your team fended once more, somehow with the assistance of the claimed prisoner Captain James Hooke, who fought alongside yourself, Fleet ensign Peter Pan, and a severely injured Commander Boyce. These events occurred while our team was docking the *Roger*."

"Yes."

Zeroing on Wendy, the Admiral swallowed. "We have corroborating reports from Colonel Commander Rashid Amin about the remaining events, including your compliance to the Fleet and your encouragement for your crew to do the same. Can you elaborate?"

"I have no qualms with the Fleet or their command, Admiral," Wendy declared over Matheson's derisive snort.

"Then can you explain your blatant disregard of our previous directive?"

"I had a soldier down, Admiral. I wasn't about to abandon him."

Glancing at Johns and Michaels beside the rest of her crew—even the Lost Boys, Wendy knew her truth. If any one of them had been on the *Ehiza*, she would have made the same decision. "As Captain, that was my charge."

The Admiral considered Wendy before glancing once more at her file, her jaw clenching before she readdressed the room. "And as Captain, did you also feel it was your prerogative to authorize the release of Captain Hooke?"

Wendy frowned. "Of course not, Admiral. His crimes were against the Fleet. That is where his penance should lie."

"Even if you felt he redeemed himself by coming to your aid?"

"I found it surprising, and it did raise some questions about my previous suppositions. But, no. I would still have left him to face the Fleet, as I am today."

"Then you claim you have no knowledge of Hooke's escape along with the abandonment of ensign Pan and his junior charge, Robert Toutolo?"

Wendy bit back a smile, knowing it would only incriminate her. "No, Admiral. I do not know how they managed to offboard the *Eterna*."

The Admiral studied Wendy, her piercing slate gaze boring to her soul. After a heavy pause, she rapped her knuckles. "Very well. Captain Darling, you understand that your testimony will directly impact the Fleet's decision on maintaining your rank as well as your potential assignment to a military prison. If there is any other evidence you would like to present to assist your case, now is the time."

"I understand, Admiral," Wendy answered, stirring the crowd's murmurs.

"So your statement, in summation, is that you directly defied Fleet orders in favor of your own personal mission to retrieve a lost officer; a mission which ultimately ended in the total loss of the *Jolly Roger*, as well as a wanted mutineer and a Fleet ensign. Is this correct?"

"And was it worth it?" Matheson interrupted with a dour smirk, her pinched lips making her look like a drowned rat.

Clenching her fists, Wendy fought to maintain her calm as she turned to the Colonel. "Actually," she began, before her retort was interrupted by a booming voice.

"I might have an answer for that."

46
CAPTAIN WENDY DARLING

Turning to the intruder, Wendy swallowed a cry. Filling the arena entrance, a hulking man in a charcoal uniform stood, his rod straight posture towering over the seated officials.

Rippling whispers swept through the crowd as the audience recognized the entrant. Glowering at Colonel Matheson through pool blue eyes, General Boyce removed his cover before searching for Wendy. Though his features remained frosted in his glare, Wendy could have sworn the creases lining his gaze softened before he turned, offering passage to a slight woman with fine golden hair. She was wearing a dress Wendy had seen before at one of her mother's many high teas.

Seeing her, Wendy frowned. Civilians weren't allowed on the arena deck, even the spouses of high ranking officials were relegated to the stands with the rest of the onlookers. General Boyce should know that more than anyone else. Unless—

Chest hitching, Wendy angled her gaze for a clearer view. Standing beside her husband, Mrs. Boyce extended her hand to a third person, taller than her, who limped heavily on unsteady feet. Stepping out of the way, Mrs. Boyce assisted the man, whose blonde hair perfectly matched hers. His face was concealed until he entered the room, and Wendy's knees buckled as she released a soft cry.

"And so might my son," the General announced, his pride evident through his stony countenance.

Dumbfounded, Wendy gaped as they approached. Isolated in the disciplinary center, Amin had banned her visitors entirely. Although she'd tried several times to get updates on Boyce, Colonel Amin's soldiers dismissed her, and the one time Johns had managed to sneak in, it had only been to inform her Boyce still hadn't woken.

That was only three days ago.

So, it wasn't surprising that her brain—which had spent the past weeks whirring through the worst possible outcomes— tailspinned when faced with the best: Boyce standing before her—albeit wrapped and bandaged, with a shiny scar tracing his hairline—with his father's blue eyes and his mother's blonde hair offsetting his perfectly chiseled features as they beamed directly at her.

"So you managed not to kill us all," Boyce murmured, leaning closer to her. "I knew you would."

Laughing back her tears, Wendy scoffed. "Now I *know* you hit your head," she said, admiring his freshly pressed suit. It hung looser than it should, but still accentuated his strong muscles and broad, open chest. "The Boyce I know would never admit that."

"The Boyce you knew was a twat," the commander murmured, reaching for her hand. "And he wasted far too much time saving face." Stroking her hand with his thumb, he added gently. "I don't intend to make that mistake again."

"Excuse me, General, but all of this is very—" Colonel Matheson's shrill cry cut through the room. Turning toward her half shriek, Wendy had to fight a snicker at the ugly puce mottling her face. Matheson spluttered as her beady eyes darted from the General to Wendy, while her fingers worked in agitated fists.

"It is very exciting to find Commander Boyce up and well," Admiral Toussant finished, saluting politely at the General before greeting his son with a grin. "Commander, welcome back."

"Thank you, Admiral," Boyce replied. "It's good to be home." He winced and the Admiral motioned for him to sit, directing Wendy to help him. "I imagine you have questions. I daresay they might shed light on some otherwise clouded areas."

"That's not—"

Colonel Matheson was quickly silenced by Colonel Osborne's stern stare. Cowed, her glower deepened, but she remained silent as the Admiral addressed Boyce, unable to hide the quirk of her lips.

"Do you believe your testimony will assist the council's deliberations?"

"I do," Boyce answered. "Particularly where Captain Darling's competency is concerned."

"Very good, Commander," the Admiral replied. "In that case, I do have a few questions. First, can you tell me how you fell victim to Itzala?"

Boyce's expression darkened, but he nodded bravely. "I will do my best, Admiral, but some things are difficult to pinpoint. I know I first became aware of its presence once we evacuated Neverland."

"And why didn't you inform the captain immediately once you realized it had breached the ship?" Matheson's snide voice interjected. Though the Admiral's eyes narrowed at the interruption, several other panel members' heads bobbed in agreement.

Boyce grimaced. "Itzala was... devious," he finished, settling on the right word. "So perhaps 'aware' is not the correct description. I recognized something was not right with me. At first, I thought it might have been an illness—the symptoms were similar enough: brain fog, drowsiness, irritability. It wasn't until I started noticing gaps in my days—full hours simply vanishing with no way to account for them—that I realized something was truly wrong. And then, came the whispers."

"Whispers?" the Admiral asked.

"Yes," Boyce affirmed, his gaze haunted. "It was how Itzala communicated, how it exerted its power. During its hold, I was always there, but at the same time, I wasn't. There were times where I felt Itzala and knew its desires—as though we were sharing space in my body—but at other points it seemed it had left completely, until it returned to overpower me."

"I see," the Admiral said after a brief pause. "Is there anything else you feel is important to share about your time under the Shadow's influence?"

Considering Toussant's question, the commander scanned the panel. After a heavy moment, he coughed to clear his throat. "There is no way that I can truly express what it felt like to be held under Itzala. The closest description I can even present is drowning in an icy pool filled with a substance that slicks to the deepest parts of your soul and threatens to swallow every bit of warmth you've ever known. It replaces those memories with hate and rage, turning you into a shade of yourself that you don't recognize, but the worst parts of you burn to ignite."

Pausing, Boyce cast a grateful look at Wendy before fixing his gaze on the panel.

"I can't say that my rescue was more valuable than the lives of any other soldier—that would be presumptuous. But I can assure you that had Captain Darling not intervened, Itzala's effects would have resulted in my complete annihilation."

"So, in your opinion, how would you classify Captain Darling's actions?"

Coughing, the commander straightened to full height, his sapphire gaze glimmering with resolve.

"I would say her actions were superior to any officer I've ever encountered. Not simply because of its impact on my life—in fact, I'd say its effect on me is the least of what Captain Darling has accomplished. Rather, her concentrated efforts against Itzala's contamination not only saved the universe but ensured its safety for the foreseeable future. It is my belief that her intervention, simply put, has saved us all."

Tears pooled over Wendy's eyes as she observed Boyce's final address. He didn't meet her gaze, but faced the panel with determination, his chin angled defiantly against the officers. A slight tremor had washed over his body as he held his stance, pushing through his pain until the Admiral's tight cough broke through the room.

"Thank you, Commander," the Admiral offered before referencing her pad. Her fingers whirred over the screen as she added a few notes, then stood to address the room. "That concludes the disciplinary hearing," she announced, leveling her gaze at Wendy. "The panel will now deliberate. You will be informed of our decision presently."

A loud rap punctuated her declaration, and the audience was dismissed, filling the circular stands with quiet murmurs. Waiting for the room to clear, the commander hovered beside Wendy, ignoring her flanking guards as he turned, his sapphire eyes blazing as he exhaled an incredulous breath.

"Wendy," he breathed, looking at her as though she might disappear like a fleeting eclipse. "What in the stars-damned universe were you thinking?"

47
CAPTAIN WENDY DARLING

"Excuse me?" Wendy asked, turning to the commander in shock. "What do you mean, what was *I* thinking?"

Staring back at her, Boyce shook his head in utter bewilderment. "Of course you'd have no clue," he let out an incredulous laugh and his piercing gaze softened. "You shouldn't have come back," he said, his brow furrowing as he brushed her cheek. "It wasn't safe."

"Wasn't safe?" Wendy challenged, her brow arched to her hairline. "I don't believe that has ever been a qualifying factor in anything I've ever undertaken, Commander."

Boyce scowled. "And that's why you keep finding yourself in these stars' forsaken situations."

Wendy snorted. "What exactly would you have had me do instead? Run back home to host a dinner party with my mother?"

"I'm quite sure that would be the worst option, all things considered."

Meeting his anxious gaze, Wendy let out a genuine laugh. "So you do understand why I had to come for you."

"I understand you could have gotten yourself killed," Boyce said.

"A feat I managed to avoid."

Boyce's frown deepened. "Narrowly," he said, slowly reaching for her hand. He traced her palm delicately, as though uncertain she was real. "There was a moment I thought I lost you."

A scoff escaped Wendy's chest. "Yeah, well, there were about a dozen times I thought the same about you," she shook her head at him in disbelief. "You always were the most infuriating cadet I've ever met."

"And yet," Boyce leaned closer, lowering his voice to a rumble. "You just couldn't let me go." His teasing smirk deepened as he looped his arm around her waist, drawing her close.

"Don't make me regret that," Wendy challenged, but its bite was lost in her smile. Examining the commander, she took in his features: all the same, but changed after the Shadow. Now there was a hardened edge, including a steel-cut in his brow that wouldn't erase. Reaching to trace the faint scar lining his hairline, she let her smile widen. "Thank you for coming back," she murmured.

"It was the least I could do," Boyce teased, gently tucking a stray curl under her cap. "Besides, it wouldn't be any fun to be in the Fleet's employ without having you there to torment."

Meeting his self-assured smirk, Wendy curled her fingers into the fabric on his shoulders, then angled her face to his, amazed by how much taller he was than her.

"You may have to get used to it, commander. The jury isn't out yet," she said, her gut wrenching nervously.

A frown darted over Boyce's expression. "We can appeal. If the panel doesn't clear you, my father will."

Wendy stilled his worry with a brush of her thumb. "It's alright. I knew the risk," she answered softly. "It was worth it— *you* were worth it."

"Captain, I—" Boyce hesitated, then with surprising speed, crushed his lips against hers, wrapping her in his strong grip to claim her with his kiss. His still healing muscles trembled with exertion, but his grip didn't loosen as he pulled her in, the kiss deepening with every passing moment. Relishing his tender touch, Wendy sank into him, his unhindered embrace finally convincing her his presence was real, and that he wasn't a phantom conjured by her grieving mind.

Refusing to break the kiss, Wendy pressed closer, hoping to convey everything he meant to her—to convince him that even if she were stripped of her title and imprisoned for a thousand years that his life was worth every stolen second. Running low on air, she finally broke free, her head spinning in a pleasant blur of breathlessness. Staring down at her, Aidan beamed, his joy finally erasing some of the Shadow's lingering weight. He leaned in to kiss her again, but a loud cough sounded behind them.

Blushing furiously, Wendy whirled toward the sound, where Lieutenant Johns waited, eyeing her delightedly.

"Johns! I—we—I—"

Before she could finish her half-worked excuse, Johns laughed. "I see exactly what *you* were doing, Darling," he teased. "Although, I can't say I wouldn't do the same in your position. But the panel has made their decision. They're heading back for the final announcement."

Finishing his message, the lieutenant looked meaningfully at Boyce's arm, still hooked possessively around Wendy's waist and winked.

"I'd loosen up there, Commander. You don't want them thinking your emotions colored your testimony."

Quickly, Wendy extricated herself from Boyce's grip and slid to her seat, straightening in time for the auditorium doors to spill open, filling the room. A soft touch brushed her leg and her heart flipped as the commander dared another gentle caress. Biting her lip, she fixed him with a silent warning, and he scooted away, forming a teasing space between them. Wendy wanted to pull him back, but before her itching fingers could hook his chair, the officer's door whirred open, admitting the panel. Sweeping a respectful salute, Wendy maintained her stance until all the officers settled in, leaving the Admiral to offer a commanding wave.

Sit.

Obediently, Wendy complied, appreciating how Boyce subtly scooted his chair nearer to hers as he did the same. Though they no longer touched, energy sparked between them like electricity, the gentle thrum softly reminding her of his presence while Admiral Toussant cleared her throat.

"Captain Wendy Darling, you stand before the panel, charged with treason, evidenced in violations against the Fleet and in turn, your loyalty to the crown. Should you be found guilty, you will be assigned a fitting and immediate punishment. Upon considering your testimony, we have reached a conclusion. Please step forward."

Complying, Wendy slowly walked to the arena's center. Her legs buckled as she walked, and she feared her knee might give out before she reached the podium. Thankfully, her muscles held and she arrived, with only the tremor in her hands revealing her terror.

Crushed under hundreds of stares, Wendy forced her attention ahead, resisting the urge to glance at her crew. Though she ached for Johns' bolstering smile and Michaels' steady quiet, she was afraid that if she looked back, she might dive into their safety. Instead, she set her chin, donning a cool mask as she calmed her shudders through sheer determination.

Bringing her hands to her mouth, the Admiral waited, considering. With a sharp cough, she placed them on the table, her expression hard.

"Captain Darling. After much deliberation and careful consideration, it is the panel's opinion that your actions showed a blatant disregard for Fleet protocol as well as its direct instruction. Furthermore, it has been suggested that such actions indicate a level of contempt for authority that if left unchecked, can only lead to further dissent pervading through our ranks."

The Admiral paused, allowing her words to resound through the room. Chest tight, Wendy tried to swallow but her mouth had become strangely dry. The Fleet was about to sentence her to a life in the brig and she had nothing to say—unlike the murmuring crowd filling the stands. Once more, she almost broke, daring to meet Boyce's steady gaze, but then, the Admiral's gaze dropped.

"However," Toussant's next word ignited a glimmer of hope. "Through those actions, you showed loyalty to your men that reflects the highest standards of leadership. Your courage and tenacity not only saved your commander, but your unwavering resolve against Itzala's threat spared the Fleet and countless others from suffering its reach."

Wendy stiffened at the Admiral's pause and tightened her lips. Looking at the panel, she could practically feel their accusing stares and Matheson's malicious glee. Briefly, she wondered how long she'd be assigned to the brig. She only hoped that she might see the stars once more before they sent her in. Swallowing to clear her throat, Wendy stamped down the thought. She would not meet her punishment with weakness. Standing resolute, she stared ahead, steeling herself as the Admiral coughed to continue her prim address.

"While we cannot condone your actions, we can forgive them. Captain Darling, you are hereby pardoned of all accusations brought against you and your rank has been fully restored, with honors. Herein, you are Command Captain Darling, Explorations Officer First-Class." In a seamless motion, the Admiral stood and raised her hand, meeting Wendy with the Fleet's official salute.

Wendy's jaw dropped and she forced her mouth closed as the rest of the panel rose, their reactions ranging from Colonel Obourne's stern propriety to Colonel Jimenez' encouraging grin. Only one officer lingered, seething as she collected her things. Gripping her files, Colonel Matheson stalked past Wendy, rigid with disdain. She slowed as she neared the door, turning as though she might argue, but before she could, the Admiral sidled forward.

"Colonel, please make sure to leave your notes before you go," Toussant instructed, glancing at Matheson's white knuckles. "As the case has been closed, there is no need for you to access Captain Darling's file."

Her words carried through the room, earning another furious glower from the colonel before she dropped her pad and stormed out, venom in her stare. Watching her exit, the Admiral's dark features pulled in a smug grin before she nodded.

"Well done, Darling," she said, offering Wendy a smile. "I must say, I am proud of the work you have done."

"Thank you, Admiral," Wendy stammered, meeting Toussant's steely gaze.

"No, Captain. Thank you," Toussant said. Smiling, she looked at Wendy, and a low chuckle rumbled from her chest. "It looks as though Lieutenant Johns was right, you just might be the best captain the Brigade has ever seen."

Sweeping a salute, the Admiral exited the room, leaving Wendy staring after her, with tears in her eyes. Overwhelmed, Wendy turned to Boyce, who stared at her with open adoration. The intensity of his gaze caught her breath, and he brought his hand to cup her cheek.

"The best captain the fleet has ever seen," he rumbled, repeating the Admiral's words, "And somehow, I get to call her mine."

His face angled in a silent invitation, making Wendy's lips ache. She leaned in, but a shout echoed through the room, followed by a booming laugh.

"Darling!" Johns' cried, swallowing her in a bear hug. He twirled her in the air, his quick circuit revealing the ragtag crew surrounding them. Prim and proper in their matching uniforms, Michaels, DeLaCruz, and Dawes beamed at her while Nibs, too, watched happily, despite looking uncomfortable in his freshly pressed suit. At the edge, SMEE hovered, his cybernetic eyes brimming with manufactured tears.

"We knew they couldn't keep you!" Johns cheered, though the relief on his face somewhat dimmed the assurance.

He dropped Wendy to the ground and her knee twinged as she steadied her balance. Having never fully healed from its first injury, her last round against the Shadow had been too much. Her leg would never be the same. But considering what might have been, it was a small sacrifice to make. Grinning past the pain, Wendy chuckled at Johns, who continued his exuberant celebration.

"After all, no other Captain could ever have such an idiotic pursuit of justice as you!"

"He's not wrong," Aidan whispered. His warm breath tickled her ear, sending a shiver down her spine.

"Yeah," Dawes agreed, "but maybe next time, don't *make* them consider it?"

"Deal," Wendy laughed, throwing her arms around the pilot before drawing DeLaCruz, then the others into a large hug. Joy bubbled inside her so completely, she was surprised to find tears in her eyes.

"Everything okay, Captain?" Arielle asked, looking at her worriedly.

"Yes, Dawes" Wendy assured, with a laugh. "I'm fine. It's just, I'm so sorry. To all of you. For everything. For making you worry, for putting you in danger, for—"

"You cut that out," Johns commanded, gripping her shoulders. "If you haven't figured out by now that any one of us would travel the 'verse with you—*for you*—then you're dumber than I thought."

"But I—"

"He's right, Captain," Boyce announced with a smirk. "And we all know that would be *impossible*." He ended his teasing with a wink before slinking his arm around her waist. Observing his silent declaration, the others burst into excited chatter, except for Dawes, who dove into Michaels' arms and kissed him delightedly.

"I *told* you she'd choose the commander," she declared, before shrinking under Wendy's accusatory glare. Blushing, she gave a sheepish shrug. "He completes you," she said.

Shaking her head, Wendy just laughed and let her crew draw her in, for once, fully allowing herself to the moment.

GROWING UP & GOODBYE

48
CAPTAIN WENDY DARLING

Hours had passed since Wendy had been declared free, and still, she couldn't believe it.

Looking around at her tiny room, once empty and sterile, filled with the people she loved, Wendy started to consider that maybe Peter had been right; emotions weren't as troublesome as she thought.

The realization struck her, and she forced a smile over the sudden lump in her throat. The others didn't notice as they happily chatted, watching Johns pantomime each member of *Phizyque*, New London's chart-topping boy band. Beside her, Boyce sat, looking more at ease than she ever thought imaginable, his broad hand covering hers as he stroked her leg with his thumb. The moment was nearly perfect, except for a nagging thought that wouldn't leave her. She'd apologized to each of her crew, but Peter's hasty departure had denied her the opportunity for the person who deserved it most. A frown threatened her plastered façade, until a loud knock sounded outside her dorm, startling everyone inside.

Surprised, Wendy looked at the visitor screen and was even more shocked to see her father's and mother's projected images.

"Should I tell them to leave," Johns asked with a growl.

"No. This is something I need to handle," Wendy said firmly, feigning a bright smile. "You guys go, it's getting late anyway."

Eyeing her uncertainly, her crew hesitated before she let out an exasperated huff.

"That's an order," she teased, waving them off. "I'm *fine*, I promise," she urged, looking specifically at Dawes. "I'll see you all tomorrow."

Hurrying them out, Wendy managed to push everyone through except Aidan, who lingered, planting himself firmly beside her. His brow creased as he studied her timid expression and bristled. Wrapping his arm protectively around Wendy's shoulder, he stepped forward, his blue gaze flashing at her parents, who waited, her mother's magnificently fabricated smile offsetting her father's agitated pout.

"Mr. Darling," he breezed, hand outstretched. "So nice to see you again."

Caught off guard by Boyce's assertive greeting, Mr. Darling returned the handshake.

"Yes, well. Very nice to see you too, Aidan. I'm glad to hear all that business with the—er—whatever…" he trailed off, his mustache twitching as he fumbled for words.

Aidan grinned. "With the Shadow?" His smile brightened, but Wendy caught the dangerous tenor underlying his genial tone. "I can't imagine what might have happened had it not been for your daughter. You must be very proud."

"Oh, we *are!*" Mrs. Darling assured, flinging her arms around Wendy in a theatrical hug, surging to catch Wendy's face in her hands. "Oh, my Darling! How we've missed you! I can't tell you how worried *sick* I've been! The ladies in West Brighton have all but given up on me, I've been so desolate! I can't tell you how *relieved* we are that this whole ordeal is behind us!"

"Yes," Aidan agreed, his grin prevailing through Mrs. Darling's selfish blathering. "I can only imagine how difficult it must have been for you, debating our well-being over Sunday Tea."

Fumbling under his pointed remark, Mrs. Darling blinked. "Well, not as difficult as it was for you, of course, dear. But one mustn't ever underestimate the effects things like that have on a mother's heart."

"If your affections are anything like my father's, ma'am, I think I have a pretty good idea," Boyce said, quieting Wendy's mother with a frown. Mrs. Darling pouted, but before she could reply, Wendy raised her hand.

"I am sorry to have worried you, mother," she apologized. "But as you can see, both Aidan and I are quite alright. In fact, he was just on his way."

Pushing Boyce towards the door, she fixed him with a wry smile.

"You didn't have to do that," she murmured, leaning close so only he could hear.

Aidan's gaze flickered to where the Darlings sat in Wendy's dorm, their noses turning at its Spartan simplicity. "No," he grinned, "but it was very fun."

Wendy looked at him conspiratorially. "Is this something I get to look forward to every time you see my parents?"

"Does that mean that I'll be given another opportunity?"

Thinking about the shock Aidan's forwardness brought to her mother's face, Wendy smirked. "It's a very good possibility," she said, "but for now, I've got to handle this on my own."

Nodding, Boyce delicately gripped her face. "Handle it quick," he said, planting a kiss on her cheek that slipped to brush her lips. Heat blossomed between them, but before it could erupt into a blazing flame, he pulled back, leaving her aching for more, "I just got you back. I'm not fond of sharing." Grinning, he pressed his lips once more to hers, then waved politely to the Darlings, before jaunting down the hall, leaving a thrill in Wendy's chest. When it finally stilled, she closed the door and turned to her parents, bolstered by Aidan's smooth assurances and intoxicating kiss.

Settled on the couch, the Darlings eyed their daughter primly, vaguely reminding Wendy of her first trip to the Academy. Straightening her posture, she angled her jaw to meet their gaze, for once, feeling their equal.

"Mother, Father. I am guessing there is a reason you haven't returned to West Brighton?"

"Because we came to see *you*, dear!" Mrs. Darling exclaimed. "I told you, it's been absolutely *miserable* with you gone."

"I have not been home for two years, mother. Certainly, you aren't just now realizing how much you've missed me."

A wounded pout puckered on Mrs. Darling's lips, but Mr. Darling blustered in a scowl. "Now listen here, young lady, you don't get to talk to your mother like tha—"

"I am neither a young lady nor am I going to allow you to tell me what I can or cannot do in my home," Wendy said, fueled by her rooting confidence. She looked at her father, and his rioting mustache, before taking a deep breath. "I am grateful that you came for the trial. It shows, in your own way, that some part of you cared enough to worry about me. But I don't delude myself into thinking this means anything has changed and neither should you."

"Of course things have changed!" Mrs. Darling said, crossing the room to pat Wendy's hand. "You have returned a hero! And a budding romance with the General's *son*? It's more than we could have ever hoped for! Just think what everyone will say!"

"General's son? You mean *Aidan*." Wendy corrected, bristling at her mother's simplicity. She shook her head, gathering her senses before forcefully retracting her hand. "Mother, I have no intention of returning to West Brighton."

"Well of course you are, Darling! You must! There are so many people waiting to see you," her mother blinked, turning to Mr. Darling for support. "Our friends…"

"*Your* friends, mother. All the people I care about are here," she said, not bothering to mask the slight. "If you really want to see me, you both are welcome to come and visit whenever you would like, but I will not be the fuel of West Brighton's gossip fire—not willingly, at least."

Looking from her father to her mother, Wendy clasped her hands, waiting for their response. They watched in confusion before her mother, beautiful even in distress, pressed again.

"But, Darling—"

Wendy sighed. "I'll comm if I decide to visit," she said, gesturing to the door. It didn't matter what she said, her parents simply would not understand, nor would they try.

Spluttering from the couch, her father stood, blustering. His mustache danced furiously as he dragged his wife to the door, muttering darkly about hiring a driver so late in the evening. Wendy didn't break as she ushered them out, until her mother's flabbergasted expression, flawless in disbelief, vanished behind the door, leaving her blissfully alone.

49
CAPTAIN WENDY DARLING

Reveling in the quiet, Wendy flopped to her couch, enjoying the steady cadence of her heart. Every other conversation she'd had with her parents—even victorious ones—had always left her queasy, but laying still, she felt nothing but calm.

Perhaps she had changed, after all.

Sitting up, she glanced around her dorm. The walls were still barren, with nothing to claim it a home, except for a new art piece Nibs had hung on the wall—a sketch of her crew on Neverland, smiling in front of the *Fiducia*. At the bottom of the page, the boy's messy scrawl declared its artist with his printed name. Smiling at the charcoal drawing, Wendy placed her hand to the hollow of her neck, where Peter's acorn hung perfectly. Touching the memento summoned a flood of memories, until her apartment became stifling. Grabbing her coat, she scrawled a brief note for Aidan and taped it to the door, explaining her quick departure.

Hurrying through the Academy halls, she waved politely at passing Fleetmen, acknowledging their congratulations as she quickly made her way to the quad. Reaching the sprawling grounds, she breathed in the cool night air, letting the faint breeze carry off her buzzing thoughts. The scent of honeysuckle danced over the fresh grass and Wendy looked up, staring into the stars dotting the twilight sky.

"I didn't think captains were supposed to cry," a familiar voice whispered, followed by a husky laugh. "Unless that's changed in the past hundred years, too."

"Peter!" Wendy cried, spinning to face the mechanic. Gingerly, she reached for his chest, and was surprised to find the taut muscles under his well-fitted jacket were certainly real. Jerking back, she looked over her shoulders, scanning for onlookers. When she found no one, she shoved the mechanic quickly behind the nearest tree.

"What are you doing here?" She hissed.

Peter chuckled again, his face lighting with mischief. "I came to see you," he said, before a furious jangle sounded deep within his coat. Pulling back the flap, he released Tinc, who swooped around them with a tirade of sparks. "*We* came to see you," he amended. "We wanted to hear how the trial went and bust you out if we had to."

"Peter, you can't be here," Wendy said in a rush before another thought struck. "*How* did you get here? I thought you and Hooke—" she glanced wildly around, half expecting the pirate to step from behind the tree wearing something ridiculously flamboyant, like a billowing crimson coat.

"James is fine," Peter assured with a snicker. "He sends his love as well. At least, his most amicable regards." His crooked grin stretched before he caught Wendy's awkward stare. Smile faltering, the mechanic scratched his head. "Which are what I wanted to send—"

Stalling him, Wendy raised her hand. "Please tell him I said thank you," she said, before looking seriously at the mechanic. "For everything."

Peter nodded, understanding her stare. "You're welcome."

Falling quiet, the mechanic shifted as he uncertainly studied the quad. After a moment of kicking the grass, he peeked at her, scratching his head.

"So, back with the Fleet, then?"

Wendy shrugged. "For the time being," she said, turning toward the Academy. "At least it's job security."

Smirking, Peter bobbed his head before he fell serious, a question in his gaze. "And Boyce, too, huh?"

Wendy shifted uncomfortably, and he attempted a smile.

"So I guess there's no talking you into another grand adventure," he joked, "Tinc promised she'll play nice."

A small chuckle escaped Wendy. "As much as I appreciate it, I've got a lot of people waiting for me," she said, remembering her quiet dorm filled with her crew's happy laughter.

"I figured as much," Peter said, his grin fading. He absently scratched his neck and Wendy noticed how shaggy his hair had gotten. "Hooke said it was a long shot too, but Tootles said we had to try."

Wendy bit her lip, picturing the small boy's deep brown eyes. Since leaving Neverland, they were the only part of the Lost Boy that had remained untouched by time—age had already lengthened his limbs and angled his features—she wondered what he might look like if she ever saw him again. "Tell them I'm sorry," she said. "And that I'll miss them."

Peter didn't meet her eyes. "They're gonna miss you. Tootles has kept Seven entertained so far, but—" he let out a sharp breath before repairing his jaunty smirk. "But they'll be alright."

"They have you," Wendy said, placing her hand on his arm.

Peter's gaze lingered on her touch for a moment too long. "Yeah. Me." Coughing, he stuffed his hands in his pockets and looked to the sky. Conflicted emotions flickered over his up-turned face, filling Wendy with guilt.

"I don't want to say goodbye either," Wendy finally admitted, voicing both of their thoughts as she flashed back to Neverland. Sorrow rippled through Peter's stare, and she could tell he was remembering the same moment.

Brushing a loose curl from her cheek, Peter smiled softly. "I think we have to," he said, studying her searching gaze. "Say goodbye, I mean." He wiped the stray tear from her cheek, then leaned forward, pressing her forehead to his. "But I promise, there's no farewell in the 'verse that could ever make me forget you."

Blinking, Wendy looked at the mechanic, who stood before a backdrop of glittering stars, his gaze smoldering like melting honey.

"Goodbye, Wendy," he whispered, grazing her cheek with a kiss so gentle, she might have imagined it, save for the tiny thimble he pressed into her grip.

Distracted by the starcaster, Wendy nearly missed Tinc's flash of golden sparks when, with a distant crow, Peter was gone, disappearing into the darkened sky.

Holding the thimble, Wendy stared into the night, appreciating the cool chill it brought to her cheeks. "Goodbye, Peter," she whispered, staring at the stars.

Unsure how long she stood under their shimmering lights, Wendy only knew it was enough time for the last of her tears to dry before hushed footsteps approached from behind.

"There you are," Boyce said, smiling warmly at her. "I was afraid I might have to call out the guard."

Turning toward him, Wendy grinned. "I'm fairly certain you had no need to worry," she teased, pleased to discover her summoned smile was genuine. "If I remember right, I'm the one who managed to find *you* in the depths of space, not the other way around."

Boyce chuckled and stepped closer, wrapping his arms protectively around her. "Oh, I wasn't worried about you," he assured, "I simply feared losing more time for this."

Leaning in, the commander touched his lips to hers, filling them with a warmth that had been stolen by the cool night air. Humming the Gentle Maiden's last stanza in her ear, he hugged her close, igniting a slow, burning fire that threatened to overtake her.

Drawing back, Wendy looked at the commander, who stared at her with open adoration. His sapphire eyes glittered in the night, reminding her of Neverland's endless pools. The thought pulled another memory and she sighed, forcing Boyce to follow her gaze, which had pulled once more to the sky.

Noticing her distraction, the commander shifted to stand beside her, draping his arm to hold her waist while she rested on his shoulder. After a quiet moment, he inhaled a shallow breath.

"Do you think he's alright?" the commander asked, guessing her silent thoughts. "He and I were never close—for obvious reasons—but I do suppose I owe him a great deal," he admitted, glancing once more at Wendy, unable to hide his awe. "I should have liked the chance to thank him."

"I'm sure he's fine," Wendy said, fixed on the stars. "And I imagine he knows. He wasn't ever the type to expect that sort of thing."

"And how about you," Boyce asked, worry edging his features. "How are you feeling about all of this?"

Wendy considered the commander's question for a long moment before finally facing him, his golden frame haloed in the shimmering night. Though part of her still ached over the loss of Peter, loving the mechanic had been a dream. A fleeting moment stolen from a timeless planet. Raw and beautiful and wild, it opened her eyes to all of the possibilities in galaxies beyond.

And to the possibility she held in her arms.

Tightening her grip around Boyce's waist, Wendy pressed on her toes to meet him in a kiss. The sudden motion caught the commander by surprise and he stiffened, before melting into her touch. Responding to her gentle embrace, he wrapped his arms around her, cradling her as the kiss deepened to envelop them both. Heat radiated from their bodies, dissipating into the spring breeze, but not even the passing of time could detract from their passion. Lingering as long as they could, they remained, entwined in the night until Wendy finally pulled back, dizzy under the commander's spell. Reaching to slick his tousled hair, Wendy smiled.

In the distance, a shooting star tore across the skyline, like a spaceship traipsing the night. For a moment, it made her think of another ship, carrying a boy, a beast, a pirate, and the most vexing mechanic.

"There is not a single place that I'd rather be," Wendy assured, tracing the small scar lining the commander's hairline.

"And what makes you so certain of that," Boyce asked, grinning over his low rumble.

Looking at the sky, she envisioned two distant stars winking at them, their shimmering green cast reflecting the hue of a familiar roguish gaze. Picturing the boy they belonged to, she grinned wider as he was joined by a swooping arc of sparking gold before he vanished into the glittering deep.

"We're living," Wendy said, sealing her promise with another soft kiss. "And living is an awfully big adventure."

EPILOGUE

CAPTAIN JAMES TIBERIAS HOOKE

LOCATION UNKNOWN

I 'd forgotten how captivating the skies could be, foolishly grown bored of them. Now that I've returned, it seems impossible. How could anyone tire of the whorl of infinite galaxies suspended against a backdrop of endless onyx begging to be explored?

Captains were not meant to live their lives in cages. I belong here, among the stars.

We will go East. Far from the Fleet and their meddlesome reach, and even farther from the Second Star. Certainly within the secrets of the deep we are bound to find a cure for this blasted disease. Once we have vanquished Hinson-Braehls, who knows what other adventures will await in the lengths of space? Perhaps one day we will land far enough that the Shadow's ghost will finally dissipate. My discussions with Pan have led me to believe as much. He no longer fears darkened whispers slinking through deserted halls, though he faces ghosts of his own.

Her memory haunts him. I see it when he searches the stars. It is not their light reflecting in his stare, but hers. She *was* captivating, I suppose.

But there are other beauties out there, and we shall attend to them all. Pan and his small companion—the tawny boy that totters after him, mimicking his every move as though the ruddy mechanic can do no wrong. It was tiresome at first, but I must admit, the lad, Robert, has grown on me. It reminds me of a time I claimed a boy of my own.

Hopefully, Pan will fare better in the role than I did. I suppose only time will tell. In the interim, I will just have to supervise to make sure. It can be wearisome, but someone must take charge. And if there is any hope of turning them into proper pirates, the task must fall to me.

How lovely it is to be home.

<<ERROR://LOCATION://x^4_CORRUPT%_s!>>

Thank you for reading

THE NEVERLAND TRANSMISSIONS SERIES!

We hope you loved it. If you did, please consider leaving a review. Your thoughts mean the world to authors!

ACKNOWLEDGEMENTS

There's a lot that goes into writing a book, even more that goes into finishing a whole series. To say that completing Neverbound was a labor of love would be a tragic understatement, and to say I did it on my own would be a complete and total lie. That being said, there is a long list of thanks that needs to be laid out, for without the help of each of these amazing people, this book (and series) would absolutely not be the same.

First and foremost, I thank God for blessing me with the opportunity to share this story with the world, and for the knowledge that even when things seem most bleak, light will always outshine the darkness.

Next, I want to thank my amazing family. Steven, thank you for your endless patience and support through all the countless hours I spent agonizing over this book, and for listening, encouraging, and loving me through it all. Brody, Zoie, Liam, and Rowynn, thank you for providing snuggles and dance breaks when I needed them the most.

Mom and dad -- thank you for giving me somewhere to escape and for wrangling the menace so I could write. She's real cute, but not easy, and your willingness to step in whenever I needed you did not go unnoticed. Mom, I hope this is the ending you wished for, and dad, I hope I've made you proud.

Diana and Paul -- thank you for always being there. Your kindness and love are so appreciated by all of us, we can never thank you enough.

For my Neverland ride-or-dies: Jessica, Katie, Ethan, Diana and Patsy. You all kept this story alive through moments I was certain it was doomed. I cannot ever thank you all enough for all your time, patience, and support. You all have influenced this story in your own way, and all I can say is that it is a million times better because of it.

For the rest of my family and friends—my inner circle—thank you for being the best support group a girl could ever ask for. Day in and day out, you put up with my shenanigans and make my life complete.

Of course, so much thanks for Owl Hollow and my AMAZ-ING editor Hannah; Thank you so much for believing in my work and me. Hannah, thank you for the endless patience and grace you dedicated to Peter and Wendy and the completion of their story. I cannot imagine how it might have turned out without your help--and honestly, I don't want to. It was a lot of work, but I think together, we created something special.

And last, but absolutely not least, I thank my incredible readers. Without you, there would have been no reason to finish Peter and Wendy's story. Although all of Neverbound's characters own a piece of my heart, truly, they belong to you.

J.M. SULLIVAN is a fairy tale fanatic who loves taking classic stories and turning them on their head. When she's not hiding behind her laptop, you can find her watching scary movies with her husband, playing with her kids, or buried in a book. Although known to dabble in adulting, J.M. is a big kid at heart who still believes in true love, magic, and most of all, the power of coffee.

If you would like to learn more about her award-winning stories or connect with J.M., find her on social media at @jmsullivanbooks—she'd love to hear from you.

www.ingramcontent.com/pod-product-compliance
Lightning Source LLC
Chambersburg PA
CBHW030759200726
48285CB00013B/301